THE INTENDED

A CULLING OF BLOOD AND MAGIC

II

The Intended by K.M. Rives

Copyright© October 2021

Cover Art: Kiff Shaik @ Solidarity Squad

Editing: Kraken Communications

ISBN: 9798498668161

This book is a work of fiction. Names, characters, places and incidents are either a product of the authors imagination or are used fictitiously. Any resemblance to actual persons, living or dead, or to actual events or locales is completely coincidental.

This book in its entirety and in portions is the sole property of K.M. Rives.

The Intended Copyright© 2021 by K.M. Rives. All rights reserved. No part of this publication may be reproduced, distributed, or transmitted in any form or by any means, including photocopying, recording, or other electronic or mechanical methods, without the prior written permission of the publisher, except in the case of brief quotations embodied in critical reviews and certain other noncommercial uses permitted by copyright law. For permission requests, write to the author.

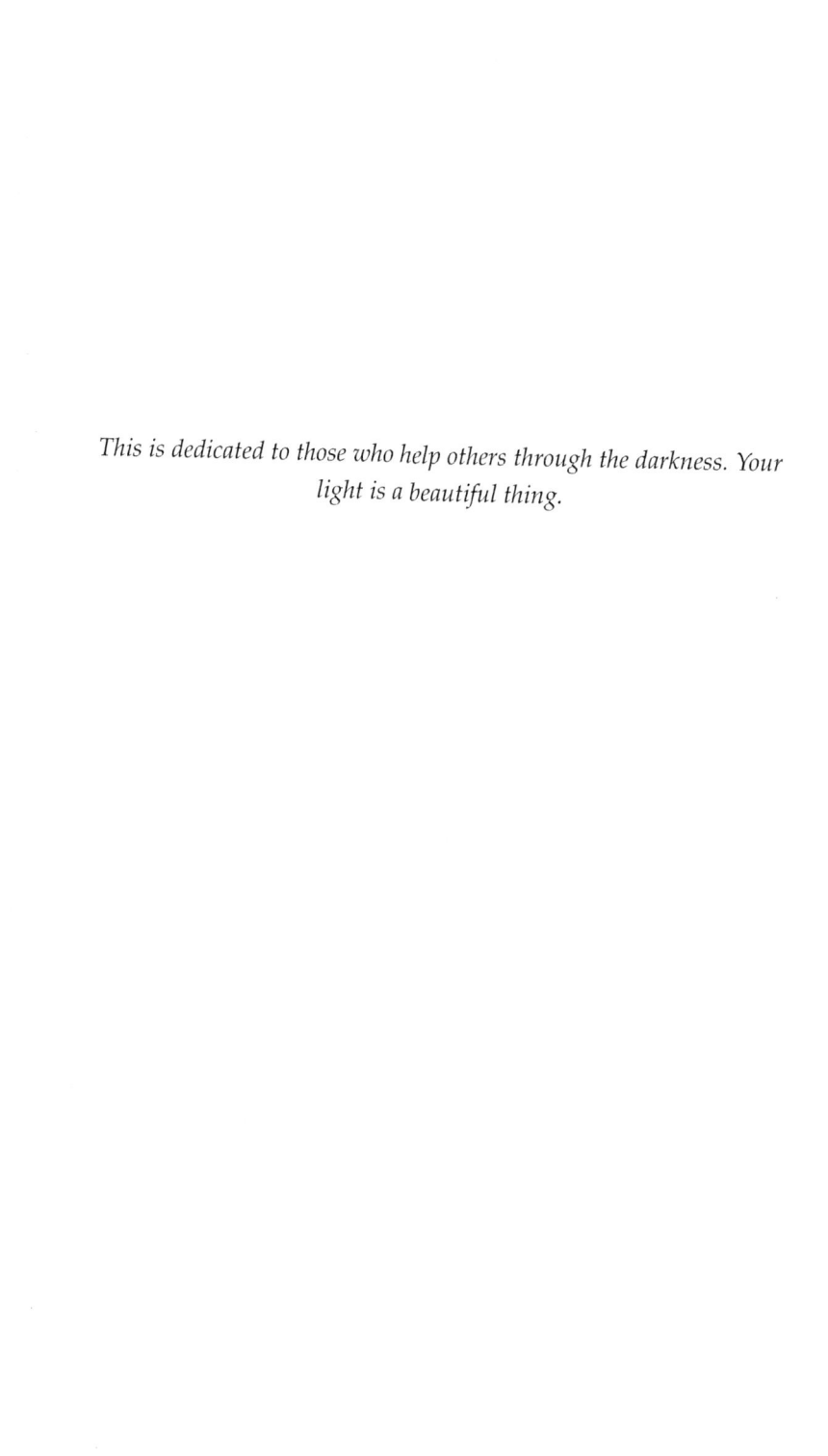

This is dedicated to those who help others through the darkness. Your light is a beautiful thing.

CONTENT WARNING

** This book contains sexually explicit scenes, adult language that may be considered offensive to some readers. Additionally, there is a moment of loss that may be upsetting to some readers.

Please proceed with caution, and always take care of yourself first and foremost. **

Chapter One

AUGUSTINE

The bloody trail started with three dead in an abandoned warehouse in Elizabethtown, Kentucky.

Seven dead in a vampire-owned bar in Memphis, Tennessee,

Twelve decapitated and arranged in a pentagram in El Paso, Texas.

Five flayed open below slot machines in a Reno, Nevada, casino.

And the latest before that night, four fledglings strewn across the highway outside of Yuma, Arizona, with looks of terror etched into their faces.

Now, the smell of vampiric blood overpowered the crisp Pacific ocean air. It acted as a beacon, leading Augustine to a back alley, hidden away behind a popular strip of bars.

He received the tip an hour ago, and when he'd arrived in Long Beach, he found the body: a newly turned vampire stuffed in a hedge off the main road with his throat cut and entrails exposed. Just like all the others.

A month of finding bodies like this, all members of his kingdom. A month of Malcolm's incessant ramblings about how Augustine was the intended heir in the united prophecy, along with his mate. The next person to mention the godsdamned prophecy was likely to have their throat ripped out like the unfortunate vampire stuffed in the bushes.

He couldn't deny it was an efficient way to kill, although messier than taking a head clean off. Then again, the goal of the cannibalistic vampire was to eat its prey, which it did without remorse. A witch quality if there ever was one.

Though the coven swore it wasn't one of theirs perpetrating the murders, witches were notorious for lies and half-truths…something he'd learned the hard way. His jaw clenched as he remembered Emery's betrayal yet again. She had lied to him, done her best to hide her true self. And now? Now she was in the wind, lost to him, though the cravings for her body remained.

Witches were always trouble. Each of the bodies they'd found carried the same remnants of magic along the jagged wound edges. There was no other faction that could be responsible for the deaths, and with Emery's recent deceit still smoldering in his gut, he felt inclined to tell every witch he encountered to fuck off.

In truth, Augustine was spoiling for a fight. He had remained diplomatic this long because Malcolm had convinced him to give his people time to prepare. They had grown soft with the last century of relative peace, Malcolm argued. Personally, Augustine had no doubt they'd rise to the occasion, but Malcolm had managed to hold him off. He reluctantly agreed to stay peaceful. At least for the time being. He would gladly kill every last one of the witches without an ounce of remorse, but he couldn't do it at the expense of his people.

But as vampires continued to be gutted, war with the witches seemed more and more inevitable.

Not that there'd be any complaints from him.

That was why Augustine had stashed Malcolm in a hotel room with a snapped neck. He'd be angry when he woke up, but it would give Augustine a head start. Contrary to what his brother thought, patience would cost them everything. They couldn't afford cautiousness, not when they were finally gaining traction in their hunt.

Augustine tapped into his senses, ensuring he and the killer were alone before he made himself one with the shadows and crept along the wall of the brick alley.

His fangs elongated, and his body thrummed with excitement, but it wasn't because of the fresh blood lacing the night air. Unlike human blood, vampire blood didn't send him into a frenzy. It was the thrill of the hunt that forced his natural instincts to the surface and propelled adrenaline through his veins.

His stomach tightened and a wicked smile tugged at his lips. The pawn he hunted was hunched over a vampire, fangs deep within her neck as her lifeless eyes stared up at the moonlit sky.

The woman probably never saw him coming. Despite the warnings to remain vigilant, his all-too-cocky subjects refused to listen. It was a reminder of how complacent his people had become.

By the time the killer became aware of his presence, Augustine was on him.

The monster dropped his victim with a sickening thud and spun, giving Augustine his first good look at the sociopath he'd scoured the country for. He didn't appear to be more than twenty years old, but his magic-laden, glowing silver eyes were brimming with the rage of someone who'd lived a hell of a lot longer, and seen far too much.

Blood trailed from his mouth, dripping to the pavement as he hissed and lunged at Augustine. At least, he tried to. Before the vampire could lay a single bloodied finger on Augustine's lapel, his back was against a wall, cracking the mortar and sending bits of brick to the ground.

A guttural growl filled the crisp air and shook Augustine's chest as he pressed his forearm against the monster's throat. "This ends here. With me showing as much restraint as you did your victims."

The man choked out a laugh. "The Mistress will always be one step ahead of you, August."

Augustine's stomach sank, but he managed to keep the surprise from his face. The man knew who he was. As did this person he called Mistress. He'd never heard that term used to describe a witch. Crone, hag, and priestess were common, but Mistress was new, even to him. It was strange—a mystery on top of a mystery.

The name was the first solid lead they'd acquired in a month.

He paused, ensuring once more there was no one else waiting to ambush him. "And, pray tell, who might this Mistress of yours be? I'd like to thank her for my cross-country vacation."

A sardonic grin crossed the cursed vampire's face. "She sends her regards and a message."

Augustine tilted his head and raised a brow. "What would that be?"

"This is only the beginning."

"The beginning of what?" He ground the words out. If she thought she'd keep killing the vampires of his kingdom, this Mistress was sorely mistaken. It was one of the few things Augustine and August agreed upon: the killings would stop, one way or another. His inferior other half lurked deep within him, all too willing to give up control of their shared body, except when it came to his precious little witch, who he refused to allow Augustine to kill.

"Your end."

Before Augustine could react, the man tilted his head toward the sky and whispered in Daelic.

The killer's eyes rolled back and he shuddered as blood bubbled out of his mouth. He choked on it, grinning like a man who'd gotten away with murder.

Which, essentially, he had.

Augustine stepped back, narrowly avoiding the blood sputtering from the man's mouth as he fell in a heap on the pavement. Inky silver magic spilled from his eyes, mouth, and nose, matching the substance pouring from the wounds of his victims.

"Fuck."

He was still two steps behind the villain pulling the strings without any evidence pointing to her next move.

Augustine reminded himself to look on the bright side: at the very least, this murderer was dead. Still, it left the lingering question of what came next.

That question was too much to consider without a drink in hand. His gums ached for blood, while his mind craved the kind of relief only whiskey could bring. In truth, he'd take either, as long as it dulled the sting of his failure and fed the rage consuming him.

He turned to follow an unsuspecting couple, intent on satisfying his bloodlust, when the steady thump of a walking bassline drifted from the nearest bar. The bluesy notes accompanied by a warm body would satisfy his needs nicely. He looked up to see the name of the establishment and his jaw tightened.

Montgomery Blues

Augustine's temper flared, while August's heart constricted deep in their shared chest.

Only when Emery was involved did August make his presence known. His increasing softness for the little witch made Augustine's eye twitch. She screwed August and left him, quite literally, after lying to him about who and what she was. It was unforgivable to Augustine, yet there August was, yearning for her through his pain.

Augustine shoved August's bleeding heart back down and focused on the implications of where he stood. He didn't have time to explore the intricacies of the mate bond. Not when their people were dying because of her and her people.

There was no way it was a coincidence the latest victim was found outside the bar owned by Emery's uncle Miles. Augustine would put money on the Mistress choosing that exact location, and he hated the mysterious bitch for it.

There was no rhyme or reason to the murders. He'd wracked his brain trying to find the pattern, trying to anticipate Mistress' next move. Until that night, there'd been no leads, which only proved the location was intentional.

Emery.

The little witch who played innocent but seemed to have a hand in all his troubles for the last three months. From the moment she walked into his life, Emery had—

Bloody fucking hell.

Elizabethtown. Memphis. El Paso. Reno. Yuma.

The cities spelled her fucking name.

Each attack methodically planned out as a calling card, naming the culprit. Emery was the Mistress. Of course she was. Augustine tightened his hands into fists as he stared up at the bar.

It didn't matter that his weaker half loved her, or that the mate bond forced a connection upon him that burned to his very soul. Augustine wouldn't be fooled by her perky tits and soft smile. In fact, he'd enjoy wiping off that smile off her face when he ripped her head from her sweet little body and fucked her lying mouth.

She deserved every bit of punishment he'd give her.

He'd bide his time. He may not be able to exact justice at that moment, not when Emery resided behind the wards of New Orleans, but that didn't mean he couldn't send her a message.

Don't.

August's single-word plea only fueled Augustine's need for revenge.

Upon stepping into Montgomery Blues, an older gentleman from behind the bar looked up from wiping the countertop. "Last call is in a few minutes, but if you're quick, you can get one or two down before closing."

Augustine strolled across the dance floor. It was significantly smaller than his club in Chicago and radiated a homey feel, the antithesis of the industrial grunge of his own. He slid onto a barstool and nodded toward the bartender. "Perfect. I'm only looking for a nightcap."

The bartender raised an eyebrow, sizing up Augustine. "What's your poison?"

"A woman. The bane of my existence."

"Ah, we've all got one of those." He reached to the top of the mirrored shelving and pulled out a small, rounded bottle. "I've never met a problem whiskey couldn't fix."

"A man after my cold, dead heart. A double, please."

The bartender tilted his head in question, but went about pouring his glass while Augustine committed the layout of the place to memory.

A dozen small booths surrounded the dance floor, a few filled with patrons saying their goodbyes. The main attraction was a stage with a small, raised bandstand and an upright piano.

Even he could see why Emery loved it. If she weren't a traitorous bitch, she would be a good compliment to August's soft nature and love of music.

Too bad she'd decided to fuck with him. She would die, slowly, painfully, along with the rest of the coven.

Maybe he'd look into purchasing the bar after the unfortunate passing of its owner. A little souvenir for August.

He waited for another of August's halfhearted pleas, but it never came. August was nothing if not consistent in his feelings for the witch. He loathed her, despised her for her lies and deceit... until it came to the conversation of air remaining in her lungs. Then he went all soft.

The bartender placed his drink in front of him, and a photo on the wall caught Augustine's eye. The bartender and a certain pink-haired witch.

Bingo.

A sly smile tugged at his lips as Augustine took a sip of the top shelf whiskey and savored the richness on his tongue. "You know Emery?"

The bartender stopped wiping the bartop, and while his lips turned upward, his eyes settled into a far off look. "She's my niece. Do you know her?"

"We've met, but we had a bit of a falling out. Have you spoken to her recently? I've been trying to reconnect." The game of niceties wasn't his style, but a full press interrogation might spook Miles.

Miles' eyes narrowed and his heart raced, but he gave nothing away. "Nope. She's been on a tour of Europe. Been saving up for ages to go explore the world."

Lie.

Augustine raised his glass and took a long sip to hide his

grin. Miles might not know yet he was dancing with the devil, but Augustine savored every calculated step. "Oh, that's a pity. I suppose I'll just have to find a way to send her a message myself. I heard she's back in New Orleans now."

Miles' eyes widened and he swallowed hard. "We're closing up, ladies and gents," he hollered, his eyes never leaving Augustine. "Grab your things and get out."

Some of the patrons grumbled but gathered their belongings and made their way toward the door.

It wouldn't matter though.

Augustine gave Miles a Cheshire grin before launching himself from his seat and snapping every neck in the bar in less time than it took for Miles to blink. Bloody hell, it felt good to take out his aggression, even if all the humans in question had done was walk into the wrong bar that night. They were witnesses, and he couldn't have any of those.

August winced from the depths, as he did every time Augustine killed in cold blood.

Augustine ignored his conscience and picked up his glass, taking a sip as Miles stumbled back from the bartop in terror, clinging to the counter behind him.

"Closing so soon?" Augustine asked. "I seem to remember you saying I still had time for another drink."

"I don't know who you are, or why you're asking about Emery, but your kind aren't welcome here." Miles' voice didn't shake, though his racing pulse gave away his fear. Augustine hadn't pegged him as the type to put up a fight, but he'd been wrong before.

"My kind are being murdered by yours." Augustine slammed his hands on the bartop and leaned forward, capturing Miles with his gaze. "You will sit down and tell me everything you know about Emery's current dealings."

Miles' had tried to turn away, but he was too slow. His

eyes widened ever so slightly under Augustine's compulsion. Miles was only part witch and didn't have immunity to a vampire's compulsion. He mechanically walked around the bar and took a seat at the nearest freestanding table. Emery's uncle strained, placing his shaking hands on the table. The muscles in his arms pulsed as he fought Augustine's command.

"I won't tell you anything." He spoke through gritted teeth. "That girl is the last pure thing in my world."

"Pure?" Augustine huffed a laugh as he shrugged off his coat. "She's the furthest thing from pure. I *personally* made sure of that."

Well August did, but they were practically the same person. He'd watched from the depths, memorizing every curve of the woman who was *supposed* to be their queen.

Miles' face scrunched up in disgust. "You're the monster she's running from. What are you going to do, kill me like you killed her sister? Like you killed the other Culling woman and the patrons in my bar?"

Fury flooded his veins. Of course that's the story the witches were telling. For all he knew, Emery killed her sister to gain access to the castle. That little mystery was never solved. Of course, the witches didn't share the part where Emery killed her best friend. Or the part where she tethered herself to August for eternity and then ripped his fucking heart out.

At that moment he knew how he was going to get his revenge. A heart for a heart wouldn't completely sate his rage, but it was a start.

Augustine was raising his hand to rip the beating organ straight from Miles' chest when the door burst open.

Malcolm stood in the doorway, awake after his Augustine-induced nap. His eyes widened, and his mouth dropped open in shock. Then he was on the other side of the bar, with Miles safely behind him before Augustine could react.

"She'll never forgive you if you kill her uncle," Malcolm said.

Augustine examined his nails, scraping a minute spec of dirt from under one of them. "You assume I want her forgiveness, brother."

"You may not, Augustine, but your better half will. If he doesn't already."

"That's debatable."

"Why don't you let him speak for himself. I know he's in there, likely wallowing in his own guilt and self pity." Malcolm raised his voice, his eyes narrowed. "You hear me, August? You are being a coward, letting this fool fight your battles and ruin the only good thing you ever had."

Augustine held back the dramatic eye roll he'd reserved specifically for Malcolm over the last two months. His brother never ceased his pursuit to bring August back to the forefront of their mind. But August didn't want to return. Not when the truth hurt and the woman he loved was his enemy. It was too much for the fragile diplomat. Augustine was made of the best parts of them*the stronger parts. And he wasn't going to be silenced again.

"We're the same person, Malcolm. I'm just in the driver's seat, and I'm not going anywhere. I'm going to rip that little witch's heart from her body, and August will sit back and watch. She's the reason we're here. She's the one behind the murders."

Augustine waited for Malcolm to deny his claim, but it was Miles who spoke up first.

"She isn't one of the coven's blind followers."

"She doesn't have to be, to have an agenda. She chose to go with them. The attacks, all the cities we've been running…

the names of the cities spell her fucking name. All the evidence points to her playing a bigger role in this. Now, I just need to draw her out." Augustine took a step toward Miles, but Malcolm blocked his path.

"There were two other attacks tonight. Neither of which have any correlation to her name."

Augustine paused. Malcolm spoke as if he knew for certain, but how could he? He'd been in a hotel room all night, practically dead. But if there were new attacks, it was significant. If only because it meant they were no longer tracking a single pawn. "What do you mean, two other attacks?"

"When I rejoined the living, I had a message from Father. There was another killing in Washington, and one in Arkansas."

Augustine's gut clenched. "That's nowhere near here."

Malcolm's lips formed a grim line and he nodded. He didn't need to say the witches were growing bolder. They'd never struck in two places at once, let alone three. If he had to guess, strategically, the first string of attacks were test runs. They would only grow more frequent and widespread as time went on. It didn't mean Emery wasn't involved, though. Augustine decided to reserve that judgement for when there was more evidence.

Augustine's phone rang and he tugged it from his coat. Upon seeing his mother's name on the screen, he answered it.

"Now's not really a good time, Mother."

"You and your brother need to come home." Panic laced her voice, setting Augustine on guard.

"What's wrong?"

Malcolm stepped toward him, and Augustine put the phone on speaker.

"It's Thea." She choked on a sob. "They tried to take her. She fought back, she really did, but they tried to kill her."

"Who tried?"

"Witches."

Augustine inhaled a sharp breath and clenched his fists as August clawed to the surface. Thea may not be their blood, but she might as well have been. She was the only bright spot left in the castle, and they both knew it.

"Is she hurt?" Worry filled Malcolm's voice, mirroring Augustine's thoughts. Gods help the witches if they'd killed his sister. He'd burn every last one of them to the ground and ensure there weren't enough to identify the remains.

"She's alive, but unconscious. We're waiting for the doctor to come check on her."

Augustine breathed a sigh of relief. "And the witch who attacked her?" Hopefully he'd get the chance to rip them apart himself.

"Dead."

"That's unfortunate. I'm glad you're safe, keep us posted on Thea, we're on our way home."

"Hurry, August."

He hung up and inhaled a long, steady breath. The witches had gone too far. Going after Thea was over the line. Thea was innocent on every front. She'd done nothing to deserve their wrath.

He was done doing the bare minimum. Done considering diplomacy to appease his brother and the weak vampire he housed within him that somehow still loved that traitorous witch bitch.

To hell with them and their peacekeeping suggestions.

The door burst open again, and another of the Mistress' vampires sped through the club. Stopping behind Miles, she grabbed either side of his head.

The vampire's glowing silver eyes met Augustine's and her blood-red lips tipped into a mocking grin. "Tick tock, Your Highness. The Mistress is waiting for you."

For the first time since he'd taken the forefront, Augustine froze, time standing still. Sweat beaded at his temple. A direct result of August putting up a real fight for the first time. He clawed at Augustine's chest, tearing holes in the impenetrable wall he'd erected to stay in control.

She'll never forgive us. She would never hurt Thea. She loves Thea. Please.

August continued to beg for Miles' life, not realizing it was all Augustine could do to fight him off. There was no room to fight August and save Miles. Not that Augustine wanted to. He didn't care that Emery wouldn't forgive them for the death of the only person who brought any joy to her shitty childhood. A heart for a heart. Even if the man whose heart she destroyed wanted to spare her a heartache of her own.

Fortunately for him, August wasn't strong enough. He didn't have what it took to tame Augustine. To be both diplomat and enforcer.

Augustine stood firm in his fight against August, giving everything he had to protect his status as the primary host of their mind. They stood by in a silent battle of wills and watched the Mistress' vampire rip Miles' head from his body and flee the club with the same speed with which she'd entered.

"No!" Malcolm's eyes darted between Miles' slumped body and the door. "Why didn't you stop her?"

"Why didn't you? I was at odds with my weaker half." He fingered the flecks of blood on his sleeve, wondering which victim dared stain his favorite coat. The reality of it was, the woman had already been holding Miles' head in her hands; neither of them would have been able to reach her before she took the older man's life. But he wouldn't point that out. "We were debating the value of Miles' life, and he didn't provide compelling enough evidence to step in."

It didn't matter that Malcolm likely tasted his lie—rage still filled his gaze for a few precarious moments before fizzling out. He hung his head and sighed. "You can't help but be the monster they want you to be."

"I am the monster, Malcolm. I always have been. Your disappointment only serves to further distance our already exasperated relationship. Just let me go, brother."

"I can't do that." A laughable amount of determination filled Malcolm's voice. "If not for you, for Em."

"She isn't one of us, Malcolm. She never will be."

He ignored the way the mate bond cinched around his heart at his declaration.

"No. She's better than us." Malcolm turned and headed for the door. "Clean up the mess you made. I'll have the jet readied."

Augustine huffed a laugh, swallowing the fear that nestled in the recesses of his mind at August's growing strength. He'd need to keep his guard up if he were going to survive this time.

He followed Malcolm toward the door and paused, surveying the carnage. Let the witches find the bodies. The time of false peace was over, and the promise of war never tasted so sweet.

Chapter Two

AUGUSTINE

Light poured in through the window of Augustine's study, highlighting the map of New Orleans. His lips curled into a smile behind his steepled fingers, his plans nearly in place.

"If we have the bombs simultaneously hit the main entrance of the compound and the south wall entrance," Augustine reached out and moved his pawns into position, "I think it'll have the most impact."

"Nicely done, son." The King nodded in agreement. "I trust everything is ready?"

"Yes, I've already received confirmation that our compelled spies are en route to New Orleans, and I'll have my men ready by this afternoon."

"I'm proud of you, son. I had my doubts that you were capable of seeing this through. I thought you'd let that witch get under your skin, but you've proved me wrong."

"Thank you." Augustine beamed under his father's praise while wrestling August back where he belonged. His annoyingly persistent other half had become more vocal since leaving Los Angeles. He didn't wholeheartedly oppose the bombing; he only cared that Emery survived. A sentiment Augustine suspected was due to the incessant mate bond between them. The damn thing nearly sank its claws into Augustine on a few occasions. He didn't like to consider the weaker moments when he'd find himself inexplicably standing outside Emery's vacant room in the middle of the night, a deep sorrow rooted in his chest.

Those were the nights he'd visit the feeders and follow them up with a decanter of whiskey.

Lucky for him, August didn't have the strength to fight him, even in those moments of weakness. Augustine suspected it was because August wasn't ready to forgive Emery. Which was fine with him, though the uptick in strength gave him pause. August was either close to forgiving or close to forgetting the little witch, and Augustine wasn't sure either boded well for him.

Ideally he wouldn't have to worry much longer. He'd taken every precaution to ensure his plan would not only work, but would hit the witches—and Emery—where it hurt most.

Where they believed they couldn't be touched.

Neither August nor the wards of New Orleans would stop him from exacting revenge—not only for his people but also his family.

"Have you been to see Thea yet?" His father tipped his glass and finished the last of the crimson liquid.

Augustine's fangs pushed against his gums and he swallowed hard to keep them in place. "No. I'm heading there now." And then he'd find a feeder. The bloodlust was worse this time around. He'd always had a penchant for the vein, but not like this. Not to the point where he constantly felt like he was missing a part of himself if he wasn't filled to the brim with the warm life-sustaining liquid.

Sweat formed on his brow, and Augustine struggled to focus on anything beyond getting his fix. How long had it been? Ten hours? Twelve? He'd fed on their short stop to the Washington crime scene before they'd flown back to the castle. When they'd arrived, he'd been in a foul mood. He was sick of the lectures from both Malcolm and August about his actions in Los Angeles, and the former's insane theories regarding his mate. They'd only fueled his need for blood, which he'd tried to ignore and channel into ensuring the safety of his family.

...Which had led to the all-nighter and a plan to bomb the coven's compound.

He shouldn't need to feed, not yet, but with his distraction sufficiently over, he wanted to all the same.

"Good, send a report after you see her. And keep an eye on your brother. I don't trust Malcolm not to interfere with our plans. While he may not be as outspoken as your cousin, he has a soft spot for the witch."

"Yes, Father."

With a nod, the King made for the door.

Augustine chuckled to himself, considering which tactics his brother would try this time. Malcolm would almost definitely continue his crusade to lure August back to the forefront. But he didn't understand; every attempt to make his *mate* more appealing backfired and only served to strengthen his resolve that she was no better than the rest of the coven.

In the past, August had allowed Augustine to take the lead when he needed to let go and allow his bloodlust to consume him—to forget his morals for a time and become the monster at the heart of every royal vampire. Malcolm had always been able to lure August back. His older brother had it down to a science. Trap him and force him to reconcile with the blood lust. At his core, August didn't want to be a monster. Which always made the light more appealing.

A month ago, August retreated to protect his heart. The mate bond was seared so deep within him that it consumed his mind. August was driven by his heart, and he'd never be able to walk away from Emery, not completely. So when the light no longer held the promise of peace, August let go.

Lucky for him, Augustine thrived in darkness.

A knock pulled him from his thoughts, and Jessi slid through the slightly open door.

She worked her body up next to his and ran a manicured hand down his forearm, light reflecting off the glittering ring on her third finger. "Your footman said you were back. I'm so happy to see you. We have so much to discuss."

Augustine managed not to recoil under her touch. He'd have to remind Clovis that while she may be his fiancée, Jessi was not on the short list of people who needed to know of his whereabouts.

He plucked her hand from his, ignoring the instant pout on her lips. "It's a short visit."

"Oh." Her voice fell momentarily before she recovered. "That gives us just enough time to discuss the wedding. I was thinking we could have it after the hunt. Everyone would already be here."

Anger rose within him, both August's and his own. He snarled and pushed Jessi back, pressing her into the stone wall behind her. "My sister is unconscious and my people are being killed by the witches. You think I give a fuck about your fairytale wedding?"

Fear flashed in her eyes before she smiled seductively and raked her hands up his chest. "You'll catch the witches, my love, and you'll destroy them. I only wished for you to be a part of the planning. But, if you'd like me to do it all, say no more." She leaned in and placed a kiss on his tightened jaw, thrusting out her half-covered breasts. "You must be so worried about Thea. I've been at her side since it happened. It's just terrible."

His fists clenched as he struggled to keep hold of his temper. Jessi was a bloody fucking snake. He didn't want to marry her—she was a means to an end. A concession to gain his father's support in hunting the witches and keep him in the loop on the investigation.

His loathing only fueled the bloodlust that pounded through his body. He inhaled sharply as she cooed against him. His fangs elongated, ready to tear into her rapid pulse. She'd picked the wrong moment to antagonize him. "Listen very closely, Jessi, because I am only going to say this once. You will never be my equal. You will be nothing more than a consort. The mother of my children, and that is it."

The "mother" part might be a stretch right now, considering he couldn't get it up unless it was one of August's nightly dreams reliving Emery bouncing on his cock, but Jessi didn't need to know that.

"But—"

"Would you rather I send you home? Because I assure you no court wants you as their own." Or they wouldn't after he was done with her. Even if he had no intention of fucking her. "You will be my wife only in name—that means you knock before you enter, and you don't lay a hand on me unless I say so."

Her eyes narrowed and a sly smile stretched across her face. "You can't send me home. While you were away your father told me just how important I am to his plans. You need me now that Emery proved to be the traitorous bitch I always knew she was." Her eyes lowered to his lips before meeting his again. "I'm the one your father picked."

"Then you can go ride his cock." Augustine pushed away from the wall and straightened his cuffs. "I don't want to see you for the rest of my stay. Plan whatever the hell union will appease my father. Nothing will ever change between us, Jessi. I suggest you get that through your head if you'd like to keep it attached to your body."

Jessi's eyes widened, but he didn't bother waiting for another of her sickeningly sweet responses before storming from the study toward Thea's suite. Jessi was a necessary evil on the road to claiming his throne—one he'd be happy to be rid of once an heir was secured.

The castle was a minefield of armed sentinels stationed to help protect the royal family. After Emery's infiltration, they'd upped their presence on the perimeter, and since the attack on Thea, there was more military presence than he'd ever seen.

A testament to the fact his father wouldn't be fooled by the witches again.

He stepped in front of one of the fledgling sentinels, who scoffed and opened his mouth to reply—and by the look of his narrowed eyes, it wasn't going to be something appropriate for the crown prince.

The young sentinel's eyes widened and he stumbled back a step before righting himself to attention. "I"m sorry, Your Highness. I didn't mean to get in your way."

"I stepped in front of you, Private…"

"Joseph."

"Joseph?"

"I mean Dowd. Private Dowd."

"Well, Private Dowd, I suggest you keep a better eye on your surroundings. I could have been a witch."

"Yes, sir."

"Do you know where General Rex and the rest of my unit are?"

"I believe they just flew in from a mission. They should be at the barracks." Interesting. Augustine wasn't aware his team had been tasked out in his absence. They should've been grounded until he returned. Though they were the best, they were a team, and his father knew that.

"Thank you. Carry on."

Joseph brought three fingers to his forehead in salute and walked away a little taller than he'd been before.

Augustine remembered what it was like to be a young sentinel. Of course, it was a different time then. A time of constant war. These fresh boys had no idea what they were in for, and he hoped they'd have what it took to face down the monsters the witches created.

The thought haunted him all the way to Thea's suite. He stowed it away as something to talk to Rex about when he found him.

Augustine stepped inside and leaned against the wall, listening as his mother sang to his younger sister. It was a song he was familiar with, one she'd sung to all her children and a favorite of his. A lullaby telling the story of a great adventure only just begun, which would carry over into dreams as one slept.

His eyes narrowed on Thea's tiny frame. All of her stuffed animals had been removed, and the sheer size of the bed left Thea looking so small. So fragile. It didn't help that the drapes were kept shut, creating a dark and dismal atmosphere.

A reflection of the situation.

The Queen finished the lullaby, and her empty gaze drifted to him. "Come join me, August."

He didn't bother to correct her. She knew he was Augustine. Somehow she always knew when her soft artist had given way to the cunning monster. Still, she loved him just the same, maybe even moreso when he was hardest to love.

He took the chair opposite his mother. Thea's breaths were

barely a whisper, though they might as well have been a roar with the way each shallow exhale filled Augustine's ears. He gently held her hand, willing her to open her eyes and give him one of her beautiful smiles.

The Queen's face was hollow, and he'd wager she hadn't moved from Thea's side since the attack. In such a short time, she'd become a shell of the woman he'd left. Thea was the last good thing she had to hold onto in a world in which she was nothing more than a pretty face.

"How is she?" It was more of a question to get his mother talking than a need to know. One look at Thea's pale skin and sunken eyes and anyone could see things were not looking good.

"The doctors said there was nothing they could do, that it isn't a physical ailment that keeps her from waking up."

Fucking witches.

He'd kill every one of them.

He inhaled a calming breath through clenched teeth, struggling to keep a calm presence for his mother's sake. Augustine would relish the carnage he'd bring to the witches' doorstep, and would stop at nothing until they were repaid tenfold.

The door to the bedroom flew open and Malcolm entered, clutching a mortar to his chest.

Their mother looked up, her mouth dropped open, and a spark lit in her eyes. "Were you able to find the herbs?"

"I think so. I'm not sure it will work but Lily seemed to think it would slow down whatever magic ails her. Unless it's a curse, and if that's the case, there won't be anything we can do without the bloodline of the witch who cast it."

Malcolm's mouth formed a grim line. He didn't need to say that would be impossible, considering the witch who'd done this to Thea was dead. If it was a curse, they were shit out of luck.

Augustine's eyes widened as Malcolm reached for the blanket covering Thea's chest. He grabbed his brother's hand and narrowed his gaze. "What the hell do you think you are doing?"

Malcolm snatched his hand back and snarled at Augustine, showing more teeth than he had in years. "Trying to save our sister. Which is more than you can say, locking yourself in your study all night."

"I was doing my part to plan our retaliation."

"While I was trying to find a way to save her."

"Both of you, stop." Their mother stood, tears streaming down her face. "If you can't pretend to get along within these four walls, then leave until you can." She shifted her focus to Augustine. "Malcolm is doing as I asked, in order to save Thea. Or, at the very least, give her more time. I couldn't care less about this stupid war with the witches as long as my little girl lies in that bed. If I could bring Lilyana here, I would. Anything to save Thea."

"Lilyana? She's one of them," Augustine spat, unable to fathom how they could trust any witch. "How do you know she isn't giving her something that will make it worse? Lilyana fled with Callum, who turned the wolves against us for his cause, whatever the bloody hell that is. He's protecting Emery. None of them can be trusted."

Callum had been nothing but a pain in his ass since he'd arrived at the castle. He may be family, but he was secretive and conniving, and as far as Augustine was concerned, he could die with the rest of the witches when the time came.

His mother pursed her lips and narrowed her unapproving gaze. "You think none of them can be trusted because you're too wounded to see clearly. That girl had nothing to do with any of this."

Augustine scoffed, but his mother only continued to berate him. "I'm not saying we don't kill every witch who harmed our people, I'm only saying, don't let your prejudice cloud your judgement."

His mouth set in a hard line, and he turned toward the door. This line of thinking would get Malcolm and his mother killed. Of course, he'd never allow that to pass. He'd protect them even if they were kicking and screaming the entire time. He'd do what it took to save Thea. She'd survive this even if he had to find a witch and make her reverse the spell with her dying breath. He would protect his people and become the king they needed him to be. He couldn't afford to be soft like the rest of his family.

"Running away from your problems again?" Malcolm taunted. "I didn't think you were one to blindly follow our father."

Shared rage coursed through Augustine and he spun on his heel, glaring daggers at his brother. "Everything I've done, I've done to protect our family. If that makes me like him, so be it. Now if you'll excuse me, I've got a compound full of witches to bomb."

Augustine had barely finished speaking when he was thrown into a stone wall. Malcolm growled, fangs elongated and forearm pressed to Augustine's throat. "You can't bomb the compound."

A manic laugh escaped his upturned lips. "The fuck I can't. You may not be able to do what needs to be done, but I have no qualms about righting the wrongs against us."

"Emery is in the compound." Malcolm's statement came out as more of a desperate plea for him to reconsider.

Unfortunately, as long as he was in the forefront and the

bond remained mostly tethered to August's heart, Augustine had zero fucks left to give.

He grabbed Malcolm's wrist and, with a shove, spun his brother so he held him against the wall, arm twisted behind his back. Augustine leaned in and whispered. "I especially have no qualms about that particular witch."

"Please, don't. She's our mate." August whined from the depths of his mind, but Augustine shut the door further on his weaker half. A mate didn't conceal what she was. A mate didn't side with his enemy. He hated the argument that Emery was his mate as much as he hated Emery herself.

Augustine may have known mates were real—as much as he didn't want to believe Callum, he felt the bond that tethered him to Emery. But the difference between him and August, his brother, and his cousin was that Augustine could live without the all-consuming love it attempted to blanket around him.

Love was fleeting. Logic was far more reliable.

But then Malcolm said something he couldn't have expected. Something that made his stomach twist. "She's pregnant, August."

Augustine stared at him, unable to process the words.

Malcolm relaxed against him, almost as if giving up. "August, you can't kill her because she carries your heir."

Augustine dropped his brother's arm and stepped away. It couldn't be true. He shook his head, overwhelmed. August screamed inside of him, banging on the door, begging to be released, but Augustine wasn't ready to give up so easily. This couldn't be; this bitch, this heinous creature who had lied to him, betrayed him… she couldn't be carrying his heir.

The tension in Augustine's gut eased as he decided that Malcolm's revelation must be another trick. "You've got to be kidding me," he snarled. "You actually expect me to believe that? Is this the best you could come up with? I expected better from you, Malcolm. She might be pregnant, but it's not with my heir."

"It's the truth, August. Call Callum. He'll confirm it. You'll know if he's lying. He scented her himself before she left the castle."

His gaze snapped to his mother, but the way her mouth hung open and tears welled in her eyes let him know she hadn't known about the pregnancy before that moment.

The mate bond tightened, and August roared within him. His chest swelled, pushing Augustine to the point he lost his grip on the metaphorical door he kept August firmly behind.

August clung to the bond that tethered him to Emery and, with everything he had, pushed his way to the front. His eyes widened and his voice was laced with desperation. "Call him. Now."

Malcolm didn't hesitate. He pulled his phone out and dialed, placing it on speakerphone.

"How's Thea?" Callum's hopeful voice filled the room. "Did the herbs work?"

August snatched the phone in his brother's hand. "Callum, I swear to the gods, if you don't tell me the truth right now, I will rip your heart out your chest the next time I see you."

"Yes, she's pregnant with your child."

No lie.

His mouth fell open and all coherent thought left.

Emery was pregnant.

He was going to be a father.

A moment passed, but it wasn't long enough to consider anything more before he was jerked back into fighting against Augustine, his strength minute in comparison to the brutish asshole. August wasn't ready to face the world just yet, but he couldn't let anything happen to Emery. To his child.

"Now, if you could get your head out of your arse, I'd greatly appreciate it." Callum's terse command was enough to distract him and cause him to lose what little control he had.

August barely managed to get out the plea before Augustine gripped his spine and shoved him back down, his words a choked whisper. "Get her out of the compound."

Chapter Three

EMERY

A guttural moan filled the library, followed by a giggle. Emery stifled a withering sigh. She should've known the stars couldn't possibly leave her in peace. Nothing seemed to go her way lately. Still, Emery put her head down and kept reading the riveting account of history according to witches.

She'd just finished a passage detailing the actual reason Marie Antoinette's head was cut off when two hands slammed on the table in front of her, and the body blocked the light from the opposite wall. Irritated by the intrusion, Emery closed the book and looked up, instantly regretting it.

Naked Double D's swung inches from her face, and if she wasn't careful she'd end up with a black eye. The woman, Emery thought her name was Marguerite, threw her head back as a male she didn't recognize rammed into her from behind. In the throes of their passion, neither of them seemed to give two shits that she was sitting at the very table they picked to fuck on.

Malcolm had warned her that witches were overtly sexual beings because of the curse cast on vampires. Sexual prowess was the price all non royal witches paid to stop royal vampires from being created outside of reproduction. Now to get a non royal vampire they had to be turned.

Emery hadn't believed a word Malcolm had said until she got to New Orleans. It wasn't humanly possible to crave sex at the level he'd described. But witches weren't entirely human. After almost two months at the compound, she couldn't doubt his words. She'd seen enough to last a lifetime, and then some.

Perky boobs. Saggy boobs. Boobs with piercings that accented their unique ability to point in opposite directions.

And that was just the females. The males were just as bad, with their free-hanging cocks rubbing up on every piece of furniture, staring straight at her while she tried to pile food onto her plate at dinner.

Witches had no shame. The moment they crossed the salt-lined threshold of the compound, they removed the majority of their clothing and went about the rest of their day in the buff. Emery had never been to a nudist colony, but she imagined it would be similar. They greeted each other with gentle caresses and open-mouth kisses, which would often lead to casual sex in alcoves or across occupied library tables.

Which is how she found herself with boobs clapping together in front of her face.

"Uh, hello." Emery waved her hand in front of Marguerite's face. "This table is occupied, do you think you could use, I don't know, any of the other tables in the library for your afternoon lay?"

Marguerite glared at Emery, and the male slowed his rhythmic thrusts. She mewled, licking her lips before looking over her shoulder. "I swear if you stop because of this vampire-loving whore, Daniel, I'm never going to let you between these sweet thighs again."

Daniel's gaze met Emery's, and he gave her a shrug. He sucked his lower lip between his teeth and gripped

Marguerite's hips tighter, picking up the pace. His eyes never left Emery's as he drove into Marguerite repeatedly. Based on the sounds coming from his partner, he was doing an excellent job of sending her into the throes of ecstasy.

Heat flooded Emery's cheeks. She wanted to look away but couldn't tear her eyes from the couple in front of her. She usually avoided the common areas of the compound for this very reason. August had awoken something primal within her, and while she didn't have any desire to join in on naked fun with anyone but him, she couldn't help the way her stomach tightened and seemed to drop to the space between her legs.

Which led to far too many solo adventures and cold showers. It had only gotten worse as the pregnancy hormones took over and forced her mind to remember the way August felt above her. Inside her. How his hips shifted against hers. The way his lips trailed across her jaw before he buried his fangs in her neck.

Emery shifted uncomfortably in her seat, her own need growing with every slam of Daniel's hips.

Daniel and Marguerite, along with all the other non-royal witches in the compound, didn't have to worry about getting pregnant. The curse took care of that, demanding infertility be thrown into the price as well. Emery, on the other hand, had become a mated, insatiable, knocked-up mess the first time she let a man between her legs.

Daniel cried out and finished with a final thrust, and Marguerite rolled her eyes. She backed into him, pushing him off her. Daniel pulled her up, pinning her back to his chest. His hand found her nipple and gave it a hard pinch.

As if she'd forgotten she didn't get off again before he did, Marguerite melted into him. His free hand found its way to her clit, and he spun soft circles until Marguerite was bucking against his hand, begging for more.

Emery clenched her fists and resisted the urge to grind her hips in an attempt to quench the need she never quite filled on her own.

Daniel smirked and raised a brow. "You sure you don't want to join us, Emery? I can make you feel things no vampire prince ever could."

The mate bond snapped to attention the moment he spoke against August, and doused the carnal need low in her belly. Anger flooded her veins.

"You expect me to be satisfied with that little thing?" Emery snapped without thinking. "It would easily take five witches to accomplish what my one vampire could."

My? Fucking mate bond. The last thing she could consider August was hers.

She hated the insane fire the bond lit within her to defend that prick of a crown prince. Or maybe she should blame pregnancy hormones. Either way she'd made herself sound like the needy whore they thought she was and managed to piss off two witches with infinitely more magic than her.

Daniel's lips curled into a sneer, and he dropped Marguerite on to the desk. She scoffed at him, but he ignored her and allowed his hands to fall to his sides, palms opened toward Emery.

Realizing almost too late what was about to happen, Emery grabbed the ancient book she'd been deciphering just in time to be hit by a gust of wind. She was thrown from her chair and slammed into the bookshelf against the wall.

Panic coursed through her as she considered the baby in her belly, and she hated the bond even more for pushing her to bait Daniel. More than that, she wished she had the ability to cast a shield as Lily had at the castle. Being useless in a world full of magic might as well have been a death sentence with the number of times she found herself at the mercy of other witches.

"Stop this, now." A female voice boomed through the small library study area.

Daniel dropped his elemental magic, and Emery slid to the floor in a heap.

Bronwyn, one of the inner circle members, stood in the doorway in a full power stance, which was only enhanced by her sexy-monk outfit: a pair of low slung parachute pants and a scrap of fabric that criss-crossed over her breasts beneath an open robe. She was shorter than Emery but her authoritative presence made her seem taller. Bronwyn's eyes darted between Emery and the two naked witches. "What's the meaning of this, Daniel?"

Daniel threw up his hands in mock surrender. "Emery attacked us! We only defended ourselves."

"With what? Her scrawny physique?" Bronwyn scoffed, her eyes narrowed. "She has no magic, and from what I could see you had her pinned to the wall. Need I remind you she is the intended heir of this coven?"

Daniel swallowed hard and Emery couldn't help but smirk.

"Get out, both of you. I'll expect to see you in my office tomorrow afternoon to discuss how you can help to make Emery's stay with us more productive."

They hurried from the room, and Emery started to snicker but thought better of it when Bronwyn's hardened gaze landed on her.

The petite redhead crossed the room, hovering over Emery while she sat up on the floor. "What the hell were you thinking picking a fight with Daniel? His family is a major contributor to the coven. They may not be inner circle members, but they could make your life a living hell."

A huffed laugh escaped Emery. "No one could make it worse than it is."

Life at the compound was not ideal, and the constant sex wasn't even the worst of it. She was an outcast. If it weren't for Ansel, she'd be completely alone.

Bronwyn sighed and extended her hand to help her up.

Emery had wanted to hate Bronwyn when she'd arrived at the compound. As a member of the inner circle, she was part of the entity that decided generations of witches in her family should pay the price for the actions of one. It was because of the inner circle that Emery had been left in the dark about her heritage. She had yet to get a straight answer as to what the hell happened between the twin sisters or how Lily ended up banished. It seemed that particular bit of information was a closely guarded secret.

Being the youngest member of the inner circle, Bronwyn was assigned all the bitch work, including Emery's immersion into the coven.

In many ways, Bronwyn reminded Emery of Flora: small yet mighty, with a fire inside that was often underestimated. It made sense she was one of the most powerful component witches of her age, and even though they were on opposite sides of the vampire-witch feud, Emery had come to enjoy the time they spent together.

Well, mostly. When she wasn't trying to get Emery to acclimate to coven life, Bronwyn was one of the few witches within the coven who didn't look at her as the vampire prince's plaything. It was one subject they didn't broach. Both because Emery didn't like talking about it, and because Bronwyn didn't care for what she had to say. Bronwyn was firmly on Team August is a Monster.

Which at that moment, Emery couldn't argue with.

He seemed to kill for shits and giggles, leaving no witness at the vampire killing crimes scenes. It wasn't like he couldn't compel them to forget, she'd seen his compulsion first-hand. He chose to kill, which scared the ever loving shit out of her. Her August was a monster of the best kind. One who understood the need for restraint and had values, only killing when necessary.

At least that's who she thought he was. The longer she was away from the castle, the more she realized how little she knew about the crown prince.

Emery absentmindedly brought a hand to her stomach and gave it a soft rub before dropping it to her side. If August was so willing to kill innocent witnesses who had done nothing to him, how would he react when he found out she carried his child?

Bronwyn's nose scrunched up and she scoffed, distracting Emery before she fell down the rabbit hole of dark August-induced thoughts. "The compound isn't that bad. It can't be worse than the castle."

Emery's lips fell into a frown. "At the castle I wasn't attacked daily."

Which was debatable if she considered the many bullshit arguments Jessi subjected her to, but at least then she'd only walked away with a bruised ego.

"We'll talk to the priestess and see if we can't get her to put some extra protection in place for you." Bronwyn paused and looked around, seemingly noticing for the first time Emery didn't have her shadow. "Where's your wolf friend?"

Her lips tugged into a smile. "Oh, he's occupied."

She raised a questioning brow but didn't push. "He needs to be with you at all times. That's the only reason the circle allowed him access to the coven at all."

Emery struggled to keep her face blank. The last thing she wanted was to get Ansel in trouble, but she'd worked hard to distract him and couldn't wait to see his reaction. She wished she could share the fun with Bronwyn, but she never knew when she was going to get inner-circle Bronwyn or the relaxed witch she could almost be friends with.

Ansel was a member of the Americas wolf pack sent to protect her while she lived with the coven. She still wasn't one-hundred-percent sure how Callum managed to get the wolves to agree to help, but she'd been thankful when Ansel showed up in New Orleans a week after she did.

He was so much more than her protector. He was the only soul in the compound who knew about the baby. Where Bronwyn was fun to talk to, Ansel was her lifeline when the weight of it all got to be too much. He was also a wicked practical joker, and loved to set up scenarios for Emery to evade or escape, claiming it was good practice if she were ever kidnapped. The way he laughed as she struggled to get out of each situation made her think it was more for fun than anything else.

She may have strategically planned some payback for the many times she'd found herself locked in a closet with no way out.

"I'll go find him now." *Before this turns into a lecture sponsored by the inner circle.*

Emery picked up the book she'd been reading on witch history and started for the door.

"Wait."

Bronwyn placed a hand in front of Emery's stomach and panic coursed through her. Emery stepped back as fast as she could—Bronwyn had been an inch away from pressing the baggy sweater Emery favored into the swell of her rapidly growing stomach.

Emery looked up at Bronwyn's face, noticing for the first time that there were signs of strain around her eyes. "Is everything okay?"

"I came down here to tell you the inner circle wants to meet with you first thing in the morning."

"Okay." Hesitation laced Emery's voice. "What's this about?"

Bronwyn raked a hand through her thick red curls. "The circle feels you aren't acclimating well. They want to speak with you about your future within the coven."

Of course they did.

The coven wanted her to learn to use the magic she didn't have. To see if she had an affinity for anything useful before they considered finding a way to unbind her magic. So far, her training sessions had been useless. They mostly entailed sitting in a room with various types of witches and hoping she'd feel drawn to one of them.

She hadn't. And meditation was not a strong suit of hers.

Between the clusterfuck that was her life and the mate bond buzzing in her chest, she was never able to quiet her mind. More often than not, she napped. Which wasn't hard to accomplish considering she wasn't sleeping most nights. Between needing to pee constantly and the nightmares of faceless beings fighting an unwinnable battle, she was exhausted every second of every day.

Emery raised a brow, hoping Bronwyn would answer her next question. "Will Vishna be there?"

The last two times she'd been called on by the inner circle, her ancestor had been conveniently busy and unable to attend. The meetings were pointless unless Vishna was present and Emery was tired of wasting her time. The circle couldn't make decisions without their priestess, and Emery was tired of half answers and untruths regarding her heritage. Vishna had been too busy since her arrival—dealing with the fallout from the attacks on vampires—to be bothered by her niece.

It was nice to know her views on the importance of family hadn't been altered by Emery's arrival. Vishna hadn't wanted anything to do with her for her first twenty-five years of life and apparently still didn't. Lily had been the only member of her family who was happy to see her, and it was Emery's luck she'd find her only to lose her moments later.

It just went to show how different sisters could be. Twins at that.

Bronwyn nodded, her hands fidgeting nervously at her sides while her gaze found every nook and cranny to avoid meeting Emery's.

"Is there something else?"

"No," Bronwyn snapped, followed by a defeated sigh. "Just be in the inner chambers at nine tomorrow morning, okay, Emery? Please don't be late."

"Okay." Emery raised her hand in a mock salute. "I'll be on time like a good little witch. Thank you for letting me know."

She sidestepped Bronwyn and walked toward the door, a strong need to flee the present company forming in her gut.

This summons to the inner circle felt different than the others—more ominous. Emery scrawled a note and left it for Ansel on her dresser before hightailing it out of the compound.

She needed fresh air and a moment alone to consider what the inner circle wanted from her. If Vishna was indeed going to be there, it had to be a big deal, and Emery was more than ready for the answers the priestess owed her.

Chapter Four

EMERY

The air was oppressive, weighing heavily on her chest and suffocating her the moment she crossed the salt-lined door out of the air-conditioned compound. Even in the dark of night, it was unrelenting in its attack. But for a few precious moments alone, she'd suffer the humidity.

Tourists maneuvered the narrow sidewalks that surrounded the compound, blissfully unaware they were in the midst of powerful witches, many of whom, with the flick of a wrist, could end their lives. Not that the witches did that often. They were content with running the shops surrounding the compound, serving the tourists and locals alike, using their talents to add to the magic of New Orleans. From specialty paper, to basic voodoo sundries, to rare herbs and spices, if it related to one of the seven basic groups of magic, it could be found nearby.

The smell of fried dough wafted down the street from her favorite café, instantly making Emery's mouth water. A craving for beignets clawed at her stomach, and she knew if she didn't satisfy it, she'd be able to think of little else until she did.

Cravings in general were a bitch, but pregnancy cravings

were so much worse. They took hold and turned her brain to mush. Which mixed with pregnancy brain basically made her feel completely useless.

Emery slid a hand to her stomach and whispered to herself. "What Mommy's little urchin wants, they get."

The nickname elicited a soft chuckle. What she'd initially said in a fit of anger after a particularly bad bout of morning sickness had become a term of endearment for her unborn child. It fit too, considering Callum had said her baby smelled of crisp ocean air. It felt like a lifetime ago he'd told her she was pregnant. Two months. Now she couldn't imagine a world without him or her in it. It didn't matter the baby leached the life out of her, she'd suffer it a thousand times if it meant they would thrive.

But before they could thrive, the baby had to survive.

Her baby continued to grow in tandem with the unease in the supernatural world, and Emery knew a time would come soon when their very existence would tip the scales. Unfortunately, if all the history she'd read recently was any indicator, war would need to come before any semblance of acceptance or peace.

Which scared the ever loving shit out of her.

Pushing away her thoughts of despair, Emery slipped from the crowded sidewalk and took to the streets, beelining for her favorite café, the VooDoo Brew, where she knew she could get her beignet fix. It also helped she adored Agatha, the old witch who ran the shop. Aside from Bronwyn and Dahlia, Agatha was the only other witch in New Orleans who treated Emery with kindness.

Out front, a green-and-purple neon sign flashed with a coffee cup bubbling like a cauldron. It served as a beacon for Emery's fluffy, fried dough dreams. The archway entrance and lattice lining the patio were covered in vines spotted with beautiful moonflowers in full bloom. While many patrons enjoyed the intertwined morning glories that bloomed in the daytime sun, Emery found it was the large white blooms that bloomed in the darkness that spoke to her soul.

"Emery!" Agatha exclaimed from behind the pastry counter as Emery entered the café. Her curly gray hair was pulled to the side in her signature braid. "I'm so happy to see you. The leaves said you would visit today."

Emery's lips tipped into an indulgent smile. "And what else did they say?"

The sweet old chrone was one of the rare few gifted with the talents of the stars which gave her the ability to prophesize through tarot or tea leaves. She really should've been a member of the inner circle, but she refused to play within the politics of the coven. Emery knew there was a story there, but Agatha remained tight-lipped the few times she'd asked. It was said the star readers of old received visions directly from the threads of destiny, but over time, their numbers thinned.

"They spoke of a big change coming to you. A new life in the making."

Panic stilled Emery, and she looked sharply into Agatha's eyes, trying to discern if Agatha knew about the baby. The older woman smiled kindly and pulled out two tea bags. "Your usual, dear?"

Emery nodded, dismissing the prediction as a lucky guess.

Agatha moved past the espresso machine and a pang of longing swept over Emery. What she wouldn't give for a double shot of espresso with a heavy layer of cream and an extra helping of chocolate sauce drizzled on top. Unfortunately, it was a craving she'd have to go without. Instead, she'd settle for the iced lemon sage tea she'd come to enjoy in its place. Apparently, caffeine intake was frowned upon when pregnant. Not that she could be sure, considering her pregnancy was a dirty little secret, and all she could go by was what she read on the internet.

Emery pressed herself against the glass counter on tipped toes and hollered back to Agatha who'd stepped around the corner. "Could I also have three of your biggest beignets?"

"For you, dear, I'll pull them fresh from the fryer."

"You are a godsend, Agatha." Emery left cash on the register for Agatha, including a generous tip, and settled into her favorite table on the patio where she would usually spread out and get lost in whatever book she'd snagged from the coven library. It was also a prime spot for people watching, which never ceased to be boring in New Orleans.

New York may be the city that never sleeps and Los Angeles the home of the stars, but New Orleans was a grown-up playground. The city thrummed with magic and lived by the beat of a steady bass guitar. On any given night, there was something for everyone. Spooky ghost tours, every type of magic reading you could imagine, historic strolls, trips through the bayou and, her personal favorite, the music. Oh, and the food. The food was unreal. In fact, she might go so far as to say the food was her favorite, considering jazz clubs weren't quite as fun without a whiskey ginger in hand.

As much as she didn't want to be with the coven, Emery couldn't deny New Orleans was something special.

She smiled and turned her focus to the book she'd grabbed from her room before leaving. It was about supernatural fertility. From what she could tell, it was mostly focused on witches and wolves, as not much had been documented and shared with the other supernatural factions when it came to vampire births. Which made sense considering most vampires couldn't reproduce, and royal vampire births were a rarity in general, happening only when there was a prince of age and a Culling.

It left her with little to go on for her own pregnancy.

Witch infertility made their pregnancies a rarity as well. But when they did reproduce, they tended to have pregnancies in line with that of humans. Nine months of getting fat and forgetting where you placed just about everything. Though she had read that if a witch were particularly powerful, sometimes they'd have the baby at eight months. It was thought their magic merged with the baby, bringing them to term sooner. Of course, there was nothing about mated witches, so even that information did little to help her prepare.

Basically, she was flying blind, hoping she and the baby would be fine until Callum and Lily could get her out of New Orleans and to the safety of the refuge they were creating.

Emery wanted to be angry at them for leaving her high and dry when they clearly knew more than she did about the whole situation. Particularly Callum. On the other hand, they were doing everything they could to create a way to protect her and her baby, so, more often than not, those hateful feelings driven by hormones dissipated into just plain missing them.

The café's patio gate swung open and a mountain of a man stumbled through, his shirt in tatters. Emery snorted at the sheer panic etched on the wolf's face. "I see you got my note?"

He glared daggers at her as he dropped to a knee and hid under the table. "Get rid of them, Emery." Ansel growled, attempting to make himself as small as possible.

Giggles erupted from the sidewalk adjacent to the café, and a scantily clad Amy and Jaime strolled past the patio.

"Oh hi, Emery." Amy waved, a fake smile plastered on her Barbie pink lips. "Have you seen Ansel? He ran off on us after we tried that thing you said he liked."

Emery stifled a laugh. She might have told them wolves

enjoyed being riled up by having their clothes torn off their bodies. She might have also added that Ansel was interested in both of them, even though she knew damn well he batted for the other team. She should feel bad, but Ansel had brought this upon himself. He was the one who pointed out the predictability of her evasive tactics. So she'd gotten creative.

Ansel's impatience while he waited for the all-clear came out as a low growl from under the table. "You know, I think I saw him run toward Jackson Square a few minutes ago. I promised to stay put and gave him the night off, so he's all yours, girls."

Jaime gave an exasperated huff and rolled her eyes. "I didn't know it was going to be this much work to bag a wolf. All we wanted to do was see if we could make him purr."

Emery pressed her lips together and shrugged, but as soon as the two of them vanished, she roared with laughter.

Ansel slid from his hiding spot and plopped down in the chair opposite her, a half-smirk playing at his lips. "Do you enjoy makin' me miserable, Emery?"

"I don't know, Ansel, they look like fun. They just wanted to see if you would purr like a little kitty cat."

Ansel straightened out what was left of his shirt and cocked a brow. "First of all, I don't purr. I'm a fucking wolf. Second, while I can admit Amy and Jaime are two of the better-looking witches in that place, you know those of the female persuasion don't do it for me. And third—" he paused, losing some of his gusto and rewarding her with a smile, "It was some of your better work. You planned their ambush perfectly, hittin' me while my drawers were down in the bathroom and couldn't easily escape."

Emery gave him a devilish grin in return. "I wish I could have been a fly on the wall. They were so eager to try and seduce the elusive wolf."

"Next time plan for someone I'd actually enjoy being seduced by. You might've had more time on your hands." He turned toward the front of the restaurant and waved to Agatha who was already on her way with her tea and a plate of beignets, more than the three she ordered. "At least you picked a place with delicious food to retreat to."

"Thank you, Agatha." Emery moved to pick up one of the powder sugared treats but Ansel slapped her hand away.

"These are my consolation prize."

Emery chuckled. "You better watch out, you eat too many and you'll lose that girlish figure of yours."

Ansel was the most muscular person she'd ever met. Where August's physique was lean, like that of an Olympic swimmer, Ansel was more akin to a body builder. His muscles had muscles and each of them were perfectly defined. Pair that with his devilish good looks and southern charm, and Emery could see why all the women, and the men, drooled over him.

He shoved a second beignet in his mouth, powdered sugar covering his lips. "So, what did ya snag from the library this time?"

Emery didn't answer because Agatha had yet to return to the register. While Ansel knew the whole story of why she was there, the witches didn't, and she needed to keep it that way. When she looked up at Agatha, ready to ask if she needed something, it wasn't the crone's usual green eyes that stared back at her. They had clouded over with a milky white film and aside from her agape mouth, her expression was blank.

"Is she o—"

Before Ansel could finish his question, Agatha spoke, her voice an octave lower and gritty.

"The time draws near, for the prophecy's might.
United intended heirs of light and night.
Together they will bring forward change for us all:
A union to stop the darkness of the fall.
Death will heal and deepen divides,
The heir of the moon, restored will rise.
The future is written in the stars above,
The heirs intended at the mercy of love."

Emery and Ansel wore matching wide-eyed expressions when Agatha blinked and smiled at them as though nothing out of the ordinary happened. "What's the matter, sugars? Did I wash my eyebrows off again? You know sometimes it just happens when I wipe the ricochet powdered sugar off my face."

Emery tore through her bag and pulled out a pen and paper to commit what Agatha had prophesied to memory.

Ansel grabbed the witch's hand. "No, you're beautiful as ever, Agatha. You feeling okay though?"

"Right as rain, you sweet boy." She patted his hand in hers and turned back to Emery. "Now you let me know if you need anything else okay. Can't have my favorite customers wanting for nothin'."

When she'd walked away Ansel turned back to Emery, his face mirroring the shock she felt. "What the hell was that?"

She stared at the words she scrawled verbatim on a scrap piece of paper. "I'm pretty sure it was a true prophecy."

"A what?"

"You know how each witch specializes in a field of magic? The one they're drawn to and gifted the talent from the stars?"

He nodded, stealing a sip of her tea. He'd taken it upon himself to learn all the things Emery did while at the compound in case it helped him protect her. "Yeah, incantation, component, illusions and elemental."

"Right, those are the main four, but there are three other rare forms of magical talents gifted to witches. Sight of the stars, blood, and necromancy."

"As in raisin' the dead?"

"Something like that. There isn't much on the subject of necromancy or blood magic since they're generally considered dark magic, and the coven doesn't permit such practices."

"So Agatha's got the other one, the sight of the stars?"

Emery nodded. "She is gifted in reading the future. Generally tarot and tea leaves. But that," she let out a slow breath, "I'm pretty sure that was a true prophecy. One gifted from the stars. They can be gifted as words or visions but typically the witch who vessels the prophecy doesn't remember doing so, at least that's what the book the inner circle made me read said. They keep hoping I'll be drawn to the sight as they haven't had a royal witch gifted with such talents in nearly a millennia."

"What do you think Agatha's prophecy means?"

Emery looked down at the words, reading through them carefully and handed it over to Ansel. "Everything I've read says prophecies are rarely what they seem, so I can't say for sure."

"The heir of the moon is Draven. He's our alpha's son, and we are the people of the moon."

"So he will aid in the quest, whatever that is."

"If I had to guess, the heir of night is the vampires, and the heir of light is the witches."

"Don't say that." The last image she had of August staring down at her with hatred in his eyes played through her mind. He wanted nothing to do with her. If their union was meant to stop the fall of darkness, then the supernatural world better get flashlights because they were screwed.

"He's your mate, Emery. There's little doubt now that the stars have plans for you."

The damn wolf didn't know when to leave well enough alone. She knew he was coming from a different perspective; wolves lived and died by their mates. But Emery couldn't say the same about her and August. They weren't the poster children for vampire-witch mates. They were the warning label.

She pushed away from the table and stood gathering her book and the paper that had the prophecy written on it. "Can we head back? I'm tired and I have a meeting with the inner circle first thing in the morning."

Ansel gave her a pointed stare, but didn't push the August line of questioning. "Are you sure that's a good idea? You spend most mornings praying to the porcelain gods."

"Vishna is going to be there. I can't afford to miss a chance to speak with her."

"She's a wicked bitch, but if it's what ya need, I'll be at your side." He shrugged and silently got up and followed her out of the café.

They walked in a comfortable silence and Emery replayed the prophecy in her head over and over.

It couldn't be about her and August. They couldn't possibly be the heirs intended.

Just before they reached the compound Ansel reached out and grabbed her hand. "I could be wrong, you know. Maybe the prophecy isn't talking about you and August, but if it is, I promise to protect you and your baby. Even from him."

Emery gave his hand a squeeze and managed a weak smile. "I know you will."

She wanted to hold onto the hope he was wrong, but deep

inside she knew he wasn't. The stars weren't kind enough for him to be wrong.

August was her mate and the crown prince of the people of the night. It only stood to reason that with Sloane gone, she'd be named the heir to the witches of the light.

The heir of light.

Fuck.

As if her life wasn't already complicated enough.

Chapter Five

EMERY

The next morning she woke and prayed to the porcelain gods, just as Ansel predicted. And he wasn't even a star-touched witch.

Pregnancy fucking sucked.

She had nothing in her stomach to expel, but that didn't stop her body from heaving until her entire body ached. Add in the forgetfulness and epic mood swings, and Emery was a hot mess ninety percent of the day.

Ansel let himself into the bathroom as he did every morning, bringing with him a damp towel. "You look like shit. You need to see a doctor. It can't be healthy to throw up so much."

Emery took the towel and wiped her face and mouth. "Women have been having babies for years without doctors. They've also had morning sickness to go along with it."

Emery grabbed her sweater from the bathroom counter. "I probably wouldn't look so terrible if I got a full night's sleep. Between needing to pee and these damn nightmares I'm up half the night, every night." She looked up to find Ansel sitting on the edge of the tub, his eyes wide-eyed and trailing over her.

"What's wrong? Do I have vomit on me?" She wiped her mouth again and wrapped her arms around herself, holding the sweater to her chest. She couldn't look that terrible.

Ansel shook his head, gaze trained on her midsection, shock written all over his face. "Your belly. It's grown."

Emery relaxed and chuckled, pulling the oversized sweater over her head. "Yes, Ansel. That's what happens to pregnant women."

"I know that, but aren't you only two months along at most?"

Emery sighed. "Yup. Almost three." She'd thought the same thing when she'd woken up two weeks after arriving, unable to button her jeans. "I can only chalk it up to parentage. I've only been able to research witch pregnancies, the other half of my child's DNA is a mystery. There's no telling how accelerated the pregnancy may be."

"At this rate you won't be able to hide it much longer."

"What choice do I have?" Emery snapped, her words harsher than she'd meant. She ran a brush through her hair, trying to tame the wavy pink locks and calm herself. "Callum and Lily have gone radio silent since pawning me off on the witches. I have no idea what I'm supposed to do besides sit and wait."

"At the very least you should see a doctor."

"In New Orleans? I can't go pee without the inner circle being informed, which at the rate I do go, I'm surprised they haven't put two and two together. Even still, I highly doubt the inner circle will take kindly to their princess bearing the vampire crown prince's child, so I can't go to a doctor here. Until we hear from Lily or Callum, I just have to do the best I can to conceal it."

She only prayed it would be soon, because Ansel wasn't

wrong. She wouldn't be able to conceal her stomach much longer at the rate she was growing.

Ansel's jaw tightened in unison with his fists, but he remained silent. He couldn't argue with her logic.

Emery exhaled a long deep breath and crossed the bathroom, joining him on the edge of the standalone tub. He meant well, and she understood his anger, but it wasn't going to change their predicament.

He hung his head, his voice barely a whisper. "You asked me during my first week here why I took this assignment. Why I would fight so hard to protect you and teach you to escape any predicament."

She had, and he refused to talk about it. "If I remember correctly, you told me it was none of my prissy ass business."

Ansel chuckled. "That's before I knew you. Before I realized you are so much more than just a knocked-up Culling girl. That you care about your child's future."

Emery waited for him to speak again, curiosity keeping her on the edge of her seat.

Ansel scrubbed his face with his palm and his shoulders sagged. When he finally spoke, he had a far-off look in his eyes. One Emery knew all too well.

"This is my first mission after losing my mate five years ago. I wasn't allowed to leave pack lands before this because I was considered a flight risk."

Emery placed her hand on top of his massive one and gave it a gentle squeeze. "I'm so sorry Ansel."

When he'd first arrived, she'd asked him if he had a girlfriend and he'd growled at her, stating he wasn't looking for anything serious. She'd later learned he was into men and figured he'd had a bad break up, which she could sympathize with. It's why she'd purposely planned for the women to seduce him the day before, not wanting to force him into a situation that might hurt him. She had no idea he'd lost a mate.

The thought of losing August nearly stopped the breath in her chest. They may be at odds with one another for the rest of their lives but just the thought of him not existing made her question her own existence. She never wanted to know what it would feel like for him to leave her world.

"When your friend Flora showed up and vowed to help our people if we helped you, I jumped at the chance. Not because I was grateful for her help, but because as soon as I heard about the child, my wolf needed to help." Ansel studied the floor as if it was the most interesting thing in the room.

Emery was still baffled at how her best friend got caught up in the brewing war. It had Callum written all over it, but still, she couldn't imagine tiny Flora taking on a pack of wolves on her behalf.

"You aren't going to tell me my child is your future mate, are you?" Not that it would be terrible to have Ansel around for the rest of her life, but it would be weird as hell.

His head tipped back, and his booming laugh filled the small bathroom. "No, your child is not my mate. Wolves mate for life. Sebastian was my one and only. What I meant was my wolf knows how important your child is to our world, to the future of all supernaturals. He or she will be the first step toward unity. Toward what Sebastian would have wanted."

"What would he have wanted?"

"Sebastian wasn't from our pack. We met while I was on a mission in eastern Europe. He was a lone wolf, not tied to any pack because of what he was. You see, Sebastian's mother was not only a wolf, she was also a witch. While in the Americas, the wolves are a neutral party, many of the older packs around the world are not. They are as ruthless as the vampires and as cunning as the witches."

Emery gasped, her hands instantly cradling her stomach. It didn't surprise her the wolves were as terrible as the other factions in the Americas. What caught her off-guard was there were others out there like her little urchin. Hybrids in a world that only recognized purity.

"I knew instantly he was my mate, and we shared a beautiful summer while I traversed the Transylvanian Alps on a mission for my alpha. I always returned to him between searches and we planned our future together. Until one day he wasn't there."

Ansel swallowed hard, and Emery gave his hand a reassuring squeeze.

"I returned to his home, to find it ransacked and covered in blood. The salt wards his mother insisted on had been swept away. Sebastian and his mother were found by the Alpha of the local pack and were murdered because of what they were." His voice cracked and his whole body shook as Ansel choked back a sob. "I wasn't there to protect them. If I hadn't been so focused on the damn mission I could've saved them."

"I'm so sorry, Ansel." Her words were filled with love, but she knew nothing she said would help heal the devastation of losing his mate. She opted for making him smile instead. "I'm sure he was incredible. Especially if he put up with you."

Ansel looked up, his brown eyes swimming in tears despite the half grin he wore. "He would've liked you." He reached out and laid a hand over hers on her stomach. "I know I sometimes come across as overbearing, but you and the baby give not only me, but so many hope. Hope for a future where we can love whoever we choose. I won't let anything happen to either of you."

She lifted a brow. "*Sometimes* you're overbearing?"

The two of them chuckled, and Emery leaned her head on his shoulder. They sat in silence, and she considered his story.

She never pictured Ansel to be the head-over-heels-in-love type, but his persona made more sense now that she knew he'd loved and lost. He'd seen the best in Sebastian, the parts that the supernatural world would never see because all they focused on was heritage. It was the most beautiful thing she'd ever heard, and her heart broke for Ansel and his wolf.

There would likely be war over her child. She'd known that from the moment she'd found out about her little urchin. But she'd never considered the hope the life of a single baby could bring.

A knock at the door shattered their solitary moment, and they both turned toward the door.

"That'll be Dahlia. She left a note saying she'd be here to walk me down to the inner chambers."

Ansel nodded and turned away, wiping away a stray tear from his cheek.

She stood, but before she moved toward the door she placed a hand on his shoulder. "Thank you for protecting us."

He stood, dwarfing her small frame. "Thank you for bringing hope into my life."

She nodded and pulled him in for a hug. She squeezed him tight, pouring every ounce of thanks and love into him that she could.

Her life may be a clusterfuck of unfounded prophecies, bitchy witches, and an asshole mate, but she didn't live her life for them.

Ansel left the bathroom, and Emery stood there alone rubbing her growing belly. She silently pledged to make it her mission to honor Sebastian's death. To make the supernatural world a place worthy of her child and any future children of mixed heritage.

AUGUSTINE

Pregnant.

She was bloody fucking knocked up with his child.

His heir.

Augustine struggled to wrestle August back into the depths of their shared mind while he drained the busty brunette across his lap.

August growled internally, repeatedly trying to overtake Augustine again. When he realized Augustine would not be giving up his moment in the spotlight, August pushed a memory of Emery to the forefront. The way she tasted under his tongue, paired with the arching of her back and the soft mewls she made as he pulled her decadent blood from her neck.

Augustine's cock stirred, remembering the way she'd felt beneath them. He may have been the one in the depths when August took her, but even he couldn't ignore the way her supple body molded to theirs, the way she tasted, or the delicious sounds she made as she came apart.

Bloody hell.

Augustine shook his head in an attempt to get his bearings. He wasn't supposed to be taken with her. He may have been present, but he wasn't the heart, August was. No, Augustine was the monster that made sure they survived. He lured them into the darkness. Into the bloodlust.

And now, thanks to August, Emery had taken that enjoyment, too.

He pulled off the woman, disgusted by her imperfection. "Why can't you just go back to not giving a shit?" Augustine grumbled to himself.

She carries our heir. How can you not give a shit?

Very easily.

Even though they both knew that was a lie. Everything changed the moment Callum confirmed the god-awful truth, and Augustine had been able to think of little else since. It was as if the bond he'd successfully classified as belonging solely to August ignored his protests and snapped into place, consuming the small part of him it held.

It didn't matter that he'd rather die than fall into the trap that was Emery's witchy vagina.

Again.

The bond didn't care. It had been easy to ignore the way it tried to twist his emotions because Augustine couldn't be fooled by its magic. But the news of a baby, his heir, had all but brought him to his knees. Forced him to consider Emery as more than just the witch bitch killing his people.

His chest constricted and fear coursed through him and he couldn't differentiate between the fear of losing his mate and the fear of losing his heir. His hatred had always been cut and dry. Easy enough to manage. And then in a single moment, he was drowning in emotions he didn't want to examine.

Which was why he'd gone directly to the feeders. Next on the agenda was drinking until he forgot the news entirely. Which he'd get to enjoy for all of fifteen minutes before he'd sober up and have to actually deal with the ramifications of August's dick.

"What, Your Highness?" The donor looked up at him with glossy eyes. He'd never understand why, when he could give them any feeling in the world, the donors wanted to feel empty.

"Nothing," he snapped, shifting her in his lap so she was sitting up.

She felt his arousal and ran her hand over his hard length. "Is there something else I can do for you?" She leaned forward so her breasts met his chest and teased her already hardened nipples through the thin camisole dress most of the feeders wore.

Augustine groaned while August growled. With a frustrated sigh, he batted her hand away. He didn't need a repeat of the first time he tried to allow one of the feeders to please him. The moment she'd taken his cock out it deflated like a three-day-old balloon.

"Just go."

"Are you sure, Your Highness?" she persisted, running her hands up his chest and batting her eyelashes.

He grabbed her upper arms and pushed her back. "I said bloody fucking go."

She scurried from his lap and out the door to the feeder's quarters.

"Are you happy?" He sounded like a petulant child, but Augustine was growing tired of August's interruptions. He was in control and he wasn't about to give it up to his more agreeable side.

This wasn't like the other times that August fought to come back to the forefront. Those times he was coming back from his desire to detach from royal life and give into the bloodlust. Which Augustine was all too willing to oblige. This time, August retreated because he wanted to avoid the ramifications of what Emery was to him, which worked in Augustine's favor until he had an opinion when it came to the witch bitch. Then he and his alter-ego were at odds.

She would be his downfall. Both of theirs.

That "witch bitch" is birthing our heir, August whispered fiercely.

"Don't remind me."

He left the feeding room, heading away from the royal residence. The last people he wanted to see were his family. While he'd sworn his mother and brother to secrecy about the pregnancy, they'd have no problem exerting their opinions on how he should handle the situation.

They were firmly on Team Emery Isn't A Lying, Murderous Bitch.

He waited, expecting August to have a retort. A need to include himself on that team, but he remained a silent passenger.

"Not convinced, August?"

If it was possible for a subconscious being to give a frustrated sigh, that's the sentiment August projected. *You know I'm not, but only because of the bloody fucking mate bond. I have no trust left for her, but no matter how much I want to hate her for what she did, what she is, I can't. She carries our heir, Augustine. I don't know if she is our enemy, but she carries our child.*

"But you can't forgive her."

August's silence said it all. It also gave Augustine the hope that maybe he'd be at the forefront for the foreseeable future.

I....I don't know. But she needs to have our child.

"She'll live to give me an heir, and not a minute longer."

Dread coursed through the deepest part of him, the same

way it raced through August when he considered killing Emery after learning of her heritage.

The mate bond. The prophecy. What if—

"Not you too. It's a fickle bit of magic she bewitched us with and nothing more."

He shut the proverbial door on August, not giving him the chance to reply.

Less than sated by the feeder, August tore through the castle. Rage simmered beneath the surface, accompanied by the newfound heat of the mate bond. The need to hit something coursed through him. August would be ideal, since he was the one who got them into the predicament, but that wasn't possible. He'd have to settle for a punching bag.

When he hit the rear terrace of the castle, he took off running toward the barracks at the back of the royal property. Ninety percent of the time they were empty with sentinels scattered throughout their kingdom, but with the factions on the verge of war and the attack on Thea, they were currently filled with new sentinels preparing for an inevitable battle.

And if Private Dowd had been correct, his own team would be ready and waiting for him.

He entered the barracks, ignoring the nods from other sentinels. They may respect him as the crown prince, but they weren't his team—the team he'd fought with in every battle since he could wield a sword. His people understood the bloodlust August faced. They didn't even blink anymore when Augustine bled into the forefront and claimed the spoils of war. They had trained together for nearly a century before his father called him home to become the crown prince. They were dispersed across the continent at various embassies, doing the crown's bidding and protecting diplomats. Augustine would have much rather stayed with them, but August, ever the dutiful diplomat, returned to the castle.

Look how that turned out. A failed Culling, a knocked-up witch, and a divide between them that ran deeper than it ever had before.

Augustine snuck through the door of the training room, hoping to catch his general off-guard. The center was filled with sparring mats, and the walls were lined with training weapons, mostly of the melee variety. Off the main room were an armory and shooting gallery for range weapons.

"Attention for the commander!" one of the junior sentinels yelled.

The entire room fell silent and every sentinel stopped what they were doing to stand at attention.

Augustine gave the at-ease command, accompanied by permission to resume what they were doing.

His general, Rex, sauntered toward him with a wicked grin plastered on his face. "I was wondering how long it would take you to show up. Didn't think it would be two months."

"I was on orders from my father. You know how it goes. I tried to get you on the assignment but Malcolm assured him we could take care of it." Mostly he wanted to keep tabs on Augustine and ensure he understood every theory he and Callum had come up with regarding Emery and the prophecy. He and Emery were the chosen ones, fated to change the world.

It was a load of shit. A bloody fucking nightmare.

Laughter boomed from Rex's chest. "How is Malcolm?"

"Still a pain in the arse." Which was really an understatement.

"And the mission?"

"Drawn out by a sadistic mistress."

Rex raised a brow and crossed his arms over his chest. "Sounds kinky."

"If only you knew. I'd bet money she's the one who sent

the witch after Thea, in addition to orchestrating all the killings across our kingdom."

"How is the littlest royal?" Rex had always had a soft spot for children. He'd had a family once upon a time in another life. He didn't like to talk about them—their end had been grim—but Augustine knew Thea reminded Rex of those he lost. She held a special place in his heart..

Augustine's mouth fell into a grim line, and he shook his head.

Rex's face fell. "Isn't there anything that can be done?"

"I don't know," Augustine replied. "The only thing I'm sure of is that I'll kill the Mistress when I find her."

"And we'll be at your side."

"Where is the rest of the team?" Augustine scanned the training room but didn't see any of the familiar faces he sought.

"Wes and Jones are on perimeter patrols, Des is at the range, and Otto is racked out from being on shift last night."

The young sentinel standing next to Rex forced a cough, catching the attention of both men.

"Oh, and this is Dorian. He's the newest recruit to our band of merry men. I even got him some of our matching tights."

Dorian's cerulean eyes widened at the mention of the ball-hugging attire.

Augustine shook his head, though a smile threatened at his lips. Hands down, Rex was the best sentinel in their army, but you'd never know it listening to him. If he could turn something into a joke and make his men smile, he did. That included Augustine.

"Don't worry, Dorian. We only wear them during team sleepovers."

Silence fell between them, and Rex attempted to keep a

straight face, especially when Dorian's eyes darted between the two of them, but it was to no avail. His general burst out laughing and slapped Dorian on the back. "The look on your face."

"Welcome to the team, Dorian." Augustine extended his hand and shook the young vampire's. "I expect you'll learn from my men and be ready when it's time for battle."

"Yes, sir."

Augustine tracked Dorian as he walked over to the wall, picked up a long sword and joined another group of sentinels. He jumped in, and though his form could use some work, Augustine could see why Rex had chosen him to add to their team.

"I know you aren't here to chat with our new recruits. You haven't been involved since the call of your Culling twenty-five years ago. Save for the few times I've visited on official business, you've been radio-silent when it came to mandatory training."

It felt like it was only last week to Augustine, but for immortals, time had a way of twisting. Augustine smirked. "I had come to work out some aggression on the bag, but seeing as you're here, I think I'd rather land a few blows on soft flesh."

"Well you won't find any soft flesh on this body." Rex made a show of running his hands down his chest. "But I could go a round or two. You probably need the practice."

He wasn't wrong. It had been too long since he had the time and a formidable sparring partner. August was always too caught up in the diplomatic bullshit to keep up with a routine, and Malcolm, while a talented fighter, didn't care to practice much.

Rex tugged his shirt over his head and Augustine did the same. It was easier to see if either drew blood that way.

The sparring ring at the center of the facility cleared as the two of them wrapped their hands.

Silently, they both approached the circles painted on the mats.

"Usual terms, Your Majesty?"

Augustine chewed his tongue to suppress his smile. Rex knew damn well the correct title, yet he chose to call him by his father's. Rex hated the King and openly voiced his opinions to Augustine. It would have been treasonous to anyone else, but Augustine understood his anger. While Augustine had earned Rex's loyalty, his father only incurred his wrath. The King threatened his human family in order to keep Rex in line. He then turned them one by one and hid them to keep him from running.

It was fucked up, but there was nothing Augustine could do. He'd tried to help Rex find them, but if his loved ones were still alive, his father had stashed them somewhere neither Augustine or Rex had yet discovered. It was the only reason Rex stuck around. That and his loyalty to Augustine.

"The usual terms?"

Augustine nodded. Bragging rights had long since become trivial. Rex learned from the King what was worth its weight in gold: secrets. Loser would give one up to the winner.

The room went silent, all eyes on Augustine and his general. He pushed all thoughts from his head. They circled each other silently, both sizing the other up. Rex was right-handed and vampires didn't age, so his body should be in peak condition as it was years before, but Rex was favoring his left side.

That's where Augustine would strike.

Rex made the first move swinging at his face, but Augustine was quick to get his hands up and block his right hook, skirting just out of reach.

He backed away, and Augustine shook out his muscles. It felt good to be back in the ring, to be with his men and be focused on the simplicity of a fight. The adrenaline high of strategy and execution coursing through his veins. A competitive smile played on his lips. "You never could wait for your opponent to strike, could you?"

Rex shrugged and brought his fists up in front of him. "Better to get the first shot out of the way, so I can take you down per usual."

Augustine threw back his head and laughed. He couldn't remember the last time he'd done so when the laughter wasn't laced with sarcasm. He and Rex danced around each other, both taking calculated strikes only to be met with well-placed blocks. Though he kept up, Augustine was feeling the months away from the ring. August hadn't trained since before he started to take his Culling seriously and he'd have the bruises to show for it.

Sweat poured down their faces as they backed away once more, an unspoken intermission so they could each catch their breath.

"You're getting rusty, Your Majesty," Rex taunted.

"I may be rusty, but you are barely keeping up. What's that say about you, General?"

"It says I've been enjoying my time away. Can you say the same?"

Augustine took two steps forward and executed a one-two punch followed by a swipe at Rex's midsection. He couldn't say the same, and he had a feeling his general knew it. "I've had better sabbaticals. Remember the South of France?"

Rex jumped back, avoiding Augustine's fist. He recovered and launched his own offensive, backing Augustine toward the boundary. "Remember?" Rex chuckled. "I tell the stories of that mission as an example for the new recruits."

"We were young and hungry." Augustine blocked Rex's punch and dodged his roundhouse kick.

"We still are, Your Majesty. We just need this war to remind us who we are."

"You have no idea."

If Augustine had any say in the matter, the war would be the end of the witches in their territory. He'd had enough of their magic. Not only for those of his people who'd been lost, but personally.

He clenched his teeth and stalked toward Rex. This was his moment. Augustine approached Rex, faking right and leaving his left side open. He reared back his fist, but before he could let it fly, the mate bond flared to life, filled with sudden panic and fear.

Emery.

August fought for control, which forced Augustine's steps to falter. *No.* He grit his teeth and focused on the fight, launching a series of attacks which Rex blocked, but only barely. He had the upper hand and went for the surrendering blow when the scent of lavender assaulted his senses.

Emery. She needs us. Augustine, she's not okay, I can feel it.

His slight hesitation was all it took for Rex to gain the upper hand. Augustine tried to recover but it was too late. Rex took out his leg, and Augustine fell to his knees with Rex behind him, his hands wrapped around his head and throat.

He tipped his head up to meet his general's harsh gaze.

Rex's hazel eyes were filled with rage. "What the fuck was that, Augustine?"

"Your quarters. Now." He wasn't about to divulge in front of his army that he had a witch baby momma with a damned bond tethering them, and there was a good chance she was in danger.

Rex offered him his hand, and they stood and silently left

the training room. As a general, Rex had a room with an attached office on the bottom floor.

Rex opened the door and gestured for Augustine to enter before following him in. The tight look on his face let Augustine know he would not be letting the incident go. "What the hell just happened?"

"Fucked up circumstances I have no control over." Augustine raked his hand through his hair, wincing slightly at the bruise he was sure had formed on his ribs.

"Bullshit, you never lose control. August, maybe, but never you."

Augustine pressed his lips together, wishing he had a retort. Rex was right, and he bloody fucking hated it. Every moment he seemed to be less in control where Emery was concerned. "Might as well get this out of the way. You need to know the stakes. But for the record, this secret clears the slate for my loss."

Rex leaned against the desk in the center of the room and nodded.

Augustine inhaled a deep breath and released it slowly. "I have an heir. Or I will. My mate is pregnant. My mate… who is also a witch."

Rex let out a falling whistle. "I did not see that coming." He hesitated and a smile tugged at his lips. "Congratulations?"

A low rumble formed in Augustine's chest and he began to pace the short length of the desk. He should be tired from the fight, but he was more keyed up than if he'd drained a human or five. "This isn't funny. She's my enemy. Infiltrated August's Culling and seduced him. I spent the last two and a half months tracking down her coven's cannibal vamps only to find out she's been hiding the secret of my child just as long."

Rex circled his lips and let out another whistle. "I don't envy your situation. Does the King know?"

Augustine stopped pacing and whipped his gaze to Rex. "Bloody hell, no, and you are not going to tell him. There is no way my father would let my child live if he did. As it stands, we are attacking the coven this afternoon, and I need you and the team ready for wheels up in thirty."

Rex nodded but didn't say anything. Augustine could see him holding back.

"I know you well enough to know you have an opinion on all this."

"You won't like it."

"Spit it out, Rex."

The general sighed. "You are a man of bloodshed, same as me, and you know I hate the witches as much as the next vampire. Your father is the reason my family was torn apart, but the witches created your line, so to some degree I hold them responsible too. But even if my kids were witches, I would still want them. They were the best thing that ever happened to me, Augustine. The best parts of me. I'm not saying to trust the witch. Hell, you should kill her the moment the babe is born, but don't forsake your child for the sins of their mother."

"He will never let me keep the baby."

"I know. But you are the future king. You are a better man than him. Claim your heir. Don't let the sins of your father stop you from being the father I know you've always wanted to be."

"The kingdom comes first," Augustine said hesitantly.

Rex raised an eyebrow. "But?"

"But I want my child."

It was the only soft side Augustine had. One too many drinks after a battle, and he'd let slip to Rex about his dream to one day be a better father than his own. It was a selfish notion. He was a monster, there was no way to reconcile that. But that didn't mean he didn't have the desire to further his line. To set his kingdom up for greatness.

The question was could he do that with Emery's child? With her dead, there was hope the kingdom might accept them. But would the mate bond allow him to kill her? Just the thought of hurting her had his chest tightening and his hands shaking at his sides.

They weren't lying when they said kids changed everything.

"The kingdom is changing, Augustine. Your father refuses to see it, but I've lived or visited all of our embassies. Your father is feared, not revered. The majority want change, and they crave peace. I fear there will be revolt if it's not granted."

Augustine knew there was unrest, but he didn't think it was so bad as to inspire uprising in the kingdom. "Peace is not without war. Our people know that and ultimately, there will be no peace until the witches are gone."

Rex scrubbed his chin with his palm, a gesture that showed his years. "The older I get, the more I question if that's true. Or is it just an archaic way of looking at a problem neither faction can fix?"

His eyes narrowed, and Augustine searched his general for any trace of dishonesty. "Can I trust you to fight for me, Rex? I need you to help me save my child. To secure the future of our kingdom."

"Always, Your Majesty." Rex pressed his fist to his chest and gave a slight bow, his honest loyalty ringing in both his words and actions. "It would be an honor."

Augustine nodded and walked out the door.

He may have Rex's loyalty and his might, but his observations of the kingdom haunted Augustine's thoughts on the run back to the castle. How had they missed the unrest in the kingdom?

We've been sort of busy. The Culling. Chasing cannibalistic vampires. Father only just let you in strategically. Up until now, it's only been out-of-country missions and court events, followed by the Culling. We haven't exactly been a present heir.

Which was their father's doing.

His stomach flipped with unease. Everything with his father had been too easy since Emery's disappearance. He thought it was because he'd finally become the heir the King had always wanted. Calculated. Logical. Ruthless. Augustine was beginning to question if it wasn't to keep him away and out of the King's master plan.

You didn't think he actually trusted you, did you? August asked.

Fuck.

He had. But once again, he was reminded that he could only trust himself—and that meant being selfish and doing what he needed to do to ensure his future, the future of his reign, and the future of his child.

Chapter Seven

EMERY

Emery walked arm-in-arm with her lady's maid, Dahlia. She kept her head held high as she navigated the compound's narrow halls. It seemed everyone knew she'd been summoned by the inner circle. Witches lined the walls and common areas as if to watch her walk a metaphorical plank. There was no way she'd let them know she was a bundle of nerves on the verge of a panic attack.

Bronwyn had said the meeting was to discuss her future within the coven. That wasn't something that warranted spectators, especially so early in the morning. Then again, the majority would do just about anything to see her fail within the coven, which only made her feel more unsettled.

A low growl filled the space around her, and Emery looked over her shoulder to Ansel walking a few steps behind her. His harsh gaze softened slightly when it met hers, a reassurance he would have her back no matter what happened. He wouldn't be allowed in the chambers, but he wouldn't stray far, and that fact was the only thing that kept her putting one foot in front of the other.

She'd wanted this meeting with the inner circle, with

Vishna, but she had the gnawing suspicion she was walking into a trap.

Dahlia leaned in close and whispered. "Are you ready for your meeting?"

"Is one ever ready to be reprimanded by the circle?"

"You don't know they are going to reprimand you. They're only trying to help."

Emery stopped walking and raised a brow.

Dahlia gave her a tight-lipped grin. "You're right. They will probably chastise you again for all the things you haven't done." She ran her hand along Emery's forearm and urged her to keep walking. "You did promise you would try to fit in better."

"Like you have?" She hadn't meant for it to come out as an attack, but being on edge, Emery wasn't capable of her typical restraint. "What was I supposed to do? Ditch my clothes and embrace my sexuality with every available male witch? Sit for hours meditating, waiting for a miracle to happen and my magic to spontaneously explain to me its many mysteries?"

The older woman gave a halfhearted laugh. "You've got me there. I supposed neither of us is adjusting well."

"That's an understatement. Nothing could have prepared us for the petty bitches who reside in this damn compound." She spoke loud enough she knew the witches lining the hallway alcoves had heard her. "At least at the castle, the only classless bitch we had to worry about was Jessi."

Dahlia pressed her lips together, suppressing a laugh.

Emery never thought she'd yearn for life at the castle or the women of the Culling, but she did. She may not have completed what she intended at the castle, considering Sloane's murder remained a mystery after Vishna declared they'd had nothing to do with her death. But Emery had found a family there and a place where she belonged. It had been in the last place she expected, but that almost made it more sacred. Best of all she'd finally found the love she searched her whole life for.

Her mate.

And then she'd fucked it all to hell.

The bond swelled in her chest at the mere thought of him. It hadn't gotten any easier to think of August. The more she did, the more hopeless she felt.

She warred with herself, remembering all the naive expectations she'd had upon leaving the castle. The first week, she hoped he'd see past what she'd done and who she was. When he didn't, she spent the second week rationalizing. He just needed time to come to terms with the fact she shared heritage with his enemy, but he would remember that she wasn't them.

That's when the needless killings started at each of the vampire crime scenes.

By the third week, she made up every excuse in the book for why he'd chosen to stay away, to give up on what they could have had. She used logic to reason away his need to kill and minimize witnesses. It wasn't until the fourth week that she'd broken down and cried every tear she had left for the man she loved. The man she'd lost.

She wanted to forget him, to move on. But no matter how hard she tried, either the mate bond or the swell of her belly brought her to her knees, and she'd start the process all over again.

At least it no longer spanned the length of a month. More often than not, she felt the range of emotions in the span of a day. Sometimes twice.

They were mates. Every fiber of her being called for her to be near him. She wanted to love him. To be by his side. To share every moment of her pregnancy and the life of her child with him. That didn't mean she should, or even would, if the opportunity presented itself.

Because as much as she wanted August, he wasn't the same man she'd met that night in the club. Nor was he the prince she'd danced with at the ball. He'd claimed every part of her and though she'd played her part in deceiving him, he chose to see her as his enemy, even though she'd never given him a reason to.

"He'll come for you."

Dahlia's voice pulled her from her thoughts, and Emery quickly moved her hands from her stomach, where they'd absentmindedly drifted to rest. "How did you know I was thinking of him?"

"I imagine he's always on the edge of your thoughts, but you get this far-off look in your eyes—one that, in my experience, only plagues those who have loved and lost."

She hated the tears that welled in her eyes and refused to turn her gaze toward Dahlia for fear they'd roll down her cheeks. She couldn't let the witches see her cry. Instead, she steeled her jaw and blinked away the tears. "You're right, he'll come, but it won't be to sweep me off my feet. That ship sailed the moment I left the castle."

"The witches will protect you, Emery. But you need to give them a chance."

A sarcastic laugh burst from her mouth. "Give them a chance?" Emery couldn't believe what Dahlia had just said, especially after everything the coven had done to her, and the fact they'd bound Dahlia's magic and sent her to live with the vampire royal family.

She dropped Dahlia's hand and spun on her, not caring that they'd stepped into the courtyard where more witches congregated. Her voice grew louder with each word, mirroring the rage she tried to keep buried deep. "The majority of the witches here see me as a traitor, and the few who don't act as though they are waiting for me to fail. To prove I am just the woman who fell in love with a vampire. The useless magic-bound heir who they only tolerate because I'm the distant niece of the priestess. They don't acknowledge the part they played in my sister's death. Or the fact the inner circle has lied to them about the true relations between witches and vampires. Not to mention they sent you to live with their enemies."

The courtyard fell silent, and Dahlia cowered, her eyes finding the ground.

Emery should have stopped there, but even though regret coursed through her, the floodgates had been opened. The tears she'd tried to hold back fell freely as she turned, no longer addressing Dahlia, but the members of the coven present. "I am not here to be your friend or to be accepted by those who shunned me my entire life, denying me a place within their ranks because of the transgressions of my ancestors."

"Enough." Vishna appeared from the entrance that led to the underground levels where the inner chamber resided. It made Emery's stomach turn how much she looked like Lily. Unfortunately there was no hint of warmth in this twin's eyes. Vishna's priestess robes flowed behind her even though there was no wind in the courtyard, and her crown of dark crystals and a twelve-pointed star glimmered in the sunlight. Her gaze narrowed on Emery "I suggest you tread lightly, niece, as you are guilty of the same transgression as Lilyana. She betrayed the coven and fell in love with a vampire. She protected them instead of siding with her family. Her coven. I have given you the benefit of the doubt, as you didn't know the finer points of our coven's laws. You have not taken the time to learn while you've been here. That is my fault for not ensuring you followed through on our plan, but do not mistake my kindness for weakness."

Emery's mouth dropped, stunned. She had no idea that Lily had been the witch whose actions had led to the binding of her entire line. She couldn't picture Lily being the cause of the incident that ruined her childhood. And how was she supposed to come to terms with the fact that it was all because she fell in love with a vampire? More importantly which fucking vampire was it? She hadn't known she was Malcolm's mate until recently.

Emery opened her mouth and closed it, thinking better of unleashing the string of expletives that coated her tongue. She placed her trust in Lily and Callum, and it was becoming clear she didn't know a damn thing about them. Her only consolation in the matter was they would, and were, doing everything in their power to protect the life inside her and that was enough for Emery to trust Lily's decisions.

Whispers grew around her, the witches in the courtyard comparing notes on what they thought would happen. Unfortunately for her, they were shit at whispering.

Her magic hummed beneath her skin, reacting to the rage flooding her veins. Her control was faltering and the rational part of her knew she should concede to Vishna and review all she'd learned, but her brazen side fanned the flame. It begged her to take a stand against the witches who'd wronged her and would in an instant wrong the babe in her belly because of something they'd never understand.

Out of the corner of her eye, she saw Ansel step up beside her. There was no doubt he'd follow her if she walked out of the compound, and as much as she wanted to do so, she'd be letting him down if she did. She needed to protect her baby and the promise of change for the future. That meant swallowing her pride, at least for the moment, and allowing the coven's wards to do the protecting.

She pressed her mouth into a line and, not sparing a glance toward Vishna, walked toward the door the priestess had come through. The whispers grew, but Emery kept going, her chin jutting out to keep her head held high.

The moment they entered the building, Emery could hear Vishna, ever the perfect leader, reassuring her people that Emery would be dealt with, and they should continue to welcome her as their heir. She spun a story of a victim who only needed the love of a coven to come into her own.

Gag me.

Emery fisted her hands tight enough her nails broke the skin on her palms, and her magic raged within her. The glow of her eyes filled the dim stairwell, and Emery struggled to keep herself in control. Her magic begged to answer the call of her true intentions, but Emery couldn't let go. A warning sounded in her mind each time her emotions brought her too close to overloading the wayward magic she didn't quite understand. She only knew that bad things would happen if she fell into its grasp. She was still bound—unable to access her magic properly—and her power would turn on her as it had at the castle.

Doubt crept through her like a snaking vine. How was she supposed to take a stand when she was powerless?

Ansel placed a hand on her shoulder and gave it a gentle squeeze. Her magic reacted to the kindness and retreated slightly, hovering under her skin. Emery suspected it wouldn't dissipate to its usual hum until the threat of the inner circle was gone.

A shiver gripped her spine and she found herself dwarfed by the ornate oak doors which marked the entrance to the inner chambers.

Vishna arrived in the small foyer, her stone gaze giving away nothing. "Inside, now." She didn't bother stopping, opening the door with a wave of her hand and entering without waiting for Emery to follow.

Emery's eyes darted to Ansel who'd taken up a stoic stance beside the door. Arms crossed, he gave her a half smile and a nod. "I'll be right here if you need me."

"Thank you."

Emery inhaled deep in an attempt to steel her nerves. A confident smirk snapped into place, and she straightened her shoulders, channeling every ounce of royal demeanor she'd learned from her time at the castle.

Fake till you make it.

She swung open the door and stepped into the circular chamber.

It wasn't what she expected.

The room was dim, lit by candelabras evenly spaced on the outer walls. She walked in toward the round crystal altar in the center of the room. She'd seen pictures of it in the library, but it was so much more grand in person. It was said to be an ancient artifact, a line of communication to the stars and their deities. It had a circle carved into the middle where sacrifices could be made within the insignias of each entity of magic.

It was stunning.

Her gaze moved from the altar to the semi-circular table that surrounded it. There sat the nine women of the inner circle. The majority of them she'd only met in passing, but still she eyed each of them. Some of them were distant cousins of hers, the daughters of Lily and Vishna's two sisters. Not that they honored their familial bonds. They didn't. And the majority of them despised Emery for filling the role of heir, which they believed should rightly belong to them.

As she worked her eyes over each member, Emery lingered

on the last seat, where Bronwyn wouldn't meet her gaze. Her sometimes-friend fidgeted nervously in her chair, giving Emery pause. She'd never seen Bronwyn look so uneasy.

Vishna lowered herself into the middle chair, which was elevated slightly above the rest. Her mouth rested in a grim line.

The priestess nodded and to the left of the table a person pushed a small television from the shadows.

Emery's heart stopped.

Standing at the edge of the inner circle was her oldest and best friend, Wren. She was torn between running to her and staying put as she was sure the inner circle expected of her. The last time Emery had seen Wren was outside a club in Madrid the night the mark of the Culling appeared on her wrist.

Wren stood tall, her pale blue eyes sunken in as though she hadn't slept in days, and she didn't wear the smile Emery had come to associate with her bubbly personality.

It was then Emery got a good look at what was on the television beside her and barely kept herself from doubling over. It was a CCTV feed of Montgomery Blues. She'd recognize the chairs anywhere. What she didn't expect was August and Malcolm standing over her Uncle Miles' dead body.

Chapter Eight

EMERY

Emery stood frozen in place.

Every time she tried to process what she was looking at, her brain short-circuited, and she'd start the process all over again, a million questions filtering through her mind.

She tried to rationalize there was a reasonable explanation for August and Malcolm to be standing over her uncle's body covered in blood, but given her mate's recent disregard for human life, she couldn't move past the obvious.

Then there was Wren. Emery had no rational inkling as to why she was standing in the inner circle's chamber. That part of her life had become a distant memory—one she purposely kept her distance from after arriving at the compound. Miles was Ada's brother, and a part of the coven. If she was honest, their short conversation weeks ago was more for her sanity than his. Even then, it broke her to hear his excitement at her finally being involved in the coven. Wren didn't deserve to be tied up in the clusterfuck that was the supernatural world.

Emery's throat bobbed, and she somehow managed to speak past the lump in her throat. "What happened?"

The rest of the nine witches seated at the semicircular table looked to Vishna, who picked up a remote and turned off the screen. "I'm sorry Emery, this isn't how we meant for you to find out. Wren showed up moments before your little tirade in the courtyard."

"Bullshit." Vishna's aloof tone sent anger flooding through her veins. "Forgive me if I don't believe you. Now tell me what happened to my uncle and why my best friend is standing in your chambers."

Vishna quickly stood and pressed her hands to the table, her whiskey eyes, so similar to Emery's, glowing a faint gold color. "You will treat me and the rest of the council with respect. You may be my niece and future heir, but you are also a member of this coven."

"Am I?" The question slipped out before Emery could stop it. "Because I was under the impression I'm only useful because my status changed from magic-bound witch to magic-bound witch with ties to the vampire royal family."

Emery's erratic breathing matched her heart beating wildly in her chest. She needed to get a hold of herself and practice the decorum she'd planned to before stepping through the chamber doors, but Miles and Wren were the last things she expected to see upon entering.

She searched for something to ground her, but in a room full of witches who wanted to see her fail, all she could grasp at was her magic or the mate bond. Neither of which was a reliable source of comfort.

"You have always been a member of this coven, Emery. As the twin of a member of August's Culling, we thought it best to keep you safe."

"By isolating me from the only family I had left? I grew up believing I was worthless to the coven, and now you expect me to believe I'm some revered heir? I'm the spare. Sloane was killed, which I'm still not convinced you didn't have a hand in, and because she's no longer alive, I'm what you've got left. Would you have come for me if I wasn't in the Culling? Or would I still be working bar shifts at Montgomery Blues? You were my family, Vishna, it was your job to raise me and you left me to my own devices with a woman who resented me. So I'm sorry if I don't believe you." For the third time that morning, Emery's core started to swirl. Only this time, her magic would not be swayed and began radiating through her limbs. "Miles was my family more than you will ever be, and I will never stop demanding to know what happened to him, so you might as well tell me."

Vishna's eyes widened and a chorus of gasps sounded from the rest of the inner circle. "Your eyes. Emery, your magic is awakened."

Of course they chose that moment to glow. Not a lick of showing up when she sat for hours meditating trying to feel the concentration of magic that spoke to her. No, it showed up in front of the entire damn inner circle and apparently meant something.

Emery blinked, her eyes would stop, but if the way her entire body vibrated was any indication they would be glowing until her magic settled. "Don't change the subject. What happened to my uncle, and why is Wren here?"

With a sigh Vishna reached up and turned the CCTV image back on the screen. "Miles was killed last night after August and Malcolm showed up to question him."

Emery sucked in a breath, and her world tilted. "No," she whispered. It didn't make sense. Malcolm wouldn't do this. He'd never purposely hurt her.

But August would.

"I'm sorry, Emery." Vishna's apology was a hollow show of sympathy.

"Where's the video? I need to see it." She was desperate for proof. Without it she'd always question if it was true. Hold on to a bit of hope the vampire princes hadn't fallen so far into hating her they'd take the last member of those she'd consider family from her.

Wren, who'd been unusually quiet, walked toward Emery and took one of her hands. "They wiped the CCTV videos. All I have is the still images taken periodically through the night that are updated to the clubs cloud network. As soon as I realized who it was, I contacted the coven with the information."

Eyes filled with tears, Emery met Wren's gaze. In her gut, she already knew the answer, but she didn't want to believe it. "How would you know to reach out to the coven?"

Wren glanced at Vishna who gave her a small nod. "Because I'm a witch, same as you, Emery. Actually, I'm your cousin. My mother was Vishna's younger sister."

Emery choked back a sob. Her whole life was a lie. Even her only friend in the world pre-Culling was in on the ruse. Everything she'd been told growing up had been an elaborate con by the coven.

"Why?" Her magic tightened in her chest, constricting her ability to breath. She gasped and her hands flew to her chest, laying flat against where her heart pounded furiously.

Wren's eyes darted over Emery and she ran her hands over the length of her upper arms. "You need to calm down, Emery."

Didn't she know that was the worst thing you could tell someone who was freaking out?

Emery's body felt like it was going to burst. Not in the same way as it had at the castle when she'd absorbed the magic of the amulet. This time her own magic was the culprit, and she got the feeling it was tired of being silenced into submission at the hands of the coven.

Wren whipped her head toward the inner circle. "What's

happening to her? Her magic is fighting against her—isn't it supposed to be bound?"

The inner circle stared at her wide-eyed. They leaned toward each other, murmuring nervously. Emery heard snippets of their conversation, since like every other witch in the compound, they were shit whisperers.

"What does it mean?"

"Should she be unbound?"

"She must be powerful."

"Is it possible she's dark?"

Powerful? Dark? Who the hell did they think she was? She was none of those things. She was just a girl who couldn't control her magic. Magic that was supposed to be bound.

"Emery, take a deep breath." Wren's voice pulled her back from spiraling. Then she repeated, "You need to calm down."

"Calm down?" Something between a strangled and manic laugh bubbled from Emery's mouth. "I just found out my entire life has been a series of lies and now the inner circle thinks I'm some sort of freak witch." Her magic swirled within her, pressing against her skin. It reminded her too much of how she felt in Chelsea's room before she exploded.

Her stomach tightened and excruciating pain shot through her.

The baby.

Wrapping her arms around her midsection, Emery turned and bolted for the door, hoping the inner circle would argue long enough she could make her escape.

"Wait!" Wren called after her, but Emery was already halfway to the door.

Emery tore from the chamber and smacked into Ansel's hard chest. Tears spilled from her eyes as she looked up at him.

His brows furrowed with worry and he looked over her

head into the chambers. "What the hell happened? Your eyes are glowing."

"The baby," she panted, the weight on her chest growing simultaneously with the pain in her belly. "I got too worked up, it's been growing all day, and now my magic is trying to release but it's hurting the baby."

"Fuck." Ansel looked around as if searching for an answer.

"I need to release it, but I don't know how. This isn't supposed to happen." Her words tumbled out of her faster than she could think. "My magic is supposed to be bound. They think I'm some sort of dark witch. I didn't even know there were dark witches, just dark magic. I can't stop it."

"Breathe, Emery." Ansel tilted his head and the corners of his mouth tipped ever so slightly.. "I've got an idea."

He swept Emery up into his arms and took off running through the underbelly of the compound, holding her tight to his chest.

The pain rolled through her in waves and she whimpered against him, her whole body shaking.

"Hold on Em, we're almost there."

"Don't call me that." She grit through her teeth as another round of pain shot through her.

August called her Em, and he was the last person she wanted to think about right then. Not when all she could picture was him standing over her uncle's dead body. Not when she considered everything he'd done since learning she was a witch. She wanted so badly to believe he wasn't what the witches said he was, that he was the man she'd fallen in love with at the castle, but the evidence was damning, and she was beginning to question if they weren't right.

Ansel moved using speed she didn't know he possessed. Not quite as fast as a vampire, but definitely inhuman. They made three more turns before he threw open a door and set her on a plush sparring mat.

"The gym?" Emery tried to focus on her breathing, but she felt her anger rising to new heights, aimed at the wolf in front of her. "Your idea of helping is forcing me to work out? Have you met me?"

"I have. And it's the best idea I've got." Ansel gave her a half cocked smile. "Now hit me."

"What?" She had to have heard him wrong.

"You heard me." He stepped toward her and puffed out his chest. "Hit me."

"I'm not going to hit you, Ansel." Emery took two steps toward the door, but doubled over when pain gripped her spine.

"You are." His hand gripped her upper arm and he gently turned her around, supporting her as he did. "We do this with wolves to release their pent up need to shift between full moons."

"I'm not a wolf though." She wrapped her arms around her stomach, and inhaled through the pain.

"No, you're not." Ansel spread his feet and took a defensive pose. "But your emotions are dictating your magic, and your magic is harming your body. So, you're going to hit me until your eyes stop glowing."

Emery rolled her eyes, conceding only because she didn't have a better idea. "Fine." She balanced herself and inhaled a deep breath, wishing she was dressed for any sort of physical activity. A baggy sweater was not ideal, but neither was the camisole she wore underneath that exposed her growing belly.

Ansel watched with an intense gaze as she pulled back her fist and thrust it toward his chest.

"Not bad for a little thing," he chuckled. "Do it again, but this time untuck your thumb. You're going to break it if you keep it tucked in your fist."

She adjusted her fist and threw another, this time hitting him in the solar plexus. Once again, he didn't budge from where he stood.

Damn wolves were just as indestructible as vampires. At least their abs were.

"Again. But this time I want you to imagine I'm the witches who angered you. Let it all go in your punches."

Emery hit him again. And again. First with her right fist then with her left. She focused on all the things the coven had done to her.

Lying about her heritage.

Punch.

Keeping her isolated and alone.

Punch.

Sending Wren to be her best friend and lying about who she was.

Punch.

Tears streamed down her face as each cathartic punch hit its mark. She didn't pause until her magic no longer jolted through her midsection or vibrated through her limbs.

"Good. Now pretend I'm the bastard who hurt you."

Emery sucked in a ragged breath and huffed a laugh. Ansel may have shipped mates, but with each passing day he became further from Team August.

Her mate was everything she wanted and everything she hated all at the same time.

She'd been able to ignore his rejection. She'd even been able to logic his murders as a way of lashing out, since they were methodical and attached to the psycho vampire attacks.

But killing Uncle Miles had been vindictive. There was no way her uncle was involved in any of the killings. Just as there was no reason for them to be present at Montgomery Blues other than to send a message. A message that was designed to hurt her.

Her punches found a steady rhythm, and Emery did exactly as Ansel instructed. She poured every ounce of emotion into each hit.

When she had nothing left to give, she hung her head and sighed, her body sagging in relief as she realized her magic was quiet once more.

"Look at me, Emery."

She tipped her head up and met Ansel's concerned gaze. He was drenched in sweat as much as she was. He reached and swept her hair away from her face, examining her eyes. "No more glowing."

Her body ached and she had no doubt she'd feel like shit in a few hours, but she managed a smile. "Thank you, Ansel."

"I told you, I'll protect you in any way I can, even if it's from yourself." He pulled her into his chest and gave her a hug, whispering in her ear. "We have an audience."

Ansel let her go and shifted so he was between her and where Wren and Bronwyn stood by the door.

"Are you okay?" Wren crossed the mats and opened her arms as if to give Emery a hug, but stopped when Emery threw her hands up.

She nodded. "I am now. Ansel was quick to find a way to give my magic release."

Bronwyn followed slowly behind Wren, her inquisitive gaze running over Emery before turning to Ansel. "Thank you, Ansel. Emery is lucky to have you."

Ansel bowed his head, the perfect southern gentleman. "It's my pleasure to protect her."

Bronwyn tilted her head slightly, her brow creased. "And just why were you sent to protect her?"

Emery's brow furrowed, taken back by Bronwyn's open hostility. They may not have been besties, but they were at the very least friendly.

"As the inner circle was informed, Emery is a potential target for the vampires. The wolves were contracted to protect her." Ansel stood tall, but with an ease about him that gave the impression he wasn't shaken by Bronwyn's line of questioning.

"But the wolves are usually neutral, are you not?"

"We are, but protecting Emery is in everyone's best interest."

"I'd beg to differ." Bronwyn's mouth gave a sardonic twist, sending chills down Emery's spine. This was not her friend. This was Bronwyn speaking on behalf of the inner circle. "If what I suspect is true and she carries the crown prince's child, the witches will have no interest in keeping her safe. Not so long as she carries the baby."

Fuck.

Holy shit fuck.

It was the moment she'd dreaded since she set foot in the compound.

A moment she knew would inevitably come, but she'd hoped to have at least a thousand miles between herself and the witches when it did.

They knew.

They fucking knew and they were going to take her baby from her. Not take. There was no chance in hell they'd let her little urchin live. They might even kill Emery. Two birds, one stone.

Ansel growled and stepped completely in front of her, effectively pulling her from her spiral. "You will not harm her or the baby. Unless you'd like to make an enemy of the wolves."

Emery dug her fingernails into her palms in a manic attempt to keep her emotions in check. The pain distracted her from the stirring in her chest and allowed her to focus on her breathing. She couldn't lose control.

Moments passed and when she was confident she wasn't going to start glowing again, she placed a hand on Ansel's shoulder and stepped out from behind him.

Keeping her face stoic, Emery met Bronwyn's glare. "How did you know?"

There was no use in lying. A simple pregnancy test would reveal the truth.

"So it's true?" Bronwyn's business facade faltered but only for a moment. "I ran after you because I cared what happened to you. I thought for sure I'd heard you wrong when you spoke to the wolf outside the chamber, but it's actually true?"

Emery nodded. The disappointment in Bronwyns's voice gutted her, but not as much as the way her lips twisted in disgust. The woman before her was both her friend and the epitome of the vampire-hating witches who would never approve of the life growing in her womb.

"How could you, Emery?" Wren belittled her in a way Emery didn't think was possible of her best friend. "He's our enemy. I know Ada and Miles taught you better."

"You don't know anything about August or me." Emery ground out. "Neither of you gets to judge me when you were complacent in the lies the coven told. What happened at the castle wasn't planned, but damn if it wasn't the best thing that ever happened to me."

"Until he killed your sister." Wren hissed, venom dripping from every word. "And your friend. Then dumped you on your ass in a dungeon and murdered your uncle. Some baby daddy you got there."

Emery took a step back, the verbal slap to the face ringing

true. Wren knew exactly what happened to her, but her assessment revealed how little the witches knew about her time in the castle.

Bronwyn placed a hand on Wren in what Emery assumed was an attempt to calm her. "It doesn't matter what happened to her, what matters now is the child growing in her womb." Her eyes narrowed on Emery's midsection, which she cradled protectively. "It's an abomination and will upset the balance of the supernatural world in unpredictable ways."

Ansel growled beside her, echoing Emery's sentiments exactly.

She had two choices: she could fight the coven to keep her child, or she could play their game in the hopes it would give them enough time to escape the city. She looked to Ansel and gave him a pleading look, hoping he would trust her.

"I haven't decided what I am going to do about the baby yet." She struggled against the panic rising within her, hoping to appear calm. "I am still very early in my pregnancy and have a few more weeks to decide what I would like to do. It is very likely my mate will know if I terminate the pregnancy, and given his murderous spree I suspect I'd be next on his hit list if I kill his heir."

"Mate?" The ridicule rolled off Bronwyn's tongue with ease. "If you are newly pregnant, it would have happened right before you left. How could he possibly know since you've been here?"

"Mates are linked by a bond." Emery silently prayed Vishna kept the inner circle in the dark regarding mates as the original witch intended. Her hairbrained plan depended on it. "He will feel the termination."

"Why do you keep calling the prince your mate? Witches don't have mates, and neither do vampires. Wolves are the only ones who mate for life."

"That's where you're wrong. You are free to ask the priestess about it, but the bottom line is vampires and witches were made for one another. August is my mate. My magic reacts to him, even though it's bound. I suspect that's why my magic has surfaced, pushing against one binding in order to complete the other." She didn't actually know this to be true, but Emery needed to buy time. "We've already completed the bond—he is mine as much as I am his."

Even if he doesn't see it that way.

"None of that is true." Wren countered, never willing to back down from an argument in which she believed she was right. "Witches and vampires have been at odds since their creation. They must have compelled her somehow. Maybe because her magic is bound."

Bronwyn remained silent, seemingly considering what had been revealed. She was a scholar, and spent much of her time researching in the inner circles's archive. It's what had drawn her to Emery initially; she always asked what Emery was reading. Bronwyn thrived on knowledge. If she questioned the plausibility of Emery's claims, it might buy them some time to escape.

Emery continued, goading Wren into questioning her further. "Have you ever considered why we can't be compelled?"

Wren rolled her eyes as if the answer was obvious. "Because witches created vampires and therefore are superior to them."

"And how would you know that? Have you ever spoken to one and confirmed your superiority?"

Wren shrugged, but didn't back down. "No, but that doesn't mean it's not true. For our safety, the coven advises us to steer clear of vampires. They are uncivilized and will attack as soon as they know we are witches."

"I can tell you they are the furthest thing from uncivilized. I'd argue the compound is more uncivilized. It's basically a sorority house filled with horny teenagers. I'd even go so far as to say the vampires are a step above. They didn't lie to me my entire life."

It was a low blow, but Emery couldn't help herself.

"No, they just booted you when they found out what you were."

Touché.

"I deserved it," Emery said, her voice cracking. "I was the lying asshole in that situation."

Wren cocked a brow, an expression Emery knew meant she expected her to elaborate, but she remained silent. She wasn't about to rehash her story with Wren, not in front of Bronwyn and definitely not when her best friend seemed to put her allegiance to the witches before their friendship.

"It doesn't matter." Bronwyn interjected. "I will take this information to the inner circle and we'll decide what will become of you and your child. Until a decision has been reached, you will remain in the compound, confined to your room."

Emery nodded in a show of agreement and watched as Bronwyn and Wren turned headed for the door.

Wren glanced over her shoulder at Emery and shook her head in disappointment before falling in step again behind Bronwyn.

Emery released a heavy sigh when only Ansel and her remained.

"We're not staying here right?"

She looked up at the wolf looming beside her. "No. We're not going to let them take our hope from us."

Chapter Nine

EMERY

There should have been indents in the wood floors for the amount of time she'd paced them. It had been almost an hour since Ansel dropped her at her room and made her promise not to leave it. Emery shook out her hands nervously and checked the contents of her backpack for the hundredth time, ensuring she remembered everything. It wasn't like she had a lot to pack, having come from the castle with nothing. Running from shitty situations with next to nothing seemed to be becoming a trend for her.

Ansel walked through the door without knocking, making her jump. "We need to go. Now."

"Where the hell have you been?" She rushed across the room and wrapped her arms around his torso. "I was worried they'd stopped you from getting back. I'm sure they've already sent someone and warded every exit."

"This isn't my first rodeo, Emery, I considered that. Yours is the only window they haven't had access to. If my plan works, we shouldn't trip any of the witch's wards."

"Shouldn't? That's a mighty big gamble, don't you think?"

"So what do you propose, my young padawan?"

Emery's lips tugged into a mischievous grin. "I know you

thought I wasn't paying attention every time you tried to teach me about tactical evasion, but I assure you I was and you're not making any sense." She pulled a small pouch from the front pocket of her bag, emptying its contents in her hand. She fingered the chain of the amethyst necklace and held it up. "I also paid attention to what I was reading when researching all things regarding the witches. This amulet from the coven's collection repels wards. I swiped it when I needed to get into the restricted area of the library. I figured it might come in handy if we ever got caught and needed to escape."

Ansel brought his hand to his chest feigning shock. "I have never been more proud."

Emery lowered herself into a mock curtsey. "Not all heroes wear capes. Are we ready to go?"

"Yes, I've already texted Callum. We'll meet him in the Bayou. He's supposed to call me with directions. It's daytime, so I don't imagine we'll have too much of a problem with the vampires. Their sentinels tend to be turned vampires, so they avoid the sun if possible."

She moved to pull the duffle over her shoulder, but Ansel grabbed it, slinging it on his back.

"I'm pregnant, not disabled. I can carry my own bag."

"And I'm a gentleman, get used to it." He moved to the window and pulled it open, looking down over the faux balcony railing. "Also, you won't be able to carry it when you're jumping from the window."

Her mouth parted and she cocked a brow. "Say what now?"

"Where do you think I was for the last hour? Brushing my hair? I lifted a car and it's waiting right down there. The witches won't expect us to go out the second story."

"*I* didn't expect us to go out the second story. I may not be disabled, but I'm still pregnant, Ansel. This is a terrible idea."

Ansel checked below the balcony and turned back to her. A smile that was meant to reassure tipped his lips. "Do you trust me?"

Of course she did, she just didn't trust the idea of jumping out a second story window when there was a perfectly good set of stairs at the end of the hallway.

The scrunch of her brow must not have been convincing, because Ansel added, "I promise I'll catch you."

Before she could list the plethora of reasons this was a terrible plan, Ansel's phone rang. He pulled it out of his pocket and his mouth formed a grim line. "It's Callum."

Ansel swiped the screen and brought the phone to his ear. "Where are we going?"

He walked away from the window and paced the same length she had for the last hour. Emery strained to hear what Callum was saying, but it was no use. She was neither vampire nor wolf, and witches didn't have super hearing.

Emery walked over to the window and looked down. *It's not that far of a drop,* she told herself a few times, hoping maybe if she thought it enough she'd believe it.

"Fuck."

Emery spun to see what had Ansel cursing. He scrubbed his jaw with his hand and swore again under his breath. "We're on our way. Be there before we are. I'm sure the witches won't be far behind." Ansel hung up and shoved his phone back in his pocket.

When he looked up at her, his features softened, but only slightly and there was no humor in his voice. "We need to go. Now."

"What did Callum say? Where are we going?"

"I'd rather not say until we are clear of the compound. Do you have Wren's number in your phone?"

"I have her old number memorized, I don't know if it's the

same. Why? What's going on?" She didn't like the way his voice no longer carried a hint of humor. A serious Ansel was cause for concern.

"Because as much as I hate the bitch for what she said to you, I still have a conscience, and you'd kill me if I stood by and did nothing."

What the hell did that even mean? Nothing he said was making sense and it only added to the weight growing in Emery's chest.

"Come on, let's go. I'll explain when we are clear of the compound."

He walked over to the window and swung his legs over the railing. "I'm going to jump down and put our things in the car. Put on the amulet just in case and then hop over the railing like I am now and get ready to jump."

Before she could protest, he was already on the sidewalk below.

Thank goodness she lived on the side of the compound that fell on the least populated street. If she were on the main boulevard, they'd have plenty of foot traffic to contend with and the last thing they needed was to explain to a tourist why a pregnant woman was jumping off a second story balcony.

Emery shook her head and slipped the amulet around her neck.

This was crazy.

She cradled her stomach. "If we survive this, I promise we'll find somewhere safe far away from all this craziness."

Steeling her nerves, she climbed over the railing and steadied herself. It reminded her of the one time as a child she worked up the nerve to go off the high dive at the local swimming pool. The nerves started in the pit of her stomach, followed by the irrational excitement that came with the thrill of doing something dangerous.

Of course, that first jump ended with her almost drowning after a dramatic belly flop.

"You ready?" Ansel called up to her and her stomach did a belly flop of its own.

Emery inhaled in an attempt to talk herself into letting go and falling, when a knock sounded behind her at the door.

"Emery, it's Bronwyn, can we talk?"

Shit.

She clamped her eyes shut and jumped from the balcony just as she heard the door behind her open.

There was barely enough time to register she was falling when she landed in Ansel's arms.

He set her down gently and gave her a smile. "That wasn't so bad."

"Don't ever ask me to do that again." She rounded the black SUV and slid into the passenger seat at the same time Ansel did the driver's. "We need to go. Bronwyn was at the door when I jumped."

"Did she say anything?" He pulled away from the curb and sped from the compound.

"I didn't give her a chance to." Bronwyn hadn't sounded angry, but there was no way she would have waited to find out. It didn't matter. Emery was never coming back to the compound. She had never felt less at home, less like herself, less like she belonged.

Emery released a breath as the distance between her and the witch compound grew. She moved to take the amulet off.

Ansel reached over and caught her hand. "Keep it on. We might need it to help sneak you past the wards at the city limits."

"Can you tell me where we're going now?"

"The southern limits in the bayou." He focused on the road, and Emery was surprised he knew exactly where he was going. She'd lived there over a month, and she couldn't have navigated much beyond the streets that surrounded the compound in the French Quarter.

It was strange to be leaving the city. It hadn't come to feel like home as the castle did, but still the French Quarter held a magic of its own that would have a special place in her heart. It was funny—the compound and her experiences there should have colored her view of the place, but… it didn't. The beignets helped. She'd miss her evenings at her favorite café with Agatha.

"Let me see your phone."

Emery handed it to him.

He rolled down his window and tossed it down an alley.

"What the hell?"

"The witches can use it to track you." He picked up his own from the center console and handed it to her. "Call Wren."

The Petty Betty in Emery considered throwing it out the window, but she resisted.

She dialed the number. When it went straight to voicemail, Ansel motioned for her to hand him the phone.

He put it on speaker and waited for the beep. "Wren, this is Ansel. Listen to me very carefully. The vampires are plotting an attack on the coven. While I don't much care for you, Emery does, so please get yourself and as many of the coven members out of the compound as you can. I don't know when they will strike, only that it will be soon."

He hung up and handed Emery back the phone. "You can toss it now."

Emery looked at him and huffed a nervous laugh. There was no reason to be laughing, but it was better than the panic that could easily turn to loss of control. She rolled down the window and chucked the phone, though the satisfaction she should have felt was lost on her.

"Are they really attacking?"

Ansel nodded, his expression somber. "That's why Callum called. They plan to bomb the compound. He wanted me to get you out. It's a good thing that was already the plan."

She brought her hand to her chest and tried unsuccessfully to rub the tightness away. "We can't let them die. They may not be right about a lot of things, but they don't deserve to die."

His knuckles tightened on the steering wheel. "Don't ask me to turn around, Emery."

Because he would. Ansel was one of the good guys.

She opened her mouth to argue with him, then shut it. It wouldn't do her any good. He may be one of the good ones, but he wouldn't put her in danger to save the witches. Emery and the child in her belly were more important than the rest of the supernatural world.

They drove the rest of the way to the bayou in relative silence. Emery stared out the window, but she was no longer seeing the magic of the city. She couldn't, not when it was possible parts of it wouldn't exist in a matter of days. More than once Ansel tried to make conversation, but Emery wasn't able to stomach small talk.

Not when everything was on the line, not just the lives of the witches.

One attack was all it would take to start a supernatural war—a war in which she not only had people she loved on both sides, but where so many innocent lives would be lost.

It wasn't until Ansel threw the SUV into park that she snapped out of her daze. She hadn't noticed the city give way to swamps, but they were now surrounded by towering bald cypress trees. Spanish moss hung like curtains, hiding another world within the bayou.

A growl rumbled from Ansel, and she swore she heard the steering wheel snap under his grip. His jaw tightened and Emery followed his gaze to where she assumed the wards of the city ended.

A narrow clearing stretched before them, and Callum and Lily stood together waiting for them at the opposite end, both of their expressions grim.

They weren't the only ones in the clearing. Blocking their path to safety stood Vishna and five members of the inner circle.

Emery's heart raced. *Of course this couldn't be easy.* "What are we going to do? We're outnumbered," she whispered.

Ansel cut the engine. "We are going to get you out of here." He turned and placed his hand over hers on the center console. "I promise I will get you out of this."

She nodded but she wasn't convinced they would be leaving the clearing.

They exited the vehicle and approached the members of the coven, each step like treading through thick mud. The coven wouldn't let her leave if they had a say, and she didn't know how they were supposed to survive six witches. Lily couldn't even help them from the other side of the wards.

Basically they were screwed.

Emery cradled her stomach and spoke softly. "I love you, my little urchin."

When they were half way between the truck and the coven, Ansel stopped and she followed suit, slightly behind him.

Emery opened her mouth to speak, but movement from behind one of the trees on the other side of the ward caught her eye.

No. It can't be.

She stood there with her mouth hanging open. If she thought her heart was racing before, it now threatened to beat clear out of her chest.

The gentle vibrations she'd missed for months—the ones that signified his presence—caressed her bare flesh and a shiver shot through her, leaving a pool of heat in her belly.

He was exactly as she remembered him. The vampire prince who held her heart in his hands. And yet the more she examined him, the more she recognized the monster who took her uncle's life. His eyes were hardened, more midnight than the crisp oceanic blue she loved, and the corners of his lips curled into a hostile smile.

A wave of sadness struck her as Emery realized the man that stood before her wasn't the August who'd held her. But she knew that. The moment she saw him standing over her uncle's body, she knew he wasn't the man she'd loved. Not because August wasn't capable of murder, but because he'd never do that to her. Still, a part of her hoped it wouldn't hold true. That he had a reason beyond his hatred of witches to justify his actions.

Blind hope was a dangerous thing. While it fueled her days at the compound, it hurt like a mother fucker now that her expectations had been confirmed as unrealistic.

August was her enemy and a threat to their child.

Emery fisted her hands at her side, finding that the strength of a mother's love was more than enough to face the monster at hand.

August took a step forward, toe to the barrier, and his voice caressed her skin with a familiar tingle.

"Hello, little witch."

Chapter Ten

AUGUSTINE

He struggled to ignore the feeling of her shock as it flooded the mate bond. Augustine was more interested in the way Emery stood there with her mouth hanging open, cradling her swollen stomach. Her presence alone had his cock surging to life. She was simultaneously the most captivating and vexing creature he'd ever laid eyes on. The way the sun peeked through the canopy and highlighted the pink she'd added back to her hair had him wanting to weave his fingers tightly through it and pull as he took her from behind.

Bloody fucking hell.

She was the only thing that did it for his depraved libido, and he loathed her for it. His body shouldn't have been so affected by her, not while he was in control. The moment she'd stepped from the SUV, his chest constricted and his skin vibrated at what he knew was the same frequency as Emery's. The bond tightened and even though both their ends were firmly shut he could feel her there, hovering at the opposite end.

His dick and his body weren't the only things affected by the witch bitch's presence. August was clamoring to be seen. He clawed against Augustine's hold, his need to get to her a tangible force. He wasn't ready to forgive her, but his softer side needed to know his mate and child were okay.

Augustine closed his eyes and fortified the walls which kept him in the forefront. August would have to wait his turn to get his hands on their little witch, because there was no way Augustine would allow him to fuck up his plans.

Emery had already done that by getting herself knocked up. While she embodied everything he'd been engrained to hate, he had no intention of letting her or anyone else harm his child. Emery was a glorified incubator at the moment and she'd remained as such until his heir was born. After that, she could burn in hell with the rest of her coven.

At least that's what he told himself.

Seeing her standing there, a breath of innocence turned protective mother, had him wanting to claim her where she stood.

It was a good thing her face was contorted in a look of disgust because if it wasn't, he might've given Rex the signal and had him kill everyone in the clearing so he could take her for himself right then and there under the looming Spanish moss.

He glanced over to the trees across the clearing and gave a slight nod toward where he knew Rex hid. As badly as he craved to hear Emery yelling his name at least once before he killed her, the only mission that mattered was keeping the baby safe.

When he turned his attention back to the clearing, Vishna stepped into his line of sight, blocking his view of Emery. "You are not welcome here, Augustine. In fact," her gaze shifted to where Lily stood, "neither are you, sister. This is coven business."

Neither Lily nor Callum moved from where they stood on the opposite side of the clearing. They toed the line of the ward as he did, Lily's hands opened at her side as if waiting for someone to make the first move against them. He wasn't sure which side Callum and Lily would fall on, but he knew they wanted to get Emery out as badly as he did, and that made them his ally in this fight.

Augustine chuckled. This standoff would be short-lived. Especially if Vishna thought he gave a shit about anything she had to say. "I would say it's very much my business as well, considering Emery carries my heir."

"That doesn't matter." Vishna scoffed and turned toward the witches who flanked her, attempting to hide the hint of a smile that threatened her lips. "The abomination she carries will be dealt with, and Emery will remain where she belongs, where we can cultivate her magic training."

Augustine chewed the inside of his cheek, only barely managing to keep his rage at bay. "The child is vampire royalty."

"As is it witch royalty, an heir in fact, but that doesn't mean it should be allowed to exist. That child will sully both our families." Vishna raised her hands and pointed toward the sky. "It's not of the stars."

Augustine wanted to roll his eyes at the hokey star bullshit the witches believed, but looked to Callum, instead needing to confirm whether what Vishna said was true. There was no possible way Malcolm left out the fact Emery was the heir to the witches.

When Callum nodded his confirmation, Augustine's mind raced with the ramifications of the news. He kept his face stoic, so as not to reveal his shock to the witches, but overall the revelation wouldn't directly change his strategies. He'd kill his brother for not telling him.

Emery would still die with the witches. Ending their direct bloodline would just be the icing on the cake.

She's immortal. She's our mate. We aren't killing her.

Augustine ignored August's claims. It didn't matter that she could live forever because he wouldn't allow it. He didn't understand how Augustine didn't see that she lied to him more than he could have ever imagined. She was the blooding fucking heir to the coven. The story she told him about her family, about Miles, was likely all a lie. Sloane was probably their first attempt to get into his good graces. Emery just sealed the deal after her death.

Air rushed from his lungs as the mate bond tightened in his chest, and his eyes whipped toward Emery.

Her eyes narrowed on him and she pushed an almost helpless emotion down the bond that matched the plea in her eyes. It crashed into the wall he'd erected at his end of the bond, nearly shattering what he'd kept in place for the last two months.

August clawed once more to the forefront, and Augustine struggled to push him down and simultaneously fend off the raw emotions of the mate bond's need to go to her.

Claim her.

Debase everything pure within her and bring her to his level of wickedness.

At least he told himself it was the mate bond. The truth was, given the numerous secrets that came to light in the last forty-eight hours, he didn't know what the hell he felt.

Augustine sucked in a breath and shook his head. He didn't have the time to discern what feelings were his own and which belonged to the mate bond.

You feel nothing for her?

"No." He ground out, tasting his own lie. No one heard him save Callum, who tipped his head. No doubt Augustine would have to explain talking to himself later.

Liar. You feel something.

He did, but there was no way he was going to admit to August, let alone anyone else, that the mere presence of the pink-haired little witch absolutely wrecked him. He wanted to both go toe to toe with her and be her solace. He was a monster and she would be his prey, and if he caught her, heaven help the world because he would tear it down for her.

But those were unfounded thoughts driven by a bond he loathed—he wouldn't dare acknowledge them. Facts were what he needed to focus on. They were the only truths he could trust. And the fact was that despite her status as his mate, Emery was his enemy. She only lived because of the child—a child he needed to save regardless of its heritage.

A shiver ran through him as he considered the ramifications of the baby's lineage. If his father knew the child was of pure witch bloodlines, he wouldn't hesitate to use Augustine's heir as a weapon against any who opposed him. He'd use it to control Augustine. The thought unsettled him. His father was already hiding things from him. He wouldn't allow his child to become a pawn in the King's game.

His chest constricted as anger pumped through his veins. The need to protect his child from his father—a father who refused to protect him—settled as his number one priority. While he strived to be the unapologetic king his father was, he refused to be the same kind of father. Family was important to him, as was trusting those around him, as he trusted his team. Neither of these were sentiments his father held.

"I'm standing right here." Emery spoke up, pulling him from his thoughts. Gone was the plea for help in her eyes, replaced by a fire he'd only ever seen in men preparing to go to war. "This child is mine. I carry it and therefore I am the one to decide what happens, and I hate to break it to all of you, but you'll have to kill me to get to my baby."

"That was always the plan." Augustine promised, ignoring

the plight of the mate bond, and the way his cock twitched at Emery's display of dominance. He'd enjoy breaking her of that. A malicious smile settled on his lips as he slipped into the persona he knew best. "But not until you've given me my heir. Until such time, you are safe from me. Can you say the same of your precious coven?"

Emery was shit at concealing her emotions. If her face hadn't already revealed everything, her tether to August did. He didn't think she realized she'd opened her side of the bond the moment he'd stepped into her line of sight. The rollercoaster of emotions was laughable. She was as weak when it came to August as he was to her. The shock, followed by disgust with a hint of sadness, was enough to make Augustine want to vomit. Her only saving grace was the anger and protective surge that radiated from her every time his child's future was mentioned. At the very least, they could agree on that.

"I was hoping it wouldn't come to this." Vishna paused, turned to the coven members who flanked her and nodded. She slowly turned back to Emery, a sinister smile on her lips. "If you will not allow us to abort the fetus, then you are no longer welcome in the coven."

"Thank you." Emery steepled her hands together over her belly protectively. "That's all I wanted. To leave and have my baby away from all the madness of the supernatural world."

"Vishna." The way Lily's voice came out as a soft plea to her sister raised the hairs on the back of his neck. "She can come with me. I'll ensure the bairn is no threat to the coven."

When Vishna nodded in agreement, Augustine's gaze narrowed on the priestess waiting for the other shoe to drop. It was too easy. There was too much at stake to allow a child of both vampire and witch royalty to walk away without a fight.

Emery took a step toward Lily and Callum. Ansel pressed

against her side, keeping himself between Emery and the witches.

Vishna's eyes were locked on Emery as she made a soft tsking noise in time with Emery's steps. "Oh sweet child." She lifted a blade from within her robes and sliced her palm, "If you aren't our princess, that makes you our enemy."

The priestess began reciting an incantation in Daelic and the two of the members of the coven stepped forward joining her in her chant.

Magic shimmered through the air toward Emery, and Augustine sucked in a breath. The magic moved quickly; even if he ordered his men to shoot, it would be too late.

Bloody fucking hell.

The little witch's eyes widened, and her steps slowed. She faltered, her knees buckling under her. The only reason Emery didn't slam into the mossy ground at her feet was the wolf beside her. He caught her and lowered her to the ground. Stepping over her body he bared his teeth and growled at the witches.

Vishna huffed a laugh. "Stupid wolf." She raised her hands and a blast of teal magic erupted from her hands and connected with Emery's protector.

The wolf whimpered and fell still beside her.

"Ansel!" Emery cried out, writhing on the ground. She reached one hand out, gripping his thick forearm, the other hand clutched her stomach. "What's happening?"

A saccharine smile stretched across Vishna's face as the other witches continued to chant, weaving the magic that shimmered around Emery. "I'm only bestowing you one last kindness. You'll need your magic if you're to defend yourself."

There was the other shoe. Augustine had no doubt that whatever Vishna was doing to Emery would not only restore her magic, but also end his child's life. Panic coursed through him, both his own and August's.

Emery fell to her knees and wisps of teal magic surrounded her, encircling her limbs and torso. With each pulse Emery's cries grew louder.

Static magic hung in the air; its earthy bitterness filled his mouth. Augustine raised his hand and gestured to Rex, giving him the fire-at-will signal.

Bullets rained down on the clearing, aimed at the priestess and her coven members, but they did little. A petite blonde witch stepped forward and waved away the bullets.

Her satisfied smirk firmly in place, Vishna twisted her hands and, magic sparks flowing from them, she opened a portal. "I'll be seeing you soon, Emery."

Emery's terrified gaze locked on his, her eyelids drooping. "My baby." Her voice barely more than a hoarse whisper.

Unbridled rage consumed him, but he was helpless to do anything.

Lily ran to Emery—she was the only one who could physically cross the wards. She picked her up and dragged her across the imaginary line set by the coven.

Emery wasn't moving. There was no fight left in her as her magic consumed her fragile human body.

When Callum knelt to pick her up, Augustine growled and pushed him out of the way. His body hummed with a need he couldn't explain. It wasn't just the need to claim her, it was something deeper. Something that could break him. It had to be because she held his child. The child he already loved with every fiber of his being.

It wasn't because she was his mate, that's for damn sure.

August paced in the back of his mind. Having her in his arms wasn't enough.

Emery shifted in his arms and opened her heavy lids. Her

normally bright amber eyes were dull and almost lifeless. The bond they shared shivered as if it were covered in the frost of death. She wasn't long for this world if he couldn't save her, which meant his child would die too.

Save her.

Augustine's fangs elongated and he prayed his venom would counteract the magic. He never wanted to be her mate, he still didn't, but if being her mate would somehow save his child he'd do whatever it took.

He pulled her up tight to his chest and bit the soft flesh at the crook of her neck, telling himself it was to save his child. They were a package deal at the moment. It most definitely wasn't because he wanted to ensure Emery's heart still kept beating so the bond wouldn't grow cold.

As her blood hit his tongue, he moaned, conflicted by his own bold-faced lie. She was his. He'd never understood how August could be so enamored with the little witch, but there in her blood was a truth he wished he could unlearn.

Her pulse weakened, and Emery convulsed in his arms, soft whimpers escaping her lips. Augustine didn't pull any more of her blood, instead focusing on pushing more of his venom into her system, willing it to heal her enough to keep her alive.

"Augustine!" Callum yelled, but all he could hear was Emery's pulse in his ears, slowing to a faint irregular beat.

He was about to admit defeat when he detected a steady pulse. It was faint and contradicted the irregular beat that still came and went.

Augustine's grip tightened on Emery and he froze, enamoured by the faint beat that doubled his own.

It was his child.

He couldn't stop the smile that formed on his lips pressed against Emery's neck.

Then another joined in and the shock brought him to his knees.

He pulled his fangs from Emery and sealed the wounds.

Callum knelt beside him and when he tried to take Emery from his arms, Augustine snarled. He may mean well, but there was no way his cousin was taking her from him. Not now.

Two.

How is this even possible?

Callum's eyes widened, and he gently coaxed. "August, you need to give her to me. Lily can help her, but we need to get her out of New Orleans."

He pulled Emery's limp form tight against his chest. "I'm coming with her."

Callum looked around as if weighing his options. "Fine, but only you. Your men can't come, and I swear if you harm one hair on her fucking head..."

"She's carrying my children, Callum. I won't hurt her so long as she does." Even after the babies were born, he might not. He wasn't ready to process everything that had happened in the last fifteen minutes.

He looked around him to find his team had surrounded them, all of them on guard except Rex who looked at him with what Augustine swore were tear-filled eyes.

"Your Majesty?" Rex rapidly blinked away his emotions. "What would you like us to do?"

"I must go with them. Return to the castle and tell Malcolm what happened. I'll return as soon as I can and we'll hunt the Mistress together."

Rex nodded and turned to his men. "You heard the man, let's move." Rex turned back to Augustine, a genuine smile on his face. "Congratulations, Augustine. Don't fuck this up."

Augustine huffed a laugh. "Thank you, Rex."

After his men walked away, he turned to Callum and Lily who whispered silently off to the side. Lily stepped forward and flicked her wrists, her green magic swirling into a portal. She walked over and offered a hand to Augustine. "Children?"

Of course Lily hadn't missed his choice of words.

Emery shifted in his arms, struggling to keep her clouded eyes open. "Twins?"

"Yes, little witch. We're having twins."

Chapter Eleven

EMERY

The pain was too much. It was as if she were tuning fork, struck hard and vibrating from the inside out. Only the pulses never stopped, and they strained her muscles to the point of unbearable agony.

Emery tried to pry her eyes open, but it was no use.

She willed her lips to part, to scream for help, but she couldn't move a single muscle.

Where was she?

It wasn't cold, so she wasn't back in the dungeons and it didn't smell of smoke, sex, or herbs so that left out New Orleans.

Her mind was clouded and she struggled to recall her last memories. Flashes of what happened in the bayou strung together, creating a narrative she knew to be true but wished was a dream.

Vishna did this. She released her magic in an attempt to hurt her baby.

Babies.

August said she was carrying twins.

And she had no way of knowing if they were okay. If she was okay.

Emery tried once more to scream for help, but her body didn't react. Trapped in her own mind, panic gripped her spine.

In a last ditch effort, she reached for the bond that tethered her to August, but if it was there, she couldn't feel it through the painful vibrations. The rapid movements created a heat that made it so her limbs felt like they would burn from the inside out.

"You're still here?" A thick brogue distracted her, and unless some other Scottish vampire kidnapped her, she'd bet it was Callum.

"Of course. She's carrying my heirs, where the hell else would I be?" August's smooth baritone washed over her, and Emery's panic settled, if only slightly. She was still royally pissed at the asshole but the fact that he was there had to mean something. Maybe she'd misjudged him.

"Your father would be planning attacks on innocents while his wife lay dying if it meant getting revenge."

"I'm not my father, Callum." August ground out, his voice low and deadly. Emery would bet his jaw was tightened and pulsing on the right side. His tell-tale tick.

"No, but you want to be," Callum baited, though Emery wasn't sure why. Everyone knew August and his father didn't see eye to eye. She remembered the way his subjects looked at him the night of the Scottish Gala. It had been with admiration when all she saw when they looked at the King was fear.

Callum continued his strikes at August. "Calculated and ruthless. You don't even see it's not what your kingdom needs. Still, you continue to strive to follow in his footsteps. The kingdom would be better off under Malcolm than under Lewyn two-point-oh."

There was a shuffling sound, paired with a deep growl, followed by a soft thud. "Because your cause is so much nobler?" August spat. "You're chasing an unfounded prophecy, and clinging to the hope you won't have to find another wife because you'll magically have a mate. Wake up, Callum. The witches are playing you, and I won't be there to pick up the pieces when you inevitably fall again."

"And what if the prophecy isn't a lie?" Callum words were barely over a whisper, hurt evident in his voice. "What if everything we've been taught has been a lie? I've seen too much to believe it's not real. And the hope for a better world is worth it, don't you think?"

"Hope is a fool's errand. It doesn't matter. A lie or not, this is our reality. It's the world we live in, and it's the world I will rule in. I have to plan for that future, not some half-baked notion of mates and peace."

"What if you could change it? Would you?"

August was silent for such a long time that Emery wasn't sure if he remained in the room. But finally his deep voice rumbled through the air. "No. I don't trust them. I don't trust her."

Emery didn't need to see him to know August was looking at her. It stung to know that even after months apart his hatred of her hadn't lessened. Then again, it made it easier to hate him in return for all the things he'd done and apparently planned to continue to do, following in his father's footsteps.

"She isn't like them."

August scoffed. "So you all keep saying. But the cities of the murders spell her name, and the coincidence of the last being outside her uncle's bar is too much to ignore."

"Do you hear yourself? It doesn't make sense. Why would she kill her own uncle?"

Emery's mind stilled and she hung on every silent moment. Did Callum mean August didn't kill her uncle? She'd seen the photos. He was standing over the body covered in blood. How could either of them possibly accuse her of having a hand in Miles' murder?

"She wouldn't." August exhaled a weighted breath.

"So she couldn't possibly be the Mistress, right?"

Who the hell is the Mistress? Emery was beginning to sense there was a much bigger game at play here than just the ramifications of her pregnancy. While she'd known that the royal family blamed the coven for the vampire killings, she hadn't paid much attention to the details aside from August's involvement at the scenes. The inner circle had assured the coven that it was a misunderstanding, and they weren't involved.

Emery hadn't believed a word they said, but she also hadn't pushed further. It wasn't her business and she was more worried about hiding her pregnancy and making sure the baby survived.

"I'm not convinced she's not involved," August huffed. Emery had to applaud August's unwavering need to make her a villain. "I have been trying to figure out her motives."

"She doesn't have any, Augustine. Only to keep her children safe. You just want her to be the villain so you can continue to ignore the fact she's your mate."

"*My* children."

"You keep telling yourself that, cousin. She's going to give you hell if you think you're taking them from her. She'll never forgive you."

Callum wasn't wrong. August would be taking their children over her dead body. Even then, she'd find a way to come back and haunt his ass. There had to be a necromancer that would enjoy pissing off the future king of vampires.

"She won't be around long enough to do so."

"Your ignorance is showing. She's your mate, no matter how much you want to deny it."

"And she's also a witch."

A soft snort filled the room followed by Callum's retort. "I saw the way you looked at her when Vishna hit her."

So had she. In the moments before she passed out, she'd witnessed an array of emotions flash over him. Everything from love and fear to pure unadulterated hatred.

"I looked at her as any father would look at the incubator keeping his children alive."

Emery winced, not because of August's words but because of the pain creeping up her spine. It was growing exponentially.

His words would have hurt once upon a time, but now, when it came to August, she knew where they stood. In fact, she was pretty sure she was going to have to kill him eventually. Screw the damn mate bond, if he thought she was just a warm body to breed his heir he had another thing coming. She was their mother and if she survived this she would make sure she kept them far away from their monster of a father.

Callum released a low growl. "She's dying, Augustine. What if she doesn't survive this?"

Wait, what? She was dying? No, she couldn't die. She finally had a purpose. Her children needed her. She needed them. The supernatural world needed them. They may still be small in her womb, but they were the future.

"As long as my children live, that's all that matters," August stated matter of factly.

August could get fucked if he thought he was going to raise their children to be witch-hating monsters.

Emery turned her thoughts to the stars. She had never put any stock in what the witches at the coven said, but she was desperate. *Please let me survive this. I will do whatever it takes to protect my children. To protect children like them. To right the wrongs of my ancestors.*

"Some people would give anything to have what you had with her..."

Pain shot through her, and Emery was sure the stars had rejected her plea. She tried to hang on, to hear August's response, but the pain was too much.

"Is she okay?" Something that could be mistaken for fear edged into August's voice. "The bond is strained and her heartbeat is slowing."

Emery fought like hell to stay coherent, but it was no use. She heard Callum call for Lily before she fell into the darkness once more.

Chapter Twelve

EMERY

She had no idea how long she'd been asleep but she thanked the stars when she gasped for air and her eyes flew open, even though her chest heaved like it would cave in at any moment.

"Lay still, Emery." Lily's voice cut through the pain, but only barely.

Everything hurt. Her head throbbed to the point of seeing stars while her muscles pulsed against her skin, pushing outward as if they no longer wished to be contained.

"Make it stop. Please make it stop," she begged, not caring if they knocked her out with a blow to the head, as long as it made the pain stop.

"I can't. It's only going to get worse unless you accept your magic."

"What?" she choked out.

Lily's eyes softened, her lips pulling into a tight frown. "My sister forced your magic upon you. I hoped to tell you the whole story before unbinding your magic, but she took that from us. Your body is fighting the magic because you are fighting what's necessary."

A scream bubbled from Emery's lips as her body contracted. "I'm not doing anything. How do I make it stop?"

Lily's eyes widened and tears filled her eyes. "You're dying, Emery. The babies are dying. They can't handle the influx of magic, and if you don't accept it, the refusal will kill you."

And them. Lily didn't need to speak the implied words.

Panic coursed through her. "Save my babies." She couldn't lose her babies. Not like this. Not at all. "There has to be something you can do."

Movement caught her attention, and she locked eyes with August standing propped up against the wall with Callum at his side. His midnight eyes were narrowed on her, and his jaw tightened like he was ready murder someone. Not for the first time she wished he was the man she met in the bar. She was scared, and needed the comfort of the prince who loved her.

"I have been siphoning magic from you and that has helped, but your magic is only growing to compensate. I can try to save you all, but there is no guarantee."

"Do it. Do whatever it takes, but save my babies."

Lily nodded and hurried to the dresser on the opposite side of the room to gather things from a bag. She spoke as she worked. "August, I need you to bite her when I tell you to."

Panic gripped her. "No. I don't want him near me. Callum can do it." There was no way she was letting August near her. He was liable to kill her himself.

"It has to be him, lass. Not only is he the twins' father, but he's your mate. If his venom can heal as I siphon and you accept, maybe the fates will be on our side and we'll be able to save all three of you."

Fuck the fates.

"You will save them." August growled. He pushed off the wall and walked toward the bed.

"There are no guarantees, princeling." Lily finished what

she was doing and joined her on the bed once more, a mortar in hand.

Emery's eyes widened as she both searched and pleaded with Lily for another answer. August may be the twins' father but he was also her enemy. Unable to come up with another suggestion, she sighed, "What do you need me to do?"

"When I tell you, you need to let go. Even if it's not consciously, you're fighting against your magic as you always have because it's been buried within you. It's been released and it yearns to consume you and become one with its master."

That's exactly what it felt like. Like she'd be consumed at any moment, and when she was, she'd no longer be of the world around her.

Lily placed a hand on Emery's exposed knee. "Close your eyes. Focus on your babies and your future. You will need to protect them and yourself. You need your magic as much as your magic needs you. A balance needs to be struck or it will consume you all."

Emery shuddered, biting through the next pulse of pain. "Please save my babies."

Lily forced a smile. "I'll do my best, lass."

August maneuvered to the head of the bed. He slipped his hands under her and lifting her with ease, he slid behind her so she leaned against his chest. Tingles mixed with the continuous pain where his hands grazed her skin. Warmth filled her, and she loathed the way her body reacted to his proximity. She craned her neck up to look at him, studying the hard lines of his face and the dark midnight eyes which should have been ocean blue. "Callum was right. I'll never forgive you. For Miles or if you take my babies from me."

August cocked a brow with a crooked smile. "Seems I need to watch where I open my mouth." He leaned in, and his breath tickled her ear. "Never is a long time for an immortal, but this isn't about us, little witch. I only care to save our children."

Never.

Forever.

She'd almost forgotten she'd live as long as him.

Still, he was right and she hated him for it. Even more so because she agreed with him. It was no longer about them and the clusterfuck that was their relationship. It was about the new lives they'd created.

Lily lifted Emery's shirt and scooped a glob of paste from the mortar onto her swollen belly. She closed her eyes and whispered softly in an ancient tongue, laying her hands on Emery's abdomen.

Green magic seeped from Lily's hands and became one with the paste, glowing on her belly. "Now, Emery. Let go."

Emery leaned into August, his warmth wrapping around her. Even playing the villain in her story, his touch provided a comfort no other could. Despite the bitterness it caused, she felt the bond swell within her and in that instant, with raw emotions flooding her already frayed heart, Emery faced the reality of her mortality.

Seconds earlier, she'd been ready to go toe to toe with August, but now, she feared they'd never get to fix what was broken. She could die if this didn't work, never knowing his love again, never telling him everything she felt for him. The fates had dealt them a shit hand when it came to destiny. Born mates and mortal enemies only to have her die before they could explore either.

"You aren't allowed to die." August tightened his grip on her.

Fucking mate bond. And even in that moment he couldn't help but be a demanding asshole.

She tensed and shook her head against August's chest. He didn't get to dictate her future. She wanted to live. Damn did she want to live, but the pain was too much. It was consuming her. Raging inside her with the need to take what it wanted most, a vessel to call home. It didn't care that it might kill her in the process. It thrived on balance, and in that moment, Emery was chaos incarnate.

August ran his hands down her arms and to the sides of her belly.

"Let go, Emery." She shivered as August whispered in her ear without any hint of malice. "For them. For me."

For him.

She wasn't sure she heard those last two words, but even if they had been imagined, the reminder that her children needed her was enough to motivate her to try and find the balance her magic sought.

"You can do this." August reassured her and weaved his fingers through hers.

She sucked in a breath and imagined accepting the pain and allowing the magic to consume her. Another wave of magic pulsed through her and when she convulsed in its wake, August held her more tightly. She gripped his hands, and he sucked in a breath against her ear as her nails dug in.

With her acceptance, the magic within her grew. The pulsing receded, becoming a constant pressure radiating from her torso. It bolted through her and every inch of her burned as though she was on fire. Emery grit her teeth, struggling to stay both in control and let go.

"One part of you at a time. Release it a little bit at a time." She clung to the calm in August's voice. "You're almost there."

There was no way he could know that, but she appreciated his attempts to soothe her.

Emery slowed her breathing and focused only on the pain. She imagined each of her muscles relaxing into the wicked pulse, starting with her legs.

Her arms came next and her grip on August loosened, but he didn't let her fall.

Lily's soft voice chanting lulled her as every inch of her slowly embraced her magic, welcoming the way it quieted the ache Emery hadn't realized existed. It reached the depths of her being, filling even the smallest spaces, probing, connecting, becoming one with her. The connection Emery felt with it was incredible.

A loud snap in her head startled her and Emery knew the moment her magic encountered the mate bond she shared with August. It swelled, claiming her mate, the bond, and August. She sucked in her bottom lip and bit down to stop the string of curses that filled her mouth. Both hers and what she assumed were August's now that the bond was blown open by her magic.

Loathing.

Fear.

Darkness.

Emery lingered on the darkest shadows between them. Such rage, capable of both war and protection. A part of her wanted to live in them. To use it to fuel the storm she planned to unleash on Vishna and weave it into a shield to protect her children.

The emotions continued to flood her.

Lust.

Pride.

Love.

Emery trembled and tears fell freely from her eyes.

The last one wasn't only hers.

Before she could consider what it meant, her magic moved

toward her core. Emery panicked, and instinctively fought back.

August's grip tightened, stopping her from reaching for her stomach. "Not my babies. Please, not my babies." She pleaded to anyone who would listen. Lily. August. The fates. She didn't care as long as her children lived.

"Now, Augustine."

Two sharp fangs pierced her neck, and Emery lost all will to fight. She arched her back, seeking more before sagging into August. He moaned against her and the warmth of his venom seeped into her, causing her to taste the sweetest caramel on her lips. She closed her eyes and floated, lighter than air until a sudden burst of light erupted behind her eyelids, and Emery was transported into what felt like another world.

The smell of an ocean breeze filled her and before her were two beautiful babies, a boy and a girl, sitting on the edge of a serene lake. They weren't entirely whole, light pouring through them from the sun above.

"Where are we?"

August's voice startled her and she turned to find him standing next to her, his eyes wide, staring at the children with what she sensed was a mix of apprehension and wonder.

"I don't know," she whispered.

The babes stopped playing and looked at Emery and August. For the first time she got a really good look at them.

They were the spitting image of her and August, right down to the girl's whiskey eyes and the boy's dirty blonde mop. Gummy grins tugged at their mouths, and Emery's heart soared. Neither of them spoke out loud, but she heard their soft voices in her mind.

It's okay, Momma. Daddy. We're going to be okay.

Emery gasped, and August's mouth hung open beside her before swinging up into the smile she'd only seen once before, when he'd looked at her the night of the ball. The kind of smile that touched his eyes and melted her soul.

These were their babies. Their twins.

"My urchins," she whispered.

Without another thought, the babies smiled and were lifted on a breeze. They swirled together, in a cyclone of air, their soft giggles filling Emery's heart with joy.

The air quickened, and Emery stepped forward, plagued by a mother's worry. The wind would be too much for their tiny bodies. When she'd nearly reached the vortex, a gust of air forced her back, and she landed in August's arms.

He said nothing as he righted her, but he kept a firm hand placed on her hip, tugging her close to him.

The wind slowed, and when the cyclone dissipated, only one baby remained. The girl stared back at them, but she no longer looked as she had before. Her eyes were no longer solid whiskey in color, instead they'd transformed. Blue along the outer edges with a ring of the lightest gold set around her irises.

We love you.

Emery's knees buckled and she fell against August as a sob bubbled in her throat. What happened to her precious baby boy?

Her vision began to blur, and she reached out for the baby girl before her. When she blinked away the tears in her eyes, she was pulled from the vision and instead of her baby girl and the lake, Lily's tear stained face stared back at her.

"Where are they? Where's my baby girl?" Her head whipped around searching for the little girl with the best parts of her parents.

"What happened?" Panic laced Callum's voice, and he moved to take Emery's hand.

"She was there, my baby girl. She was there, by the lake."

Her voice bordered on hysteria. "And my baby boy. He was taken by the storm. Where is he?"

August didn't say a word, but continued to hold Emery against him, and she was no longer sure if the panic she felt was hers or his, only that it was all encompassing.

Lily's eyes widened, the only indication she was worried as her voice remained calm. "Emery you were amazing, but I..." she hiccuped a sob. "...I couldn't save them both."

"What do you mean? My babies. They were both there. And then he was gone and she was the best parts of them. But now she's gone too. What happened? Where are they?"

"You...you saw them?"

"Yes, Lily. I saw them, now what do you mean you couldn't save them both?"

"Your magic was too strong. Too much for their tiny bodies to take on and I could only siphon so much. To live, you needed to accept your magic, but they were not ready. Babies aren't born with their magic, the earth gives it to them as they grow." Lily's shoulders sagged and she bowed her head. "I couldn't save them both."

"No." Emery shook her head. "No, no, no, no." This wasn't happening. She couldn't lose them.

"Lass, I couldn't save them both, but I was able to merge their essence. The night and the light. Only one babe remains, but she is made up of all the best parts of both of them. And the both of you."

Her eyes. Her baby girl with the blue and amber eyes.

"So the baby is a girl." August's voice was low, almost deadly.

Lily nodded, a smile tugging at her lips. "It's a miracle."

A miracle?

Emery's heart warred in her chest. The walls around it shattered for the briefest of moments by the love of her children, only to be refortified by the loss of her son. How could Lily say it was a miracle? She had lost her son. Her beautiful son who had his father's eyes.

August's emotions mirrored her own, angry and confused with sorrow woven in the space between.

Emery craned her neck, and met August's blank stare. His haunted eyes told her he was just as lost as she was.

She swallowed hard, choking back tears as she tried to get a read on where he was. He'd been kind, almost loving during the whole ordeal. They were connected through the mate bond, and as much as she wanted to hate him, there was now something holding her back from writing him off completely.

An inexplicable sliver of hope.

"I want a paternity test."

Her mouth dropped. "What?" Those were the last words she expected to come from his mouth.

"I want to make sure the baby's mine." He untangled Emery from his arms. "You've been in New Orleans for two months, and I have reason to believe it's not my child."

"Are you fucking kidding me, August?" Emery shoved him away from her, needing to put as much space between her and her thick-headed mate. "You are the only person whose baby it could be."

"Augustine," Callum stepped toward where they sat on the bed. "I know what you're thinking, but you're mates. We don't know what happens when you procreate. We'll reach out to Lily's grandfather, see what he knows."

August stood and rolled down the sleeves of his shirt. "Vampires can't sire females, Emery. If you are so sure, you'll have no problem with the test."

"Go to hell, August. You saw her," Emery sobbed, hating she couldn't hold back her raw emotions. "She is the best parts of you and me. Well, at least me. I pray she got nothing from you."

It wasn't true. She hoped her child got his resilience and his loyalty, even if he reserved none of that for her. It seemed she'd always be a toy to him. One he could turn on and off at will when it suited him. Enemy and mate, but never a partner. She might as well get used to the sting of rejection.

August's lips curled into a sneer. "We'll see." He tore from the room, slamming the door as he went.

Emery stared at the door, not bothering to hide the tears that fell. She needed to let them fall, all of them, so the next time her asshole mate came at her with hearts in his eyes she'd have none left.

Callum sat on the bed next to her, pulling her hands into his lap and running his fingers over her palms. "He'll come around, lass. It's a lot to process and he hasn't exactly been himself lately."

"He's the monster he wants everyone to believe he is."

"Aye, lass, Augustine is that, but August is in there fighting, and he always comes out on top."

Emery cocked her head and almost asked if Callum was feeling alright. "What the hell does that even mean?"

"I'm not excusing his actions. As far as I'm concerned he needs to get his head out of his arse. " Callum sighed, his face falling into a frown. "It's not my story to tell, but August didn't have it easy growing up as the crown prince. The King held him to an unattainable standard, and thus Augustine was born. The worst parts of August pushed to the forefront to deal with the hardships thrust upon him. War. Politics. Bloodlust. Usually August pulls himself out, but this time, the light broke him. He fell apart when he found out what you were and he hasn't been able to find his way back."

"So this is my fault?"

"No, lass. His actions are his own. He just needs to find his way back. He needs his light. He needs you."

"Most of the time he wants to kill me." She placed her hands on her stomach. "This baby is the only thing keeping me alive at the moment."

"We won't let him harm you or the baby." His voice fell off and Callum searched her eyes, for what though she wasn't sure. "I'll talk to him, but I don't think it will do any good. It's you he needs, lass."

"I'll take it under advisement, but until he gets his head out of his ass he might as well kick rocks."

A soft chuckle escaped his lips. "Get some rest, Emery." With that, Callum stood and left the room, leaving her alone with Lily.

"Could my life be any more fucked up?" she groaned.

"I'd like to say no, but I don't think it's wise to test the universe." Lily pulled Emery's shirt down over her belly and helped her get under the covers. "You need to rest so your body can regulate to its new normal. We'll discuss your magic later."

Emery caught Lily's hand before she could leave the bed. "Thank you. For everything."

"You are the only family I have left, lass. There isn't anything I wouldn't do for you." She gave Emery's hand a squeeze and stood. "I'll have Ansel keep watch for any broody vampires. Augustine will come around. Until then, rest easy."

She expected to have trouble sleeping, but the moment her head hit the pillow, a blanket of sorrow cocooned her and for the first time in months, she fell into a deep and dreamless sleep.

Chapter Thirteen

AUGUSTINE

Go back in.

"No."

Augustine slammed the front door of the cottage and took off at a full sprint toward the loch off the back of the property.

He followed the river, allowing the crisp air to tease his lungs and radiate a calm only the air of the Highlands could bring. It should have doused the fire within him as it had so many times in his youth, but it didn't. He was too far gone, too broken to be soothed by his homeland.

The heather fields were in full bloom, a blur of purple on either side of him. As children, Malcolm and Augustine played in these fields during the summer months when his father would tour the countryside. They were just far enough away that they were off the royal family's radar, but close enough to access easily. Those were simpler times. Times when he could wholly be himself, instead of the split entity he'd become.

Let me go to her.

It really was quite genius for Callum to use this location to hide Emery. Fortified with the spells Lily had woven, they were right under his father's nose and neither the Scottish King nor his brother would ever know it.

Augustine, she needs us. Don't bloody fuck this up. You let your guard down. I know you want her as much as I do.

Augustine ignored August's pleas. He knew he'd been unable to stop himself from comforting Emery, but he wasn't ready to examine why. Not now. Maybe not ever. He'd sooner chalk it up to a mate-bond-induced moment of insanity.

When he reached the loch, he ran faster, circling its widest part. He slowed to a jog when he reached the inlet from the mountain stream. It raged with the melted snow brought on by summer. It was late, but the June sun hadn't completely set, leaving the sky painted with beautiful pinks and purples.

"Remember when I drained that group of Highlanders here? Didn't you fancy one of the humans that summer? Her blood didn't call to you like Emery, but she was a great lay from what I remember." He enjoyed the annoyance that seethed through August, ruining the serenity of the moment.

Are you fucking kidding me? I swear on the stars and all that is holy, you need to fix this. You know it's our child. Not only did you see it as plain as I did, but you were with me when we fucked her. You were always there. She would have trusted us. Would have proved you wrong in every way, but you had to go and open your big mouth and ruin it.

Of course he did. The child may be theirs, and he may have already loved his child more than life itself, but her mother was a conundrum he'd yet to master. One who could cripple him as a man and king.

And then there was the ache—the impossible, unending ache—for the son who would never be born. Emery's agony had matched his own. It was too painful, too real. Lashing out was a perfect way to cover the pain. Asking for a paternity test changed the pain to conflict; conflict was easy.

"She is still our enemy, August. How is it you don't see that?" Augustine picked up a rock and ran his fingers across its smooth surface before skipping it across the glassy lake. "We need to keep her at a distance until our child is born."

Our daughter.

"Yes." His jaw tightened and he struggled to get the words out. "Our daughter."

Why is that so hard for you to accept? Lily is right. This is a miracle. If we can have a daughter it will change everything.

"What will it change? We'll have to breed with the witches. We'll be shackled to them and their magic for eternity. They are our enemy for fuck's sake." The ramifications of vampire royals being able to sire female children were vast.

Right now. They are our enemy right now. What if they were never meant to be? What if everything Callum told Malcolm is true? It's possible we have it all wrong. That vampires were made for witches. We're having a daughter. Something that is supposed to be impossible for our kind. We could do away with the Culling.

"Do you actually think our father would allow that? He thrives on control. All vampires do. Except maybe Malcolm. Still, he would enslave the witches before we were ever allowed the freedom to breed between the factions."

Augustine paused, remembering the way Emery felt pressed against his chest. In that moment, while she lay dying, he wanted her more than anything in the world. He'd have done whatever it took so he'd never have to live in a world without her. Every bit of his hatred for the little witch had been dampened only to return when he left her side, albeit with far less gusto than before. Everything about it was wrong, but he couldn't help it. She'd gotten under his skin.

He shook his head, freeing the thought, telling himself it was just the mate bond. "There is too much bad blood between vampires and witches. None of the factions will ever let that truth exist. They've already rewritten history once, what makes you think they won't do it again?"

And you call me the coward.

"I am doing what's best for our people."

Do you even know what that is? As far as I can tell, our father has been lying to us about the state of the kingdom. They want peace. They want unity. And what about what's best for us? For Emery? For our daughter?

"We failed to protect Thea, how are we supposed to protect our own little girl from the war that is brewing? Not to mention our kingdom. If we don't win, we won't have a kingdom left. The witches will take everything."

Together. You and me as one. Not to mention Callum, Malcolm, and Lily. Even Emery is powerful in her own right. I know you noticed the way her magic pressed against us. She is not weak. She is so much more than what we expected.

He wasn't wrong. Emery was so much more, and he hated that it gave him pause—that in the last three days, every time he considered himself taking the throne, it was with her by his side, his babies continuously in her womb. Ever since her magic flooded their mate bond, he'd been fighting between thoughts of claiming every inch of her and destroying her.

From the moment he'd seen her, everything about her taunted him.

Fucking mate bond. That was the only answer. As time went on it continued to twist his view of the little witch. Her proximity made it worse. Even thinking of her as the witch bitch now left a bitter taste in his mouth when just days before he'd wanted to set her on fire, just to watch her burn.

"She makes us weak, August."

Your failure to accept what's in front of you makes us weak. That woman is our everything.

"Our daughter is our everything, and for the moment she is tethered to Emery."

I'm done denying what Emery is to me. To us. We almost lost her, Augustine. I can't lose her. You may not be willing to concede, and I may not be strong enough to take the forefront. Not yet, at least. But when I do, and I will, she will be our queen. She is our future.

"I will not fall prey to the mate bond." Despite how much his cock wished he would. "It's not real love. It's a cruel infatuation created by a witch who thought to meddle with the fates."

Is it?

The question hung between them, a metaphorical stalemate in which neither would yield. August was ready to jump in with both feet and play family with their little witch, while Augustine wasn't sure he'd ever be wholly convinced magic hadn't coerced him.

At least that's what he told himself. The truth of it was Emery was so much more than he imagined. She had no problem going up against Vishna, a witch who could break her with the snap of a finger. And she often challenged him for the sake of their daughter. It was evident she would always put their child first—what more could he ask for from her mother? But he wasn't ready to admit that out loud. Not even to the deepest parts of himself.

August didn't press him or question his thoughts.

The silence was broken by the sound of his phone. He dug it from his pocket, swiping across Malcolm's smug face.

"What?"

"How's Emery?" The eagerness in Malcolm's voice had Augustine biting back a growl. He needed to get a fucking grip.

"She's fine," he ground out, crushing the rock in his opposite hand.

"And the babies?"

"Baby." Augustine's voice fell, the memory of the son that would never be playing in his mind. "We lost one. My son."

"I'm so sorry, brother. If you need me…"

"I don't." He wasn't ready to consider the loss of his son. He'd only ever imagined a little boy in his future. One he could love and nurture in a way his father never did. A son who would rule after him, a fair but fierce king. So many of the things he'd dreamed of were ripped away from him in a single moment. Because of Vishna.

The priestess would pay for what she'd done. A life for a life wasn't enough when it came to the loss of his son. No, Augustine's rage would see nothing less than the complete decimation of the coven.

The frame of his cell phone creaked against Augustine's tightening hand, and he pushed his dark thoughts away for another time. He changed the subject and took a jab at Malcolm. "I know your next question is going to be if Lily has asked about you, and she hasn't."

His poor brother was obsessed with the ancient witch, had been since he'd met her at the garden party months ago. He swore she was his mate, but she'd avoided him at all costs, leaving Malcolm to pine in a way that irritated Augustine. He had tried to tell his brother that he dodged a bullet on the whole mate thing, but Malcolm wouldn't be swayed.

"Noted." Malcolm's voice was tense and Augustine expected him to argue. "I take it you fucked things up somehow?"

"Now why would you think that?"

"Because I don't hear Callum or Emery in the background, which means you likely stormed out for fresh air, and you only do that when you're either angry or you fucked something up. I'm going to guess both."

Augustine ignored his brother's too true assessment. "How's Thea?"

Malcolm was silent, before letting out a weighted sigh. "She's not any worse, but she's not getting better. The herbs are keeping her comfortable, but she still hasn't woken up. She's become restless, flinching in her sleep."

One more reason he was going to kill the witches. They were running out of time and still had no clue how to save his sister. "How's Mother?"

"She's a wreck. Between the constant stress of Thea, your absence, Emery's pregnancy, and Father's constant attacks, she's withering away."

Augustine abruptly stopped his pacing. "What attacks?"

"After the first attack on the coven's compound, the wards around the city fell. It's been a war zone of witches and vampires every night. The majority fled to smaller compounds throughout the United States, seeking refuge. Father started his attacks on those two nights ago. He's on a rampage to end the witches."

Bloody fucking hell.

He wasn't exactly surprised—his father wouldn't stop until all the witches had paid for what they'd done to his family. Not only recently but all those years ago in Scotland. But the attacks weren't part of the plans Augustine had laid out. They were supposed to wait for the witches to retaliate. To make sure they had the upper hand to ensure minimal lives lost.

"Why did no one tell me?"

"Father doesn't know where you are. I told him you were investigating the identity of the Mistress and it required you to go undercover. He expects you home in a few days."

That's why he hadn't been consulted. He'd been too busy worrying about the lives of his child and his mate, and as a result, lives had been lost. He was torn between regretting his decision to come to Scotland and the knowledge that if he hadn't his child and mate would likely be dead. How was he ever supposed to reconcile that he'd put his children before his kingdom? Worse still, he'd do it again. That sort of decision made him weak. It was something his father would never have done.

And he is feared, not revered, August interjected.

"Thank you for keeping my location to yourself," he said to Malcolm, choosing to ignore August. More likely than not, Malcolm's lie would likely come back to bite him in the ass when he finally did make it back to the castle, but for now, it had protected Emery and the baby.

"Don't thank me. Get your head out of your ass, and fix things with Emery."

What he said. How many people need to tell you the same thing before it sticks in your thick skull?

Augustine's jaw tightened with a soft growl. "I'll take it under advisement." He wouldn't. "In the meantime I have a favor to ask of you."

"What is it?"

"I need you to go into our private collection and search for the name Octavian Winterstar."

"Okay." The faint sound of a pen scribbling on paper came through the receiver. "Who is he?"

"He's Lily's grandfather and, according to the witches, the sire of all turned vampires. I did some reading of Lily's texts while I was waiting for Emery to wake. I need to know if he's still alive."

Malcolm let out a low whistle. "You know he'll have been erased from the castle texts. Anything surrounding the original witches and vampires has been. It's all hearsay, stories passed on filled with half truths."

"I know." It was a long shot but Augustine needed to know the truth of their origins. Needed to know if there was any factual evidence for the mate bond that plagued him. "But I am sick of the lies perpetrated by our forefathers."

"I'll see what I can come up with."

"Thank you, brother."

Malcolm paused, hesitancy laced his voice. "When will you be back?"

"Soon. Tell Mother if she'd like, we can bring her and Thea here."

"Really?" Malcolm asked, surprised. "With the witch there?"

"Yes," Augustine said. As much as he didn't trust witches, Lily had always put his family first. "She saved my daughter and I fear she'll be the only one who can help Thea now."

"They'll be ready to go upon your return."

They traded goodbyes. After he hung up, Augustine sat in the serenity of the Highlands, trying to ignore the pull of his mate at the cottage. He opened the bond between them and though it was still, as if she were sleeping, sorrow and regret slipped through in a steady stream.

He warred with himself, the need to comfort her both intense and infuriating at the same time. Augustine would not go to her, would not give in and allow Emery to alleviate the pain that consumed him. He sat on the edge of the lake, and his head fell to his knees.

There in the silence, he dropped his walls and mourned the loss of his son.

Chapter Fourteen

EMERY

It was still dark outside when she woke. Her body ached, her head throbbed, and her mouth was drier than the Sahara.

Emery blinked repeatedly, trying to gather her bearings. She switched on the light beside the bed and was surprised to find a tall glass of water and a note.

You're going to feel like you've been hit by a truck until you learn to trust your magic.
Pull it to the surface. You don't need to release it, but test it, feel it. Doing so will help you to accept it.
It won't hurt the baby. You are one now.
Come find me if you need help.
Lily

We are one now.

Her stomach sank.

But at what cost? She'd found everything she'd ever wanted without her magic. A family. Friends. Even love. All magic had done was take from her the few things she'd held dear, leaving her with pieces of a life that might never be whole again.

Emery's chest constricted and a sob bubbled as the memory of her little boy flitted through her mind. His perfect eyes and tiny nose. The way he looked just like his father. Magic took him from her. She'd never hold him, never teach him to play the piano, never swaddle him close as he fell to sleep and whisper in his ear, telling him how loved he was.

Her hands dropped to her stomach, cradling his sister in her belly. She was all Emery had left of her son. Lily had said she would be all the best parts of August and her, but she wasn't sure that would ever be enough.

A sob broke from Emery's throat. What the hell kind of mother was she, to think her daughter wouldn't be enough even before she was born? It wasn't that she didn't love her daughter. She did. More than life itself. Emery would do anything to ensure she thrived in the world. But she feared a part of her would always yearn for her son. No matter how much of him was in his sister, his life was cut too short at the expense of her life. At the expense of her magic.

As if in response, Emery's magic fluttered in her chest, causing her to inhale sharply. Unbridled hatred coursed through her. She had always imagined her unbinding would be a joyous occasion. One that meant she was accepted, loved, and a part of something bigger than herself.

While all those things may be true in some sense, she was fractured. Left in pieces by the life she thought she wanted. Magic hadn't equated to the happiness she thought it would. There was power, but it always came at a price. Every time she'd encountered it, nothing but death and destruction reigned in its wake.

And now she was supposed to accept it. To become one with the thing that consistently fucked up all the good things in her life.

At one point she would have been strong enough, but in the silence of night, alone in her room, it was easy to admit she was no longer the woman who stood strong in the light of day. While her exterior remained the same, she was the shell of the person she once was. The only thing keeping her above the abyss of darkness that threatened to consume her was the remaining life within her.

The throbbing in her head increased. Her magic taunted her, reminding her it would not hesitate to take what it demanded if she rejected it again. It held no mercy for her or what she wanted. Just like every other aspect of her life.

Her hands fell open in her lap, palms up, and Emery looked at them, unsure what she was supposed to do next. She hesitated, wishing there was another way besides accepting the magic she knew would likely continue to demand more than she could give. If it weren't for her daughter, she might choose to forsake her magic completely. But that wasn't an option.

Emery inhaled the still night air and closed her eyes. Slowly exhaling, she imagined her magic rising to the surface, just under her skin. It moved within her, like a thick fluid, lackadaisical as it tested its way through her veins. She probed it gently, forming it and willing it to move only toward her hands.

Heat formed in her hands, and she dared to peek through her lashes to find a golden glow filled the dim room. Sitting in her palms were two glowing spheres of magic. She choked out a sound that was a mix of a laugh and a sob. She may hate everything her magic represented, but she couldn't deny its beauty. Where Lily's magic had been green, and Vishna's teal, hers reminded her of the sun. A soft yellow that glittered as it circled in her palms.

What struck her as most beautiful, though, was the almost phantom-like stain that swirled through it. A darkness which matched the emotions she'd felt in Augustine. It not only threaded its way through her magic, but tethered itself to her soul, urging her to take revenge, to feed it so it may grow.

And she wanted to. More than anything, she wanted to latch onto it and allow it to fuel her revenge.

"You are mine," Emery whispered, claiming her magic. "No more going off the rails. In all we do, we work together or not at all."

Her magic didn't react, but obeyed her movements as she closed her palms, extinguishing it. Quickly, she opened them again, and the spheres appeared instantly, much to her surprise. The magic ebbed and flowed at her command, embracing her as its master.

After a few more minutes of testing her magic and absorbing its heady power, Emery's headache was gone and her body relaxed, at peace in its merge with her magic.

She finished her glass of water and slipped from the bed.

The room seemed smaller now that everyone in the house wasn't hovering around her. It didn't offer much in the way of extra amenities, the king bed taking up the majority of the space, along with a dresser that—upon closer inspection—she found to be filled with clothes in her size. It also housed male clothes, but she couldn't bring herself to assume what Lily and Callum were thinking when they stocked the bedrooms.

She also didn't want to think of the male they'd likely intended them for. He'd stormed out after cheapening her to that of a knocked up whore. As if they hadn't shared an epic connection through her magic and the vision of their children. He could rot in hell as far as she was concerned.

The mate bond reverberated in her chest, protesting her thoughts. It had strengthened, and she longed for August in a way she hadn't before her magic was unbound. Before, it was an emotional attachment, superficial in comparison to what it would become. It now consumed her on a visceral level, almost begging for her to find him and claim him.

Another thing to add to the list of shit circumstances.

She'd never put much stock in the stars or the fates, having grown up outside the coven, but she'd appreciate it if they'd leave her alone. They'd already fucked her enough for one lifetime.

After a quick shower filled with more tears lost in the stream of hot water, Emery set out to explore the house. Or at least she tried before she was halted, nearly tripped over someone outside her door.

When she righted herself against the doorframe, the light from the room illuminated a dozing vampire.

"Callum?"

He scrubbed his face and rubbed the sleep from his eyes. "Hi, lass. What are you doing up? Shouldn't you be resting?"

"The better question is, what are you doing sleeping outside my room?"

Callum stood and leaned against the opposite wall. "Ansel made me promise to keep an eye on you while he went for a run."

"Ansel?" Emery searched the hallway even though Callum had just said he'd gone for a run. "Where is he? Is he okay? And the witches? Did the vampires attack the compound?"

The last time she'd seen her protector, he was sprawled out on the bayou floor beside her, unmoving. She'd been too out of it to notice he hadn't been there the night before, which was unlike him. Ansel would move hell or highwater to protect her and her child.

"Calm down lass, he's fine. Vishna did a number on him, but he recovered after a few days rest. He's given Augustine a run for his money trying to protect you."

Emery laughed. That sounded like Ansel. But it didn't sound like Augustine. Not after the way he stormed out. "And the witches.?"

Callum shook his head. "The attack went on as planned. Many of the witches were able to escape and seek refuge elsewhere, but not all were so lucky. As soon as I have any more information, I will let you know."

The few witches she cared for—and even a few she didn't —filtered through her mind: Bronwyn, Agatha, Wren. She prayed they made it out alive and were somewhere safe. She raised a brow in Callum's direction. "So you got tasked with protecting me? I somehow thought that would be below you."

Callum brought his hand to his chest and leaned against the wall as if wounded. "You slay me, lass."

"You only do what is in your best interest, Callum. Don't think I've forgotten the castle." Her eyes narrowed in suspicion.

He shrugged his shoulders and picked an invisible piece of lint from his chest. "And keeping you safe suits me."

"Why is Ansel running in the middle of the night?" she pressed. Her trust in Callum only went so far. "The full moon isn't for a few days."

"Aye, but he can shift whenever he wants now, thanks to your little friend Flora."

"Flora?" Emery tried to keep the excitement from her voice but failed. She hadn't heard anything about her friend since Ansel arrived at the compound. Not that she hadn't tried to find out where she was. All she was told was that she was safe with the wolves and had to remain off the grid, same as Callum and Lily. "What does she have to do with any of this?"

"She's a part of my court now. Well, was a part of my court." He brought a finger to his chin and looked away, thinking. "I suppose she has a new hierarchy to follow now. Anyways, she completed her mission with the wolves and now that the moonstone is intact, the wolves can shift at will once more."

She cocked a brow, having trouble believing her shy friend did all that. Flora wasn't exactly the adventurous mission type. She was a prim, castle-raised princess who loved horses and would keep you on your toes with her fiery attitude. "Flora did all that?"

"Aye, lass. Your friend has been on an incredible journey. She'll have a story to tell when she arrives."

"She's coming here? When?" Excitement coursed through her. The last few days had been filled with nothing but shit experiences, and while Ansel was a great substitute, and Lily would no doubt try, there was no replacing the bond she'd formed with Flora at the castle.

"I'm not sure, but soon. You should head back to bed, you need your rest."

That was a laughable thought. There was no way she could possibly rest with her emotions swirling around her like this. She needed a distraction. "I've rested enough over the last day, I need to stretch my legs."

"Three days, lass. You were out for three days, and then you nearly died. Give yourself some time."

She clenched her fists at her side. It didn't matter that he was only trying to help, she didn't want his concern. "I don't need time, Callum. I need action. I need to make Vishna pay for what she did. I need to make this world a place where I can raise my child without fear."

"And you will. But you won't do it tonight."

Emery lowered her eyes to the floor, trying to calm her racing heart. It didn't matter that he was right. She didn't have a plan beyond going to New Orleans and ending Vishna—a plan she couldn't even execute since she didn't know how to use her magic. Balls of light weren't likely to stop the priestess. But the thought of going back into that room alone with her thoughts was too much to handle. She needed to stay busy, to distract herself from the pain that threatened to swallow her if she dwelled in it too long.

As if sensing her turmoil, Callum stepped forward and placed a hand on her shoulder. "But if you must plan your revenge, I suggest a walk around the grounds. The Highlands are magical this time of year."

"We're in the Highlands?" Wonder danced in her voice and a shiver ran through her. She loved the Highlands, but it was no longer only for the crisp air and rolling hills. They would forever remind her of a certain vampire, and now she was here. With him.

Well not with him. He would be okay with her falling off the face of the earth at the moment, and she would not argue against the same fate for him.

"Aye, lass. Explore the cottage. Go for a walk under the stars. You might find clarity you didn't know you needed." Callum tipped his head and turned to walk away. "Just stay within the wards."

"Wait." Emery stopped him and grabbed his hand, pulling him into a hug.

"Whoa." Callum threw his hands up, as if unsure on how to react. "What's this for?"

"Thank you. I may not ever forgive you for that stunt you

pulled at the castle, but you created this place for me and my child, and you showed up when we needed you most."

"Don't thank me, Emery. I'm still the asshole who bit you and I'd do it again. There is war coming to our world, and you and your child are going to be a key part in our success. You are the future, and I don't plan on letting you throw it away over a man who can't get his head out of his ass. Use your pain, harness it, and redirect it to those who think to hurt you or anyone you care about. You are so much more than you've been led to believe."

She gave a subtle nod, not fully subscribing to his delusion, but feeling the spark of hope in her chest that she'd be able to succeed. She opened her mouth to ask him what he meant, but Callum cut her off.

"I made cookies and left them on the counter. Help yourself. I'm told chocolate fixes everything."

Emery couldn't get the image of Callum in an apron and chef's hat out of her head, but before she could say as much, he'd stepped into the nearest bedroom.

The fucker was a mystery—a mystery who apparently baked—but at the end of the day she was glad he was on her side.

The hallway split in the middle and led to the bottom floor of the cottage, though that was the last thing Emery would have classified it as. Cottages were small and quaint homes hidden in the woods. The house she attempted to navigate was none of those things. Six rooms lined the upper hallway and, given their spacing, she assumed they were all the same size as the one she'd been in.

She descended into an open floor plan. The focal point was a large hearth with dark brick and a dwindling fire. It was surrounded by a sectional and three plush chairs which beckoned to be lounged upon. She could imagine curling up with her journal or a good book and getting lost for hours in the pages.

On the opposite side was a fully stocked kitchen with new appliances and a dining table big enough to seat at least twelve. Despite the dark brick and cabinets, the space felt light and airy with crisp white paint, and windows that ran along the majority of the adjacent walls.

Emery zeroed in on the giant chocolate chip cookies. She debated having one, considering Callum claimed to have made them, but chocolate won in the end.

The cookie had the perfect consistency and cookie-to-chocolate ratio and she'd probably have to beg Callum to give her the recipe, but there was no way she was leaving Scotland without it.

The snow-capped mountains out the front window caught her eye, and Emery instantly moved toward the door. She needed to be outside, to feel the wind and breath in the fresh Highland air. She finished her cookie and wandered onto the wrap-around porch, each step a war in her mind between fulfilling the need within her and the unwarranted longing for the stolen moments in August's bed when he promised to show her his homeland.

Every part of her life seemed to begin and end with him; no matter how hard she tried to distance herself, he was never far from her thoughts. And yet he seemed fine to push her away, as if the bond between them was just a minor inconvenience. The prick was probably sleeping upstairs, dreaming of all the ways he'd kill her the moment their daughter was born.

Emery huffed, her rage rising in tandem with her magic. She needed to learn to control her emotions or at the very least learn to channel her magic otherwise she'd likely implode at the peak of a mood swing. And right now, she was having a lot of mood swings.

She stepped off the porch, and the wind whipped around her. She quickened her pace, ignoring the hum of her magic, needing to separate herself from her fucking mate.

Fucking mate. She chuckled to herself. *That's what got her into this mess.*

That and the lies of her ancestors.

When she made it to the water's edge, she kicked off her shoes and climbed on top of a small boulder. Tugging down the sleeves of her long pajama shirt, she wrapped her arms around herself, wishing she'd thought to grab a jacket or at the very least a blanket. She tipped her head up and gazed at the endless stars blanketing the pitch-black sky.

"Fuck you." She sneered at the stars, knowing the balls of gas had little to do with her fate.

A wave of despair washed over her ,and Emery almost mistook it for the stars sending her a message until a figure stepped out from behind the boulders next to hers.

"You shouldn't be out here alone. It's not safe."

Augustine's voice sent shivers down her spine that pooled in her lower belly. "Because you all of a sudden care about my well being?"

He sauntered up to where she sat and crossed his arms. He was wearing the same clothes he had the night before: low-slung jeans and a fitted white shirt, only he'd added a leather jacket. "For the next three months, and for as long as my daughter is in your care, I will ensure you are doing what is best for her, and yourself."

Inhaling a sharp breath she looked away from him, not wanting him to see how his words affected her. His need to care had nothing to do with her and everything to do with their daughter. Which was almost worse. The mate bond and pregnancy hormones twisted her perspective, and seeing him as a protective father almost made her forget all the terrible things he'd done.

Almost.

Each time the bond surged, it left her somewhere between loathing and the intense desire to ride his cock like a pogo stick. At least he'd answered the question of how much longer she had to go in a vampire pregnancy. Three months. She just had to make it three more months without giving into the intensified emotions of the mate bond.

Emery ignored the way his eyes roamed over her body, searing her from the inside out. "So you admit she's yours now? Well I'll have you know, she's my daughter too, August. Or is it Augustine now? A pretentious name to go with the stick up your ass. And don't talk to me about protecting our child. Up until this point, I have done everything in my power to protect her. " A soft glow radiated from her eyes, the outward indication of her magic reacting to her rage.

He was on her in an instant, laying her back so she was pressed into the boulder, but careful so as not to put his weight on her belly. "Calm yourself, little witch. Tonight is not the night to test me."

"And why is that? The only thing I have left to lose is something you want, I might as well take out my heaping piles of resentment on the person who has caused at least half of them."

"Because I am not the monster you think I am, at least not at the moment, and I am not only fighting the grief of losing our son, but the mate bond's need to take you right here on this boulder. You deserve better than that, and you wouldn't trust me even if I tried."

Emery stilled under him. Her gaze traced the line of his

jaw, the curve of his kissable lips and landed on his oceanic eyes.

Oceanic, not dark like the midnight sky.

"August?" Her voice held more hope than it should. He was still her enemy, even if in that moment he was the man she'd fallen in love with.

She swallowed past the tightening in her throat as he lowered his head, his breath fanning her lips. "Princess."

Chapter Fifteen

EMERY

His nickname was her undoing.

Emery closed the distance between them, her lips crashing against his. There was nothing soft about their kiss, both of them seeking the reaffirmation of what they were to one another, despite all the bullshit that had transpired. Their connection was raw and carnal, charging the emotions that filled the air around them and consumed their bond.

August's hand gripped her hip and he ground his growing length against her inner thigh. A growl tore from him, and Emery's nipples peaked against his vibrating chest. He probed her mouth, deepening their kiss, and she shivered as his fangs lengthened against her tongue.

She should stop him. There were far more important things she needed to discuss with August, but everything about this felt right. Maybe it was the mate bond. Maybe it was the hope the man she'd fallen in love with had returned. Or maybe it was the need to feel anything but the intense grief and rage that plagued her. It didn't matter—right now, the only thing Emery was concerned with was living for one more stolen moment with him.

August tore his lips from hers, his pale blue eyes filled

with desperation. "Tell me you don't want this. Say the word and I'll walk away."

Her reply was breathless, caught between kisses. "I do."

The bond swelled in her chest with every touch. Magic hummed in the air, shimmering and growing stronger as their limbs tangled, each clamouring to feel more of the other, to fix the strained bond between them, even if they both knew it was a temporary reprieve.

Emery ripped his jacket from his shoulders and tugged his shirt over his head. She splayed her hands on his chest and took her time, running her hands down the ridges of the abdomen she'd dreamed about more times than she cared to admit.

August sucked in a breath and caught his lip between his fangs. She propped herself up, wanting to see just how far she could push him, just how much he'd let her take. She craved his reactions, the little things that gave away his need for her. Her tongue darted out teasing his nipple. She sucked it into her mouth and savored the hiss that fell from his lips when she rolled it between her teeth.

He rocked his body against her and in one swift motion, August flipped them so she was straddling him. He reached between them and tore the front of her pajamas open, exposing her breasts to the cool Highland air.

"Two can play that game, Princess." He grinned, then lowered his head to latch on to her nipple, his fangs teasing the overly sensitive bud as he sucked. Emery arched her back and a moan escaped her, floating on the winds of the Highlands. His fingers danced along the hem of her pants and she pushed her hips forward in an attempt to urge him down to where she wanted his hand's attention.

"Needy, little one?"

"And whose fault is that?"

August growled against her lips and tugged the hem of her pants, pushing them down. He pinched her clit.

Emery yelped and jerked away, but August's hand against her back held her in place. "You better keep quiet," he whispered against her ear, his fingers tracing expert circles on the bundle of nerves he'd jolted to life. "If not, everyone will know exactly how you sound when you find your pleasure."

She should be upset, should care that everyone would hear, but she wasn't. She wanted them to hear. Wanted the entirety of the Highlands to hear her pleasure. That, and it was too late for her to care. The waves of pleasure at his hand rushed through her and she leaned forward and buried her face against his mouth, crying out as the orgasm she'd been dreaming of for months tore through her.

Not giving her a moment to rest, August slipped a finger inside her, forcing her to chase the pleasure only he could provide. Emery's nails dug into his shoulder while the other hand tangled into his hair. She gasped when he slipped a second finger in, and using him as leverage, she rode his hand until the coil in her belly tightened again and she was on the edge once more.

"August," she whispered his name as if she was praying for release. "I need you inside me."

"I will be." He slid another finger in her and hit the spot that made her knees tremble. "But right now, I need you to come for me, Princess."

Emery arched her back and closed her glowing eyes, giving into the pleasure only August could give her. She whimpered his name and spread her body further for him, coming apart on his hand.

The wind whipped up around them, and when she came down from the high, Emery opened her eyes to a whirlwind of glowing gold magic circling their bodies.

She clung to August and a soft chuckle fell from her lips. "That's never happened before."

"You didn't have magic before."

Emery stilled and waited for the backhanded comment that would end with him running from her just like he did every time he was reminded she was anything but human. But it never came.

He looked at her with love and sheer desperation in his eyes and it nearly brought tears to her own.

When the magic wind died down, a shiver ran through her and her skin pebbled. August wrapped his arms around her and pulled her tight against his chest. "You're cold. Let me get you inside."

Emery shook her head. "I'm not." It was a lie, the wind sent a chill through her and her lack of clothing was taking its toll. But she needed this. It may have started as a distraction but every moment with August proved how much she needed him. She wouldn't survive if he ran from her now.

August dug one hand into hip and the other caught her chin, tipping it upward until she met his gaze. "Don't lie to me, Emery. We don't do that. Not anymore."

She studied his eyes, the hurt she put there with her lies. There was no denying they had a long way to go to repair what she'd broken. What he'd set into motion when he unleashed Augustine. Sex was easy, living with the past was harder.

Emery nodded.

"Say it."

"Not if it means this moment ends. I need just this moment."

"It won't." He tucked a flyaway hair behind her ear and cupped her face. "I'm here. And I'm not going anywhere until I have you screaming my name and coming on my cock." He pressed his forehead to hers and smiled. "I need this moment as much as you do. But I need you to say it. No more lies. Even when I'm not me. No more lies. It doesn't matter how much I want you, I can't get back if you shut me out. And I bloody fucking want to. I want forever with you."

Emery leaned back, studying the lines on his face. Not for the first time she wished she could detect lies as he did. "Do you mean that?"

A half smile tugged at his swollen lips. "I've already lost too much. You and our daughter are my forever, Em. I'll do anything to fight for you, not against you."

"No more lies," she agreed.

"None between us."

"But Augustine—"

"Will get in line. He will see what I see." August pressed his lips to hers, and trapped her lip between his fangs as he pulled away. "Let's not talk about him. Right now, I need my mate."

Mate.

He cupped her ass and grinned. "Hang on."

Emery wrapped her arms around his neck and August slid them from the boulder and took off toward the house. His cock strained against his pants at her core and she shifted her hips against him. August growled against her neck and nipped her soft flesh. "Brat."

She giggled and held him tighter, wishing the moment could last forever. This was how it was supposed to be with them.

Moments later they were in her room. August lay her back on the edge of the bed and hooked his hands on the hem of her pajama bottoms. His eyes raked over her, the heat in them sending warmth to pool in her lower belly.

"Fuck, Emery," he purred, his voice strained and low. "You're the most beautiful thing I've ever seen."

"I'm fat, but thanks for thinking so."

August scoffed and fell to his knees between her legs. He ran his hands over the swell of her belly, his fingertips tracing the outline of her womb. "You carry my child, which is by far the sexiest thing I've ever laid eyes on in all my years on this earth." He leaned forward, trailing kisses on her small bump and whispered something in Gaelic.

She ran a hand through his tousled hair. "What did you say?"

"I told our little girl she's the moon in my sky."

Love enveloped their bond, and Emery wasn't sure where hers began and August's ended. Tears sprung from her eyes and rolled down her cheeks.

Suddenly the moment was too much. August was going to leave her, giving his consciousness back to Augustine, and she'd only be left with the image of the love she could've had. The love they should be sharing over both their children. She had started out needing this distraction, needing him, but this was too much. For the first time she understood why August let Augustine out in the first place because feeling fucking sucked. It hurt and wasn't something she was ready to face.

"Emery, what's wrong?"

She shook her head, needing to ruin the moment so she wouldn't be sucked into the what-ifs when he was gone. She promised she wouldn't lie to him, and she wouldn't, but she couldn't tell him how much seeing his love would break her when he inevitably lost control to Augustine. Each moment with him reaffirmed he wasn't just her mate, he was her everything. Whether it was fueled by the bond or the man she wasn't sure, but it didn't matter.

Augustine studied her tear-laden face, waiting for her

answer. Emery silently vowed to one day find a way to keep the man in front of her at her side, but today was not that day. In that moment, she didn't want to feel the hurt or the anguish. She needed to fuck. Raw and hard until she couldn't remember her own name. She needed to feed the mate bond and cement herself to him so that she'd have the strength to fight and bring him back to her.

Emery sat up and cupped August's face and brought it to hers. "Fuck me," she whispered against his lips. "Remind me why no one else will do."

"Gladly, Princess."

He pushed her back onto the mattress, and when he stood, she savored every moment of watching him discard his jeans. She caught her lower lip between her teeth as he freed his rigid cock and it sprung up toward his belly button.

Damn I've missed this. Both him and his cock.

August knelt between her legs, and trailed barely there kisses from her knees up her thighs. When he reached her core, he traced her slick folds with his expert tongue and sucked her clit hard between his lips.

Emery gasped a moan, arching her back and grinding her hips into the simultaneous pain and pleasure he offered. She was almost there when August released her and his gaze locked with hers.

"Someday, I'm going to bring you to the edge, and just when you are about to come, I'm going to bite you, here," he placed a kiss on one side of her clit and then on the other. "And here, so I can taste all of your essence on my lips at once."

Emery's tummy dipped and she clenched her core in response. She should be appalled at his suggestion, but she found she wanted every bit of what he'd promised. Her mouth watered at the memory of his bite—the way it felt when he shared his blood with her. She'd yearned for it every time she pleasured herself the last few months. August was her own personal drug.

"Would you like that?" August pushed himself up and captured his lips with hers. She could taste herself on him and it only fueled her need.

"Please, August."

He rocked his hips, teasing her exposed clit with his length. "Tell me what you want, Princess."

"I want you to fuck me. You've already ruined me, but remind us both why there is no one else. Remind yourself I'm yours."

Vibrations rolled through them as he growled. "Mine." The bond echoed his sentiments.

In a single thrust he seated himself within her, and Emery couldn't stifle her cry. She clenched around his shaft, memorizing the feel of him as she adjusted to his girth.

August released a guttural moan, and that split second was the only reprieve he gave her.

His hands gripped her hips and he pulled her closer to him, pressing himself into the deepest parts of her. "Mine," he whispered and slowly pulled out of her until the tip of his cock was all that was left.

Emery gave him a seductive smile. "Yours."

He angled her hips and pistoned back into her, finding a glorious rhythm that allowed him to slam against her sweet spot. He hammered into her, reminding her with each thrust the claim he had on her body. "Bloody fucking hell, Emery."

The bond between them tightened, the magic recognizing the union of its two mates. Emery's pulse skyrocketed, and she dug her nails into August's forearms, clinging to him like a lifeline as she rode the storm their bodies produced.

August stretched her, filling her as only he could. He

palmed her breast and rolled her nipple between her thumb and forefinger, and Emery moaned his name, begging him to take her over the edge.

An unguarded smile tugged at August's lips. "Come with me, Princess."

Words failed her, but she gave him a firm nod.

August bit his opposite wrist and offered it to her, never ceasing his thrusts. The moment his blood hit her lips, he pinched her nipple, sending her pleasure crashing around the pain. Her sucking was accompanied with muffled cries of ecstasy as she rode the waves of her orgasm.

August buried his face in her neck and pierced her with his fangs, moaning as he claimed his own release.

Both of them stilled when light burst behind their eyes and a vision of the bond between them filled her vision. Silver and gold vines entwined together, melding until gorgeous pink poppies grew from their depths.

There was another burst of light and the bond flooded with ecstasy, returning them to the height of their love making. August thrust into her, fast and brutal, and Emery clung to him as they rode the endless pleasure of their union together.

When the bond retreated, they both gasped and fell into a tangle of limbs on the bed. August sealed her wounds first, then his own and pulled her up to his chest. He captured her lips and whispered. "Forever."

"And ever," she replied, silently hoping they would get the chance to make it a reality.

He rewarded her with five more orgasms before they once again fell into the mattress and the first hints of dawn spilled through the window. If the ache in her core was any indication, Emery had no doubts she'd be feeling the memories of August between her legs for the next few days.

He'd taken her every way imaginable, making up for their time apart. August had fed her need to feel anything but loss and grief. He'd fucked her with the fury of a broken man who'd found a treasure he'd thought lost, but still managed to remind her she was the center of his world. The bond hummed between them, thrilled with the connection they'd forged.

A piece of her hair tumbled in her face, and August reached up and tucked it behind her ear. "I love the pink."

At the same moment butterflies took flight in her stomach, an unnatural force of wind blew open the shutters and danced around them, tossing her hair up.

August's hearty laughter mixed with hers and the carefree moment between them felt right. She didn't want it to end.

But wants were rarely considered when it came to fate.

August's lips twisted into a wince and he sucked in a breath. His eyes widened, locking with hers. "I'm sorry," he whispered, "That I let him out. That I couldn't save Miles."

Emery cupped his chin and turned his head so his eyes met hers. "I know it wasn't you. It was him."

"No. It was us." August reached up and placed a hand over hers and brought it to his lips. "I am him, and he is me. I have always struggled to accept what I am. What I am supposed to be. That's why we are separate. I'm afraid to be him, to lose myself in the darkness. Just as he's afraid to love and show weakness. We are the same person, Emery. You'll get both of us, not just me."

The reality of his words sank in. All this time, she thought she'd be fighting to get back the man she'd fallen in love with at the castle, when in reality she'd be getting them both. August and Augustine. If she wanted this, wanted his love, she'd also have to survive the darkest parts of him.

But the flip side was also true. She wasn't pure light, not any more.

Her magic swirled in her chest, and she could feel the tendrils of her own darkness keen to the idea of embracing Augustine.

"I'll embrace your darkness if you embrace mine."

"Em, you are all that is light in the world."

"Not any more." Emery untangled herself from him and sat up, bringing her knees to her chest. "There is no way I could remain the girl you knew in the castle. I didn't belong there, and I don't belong with the witches. All the tiny cuts along the way have grown into deep scars, and last night was the final blow. Rage consumes me, the need to let go and give into the darkness that plagues not only me but my magic. I'm only afraid if I do, it will devour me and I can't let that happen. I have to bring our daughter into the light."

August propped himself up on the bed and searched her eyes. "Let me be your darkness."

She wanted to say yes, but couldn't. "I can't ask that of you."

"You don't have to. Em, I need you to be my light. My way back. Because no matter how much I want to be only the man I am right now, this will always end with me joining with him. Augustine can be what you need. He is cold and calculated, but he loves you. Even if the fool is too damn stubborn to admit it."

Emery didn't want to believe him, but she couldn't deny what she'd felt from Augustine when her magic had flooded their bond. He was August, albeit a more prickish version of him. But she believed he would protect her.

August leaned forward and placed a soft kiss to her lips. "I can't hold on much longer. Augustine is clawing his way to the forefront and I don't have what it takes to hold him back forever." He skirted off the bed and pulled his pants on, sorrow in his eyes. "I should never have let the darkness consume me. But know I'm always there, and I'm fighting to find a way back to you. Be patient with him and me. My light. My intended."

"The darkness doesn't scare me, August. Come back to me as a whole. You are mine, all of you."

His eyes widened in slight shock, and she was rewarded with a genuine smile. "I promise. Don't give up, Princess."

Emery nodded just as August winced and closed his eyes for more than a beat. When he opened them they no longer held the brightness of a calm sea. They raged with the power of a violent storm.

Augustine.

"Hello, little witch."

In that split second, Emery slammed up the walls she'd let down with August, only letting through the bond which the emotions she deemed necessary. Augustine was still her adversary, even if he'd moved down ever-so-slightly on the hatred scale due to August's *glowing* recommendation.

She shifted to her knees, grabbed the sheet and wrapped it around her naked form.

"No need to be shy. We are one in the same, as August so eloquently shared. I'm just the monster he kept leashed. The darkness he continuously tried to stifle. When you broke him with your lies, he no longer cared to be the man you needed and let me take the wheel. While I'll admit, your return has given him a strength I didn't think he possessed, he isn't ready to be the man he needs to be."

Emery doubted that, but she couldn't argue that August needed to return on his own terms. But she liked the idea that Augustine might still be useful to her. "And what if what I need now is both of you? The darkness that will protect what's ours, and the light to lead us home."

"I'm not sure he's ready, but for our little girl?" Augustine reached out and Emery froze when he rubbed her belly with a gentleness that surprised her. "For her we'd move the bloody fuckin' stars."

"Good. Don't mistake our understanding as forgiveness. You have royally fucked up everything you've touched since you've come to the forefront, but if you are what it takes to keep our little girl safe, so be it. The witches took from me that which they had no right to take, and I want them to fucking pay. I want Vishna's head on a pike, displayed as a warning for anyone who comes for my baby."

Augustine's brow raised, and his lips tugged into a wicked grin. "I think we can manage that."

"Good. Now if you'd leave I'd like to shower before the rest of the house wakes up and realizes what August and I did last night." Keeping the sheet around her, Emery swung her feet off the bed and made her way to the bathroom.

Augustine cocked a brow and a sly grin formed on his lips. "I think I'll stay. You might need help cleaning up."

Emery huffed a laugh. Now that she had a better understanding of the situation, she didn't fear Augustine. He was an extension of August, and she knew how to deal with August. "Don't pretend you care now, Augustine. You've made it very clear who you are, and what I am to you. Which is a damn shame."

"And why is that?"

"Because if you were August, you'd be going for round two." Emery opened the hand that held the sheet, allowing it to fall to the floor. "And I hear shower sex is the best kind of sex."

Augustine sucked in a breath and caught his lower lip between elongated fangs. He blew it out on a low grunt.

She knew what she was doing when she stepped out the pile of sheets, giving him a shrug and a wink over her shoulder as she walked into the bathroom. She was playing with fire, testing to see how much of the mate bond belonged to Augustine and how much it would take for him to give in to her.

He may not trust her, but attraction was a very powerful tool. One she intended to exploit with August's grumpier half.

Emery had only crossed the threshold when she was halted, her back pulled against the chiseled chest she'd only just run her hands down minutes before. One of Augustine's hands wrapped around her, cradling her stomach while the other tangled in her hair and tugged her head back.

His lips found the sensitive spot behind her ear and it took everything to keep herself from moaning.

"I could have you if I wanted you, little witch," he growled against her skin, sending a shiver through her.

A malicious grin curled at her lips and she shifted her hips, teasing his engorged cock trapped in his jeans. "It's a good thing you don't, then."

She pushed off of him and rounded the corner into the walled off shower, only sparing a fraction of a second to glance back at Augustine. His jaw tightened, and he balled his hands into fists before he turned and stalked off.

It seemed she had struck a nerve.

Chapter Sixteen

AUGUSTINE

He was more sexually frustrated than a fourteen-year-old going through puberty.

Bloody fucking August had to go and get him riled up. And the blasted mate bond kept him there. Followed by that damned pink-haired little minx of a witch who fueled his sexual frustrations to a new level of toruture.

Augustine sat at the dining table and eyed the glass of blood in front of him. He'd poured it out of habit, hoping his routine would ground him. At the castle he'd start his days in the feeders lounge, and felt zero remorse in feeding his bloodlust. What a way to start the day. He lived for the way it coated his throat, and not only sustained him, but fueled the darkness within him.

The problem that morning was he didn't need to drink. Not that he didn't want to, but for the first time in his life he didn't need to. There was nothing left to quench. The darkness was still there, and he was fully sated.

August's taking of Emery's blood the night before fulfilled him in a way he hadn't known was possible. Augustine had only tasted a minute amount the two times he'd bitten her to save her life. Not enough to sustain him. If he had known how he would thrive with her running through his veins, he might have re-thought the short duration of those bites.

The only downside to August consuming Emery was it further cemented the bond between them. He invited her into their body like a schedule-one drug, and she flowed through them, enticing the most addicting mix of freedom and imprisonment.

The hold she had on them—on him—went far deeper than any he'd previously encountered. Her blood calmed their monster and her body fed the deeply seated need the bond created. The bond he desperately wished he could sever, but even the thought of doing so made him nauseous. It may have fed August, but Augustine could do without the crippling need to bury himself within the damned little witch.

While their bloodlust may have been quelled momentarily, the sexual relief didn't carry over to Augustine's consciousness. While August relaxed in the depths, well-fucked and sated, he was left to remember every bloody moan that escaped Emery's lips and the way her ass perfectly cradled his cock.

The little brat knew what she was doing too, dropping her towel to give him a view of her naked flesh. August wasn't wrong when he'd claimed her rounded belly was the sexiest thing he'd ever laid eyes on. Augustine wanted nothing more than to claim the round two she promised August, if only to sate the needs she'd sparked the moment she'd walked back into his life. It had been months, and his dick would've thanked him.

He looked down at the tent in his pants and tried to force himself to think of anything but Emery. It proved impossible. She was an enigma he both wanted to dismantle and covet. Neither of which were possible as long as she carried his child and remained a witch.

She was his enemy.

He chuckled at the lack of enthusiasm behind the thought.

A week ago, he wouldn't have hesitated to kill her on sight. August would have winced but ultimately Augustine had believed he would've survived. After feeling more than a sliver of the mate bond though, Augustine was no longer sure they would have. Because as he sat there, knowing she was upstairs showering her naked flesh, carrying his child, Augustine was no longer convinced he'd be able to pull the trigger.

One night with her, and he was a dinghy lost at sea. Augustine hadn't even spent the night with her. August did. He was there though, on the fringes of their consciousness, detesting every moment while still savoring the presence of their love.

He'd fucked up when he lost control. One moment he was lost in the grief of losing his heir, considering how he was going to sate his need for a vein and the next he was staring at a teary-eyed Emery perched on a boulder.

She'd caught him off guard, not only with her outward show of grief, but the love that intertwined itself with the sorrow rolling off of her. That woman felt deep. With more emotion than Augustine ever allowed himself to feel. It both repulsed and fascinated him, but in that wretched moment, all he wanted to do was comfort her when he should have wanted to kill her.

That single hesitation was all it took for August to lurch forward and knock him from the forefront.

He'd rushed to her and although Augustine could have taken over at any time, he chose to let their reunion play out. To see what his other half would do and how the bond would react. He held onto the slight hope that once August was sated, Augustine would be free of its tumultuous pull.

At least that's what he'd continue to tell himself. The truth of the matter was, for the first time since taking over, Augustine struggled to get back to the front.

Much like August was doing at that very moment. Pacing in the depths of his mind, Augustine could feel the rage that radiated through August as he silently planned his way back to the front.

August had proven he was willing to fight for Emery. For their daughter. But Augustine wasn't about to let him take over. Not when there was so much left to do. Emery needed him as much as she needed August. If not more. Until August could come to terms with who and what he was, he'd never have what it took to stand by her side or rule their kingdom. Augustine wouldn't be silenced, not again.

"You waiting for that to get cold?" Callum's voice pulled him from his thoughts and Augustine looked up to find him towering beside him. "I thought I taught you better than that, cousin."

Augustine pushed the glass away. "I'm not hungry."

Callum picked up the glass and downed it in one go. "Not going to let a perfectly good bag of A positive go to waste. Although recently I've become accustomed to O negative. It has a nice hint of spice."

Augustine nodded and looked out the window, hoping Callum would take a hint and leave him be. The last thing he wanted was a lecture on why Emery was the future of their kind. Between Callum and Malcolm, Augustine could recite every way they believed she was his savior. They too often forgot, though, that he wasn't August, and Emery was no longer untouched by the stain of the supernatural world. Their plans had him bowing to the little witch and playing nice in the sand box with the coven. That wasn't what was needed or wanted by their so-called 'power couple'. His plans included exactly what Emery asked of him: the priestess' head on a spike. Revenge. Fear. Then the real fun could begin.

The chair beside him creaked across the wood floor and Callum plopped down next to him.

So much for a moment alone.

"How are you doing?" His voice no longer playful, Callum placed a hand on Augustine's shoulder. "Yesterday was a lot to handle."

Augustine shrugged him off. "I'm fine." Callum didn't give two shits about his mental state. He was more interested in how it pertained to his plans.

"Whatever you need to tell yourself to sleep at night, Augustine." Callum stood and sauntered toward the kitchen. "Or not sleep."

Augustine raised a brow at his cousin's taunt, and Callum's lips tipped up into a knowing smirk.

"I'm just saying. For someone who hates their mate as much as you claim to, there were a lot of extra-curricular activities going on this morning."

Bloody hell.

He was never going to hear the end of it. Augustine was about to tell Callum to mind his own bloody fucking business when the front door swung behind them, and Lily walked in, fresh herbs in hand. "What activities happened this morning? Did I miss something?"

"No," Augustine snapped.

"Only the carnal tango, starring Emery and Augustine." Callum opened the fridge and mumbled under his breath, low enough Lily wouldn't hear, but Augustine did. He pulled out bacon and eggs and went about prepping breakfast. "I was just saying Augustine should stick around to help Emery adjust to life in Scotland. There are plenty of activities he can help her with as she adjusts to her new normal."

Lily stood with her mouth hanging open. "Ye have seen them together right? They get along about as well as Kipton and I did when we first met."

It was the first time he'd heard either Callum or Lily mention their history with his half-brother since he'd been at the cottage, and he got the feeling he wouldn't like the comparison being made.

"I seem to recall a wing of the castle burning down after one of your more epic arguments," Callum said with a smirk.

One hand whipped to Lily's hip, while the other wagged a pointed finger in Callum's direction. "Listen, I told you both, there was no way I could have known the plate would hit the chandelier's chain and cause it to fall. And doesn't that prove my point? We were toxic together."

Laughter radiated through the kitchen. Augustine couldn't recall the last time he'd seen Callum have a genuine carefree moment.

When he caught his breath, Callum tipped his head toward Lily. "And yet I've never seen two people more in love when all was said and done. Well, except maybe Augustine and Emery."

"Maybe when he was still the decent half."

"Oh, I've heard them together," Callum said with a calculated smirk. "And that's my point, I just think their hatred should be worked out in the fresh Highland air. Don't you think, Augustine?"

A growl rumbled in his chest, but he didn't answer. Callum would detect the lie if he told him he didn't want to spend time with Emery, and Augustine wasn't ready for the ramifications of that notion.

Lily scoffed and made her way into the kitchen and set about separating the herbs. "Emery needs to focus on learning and honing her magic, not on a mate who wants her dead."

Callum threw the bacon in a skillet, but whispered through the sizzles, "He may want her on her back, but dead is the last thing he wants her to be."

Augustine threw his weight back and stood from the table, ready to storm into the kitchen and pummel Callum with his fist. He'd made it two steps when his crusade was interrupted by a voice that sent electricity running through him.

"Good morning, everyone."

The room grew silent and everyone turned to watch Emery walk down the stairs and into the kitchen. There was a slight hitch in her step and he'd bet it was due to the rounds August had put her though. He bit back the groan as the memories played through his mind.

She wore shorts that accentuated her long legs and an oversized sweater that dipped low enough in the front to reveal the swell of her breasts, which had grown too large for the bra she currently wore. Her hair was still damp from her shower, but she'd pulled it into a knot on the top of her head with a few small whisps hanging down.

Her amber eyes locked on Augustine and then fell to the bulge in his pants. They flitted back to his, and she smirked and bounced toward the table.

What the hell was she playing at? They were mates, but they were not on the same page. Hell, they weren't even in the same book. She should not be looking at him like that. With eyes that made his cock strain against his jeans and lips that dared him to carry her right back up those stairs and take what she wouldn't give him. He'd show her every way he was the darkness August claimed he was. And before he was finished, she'd beg for it. For him.

Bloody hell, he shouldn't want that as badly as he did.

"Good mornin', lass. How are you doing?" Lily's voice

pulled him from his fantasy and Augustine shifted uncomfortably on his feet.

He needed to get a fucking grip.

"I'm fine." She didn't expand any more than that, but Augustine didn't miss the way her fists clenched at her side or how her shoulders rounded forward as if retreating from the situation. There was no lie to her words, indicating she believed what she was saying, but her body said otherwise. She was anything but fine.

Emery stopped at the kitchen counter and leaned over, giving him a view of the way her shorts perfectly cupped her beautiful ass. "Are you making breakfast, Callum? If those eggs are as good as your cookies, sign me up. I'm starving."

"Glad to see you're hungry. You must have really worked up an appetite on that walk of yours."

Pink tinted her cheeks, and her eyes whipped to Callum, narrowing as waves of annoyance rolled off of her.

Interesting. She hadn't closed the bond on her end.

It was the first thing he'd done upon walking away from her. His emotions where she was concerned needed to remain his own. Especially now that August had gone and planted a seed in her pretty little head that he would return. That they could become one again.

That was his hell. He wouldn't be pushed back again only to be let out when a situation became too much for August.

The room remained silent as Emery padded through the kitchen, placing fresh fruit in a bowl and pouring herself a cup of tea. Augustine returned to the table, but his eyes remained firmly on Emery. She moved effortlessly, as if she hadn't lost her child the night before or reunited with her lost mate.

Even the bond radiated her contentment, and it made his nerves stand on end. She always felt so wholly, and at that moment it was as if she was just floating through life without a care in the world.

Both women joined him at the table, followed by Callum who brought plates of scrambled eggs and bacon. She ate her breakfast as he, Lily, and Callum watched, waiting for her to say something. Anything to give them a hint at her mental state.

Emery finally looked up, noticing she was the center of attention. "You guys don't have to treat me like I'm a bomb ready to go off at any moment. I said I'm fine. I don't want to dwell on what happened yesterday."

No lies. In the time she'd showered she'd managed to bury her feelings so deep not even she believed they existed. But to what end? She could claim all she wanted that she wasn't a bomb ready to explode, but in all his years, he'd never seen a situation like that end well. Not when someone felt like Emery did.

It was why he didn't feel. He had priorities and those he would protect with his life such as his mother or Thea, but he didn't do attachments. He left that side of him to August. Or at least he had before Emery got inside his head.

Her eyes locked with his from across the table, and Emery pursed her lips around a strawberry, biting it slowly. Damn if it wasn't the sexiest thing he'd ever seen.

Augustine bit his lip, stifling the moan that threatened to escape.

Emery tipped a single brow upward, her lips parting in a half smile.

Fuck.

Fuck her.

Fuck the mate bond.

Augustine averted his gaze to the mountains out the

window, trying to ignore the way Emery was sucking fruit juice from her fingers like it was the tip of his cock.

She continued talking as if she wasn't putting on an erotic display just for him. "Vishna did this with the intent of killing my children. That is a punishable offense, and I plan to exact my revenge on those members of her coven who took part in the unbinding. Augustine is going to help me with that."

Callum snorted and Augustine's brows shot up. "I am?"

"You are, because he was your son, too. The vampires have just as much right to revenge as I do. I can admit when I need help, and you, mate, have the exact talents I need to rip Vishna's head from her body."

Augustine nodded. She was a damn queen if he'd ever seen one. Calculated and precise in what she wanted.

"Glad you see it my way." She popped a piece of pineapple in her mouth and after licking the stray juices in the same sinful display, continued. "Then I plan to do everything in my power to make this world a place where my daughter is going to flourish. If that means tearing down every archaic belief in the supernatural world, so be it."

"Aye, lass." Callum raised his glass. "You shall have my sword."

"Thank you, Callum. But I swear if you pull another sideways stunt like you did at the castle, I'll castrate you myself."

Callum laughed for the second time that morning. "Noted."

Emery continued to eat her fruit, sucking each piece between her capable lips as if she hadn't just declared war on those who opposed her.

His heart swelled in his chest and he honestly wasn't sure if it was him or August who'd felt the pride first.

Who the fuck was this woman and what had she done with the witch he was determined to hate?

It wasn't the mate bond that had broken him.

It was her.

She was incredible.

And he hated her for it.

Chapter Seventeen

AUGUSTINE

Augustine shook the thoughts from his head. Emery was still a witch. She was his enemy. He repeated the mantra in his head, hoping it would stick to something. Anything. Because his heart was rapidly being consumed by the mate bond and the woman it was attached to.

Her heritage was the only argument he had left to hold on to. She wanted the same thing he did: to stop the witches and protect his daughter. He suspected she'd go to the same lengths he would to ensure it happened.

"Those are lofty goals, Emery." Lily stirred milk into her tea, unphased by Emery's declaration that she planned to murder her twin. "First and foremost, though, you need to learn your magic. Learn where your strengths lie. We will stand behind you when you are ready."

"Aye. You are the future, lass," Callum echoed. "The prophecy is at hand."

There Callum went again with his damn prophecy.

"I know, and I'm ready to do my part."

Callum swiveled his head to Emery, his brow furrowed. "Do the witches think you are the heir?"

Emery shrugged. "I can't pretend to know what the coven

thinks. They didn't tell me anything. But my friend Agatha bestowed a prophecy upon me when I was in New Orleans. I know what I have to do."

Lily choked on her tea, nearly spitting out what was in her mouth. "She did what?" Her eyes were wide with disbelief, though Augustine wasn't making the correlation as to why this was more shocking than murder. "Do you remember what she said?"

"Yes, why?" She brought her mug to her lips and sipped her tea. "You look as if you've seen a ghost."

Lily dabbed her napkin at her lips, her age showing in her mannerisms. "Prophecies are only revealed to those who are star-touched. Most blessed with the talent of the stars only are able to perceive minor futures such as tarot readings or tea leaves. It's why prophecies are so rare. I've only ever heard of one other true prophecy being revealed in my lifetime and it was given to my grandmother."

"The prophecy of the united," Augustine and Callum whispered simultaneously.

It was a thing of fairy tales, handed down as a story to both vampires and witches throughout the ages. He'd heard Malcolm repeat it too many times to count over the last two months. It was the basis of Callum's entire mission.

"The prophecy of the united?" Emery looked at them like they were all crazy, and he supposed to someone who'd grown up outside of the supernatural world, the idea was a bit insane.

"It's what fairytales were based on, lass, promising peace in the supernatural world at the hands of the united." Callum stood and scanned the bookshelf along one of the walls by the hearth. He pulled out a dusty old tome and placed it in front of Emery. "Or at least I always thought it was a fairytale, until an old text was delivered to my keep recounting the truth of witches and vampires."

"The truth?" Augustine scoffed. "That's a bit of a stretch. It's a story, one told by those who believe the prophecy is fact. If it were true how it came to be, and witches created vampires and then cursed them, resulting in split factions and the need for the prophecy, how is it we've gone this long without figuring it out?"

"Because we didn't want you to." Emery ran her hands over the supple leather, her eyes transfixed on the book. "Our ancestors put everything in place so you would never question the true relationship between our kinds."

"She's right." Lily beamed. "You were never supposed to exist. You were a mistake made by my grandmother. It's all in the book."

A deep growl rumbled from Callum, matching Augustine's.

"I'm not saying you shouldn't exist now, you thick-headed buffoons. At the time though, my grandmother intended to end you, but my grandfather wouldn't have it. He'd come to love the warriors she'd created for him and in a time where war was prevalent, he wasn't keen on giving them up. In order to protect them he went behind my grandmother's back and had her sister bind his life to the original vampires, becoming one himself. If my grandmother killed his warriors, she'd kill her love, too. And thus the first mates came to be."

"So it's true," Emery whispered, a hint of awe twinkling in her eye. She opened the book and ran her finger down the seam. "I looked for something like this in the witches' libraries, but I could never find any hint that confirmed it as truth."

"Aye, lass. It's all true." Callum sat down beside her and flipped the pages to the middle.

Emery looked down at the text, then back up at Callum, her eyes wide. Augustine's fist clenched and he struggled to bite back the bond's jealousy, caused by the awe in her eyes as she looked at his cousin. "Is this the prophecy?

Callum nodded. Emery began to read:

"The course has been set for war and divide.
The faults of the firsts driven by pride.
Death and destruction will curse the centuries of all,
With truth in distant memories peace will fall.
Three factions in chaos,
Each falted by past.
Losing everything dear if the lies should outlast.
The mates of the firsts will cause turmoil increased.
The heirs intended the only hope for peace.
The stars have written a future anew,
The witches, the wolves, and the vampires true."

"Aye." Callum spoke, but his eyes were lost in whatever thought he clung to.

"That's what your fairytales are based off of?" Emery grumbled. "And I thought Cinderella's stepmother was bad."

Emery's amused chuckle shot right through him, her smart mouth was an absolute joy.

Augustine smiled, remembering how his mother used to use the prophecy against Malcolm and him as children. "The queen used to tell me that I would wake up alone if I lied to her. It took me ages to figure out it was just a line in a story."

"Only it's not a story," Emery teased, her eyes turning in his direction. "All these things have come to pass. Faults of the first. Factions in chaos. The mates of the firsts, causing turmoil. What's more turbulent than a hybrid child of royalty? The heirs intended, the only hope."

Augustine's jaw tightened as she met her stare. He didn't want to believe they were right. Even with all the facts right in front of him, he didn't want to believe it. There was no way his entire life had been formed around a lie. He'd fought countless wars throughout the ages with the understanding that witches were his enemy. He'd watched them kill his brethren with zero remorse, and he'd returned his sword in kind.

Callum shook his head. "We know that now, lass. Up until I met you, I wasn't sure it would ever come to pass. If only we knew what comes next."

"Good thing Agatha's prophecy tells of the future."

"The future?" Lily asked, her voice barely more than an awe-filled whisper. When Emery nodded Lily tugged the book from in front of her and flipped to the back. She pulled out a pen from her dress pocket and nodded. "Go on lass, what did the crone tell you?"

Augustine listened carefully, hanging on Emery's every word as she recited the prophecy bestowed to her, telling the future of the heirs intended. There was no doubt it referred to them, and the heir of the wolves. He'd never met Draven, but rumor had it he was as fierce as his father, the alpha. The wolves may be the neutral faction, but they had a bloody history that rivaled the vampires.

Together they will bring forward the change for us all. A union to stop the darkness of the fall.

August repeated the words in his head.

Are you ready to admit she is made for us? I've heard your inner turmoil, I know you are questioning everything you thought was true. If you can't do what's right for our people and stop what's coming, then let me do it.

"No."

"No, what?" Emery asked.

"Nothing. I was just thinking."

She tipped her head and the messy bun fell from the top of her head. "Care to share with the class?"

"Not particularly." He raked a hand through his hair, considering his words carefully. "Prophecies aren't gospel, they can be interpreted in many ways."

"You're right," Emery agreed, but the look she gave him told him she didn't agree, because of course she didn't. She'd buy into anything that saved their child. "But I'm sure you have a very different interpretation than the rest of us."

Before Augustine could respond, Callum slammed his hands down on the table. "Get your head out of your ass, Augustine. This couldn't be any more clear. The heirs intended. You and Emery. If you would just stop being blinded by the rage you think is justified, you would see you have something the rest of us can only hope to have someday. She is your other half. The one who will make you whole. Augustine, you are not only hurting yourself but the future of the supernatural world by resisting what was written in the bloody stars."

He might be right, but Augustine wasn't ready to concede, even if that made him a stubborn fool. Not yet; not when he didn't know what the end looked like. There was little doubt Emery was his mate, and his whole life was built on a lie, but he couldn't blindly put his trust in the prophecy of a witch, or in the stars who'd already dealt him shit hand after shit hand. "Fate is a fickle bitch. You have to believe she has a say in your life in order to follow her ways."

Callum let out a string of curses in Scots Gaelic. Augustine didn't catch all of it, but there was something about being a stubborn flea on the ass of a donkey. When he was done, Callum stood and stormed from the table and out the back door, slamming it behind him.

Lily stood and shot Augustine a glare. "He's lost just as much as you, Augustine. The difference is he hasn't lost hope in our kind. I suggest you find something to believe in, or get the fuck out of Scotland, because whether you like it or not, princeling, the war of the prophecy is coming. You best decide whose side you're on."

She turned and set her tea on the counter before heading out the backdoor after Callum, leaving him alone with Emery.

Augustine clenched his jaw. It wasn't like Callum to storm out in a rage. His cousin's reaction was about more than Augustine's inability to conform to what was expected of him. Augustine just didn't know what else was wrong.

Lily was right that Callum had lost as much if not more in his lifetime. His mother. His wife. His child. It was incredible that there was any hope left in him. Still, Augustine couldn't bring himself to hope in something plucked from the mouth of a witch. He didn't want to go to war against Callum or his cause. He only wanted to save his kingdom and his child.

If, and it was a big if, the prophecy was true, then he and Emery played an integral part in the future of the supernatural world. He should probably keep her at arm's length until he knew what their roles would be in the upcoming war. He was playing more than one game, and the playing field grew more complicated by the day.

The bigger question was: did he want to stay away from her?

I could answer that for you.

"Shut the fuck up, August." He muttered under his breath.

"Talking to yourself again?" Emery glanced at him with a mocking smile.

"Mind your own bloody business."

"What was it you told me?" She twirled a piece of her pink hair that had fallen between her fingers. "As long as I carry your babe, I am your business. Well the same goes for you, Augustine. I need to know my baby daddy isn't bat-shit crazy."

Emery met his glare and didn't back down. She would be a force to be reckoned with and that thought did little to soothe the hard-on raging in his pants from the moment she'd come down the stairs.

"I think you're conflicted, Augustine." She ran her finger across her collar bone, pushing the hem of her sweater to the side and exposing his favorite part of her neck. "August's little takeover has you shaking in your boots, and now you're forced to face all the truths you'd rather bury."

He hated just how fucking right she was. He'd never been more conflicted in his life. Not when he'd been forced to change Malcolm, or even when August agreed to start his Culling, chaining them to a wife for the rest of their life. He'd always been the calculated and logical one. The problem was logic was beginning to align with the side that questioned the entire belief system of who he was as a being. There was a distinct possibility that the entire purpose of his existence was a lie. And where did that leave him?

"I need some air." Augustine pushed away from the table and made for the front door.

When he opened it, a shaggy brown wolf he recognized as Ansel stood in his way.

A low growl rumbled from the wolf, and Augustine returned one in kind. His fangs lowered and he widened his stance.

Magic permeated the air, but not in the same way Lily's did. It was light and almost glistened against his skin. The crunch of popping bones was loud in his ears as the wolf shifted into a man before them.

Ansel stood naked in the doorframe. "I was just coming to get you all."

"Holy shit! Ansel!" Emery cried and darted from the table. In an instant, she was in the arms of the very naked wolf.

If he thought he'd been jealous over a stolen glance at Callum, he'd been wrong. Seeing Emery tangled in the arms of another man had him seething. His heart pounded in his chest and when Ansel nuzzled his nose into her neck it took everything in him not to rip the wolf's head from his body.

Augustine lowered his voice to a deadly octave. "Take. Your hands. Off her. If you'd like to keep them, that is."

"Excuse me," Emery whipped her head around, and anger rolled off of her in waves. "While you were off galavanting and killing innocent people, Ansel was protecting me and our daughter. He can hug me, kiss me, and do whatever he'd like to me."

Ansel raised a brow and gave Emery a pointed look. "A bit much, don't you think, Emery?"

Emery shrugged, her defiant stare pinned on Augustine.

His vision went from green to straight red. "Don't test me, little witch."

"You made it very clear where we stood this morning, you don't get to decide who I spend my time with or what we do. If I'd like to befriend every man in Scotland, I'd be well within my rights considering I don't belong to you."

The hell she doesn't.

Augustine held back a snort. Possessiveness was a trait both he and August shared. "What would August think?"

"He'd trust me enough to know I'd never do anything to betray him. You, on the other hand, are incapable of trust."

The fuck I would. I'd haul her ass back to the cottage and show her exactly who she belonged to.

"I don't think you know your mate as well as you think

you do, Emery. Trust is earned, and you don't exactly have a great track record."

Callum stepped up on the porch behind Ansel, his composure once again firmly in place. "Everything okay here?"

"Mom and Dad are fighting." Ansel unwrapped his arm from Emery' waist and turned toward Callum.

Without missing a beat Augustine pulled her flat to his chest and inhaled her scent, needing to replace the wolf's remnants with his own. He growled against her hair, hating the way the bond between them calmed the moment it registered her presence against him. She was a weakness he couldn't afford.

Emery tried and failed to wiggle from his grasp. "What the hell, Augustine?" she yelped.

He ran his nose over the space behind her ear, loving the shiver that ran through her as he whispered, "You don't belong to him."

"He's gay, and one of my closest friends, you overgrown bat." She pushed herself from his chest and righted her sweater. "And for the record, I don't belong to you either."

He'd just have to see about that. He may not be able to keep her once he was king, but after feeling the hot rage that ran through his blood at seeing her in another man's arms, he sure as hell wasn't going to let anyone else have her. August's idea to lock her up and only take her out when he needed a fix wasn't sounding like a terrible idea. "I don't like him touching you."

August growled agreement in his mind.

"Well, get the hell over it." She gave him her back and walked over to where Callum and Ansel stood, pretending not to listen to them argue.

Fucking children. All of them.

Ansel eyed Augustine, giving him a glance that said he wasn't a threat, but he wasn't letting Emery go either. "I came to tell you all, the wolves are here."

"Flora's here?" Emery didn't wait for a response and ran to the railing of the porch. "Where is she?"

Ansel snorted a laugh and padded toward the steps. "Follow me." He looked over his shoulder and gave Em a smile. "And you owe me some beignets for taking a bolt of magic to the chest."

Emery tipped back her head and laughed as they all watched Ansel jump from the steps and shift into his wolf form by the time he hit the ground.

"That's so damn cool," Emery whispered, awe in her voice. She then followed Ansel's wolf out toward where the wards ended on the south side of the property.

Augustine ran a hand through his hair and shook his head, fighting the bond's need to be close to her.

You're slipping, Augustine. She's got her hooks in you and it won't be long before you're just as helpless with her as I am.

Augustine ignored August's jab. Mostly because he didn't want to admit he might be right. Emery was nothing like he had expected—in fact, he was starting to believe that she was everything a queen should be. He needed to get a grip if he was going to survive the little witch.

Chapter Eighteen

EMERY

Ansel's shaggy wolf padded in front of her, wagging his tail, and Emery couldn't tear her eyes from him. His wolf was beautiful. There was no way he could be mistaken for a native wolf as he was easily double the size, and even though his brown-and-red-speckled coat matched a standard pattern, it glimmered in the sun in a way that was reminiscent of magic's glow.

Emery jogged a few steps so she was walking beside him, and Ansel tilted his head in her direction, giving her a playful yip. She ran her hand along his back, which came up to just above her hip, and her magic tingled beneath her skin, welcoming the energy that flowed from the wolf. If she hadn't seen him transform with her own eyes, she wouldn't have believed he was her protector in wolf form. At the same time, his wolf fit him. Big and full of brawn, but with kind eyes and a playful heart.

She tufted the hair behind his ears. "I suppose I shouldn't tell you you're a good boy?"

Ansel bared his teeth and gave her thigh a gentle nip.

Augustine growled behind her, and all Emery could do was tip her head back and laugh. Even with everything going to shit in the world around her, she could appreciate the simplicity of the moment. Her mate was jealous of the only man he shouldn't be, and they were walking to find her best friend. If she left out the fact that Augustine was a vampire and Ansel was a wolf it almost seemed like a normal situation.

The wind tangled in her hair and the sun warmed her skin, giving her a renewed sense of life. She'd never been one to crave the outdoors. Not that she hated it, but it didn't call to her as it did some. Walking through the Highlands though, the world around her seemed to come alive in a way it never had before. Her magic rose until it hummed in her chest. She opened her palms, and gold tendrils snaked down her arms. Her magic pooled in her hands, begging for her to do more than just tap its well.

She started to call it forward, but halted when two wolves crested the hill beyond the shimmering green magic barrier, about fifty feet away. The larger one had fur darker than the blackest night, while the other could blend in with the snow-capped mountains that surrounded them.

They were beautiful, standing in the morning sun, their intense gaze narrowed on her. Magic radiated from them and everything inside her wanted to run to them, to welcome them, even though she had no idea who they were. Ansel looked back at her as if to tell her to stay put and then took off running toward them.

She held her breath as Ansel approached and crossed the barrier. He stopped in front of the new wolves and lowered his head, bowing to them.

The black wolf nodded his head, and the two stared at each other as if having a conversation.

When they'd finished their silent exchange, Ansel turned and padded back to where she stood. Though she'd just seen him shift, her mouth hung open through the cracking of his bones until he stood in front of her in his human form, smiling ear to ear. Augustine appeared beside her, a scowl firmly in place.

Fucking men. Emery nudged Augustine with her elbow. "Down boy. He's not the enemy."

He scoffed and stepped closer to her.

Promising her death one minute and possessiveness the next, Augustine's whiplash of emotions was enough to make her roll her eyes. And yet, she understood him completely. Both love and hate ran through her veins for the crown prince —it made every moment near him confusing as hell. But she needed both sides of him. The brutal nature of Augustine and the love of August. She didn't know how, but she'd have them both.

"She's right, Augustine. I'm not the enemy, but I am Emery's protector. So cut the shit. We are on the same side so long as you don't hurt her."

"As long as you remember your place, guard dog."

"Oooh how original. Trust me she's not my type." Ansel huffed a laugh and Emery couldn't help but picture him trying to hit on Augustine. Which led to her trying and failing to suppress a laugh.

Ansel shifted his gaze to Emery and she regained her composure. "I'd like for you to meet the son of the alpha to the Pack of the Americas and his mate." He gestured toward the wolves beyond the barrier. "They'd like to meet you on neutral territory before they join us at the cottage."

Augustine stepped in front of her and wrapped an arm behind him so she was pressed to his back. "She is not going beyond the barrier, not so long as there are people who want to kill my child."

Holy hell Augustine needed to decide where he stood before Emery lost her damn mind. She stepped out from behind him and grabbed his arm, forcing his attention to her. "Listen to me Augustine, because I am not going to say it again. The wolves have done nothing but keep me safe, they are not the enemy. Lily was right when she told you that you needed to decide where your loyalties lie, because I can tell you mine are with those who want a future for our child. Mine are with the wolves. So as far as I'm concerned, you can get fucked if you think I'm not going to welcome my allies with trust and open arms. It's more than I can say I have for you."

She huffed and spun on her heel, giving Augustine her back even though she really wanted to savor the shock on his face. He needed to know she would not bend to his archaic antics fueled by his inability to come to terms with what they were.

Ansel's lips were pressed together and he looked away, trying not to laugh. Emery walked toward him and he gave her a hidden high five when she reached him. She let out a small laugh and bumped Ansel's shoulder as they walked toward the wards. Augustine followed behind, and Emery could feel the heat of his gaze at her back. "I'm absolutely honored to meet your second in command, but I thought you said Flora was here."

"She is." Ansel tipped his head toward the wolves waiting for them. "She's his mate."

Emery's mouth fell, and her gaze narrowed on the smaller white wolf. It shifted, tamping its front paws in an almost anxious manner.

"No way," Emery murmured.

And yet, the more she studied the wolf, the more like Flora she seemed. Flora's wolf was small in stature and her stare was soft in a way that didn't match that of the alpha next to her. And yet she still exuded a confidence that Flora was only just beginning to find before everything went to shit at the castle.

Emery took a step forward toward the barrier and then another. By the third she was sprinting toward her best friend.

Flora looked up at the alpha and when he nodded she began to shift. A glimmer of magic shimmered through the air, and though Emery couldn't feel it on the other side of the ward, her magic told her it belonged to the moon. She knew that it was the foundation of the wolves magic, but Flora's wasn't pure like Ansel's. Neither was her mate's. It was similar, but tainted with a darkness that clung to the edges like frost on a window.

Emery reached the barrier just as Flora finished shifting. She didn't wait for Flora to dress, nor did she have any inkling of the permissions or protocols related to wolf royalty. Emery crossed the wards and pulled Flora into a hug.

Both women shook with what came out as half sobs and half laughter. They stood there in each other's embrace with so many unspoken words between them, but it didn't matter. They were bonded in the Culling and no time or distance would change their sisterhood.

Flora chuckled against Emery's shoulder. "Do you think I could get dressed? I don't think August needs to see me naked."

Emery had forgotten the two men were behind her. She was surprised Augustine hadn't plucked her back across the barrier the moment she'd crossed it.

"Oh shit. Yeah, I'm sorry." Emery stepped back and wiped a tear from her cheek.

Flora reached down and picked up a flowy satin dress Emery hadn't realized was there. She slipped it on, and it fit her like a glove.

Emery studied her closest friend. She wasn't the same

woman she'd seen the night of the ball. The woman before her stood taller, with her shoulders held back and her jaw set with conviction. She was no longer the meek girl who allowed Jessi to bully her. Her strength was beautiful, It wasn't an extension of the alpha beside her. It didn't come from anywhere else. Flora was exquisite in her own right. Emery wished Jessi would try the woman before her because she had no doubt that Flora would come out on top.

The smile that tugged at her lips faltered when Emery's gaze met Flora's. While everything else about her radiated, her soft blue eyes didn't hold an innocent sparkle like they used to. They now housed the haunted shadow only present in someone who had seen the horrors of the world.

Emery opened her mouth to ask what the hell had happened to put the darkness in her eyes, but Flora shook her head slightly and looked away. When she looked at Emery a second later, she had an award-winning smile firmly in place.

Flora's hands reached out and hovered over Emery's belly, asking permission to touch her bump. "You're pregnant."

Emery huffed a laugh and nodded. "Guilty. And you're a wolf."

"And a vampire," Flora said with a shrug like it wasn't a big deal.

"Um, what?" Emery's brows reached her hairline and she was sure her eyes were widened so far they'd pop right out of her head. There was no way she said what Emery thought she did. "A vampire?"

Flora smiled and her canines elongated into cute little fangs.

Emery gasped as Flora's incisors also elongated into smaller points.

"How?" Emery whispered. "You're like…" Her hands drifted to her belly and covered where Flora's hands sat.

"Your baby." Flora smiled but it didn't reach her eyes. "Yes, I'm a hybrid now."

"But how?" Augustine stepped up beside her, his eyes locked on Flora. "Does Callum know? You're a member of his court now. Were you turned against your will?"

"That's a story for behind the wards." A deep voice, attached to a very naked man, interrupted. He took a step toward Flora and wrapped his arm around her, pressing a kiss to her temple. He extended the other toward Emery. "I'm Draven, and I assure you, Flora practically begged me to change her."

"I seem to remember it a bit differently, but I wasn't turned against my will." Flora rolled her eyes and pushed his hand away, untangling herself from him. "Put on some freaking pants, Draven. You are speaking to a future queen."

Emery winced and kept her gaze firmly focused on Flora. She was the furthest thing from a future queen, but that didn't mean her ego could handle the rejection she was sure was plastered all over Augustine's face. Didn't Callum tell her what happened?

Draven snarled at Flora. Picking up his pants, he slid them on.

Emery bit back a laugh. There was the snarky Flora she remembered.

When Draven righted himself, Emery offered him her hand, hoping there wasn't some weird wolf protocol that made shaking hands an offensive act. She really should have asked Ansel more questions before charging head first into the meeting. "It's very nice to meet you, Draven. I'm Emery, and I assure you I am not a future queen, but I am going to change the supernatural world."

He tilted his head with a cocked brow. "So Callum says. Just what do you plan to do, little witch?"

She felt Augustine's stare in her peripheral vision, and imagined he was interested in her answer as well.

"I don't know yet." Emery's voice faltered, once again faced with the grim reality that she didn't have a clue what she was doing, only that she was determined to succeed. She met Draven's questioning stare and spoke from her heart. "I'm new to the supernatural world. I don't know the ins and outs of its politics, and there are times I don't quite grasp the gravity of each situation. To me, it's simple. The lies of our ancestors need to be brought to light. Our peoples deserve the right to decide the future with all the facts on the table. In addition, my child deserves the chance to live in a world where hybrids aren't murdered for what they are. Monsters aren't born, they are made. I understand how we got where we are now, but we don't have to remake the mistakes of the past."

"You're not what I expected, but I think you might be everything I hoped to find." Draven grinned, his doubled fangs flashing white against his tanned face. "I am looking forward to working with you, Emery."

Ansel stepped up between them, still wearing only his birthday suit, and clapped his hands in front of himself. "Now that everyone's been introduced, shall we go to the cottage? Even in the sun, it's not exactly warm."

"It's not our fault you didn't bring any clothes," Augustine huffed under his breath. He stepped in front of Emery and extended his hand to Draven. "I'm Augustine."

"I know who you are." Draven looked at his hand but didn't extend his own. "I once admired you, thinking your reign would be a breath of fresh air, but as of late you are proving to be no different than your father before you."

Augustine growled and stood toe to toe with Draven. The

two heirs stood at the same height and stared each other down, neither backing down.

Fuck. If there wasn't too much riding on a working relationship between them and the wolves, Emery might let them work out their insane testosterone on their own. Instead, she reached out and placed her hand on Augustine's shoulder. She sent calm waves through their bond, relaxing only when he accepted her emotions. He allowed her to slide her arm into the crook of his elbow though he hesitated when she tried to tug him back.

"Please, Augustine, I want to catch up with Flora, and I'd really like it if Ansel could put some pants on."

Flora was doing much of the same, trying to calm Draven down. "And I want to rub that cute little belly Emery has going on."

Draven stepped back and pulled Flora to him, and Emery's heart melted. While there seemed to be some tension between the two, it was clear how much Draven cared for Flora. She was happy for her best friend. Flora deserved to find love and happiness.

Emery craned her neck and watched as Augustine observed the couple. When his gaze fell to hers, he dropped her hand and stepped back. She instantly mourned the loss of his touch, but kept her face and the bond free of the rejection that pierced her. He didn't need to know how much her heart bled for her mate after the night before.

"Shall we?" Augustine extended his hand toward the cottage.

Flora hesitated, her gaze finding the ground. "I can't cross the barrier until I tell you the truth. Then you can decide if you want to welcome me into the safety of your wards."

"What truth? Of course I want you to come in." There

wasn't anything Flora could say that would stop Emery from wanting her by her side.

Flora looked up at Draven who gave her an encouraging nod, then back to Emery. Her hands twisted in front of her and she took a deep breath. "I don't know how to say this, so I guess I'll just spit it out. I killed Sloane."

Emery's lips fell apart and though she tried to find words, none came.

She took a step back and Ansel grabbed her elbow, grounding her and preventing her from stumbling. Her world was falling apart. It wasn't enough she'd lost her child and her mate. Now she was forced to hear that her best friend killed her twin.

"What do you mean you killed Sloane?" Augustine ground out.

Emery reached for him, knowing August took Sloane's death personally. She died under his watch, and he'd never been able to reconcile that he'd let it happen.

"As you both know I was in the stable that night. I didn't think anything of it and told you both the story I remembered. Only, as it turned out, that's not actually what happened that night." Flora swallowed hard, her eyes darting between Emery and Augustine. "Sloane was in the stable, and she did meet with someone in the loft, though I don't know who and couldn't hear what they talked about. All I remember is a bright red flash before it went silent. I went up the stairs to the loft. Sloane's back was to me and she was busy tipping back a vile of a dark crimson liquid. When she turned and saw me her eyes were wide, and she asked me what I was doing there. I tried to answer but I couldn't. It was as if I couldn't control my own body. I walked right up to her and pushed her over off the loft. The loud crack I remember was her head hitting the floor."

Tears filled Emery's eyes as she turned to Augustine. "Is she telling the truth?"

She prayed he would say she was lying. That there wasn't a hint of truth in her words. This wasn't Flora. Her best friend wasn't capable of murder.

Augustine's mouth formed a grim line and he nodded, confirming her fears.

"Why did you lie to me, Flora?" Emery searched her eyes, trying to find an explanation for Flora's actions. "I thought we were friends."

The petite blonde hiccupped a sob and started to step forward, but Draven held her back the same moment Augustine stepped in front of Emery.

"I didn't mean to," Flora sobbed, tears streaking down her pale cheeks. "I didn't even know what really happened until Draven turned me. All of my memories came flooding back to me. I was compelled to kill her."

"By whom?" Who would want to kill Sloane? Emery almost laughed the second the thought slipped through her mind. Sloane had as many enemies as she did in the castle. Literally anyone who found out that she was a witch would have wanted her dead.

"The King," Flora whispered.

"That is a treasonous accusation, Flora," Augustine growled, and for the first time Emery worried for Flora's safety.

"I know, and if I were a member of your court, or even Callum's, I'm sure your father would find a way to have me killed for the memories I had returned to me."

"Why? Why would my father kill Sloane?"

"I don't know. He didn't give me a reason when he compelled me. He only said to go to the stables that night and to kill Sloane. If she left alive, he'd return me to my family."

Fear flashed in Flora's eyes and a visible shiver ran through her. Draven pulled her against him, and Emery wondered what her home life must have been like to cause such a visceral reaction from her. Flora never talked about her life before the castle; Emery had just assumed she was too young to remember much.

"It doesn't account for the fact that she didn't have any head trauma when we arrived the next morning."

"I don't know, August. I only know what I did." Flora sidestepped Augustine and directed her gaze to Emery's. "You are my best friend, and I understand if you can't forgive me, but I wanted you to hear it from me and know that I would never do anything to hurt you or your baby. I also can't be compelled now that I've been turned, so you never have to worry about me betraying you again."

Emery placed her hands on Augustine and Ansel's shoulders and gently moved them from her path. She stepped forward and took Flora's hands in hers. "I love you, Flora, and I believe you when you say you'd never hurt me or my child." She looked over her shoulder and locked eyes with Augustine. "Your father, on the other hand, will answer for his crimes."

Augustine's jaw tightened and he gave her a stiff nod that didn't seem to confirm or deny whether he'd be helping her lead the crusade to bring his father to justice for killing her sister.

Emery pulled Flora into a hug. "Let's go back to the cottage, and you can tell me about your time with the wolves."

"And you can tell me all about the baby and what I've missed."

Emery winced internally, but gave Flora a forced smile. Her story wouldn't likely be as exciting as Flora's, and it would most definitely not include the happy ending her best friend had with her mate.

Draven wrapped an arm around Flora and followed an already-shifted Ansel back down toward the cottage.

Emery turned to join them but a firm hand on her shoulder stopped her movement.

"May I have a word, Emery?"

"Ooh so formal now are we?" She spun to face him and crossed her arms over her chest.

He smirked, and Emery had to ignore the drunk bees that took flight in the pit of her belly. Augustine was a sight to behold against the backdrop of his homeland.

"I'm leaving to go back to the castle when we get to the cottage. I don't know how long I'll be gone, but I need you to stay here and not do anything stupid to hurt our child while I'm not here to save you."

She rolled her eyes. "We've made it this far without your help, I think we'll survive the time you're gone."

In an instant he was on her, and taking her chin between his fingers, he tipped her gaze to his. "Do. Not. Roll your pretty little eyes. At me." With each articulation his face closed the distance between them until he was a hair's breadth from her.

She shouldn't push him, but she couldn't help herself. Which is why she closed the distance so her lips touched his as she whispered, "What are you going to do about it?"

Chapter Nineteen

AUGUSTINE

Augustine inhaled sharply, his lips dancing over Emery's. The things he'd like to do about it were all things he shouldn't. He'd like to tangle his hand in her bubblegum pink tresses and force her to take his hate-filled kisses. He'd like to rip the sweater she loved so much and take her sensitive nipples between his teeth until she screamed his name through her pain and pleasure.

And that would only be the start.

He'd like to punish her tight body until she remembered that the only thing that should roll is the waves of her orgasms at his hand. Or other parts of his anatomy.

But those were the things he'd like to do. The things he'd do to his mate and queen. Emery was only the former and could never be the latter.

"You're going to push too far one day, little witch." His lips danced over hers, not quite touching them. Torturing them both. "And I won't be held responsible for what happens when you do."

"Noted," she said. He started to pull away, slightly placated, when she added: "As is your cowardice." Her soft lips curled up in a self-satisfied smile, and it was more than he could handle.

Augustine gripped the back of her neck and crashed his lips against hers. The breathy moan that escaped her fueled his absolute possession of her mouth.

She kissed him like she was waging war against him. And maybe that's where they were meant to be. Forever on opposite sides of a war against fate. He wasn't made for the lovey dovey bullshit August spewed, but this... The destruction of Emery's perfect little body? This was exactly what he was made for.

Her hands tangled in his hair, gripping, tugging and begging for more.

Augustine's lips trailed harsh kisses and nibbles down her jaw and throat, coveting every inch of her flawless skin. His hand slipped under her sweater and cupped the breasts he adored, his fingers finding her nipple. He rolled the sensitive bud between them and when Emery threw back her head and groaned, he pressed his mouth to hers, capturing every bit of her pleasure.

Then, using every bit of restraint he had left to ignore his growing cock and the need to ravish every inch of her body, he stopped. Warring against every instinct, he stepped away, leaving them both breathless and wanting more.

"What the hell was that, Augustine?" Emery's shoulders rose and fell as she struggled to force air into her lungs, all the while glaring at him. Her eyes held the same hatred and desire that coursed through him.

"That?" His lips tipped into a wicked smirk, and he hoped she heard the malice in his words. "That, little witch, was just a taste of what I'll do if you push me too far. You are my mate, and so my traitorous body craves your tight cunt, but don't mistake that for tenderness. I want to wreck you. Destroy you in the most delicious ways. I am not your fucking prince charming."

Emery's lips curled into a sneer. "I'm not asking you to be," she ground out.

"You're not," Augustine agreed. "In fact, I can smell your arousal. I know exactly how much you'd like to taste the darkness only I can give you."

A beautiful pink color flushed her cheeks, but Emery stood her ground. If it wasn't for his superior senses, he wouldn't be able to tell how affected she was. Her fierce stubbornness only made his cock harder. It didn't matter how much he threw at her—on the outside she kept it together.

But the bond told a different story. He hadn't realized it at first, but she was only projecting the things she wanted him to feel. Until he kissed her. When he took her mouth with his, she couldn't hide from him. He'd felt every bit of the conflict within her. Fear. Passion. Hope. Hatred.

"You flatter yourself, Augustine." Emery shifted her weight and scoffed. "I don't need a prince charming, I need a monster to remind me what we're fighting for and against. And just so we're clear, wanting your cock is not the same as wanting you."

Her truth was laced in lies, and Augustine could only imagine which of her words were honest.

"So you want my cock?"

She huffed, and almost rolled her eyes before catching herself and narrowing them on him. "You and August both suffer from selective hearing."

He shrugged. "One in the same, little witch."

"Was there anything else you needed from me? If not, feel free to remain in Chicago as long as you want with your dick of a dad."

Reality came crashing down, piercing the bubble of lust

around them. There was no world where he could explore the bond they shared, or the electric chemistry between them. Stolen moments of passion and rage were all they'd ever be awarded.

He shook his head, stifling the growl caught in his throat. "No, you are free to go."

Augustine looked away from her and scrubbed his face with his hand. He wasn't ready to process the bomb Flora had dropped. His father was a lot of things. Murderer could absolutely be added to the list and it wouldn't surprise him. What hurt more was he allowed his own son to suffer, believing he'd failed. The king knew how deeply August cared about his people, and the Culling women fell under that purview. He'd beat himself up over Sloane's death, even more so when Emery had come into the picture demanding retribution.

It's just another example of how he's been lying to us all along. He isn't who we thought he was.

He wasn't as quick to write off his father as August was, but he couldn't deny it seemed they were being kept in the dark on every front, and he was bloody sick of it. He'd demand answers as soon as he returned to the castle.

When he looked up, he was surprised to find that Emery was still standing in front of him, studying him. As if she could read his mind she whispered softly. "You don't have to be like him."

"What?"

"Your father. It's written all over your face. The king is a piece of shit, you have to know that. And he isn't the end all be all representation of a king or a father. I've never had either, but honestly, looking at him, I don't feel like I'm missing out on much. You have everything it takes to be the king the vampires need and the badass warrior our daughter deserves.

She'll be lucky to have you fighting for her, if you choose to do so."

"You have no idea what I'm up against," he spat, his brow furrowed. She couldn't imagine the pressure of holding the future of his kingdom in his hands. Especially following a ruthless king like his father.

"Don't I? The vampires don't want me. The witches don't want me. And the entirety of the supernatural community will likely shun my daughter for what she is."

Augustine let out a low growl at the thought of his daughter being excluded. She was royalty, damn it. Yes, she would be half witch, but that wouldn't make her any less his child. "One thing I can guarantee," he said. "I'll never abandon our daughter. Or my kingdom."

Emery's eyes softened for a moment at his words. "I appreciate that," she said in a low voice. Her expression turned hard, and she took a deep breath before continuing, "But for the record, I do think I have an idea of the kind of pressure you're under. The difference is I know I'm not alone in the fight. I haven't lost sight of what it means to count on those around me and let them in."

Augustine clenched his fists. He was torn between wanting to put her in her place and wanting to reward her for the use of her glorious mouth to call him out. Too bad he'd never give her that kind of power over him willingly.

He narrowed his eyes and slowly crossed the space between them until he stood an arms length away, not trusting himself to get any closer. "And who do I have? You? A knocked-up heiress who doesn't even know how to use her magic? Who hides behind the fake smile she plasters on her face so everyone won't see the cracks in her armor? So they don't know she's breaking? I see you Emery. I see the winces you think you hide so well and the sideways glances when anyone brings up our son. You want everyone to believe you're in control, but you aren't. It's reckless and it's why I only count on myself and my men. The rest of the daydreamers at the cottage can have their hope for a better tomorrow. I'll stick with the facts, and so far I have heard nothing except I'm attached to you for the rest of eternity."

Emery's eyes welled with tears, and if he was a better man he'd apologize for putting them there. But he wasn't a better man, and it was high time she realized that. She had goaded him, implying that he was without faith. She had forgotten to whom she spoke.

Emery's eyes ignited with a golden glow, and her bottom lip trembled. "Keep your facts, asshole. I may have to pretend I'm okay to make it through the day, but at least I'm not so stunted in my emotions that I can't recognize what's breaking me. Your head is so far up your own ass that you can't see that you're in pain. When you come crawling back to me because your logic falls apart, it better be on your fucking knees."

Rage coursed through him, but when she turned and walked away, he let her go. He told himself it was because she was wrong and he didn't trust himself to put her in her place without hurting her, but the reality was he feared everything she said was true.

He watched as she walked down the heather-covered hill, each step pulling the incessant bond between them tighter. Weren't there scissors they could use to cut their bond? To rid them of the underlying need to appease each other? How was he supposed to fix the damn world with that damn witch under his skin?

Emery was nearly half way back when she paused and swayed on her feet.

Augustine tensed and listened for her heartbeat. It raced, but it could be because she was pissed. Still, his anger dissipated slightly, replaced by worry. When fear flooded the bond, and Emery's knees buckled beneath her, he tore down the hill in her direction.

By the time he reached her, she'd fallen to the ground, and lay sprawled in the heather. Her eyes were closed, and her skin ashen. If he hadn't been able to hear the steady beat of her heart and that of his daughter, he'd have questioned if she still lived.

"Emery!" he yelled, but got no response.

Augustine shook her shoulders and pulled her into his lap, with the intention of biting her and using his venom to heal and calm her, but the instant he touched her skin, his world went black.

He blinked through the darkness for long moments before his vision cleared. When he could look around, he found that he was no longer in the field with Emery. Instead, he stood in one of the rooms at the cottage. The light of the full moon spilled in through the large bay window, blanketing Emery in moonlight where she sat on its ledge, staring down at a potted flower in her lap.

He rushed across the room, and his eyes raked over her, trying to assure himself that she was okay. When he found her unharmed, he let out a sigh of relief and barked at her. "What the hell, Emery?"

She ignored him, looking straight through him toward the bed. "Hurry Lily, we don't have much time before it closes."

Emery lifted a pot in her hands, admiring the small purple flower that bloomed inside. It shimmered in the moonlight, a soft pink dust falling from its inner petals onto the dirt below.

He followed her gaze toward the bed and sucked in a sharp breath when he saw the small frame he'd previously mistaken for a pile of blankets. Thea lay in the middle of the queen size bed, her cheeks hollow and and her closed eyes sunken in. Her little hands were folded over her chest, looking as though she was already one with the grave.

Augustine rushed to the bed and sat beside his sister's frail form, a wave of helplessness overtaking him. This was his fault. If he hadn't insisted he be the one to hunt down the Mistress' cannibals, he would have been there to protect Thea. She wouldn't be death's for the taking.

Lily skidded out of the bathroom and plucked the flower from Emery's hands. She brought it to the night stand and meticulously pulled three golden pebbles from the depths of the flower's center.

"Emery, you did it! I can use the seeds to save her."

A smile curled across Augustine's face as realization hit. This was a vision. This was how they were going to save Thea.

"Emery?"

When she didn't answer Lily's call, both of them whipped their heads to where Emery had been sitting. Only she wasn't there any longer. Emery lay prone on the floor, her wavy pink locks strewn over her face.

What the hell was it with this woman and falling to the ground?

Augustine ran to her, even though he couldn't do a damn thing. He couldn't hear her heartbeat in the damn vision. He moved to grab her wrist to check her pulse, but his hands passed through her as if he were a ghost.

Bloody hell.

He studied Emery's chest, waiting for any sign of life. He tore his eyes from her for a split second, rage bubbling that Lily wasn't doing a damn thing to help her.

Lily's eyes darted between Emery, Thea, and the sparkling flower seeds. Even he could see they were losing their shimmer, dimming to a dull brown.

"Help!" Lily called out, panic flooding her voice. "Someone help!"

His vision world counterpart appeared in the doorway seconds later. The moment he saw Emery laying on the floor, he rushed to her and pulled her into his lap. "What the hell happened?"

Lily's back was to him as she hovered over the flower. "She opened the flower and I'm guessing over-exerted herself. I need to get the seeds prepared before they lose their magic. Emery will be fine but you need to get her something sweet or give her your blood quickly to help replenish her. She hasn't mastered pulling energy from the world around her yet."

Lily continued muddling the seeds in a mortar and by the time Augustine's eyes had swiveled back to his doppelgänger, she'd started a rhythmic chant over the components.

Vision Augustine wasted no time and bit into his wrist. Forcing her mouth open, he placed it to Emery's lips. Seconds passed, but it might as well have been an eternity.

"Come on, little witch." His counterpart whispered against Emery's forehead, placing a soft kiss to her flesh. "You don't get to leave me here to deal with all this shit on my own."

Augustine's mind raced. She had to be okay. The stars wouldn't gift her a vision of her death right? Lily said she would be fine but—unlike most witches—Emery's magic had proven to have a mind of its own. As ever, Emery was anything but the norm.

Finally, after a minute of pure torture, Emery coughed, sputtering droplets of blood as she returned to consciousness.

She shot up, her hands clinging to her stomach, and her eyes darting in every direction. "Did we do it? Did we save her?"

Lily stopped chanting and took a step back from where she'd been hunched over Thea's body.

A tiny movement caught his eye, and Augustine held his breath, not daring to hope it wasn't just a trick of the light. But then another movement came, and Thea's arms left her chest and reached out to Lily.

Lily choked on a sob. "You did it, Emery."

Augustine stood and swallowed past the lump in his throat as he walked toward the bed. Thea was alive. Her deep brown eyes looked right through him to where Emery lay with him on the floor.

She raised her hands to sign, but before he could see what she was going to say, his world tilted and went black.

When he blinked open his eyes again, the sun blinded him and he was back on the hill with Emery in his lap.

Her eyes widened, and she dug her nails into his forearms, her voice laced with desperation. "We need to get Thea to Scotland."

Chapter Twenty

EMERY

A wave of nausea caused her stomach to roll.

They had to save Thea.

"Are you okay?" Augustine pulled her tighter against his chest, and while usually she'd drink up the chance to be pressed against debatably one of her favorite parts of his body, each step where she wasn't grounded surged the need to hurl.

"I'd be fine if you would set me the fuck down and let me walk."

"You can hardly stand on your own, and you are shit at hiding the pain you're in."

Emery rolled her eyes, knowing how much he loved when she did that. "Then why did you ask?"

"We'll address that eye roll later, but for now I need to know I can trust you."

"Trust is earned, Augustine."

"And you just failed spectacularly at earning mine," he retorted.

Augustine ripped the front door from its hinges and stormed into the cottage. With more gentleness than she thought him capable, he set her down in one of the armchairs and bit his wrist. "Drink."

"No." If he thought he was going to boss her around just because she'd had what she was pretty sure was a vision, he had another thing coming.

Why couldn't her magic cut her a fucking break and allow her some warning before going off the handle? She was fine with visions. Especially if they helped her heal those she cared about. Visions galore, she was happy to have them. *But maybe next time, give a girl a chance to sit down*, she thought to her magic chastisingly.

"Emery, drink the damn blood. You're feeling like shit because you're depleted, and I know for certain my blood will help. If not for your stubborn ass, do it for our daughter. She needs you at your best."

That was debatable considering how many times she'd spent her mornings with her insides becoming outsides as a result of their daughter's occupancy.

Emery stared at the two blood-welling holes on the underside of his wrist and considered refusing, but there was no denying she felt like she'd been hit by a train. Her head was pounding, and any movement threatened to end with her breakfast on the floor.

She grasped his wrist and brought it to her mouth. The instant his blood hit her tongue a groan rattled her chest, and she sagged into the couch. Augustine's blood was her lifeline. It penetrated her very soul, filling her with life and satisfying needs she couldn't very well address in the living room of the cottage. It wasn't like when she exchanged blood with August during sex, or the other times Augustine had fed her to save her. Each of those times had been accompanied by an orgasm or a life or death situation. Willingly taking his blood fed something deep within her. It excited her magic and her body in a way that connected them on a profound level.

Emery peered up at him through her lashes as she drank, daring to see if Augustine felt anything from the interaction.

Darkened pools of midnight stared back at her. Augustine's chest heaved slow heavy breaths in time with each suck at her lips. He chewed his bottom lip which allowed a fang to peek out. Her eyes trailed lower to where a bulge strained against his zipper, which was coincidentally at eye level.

He was just as affected as she was.

A warning growl fell from his lips, and Emery quickly averted her eyes from the cock she wouldn't mind relieving of its hardness.

This damn mate bond was going to make it impossible to be around him. The sooner he left the better.

Just then, Lily appeared in her peripheral vision along with Callum, Ansel, Draven, and Flora. "What the hell happened here?" Lily asked, pointing at the ruined door. "And why are you feeding Emery your blood?"

Great. Just what she needed. All her friends witnessing her borderline sexual experience at the hands of the mate who hated her with mostly every fiber of his being.

She began to pull away, intent on sharing what she'd seen, but Augustine gave her a stern 'don't fucking test me' look and kept his wrist firmly pressed to her lips.

"What the hell happened is that Emery fell to the ground and sucked me into a vision of how we're going to save Thea, and now she's physically exhausted and you told me in said vision my blood would restore her energy."

Lily's eyebrows shot up, and her eyes darted between Emery and Augustine.

"Is this true, Emery?"

Emery shrugged, her lips still attached to Augustine's wrist. She hadn't even been sure it was a vision. This was the first she'd heard of Augustine seeing everything that played out in her mind. Being star touched was rare, and even though she'd been gifted a prophecy from Agatha, she didn't think that meant she, too, would be prophetic. Nor did she particularly want to be. Falling prey to that vision was scary as hell. One minute she'd been stalking off from her fight with Augustine, the next her magic reared up, and she'd lost control. It was only worth it because it may help save Thea.

"You're star touched." Lily whispered, her wide eyes glued to Emery like she'd grown a second head. "Sweets or sleep is usually how we help young witches with magic exhaustion. But we don't usually have the option of vampire blood. Is it working?"

Emery nodded her head and took another shallow pull of Augustine's blood. The nausea had settled, and her headache had disappeared, but she wasn't ready to give up the connection she had to Augutistine. Not yet.

Guilt crept into her heart. She shouldn't want any connection to him. Not after he'd pushed her away. She'd meant what she said when she told him he could crawl back to her on his damn knees. That didn't mean she didn't crave what the bond so desperately needed. She didn't have to like it, but unlike Augustine, she'd begun to come to terms with the fact they were mates, and concessions would need to be made if they both wanted to survive the connection between them.

"Fascinating," Lily mused.

"What does that mean for Emery?" Flora asked, her voice filled with concern as she stepped forward to sit by Emery, only to be pulled back by Draven and led to the opposite couch.

It seemed Flora's mate was as protective as her own.

Emery hoped that didn't mean he would start acting like a douche canoe, too.

"Emery has been gifted a rare form of magic," Lily replied. "Being star touched means the stars will work through her, gifting her visions as they see fit. She may also excel at other prophetic practices, like tarot or tea readings."

Callum rounded the other armchair and plopped down. "Are the visions accurate?"

"From my understanding, mostly. Unlike prophecies, which tell of individual destinies, visions are what will transpire in the future at that moment for everyone involved. But free will plays a part, and should the players choose a different path, the future may change." Lily's eyes then narrowed on Augustine. "You shouldn't have touched her. She was tethered in the vision, but you wouldn't have been. The stars are particular about who they allow to see their will. Souls have been permanently lost in the visions of other witches."

"I'm fine." Augustine ground out, and Emery could sense his impatience. "Now would you like to know what we saw? Because we have exactly five days until the full moon, which is when we save Thea."

Every mouth in the room fell open except hers. Emery pretended to keep drinking as Augustine lifted her and arranged her in his lap. She tried to fight him, but his stern glare and tightening hand on her hip told her it was a lost cause.

He recounted the vision from his point of view, and Emery was shocked he'd actually retained more information than she had. Then again, she'd been slightly freaking out during the whole ordeal, unaware what the hell was going on. Augustine was cool and collected, though, recalling the most minute details regarding the flower they needed.

Emery's eyes grew heavy, and she closed them as the group began to argue about what came next and how they were going to find the flower no one had ever heard of and get Thea to Scotland. She was vaguely aware of Augustine pulling his wrist from her lips, and her halfhearted attempts to stop him, but sleep trumped her ability to care, and she sank back into the couch wrapped in a cocooning warmth.

"Emery?"

A deep voice pulled her from her sleep. She opened her eyes to find herself pressed against Augustine's chest. She tipped her head up and met hard midnight blue eyes.

"I need to go, and you need to eat."

Still groggy from sleep, Emery furrowed her brow at Augustine, unsure what one had to do with the other.

He reached up and pushed back a piece of her hair that had fallen in her face, tucking it behind her ear. "Which means you need to stop using me as a pillow."

"Oh." She scrambled from his chest and pressed herself against the wall of the oversized armchair. Which really didn't do much good, considering the chair wasn't big enough for the both of them to begin with. Emery looked around and saw they were the only two left in the living room. "Where did everyone go?"

Augustine untangled his arm from around her, slid out from underneath her, and stood beside the chair. "Lily is portaling Draven and Flora back to Tennessee to see if they can find any information regarding the flower with the wolves, and Ansel is with Callum searching his own records."

"Oh."

"Something wrong?"

"No." She didn't need to see the raise of his brow to know he's tasted the lie.

The thing was, she had only just gotten Flora back, and

now her best friend was already gone. Emery was a hot mess, with a list of problems she didn't know how to fix, and she'd hoped some quality girl time would at least help her wrap her head around a fraction of the issues. At the very least it would have provided a good distraction.

"Well, then." Augustine stepped back and grabbed his coat from the back of the sofa. "I'm heading back to the castle. I'd bring you with me, just to make sure you don't get hurt when you inevitably find yourself in trouble again, but the King would probably kill you, and I want that honor to be solely mine."

"Be careful Augustine, a girl might think you care."

He chuckled, and gave her a sly grin. "I assure you my motives are purely selfish."

"I'll see you when you return then." The mate bond tightened within her, and she struggled not to wince. Somehow it knew they were going to be apart and wasn't okay with the notion. It urged her to beg him to stay, if only to cease the longing pain it knew was coming, but she wouldn't dare. Augustine didn't deserve the knowledge of her pain.

"I'll be back before the full moon." If Augustine felt the same pull on his end, he didn't show it. He turned his back and started toward the doorway, but then stopped and turned toward Emery again. He moved closer, and Emery sucked in a breath as he leaned down to whisper in her ear, his voice low and sinful. "And don't think I've forgotten about that eye roll of yours, little witch."

She clenched her thighs together, remembering the searing kiss they'd shared after her first offense. The way he'd wrapped his hand in her hair and demanded retribution. His voice held the promise that her next punishment would be so much worse, and even though she should loathe the idea, the promise of pain and darkness lit a fire within her.

"You're an asshole," she goaded, though it came out sounding more like a whimpered plea.

Augustine brushed his lips against her ear. "Now you're getting it. Be a good girl, Emery."

Without another word, he sped from the cottage, presumably to where Lily waited to portal him back to the castle.

Her heart raced and she gripped the leather arms of the chair in an attempt to steady herself. Not that it helped much. She kept telling herself the mate bond was to blame, but deep down Emery knew she absolutely craved this darker side of Augustine all on her own.

August offered her the light, and while she needed to remember the good in the world to fuel her hope, it was the darkness she craved. Augustine had given her a glimpse at the forbidden touch of her enemy, and along with it, the wickedly delicious potential of pain and revenge.

"Are you okay?"

She didn't know how long Lily had been standing in the doorway watching her muse over Augustine, but she was thankful she couldn't smell arousal like vampires could. "I'm fine. Just a little tired." Her stomach chose that moment to growl loudly. "I may also be a bit hungry."

Lily smiled. "I'll fix us both some lunch."

Emery joined her in the kitchen, sitting at the kitchen island as Lily fixed sandwiches and made small talk. "Augustine made it back to the castle. He'll let us know when he needs a portal back."

The words felt stilted and forced, and for the first time Emery realized even though she trusted Lily with her life and the life of her daughter, and they'd been through two life-or-death situations, she hadn't actually spent much time getting to know her.

"That's good," Emery nodded. The last thing she wanted to discuss as a get-to-know-you topic was Augustine. "Do we have any idea where to start looking for the flower?"

"Everyone is looking for information, but it's not anything we've ever seen or heard of in all of our many years combined."

"We only have five days." Emery's voice edged on panic. In her vision it hadn't looked like Thea had long. She wished there was a way to share the images she saw, to impress on Lily the gravity of the situation. Not that Augustine hadn't done a great job threatening everyone in the room with their lives if they didn't find the damn flower.

"We'll figure out how to save Thea." The calm Lily radiated irritated Emery. How could she not be panicked when Thea's life hung in the balance? "We're doing all we can. In the meantime, the best thing you can do is hone your magic."

A groan escaped Emery's lips. That was absolutely the last thing she wanted to do. She still wasn't fully on the same team as her magic. So far it had taken her son from her and left her on her ass in a heather field. It didn't exactly have a great track record, and Emery would've much rather ignored it completely.

...Then again, she considered, learning to wield magic might be fun. She'd seen a few young witches pelting each other with balls of magic, and she could think of one particular vampire she'd love to hit.

"I know it's daunting, and the exhaustion is not fun. Especially with Augustine gone. You'll have to fight through it the traditional way. The upside is it involves lots of chocolate."

Emery raised a brow. "Go on."

"While your mate's blood seemed to do the trick the

fastest, sleep is the best remedy for exhaustion, and sweets will work in a pinch. Think of it as pushing your body to its limits in a short period of time and needing to recuperate. The sugar in sweets feeds the magical properties within us and helps to speed up the process. Like taking a supplement for muscle fatigue."

"You aren't going to have to twist my arm to get me to eat copious amounts of chocolate. But what about the baby? Won't pushing myself to those extremes hurt her?"

Her magic hummed strong in her chest as if to reassure her of its commitment to her, and Emery rolled her eyes. So much for being able to ignore it completely. She despised the way it completed her. Like a missing limb she hadn't known was missing her first twenty-five years of life and now that it appeared she couldn't imagine it being gone. But it didn't change the fact she'd cut off that limb if it meant hurting her daughter.

"I don't think so. Last time, when… that… happened, the bairns hadn't ever encountered magic before. As you know most witches gain their magic at a young age so if they get pregnant their children would already be exposed to the magic inside their mothers from the moment of conception. Yours weren't, which is what caused…." Lily didn't say it, but they both knew what the influx of magic within Emery had caused. "…but we'll keep an eye on your training. I promise the bairn's safety will be my first priority."

Emery set down her sandwich and locked eyes with Lily, her voice wavering slightly. "I can't lose her too, Lily."

"You won't. And your son is still within you, Emery. Within your daughter. He'll live on through her."

Rage and sadness swept through her, and Emery fisted her hands on the table in an attempt to keep her emotions in check. She felt her magic rising within her ready to help her eliminate any impending threat. Only there was no one for her to unleash her anger on. No one to hold accountable. At least not in Scotland. Tears welled in her eyes and she blinked them away.

Lily reached out and placed her hand over one of Emery's. "You must let go of this, Emery. Your anger will seep into your magic. The resentment will grow, and the darkness you harbor will consume you."

"I need the darkness to do what needs to be done," she whispered, her walls dropping slightly. If anyone was going to understand her need for vengeance it should be Lily. The witches had shunned her the same way they'd abandoned Emery. "Vishna and the witches need to pay for their actions."

"I agree, my sister has done a lot over the years that deserve retribution, but giving into the darkness is not the answer. Look what it's done to August."

"That's not the same." Emery scoffed.

"Isn't it? His anger and resentment drove him to fracture himself so wholly he's not able to control his own darkness. If you give in, it will haunt you for the rest of your life."

"How could you possibly know that?" She may not want to live in the darkness, but Emery wanted to feed it. It should scare her, but the deepest parts of her knew she'd need every ounce of it to rectify the wrongs not only in her life but the supernatural world. Light needed the darkness, just as the darkness couldn't survive without the light to draw its boundaries, and she held both within her. A catalyst for change.

Lily's eyes softened and she pushed away the second half of her sandwich. When she spoke, her voice was distant. "Because I've tasted the darkness and since then it's a conscious decision everyday not to give into its sweet temptations."

Shit. Emery chewed her lip as the revelation turned over in her head. Lily wasn't innocent, but she knew that already even if she hadn't wanted to believe it. She shuddered at the thought. Lily was supposed to be one of the good guys.

Emery inhaled a shaky breath. "Vishna said you were the reason our family was cursed with bound magic. She said it was because you fell in love with a vampire. Would it have anything to do with that?"

"Aye." Lily's gaze shifted to the window, avoiding Emery's. "Come lass, grab a blanket and walk with me. We'll start your training, and I'll tell you a story."

Emery hesitated. She'd much rather finish the nap she started on the sofa than have a magic lesson, but she was nothing if not curious, and Lily had piqued her interest. She finished the last two bites of her sandwich, plucked a quilt from the back of the sectional, and followed Lily out the back of the cottage, ready for the secrets Lily was about to divulge.

Chapter Twenty One

EMERY

They walked in silence toward the treeline, traversing the thick forest. The wind rustled the leaves of the trees, giving the appearance that the branches were dancing to a song only they could hear. A gust circled Emery, whipping through her hair and pulling free more of her pink tresses.

Emery laughed as she twirled in the caress of the wind.

"Wind." Lily turned around and smiled as the wind caressed the skin on Emery's legs, sending a shiver through her. "Interesting. I wasn't sure you'd have a second concentration, but it seems you are full of surprises."

"I'm an elemental?" Emery cocked a brow and grinned.

"I suspect you might be." Lily gave Emery her back and continued walking.

An elemental.

A twinge of excitement creeped through her. She'd often envied the witches at the compound who could manipulate the world around them. It was extremely useful during the late spring storms. While she would be soaked from head to toe, the elementals managed to part the rain or at the very least could blow-dry their clothes with wind before entering the compound.

Lily halted when they reached a small clearing. She took the blanket from Emery and spread it on the mossy ground.

"Sit."

Emery plopped down cross-legged, regretting instantly the choice to sit on the ground. She'd reached the point in her pregnancy where getting up was a downright chore. Lily joined her, sitting as a proper lady should with her legs crossed and knees bent off to the side. It was eerie how similar they looked. Even with the pink in her hair, there was no doubt they were related. But the more time Emery spent with Lily, the more she was sure that's where the similarities ended. Lily radiated an old world simplicity and always seemed to have her shit together, whereas Emery was a classic example of a modern hot mess express with her disheveled outfit and messy bun.

Lily closed her eyes and placed her hands, palm up, in her lap. "Put your hands out and call your magic to your palms."

Emery did as she said. She was surprised when only solid gold light appeared. The tainted streaks she'd witnessed the night before were no longer interwoven. She still felt where the darkness lingered, but it wasn't making its presence known, as if it knew Lily wouldn't approve.

Emery willed it to release itself, wanting to train with both dark and light, but her magic resisted.

I thought you were going to listen from now on?

Her magic didn't respond either way, which only served to annoy Emery more.

While she was arguing with her magic, Lily had summoned hers. Emery tried to put her own frustrations aside, concentrating on observing Lily. Where Emery's magic was gold, Lily's was a soft green with dark silver flecks throughout.

"What type of magic do you have?" Emery inquired,

unsure if it was impolite to ask. She had never asked anyone at the compound, and no one had ever offered any information to her. Mostly she learned by watching what the other witches did and keeping a mental catalogue of their talents.

"All witches have access to every concentration. But for most witches, there are certain kinds of magic that come more easily." Lily shifted her magic, letting it pool in one hand and with a gentle motion, passed it between her hands like a ball. "I specialize in illusions and incantations."

Emery concentrated on her own magic and willed it to move in the same manner. It felt sticky in her hands, like silly putty that had been left out in the sun. And although it moved as she'd asked, it didn't flow effortlessly as Lily's had. "Which is how you were able to conceal your identity for so long at the castle."

"Correct." Lily closed her hand, extinguishing the light green glow. She leaned forward and placed one hand on each side of Emery's. "Let go. Your magic wants to respond, but your hesitancy is evident. When you call your magic in its most basic form to your hands, connect with it, allow it to become an extension of you."

Emery exhaled past the frustration that always seemed to form when someone told her to just 'let go.' If it were so easy, she would have already done so. Still, she gave it another try and with more than one frustrated sigh, she spent the next five minutes in silence attempting to connect with the magic she barely knew. She closed her eyes and did as Lily said, but her magic still didn't flow easily.

"You aren't letting go."

Rage flooded Emery and she shrieked when her golden magic burst into flames.

Lily snorted, shaking her head as Emery shook her hands out. "Let's take a break."

Emery examined her hands. They weren't burned as she expected them to be, but the flames had provided a definite heat she'd felt to her core. "What the hell was that?"

"You're an elemental. While you can use your magic in its most basic form, your true weapon will be mastering the elements. A difficult concentration, but one of the most vital in battle." Lily got a far-off look as if she was remembering something, but just as Emery was about to ask, she shook her head and continued. "Just as your magic at its core is fueled by your emotions, each element is also fueled by a specific aspect of your being. Fire is fueled by rage, which you were exhibiting when you lost control."

"And the other elements?" she asked, regretting she hadn't taken the time to study more about magic during her time at the compound.

Lily's mouth parted and her brows shot up. "Did they not teach you anything at the Coven?"

"They were waiting to find out what concentration I was drawn to, and in my spare time I was too busy researching vampire and witch pregnancies to care about magic I didn't have. To be honest… I didn't think there was a way to unbind my magic."

"I see." Lily nodded. " I suppose we'll start from the beginning on all magic lessons then. Wind is fueled by passion."

Heat filled Emery's cheeks, remembering the times wind had shown up unexpectedly. That explained why it often made an appearance during her time with August.

"Water is fueled by your dreams."

"My dreams?" They were filled with war and death or

dirty thoughts of Augustine, neither of which seemed relevant to water.

Lily nodded. "Not dreams that we have as we sleep. Think of it as always changing. Just as your dreams and goals evolve, so does water between its different states. So you would pull from the emotions tethered to those dreams."

"You know that makes zero sense right? How can a concept fuel my magic?"

"You'll have to ask another elemental." Lily shrugged and reached for a piece of chocolate, tossing Emery one as well. "I'm just teaching you what I know to be true. This isn't my area of expertise. Vishna was the elemental of our family."

Of course, she was.

"And earth?" Emery unwrapped the candy and pressed it to her lips, savoring the chocolate and the way her mouth watered instantly.

"Earth is fueled by your heart. It's the most difficult to master because in order to grasp its magic, you must be honest with yourself about what your heart wants most and use that to fuel it."

"Great," Emery grumbled, her voice dripping with sarcasm. It looked like she and earth would not be acquainted any time soon. Her heart was a clusterfuck of a maze at the moment and that wasn't likely to change.

"Let's not worry about that just yet." Emery didn't miss the undertones in Lily's voice, which gave the impression she should very much be worried about mastering her earth magic. Her hands twisted in her lap, and she looked away from Emery. "I'll do my best to help you understand your magic, but I don't know everything and it's been a long time since I've trained a fledgling. To start though, it's time I tell you the story of how our line came to be bound."

Emery stilled and looked up at her for a long moment

before nodding her head. This was it. The story that shaped her life and set her on the journey of being cast out. She inhaled to settle her nerves.

Lily popped a piece of chocolate in her mouth and slowly exhaled. "This was a long time ago. Long before Augustine was born. Back when things were both simpler and infinitely more complicated. I was young and ambitious. I thought I knew everything there was to know and was ready to take on the world. As the heir to the coven, I was expected to take the helm, and I looked forward to it. It was my job to protect the secrets of the witches and guide them in the ways of our ancestors. As the heir, I would be entrusted with carrying the most closely guarded secret of our coven: the truth about vampires. Our true mates."

Emery's eyes widened. "You knew?"

"Aye, I was entrusted with the secret right before my grandmother died. My mother became the priestess, and as the next in line, I was in a position where I would need to know in case anything happened to her."

"I thought the royal line of witches was immortal."

"Immortal yes, but that doesn't mean we can't be killed. We were told she was poisoned, likely by the vampires, although I've always had my suspicions that it was an assasination attempt by another. It wasn't the first attempt on her life. On her deathbed, my grandmother told me that she'd recently had second thoughts about her role in the creation of vampires. In the separation of mates. She regretted her separation from my grandfather. But there was nothing she could do, and my mother didn't feel the same way. When my grandmother passed, everything remained the same, but I never forgot the way she spoke or how the prophecy could be fulfilled by the mates we tried to hide."

"Even then you knew," Emery whispered, the weight of

Lily's admission hanging heavy between them. "Callum wasn't the only one who had hope for a future of peace was he?"

"No, he wasn't." A weak smile tipped her lips, a hint at Lily's view of her memory. "At the time, I believed with as much faith as Callum has now. I truly thought I could be the heir of the light."

"Is there an heir of dark?" The question slipped from Emery's mouth without thought. It only made sense to her though. Light opposed dark, and balance seemed to be a thread in the stars, but she'd never heard of a dark heir.

"Aye. Long ago, my grandmother's twin was the queen of dark. She chose to practice dark magic, and her life was forfeited because of it. It's always possible for a witch to go dark, but almost all practice in the light now. The ways of the dark have been forgotten."

"Oh." Her gut sank and Emery tried not to show her disappointment that there wasn't more information. If Lily noticed, she didn't say anything. Still, Emery couldn't help but hang on to the notion that there should be an heir of the dark. Everything needs balance, even light.

The mention of dark magic had the tainted portions of her own coming alive. The darkness within her hummed and instead of lingering on the fringes of her magic, it gripped her spine, sending a shiver through Emery. She bit the inside of her cheek and inhaled a shaky breath and tried her best to focus on Lily's words.

"There were two possibilities for the heir of night—one with the wolves and one with the vampires. But seeing as the heir of the wolves at the time was a baby and couldn't possibly be my true mate, I didn't think he and I would be solving the world's problems together any time soon. So I set my sights on the vampires.

"By that time, my mother had taken over. She hated the vampires almost as much as Vishna does now. She believed they were responsible for the death of my grandmother. So when I came to her with the plan to infiltrate Kipton's Culling using my talents for illusion to trick the vampires, she jumped at the chance."

Lily swallowed hard as tears formed in her eyes. Her lip quivered, and Emery wanted to tell her she didn't have to continue, but she didn't. Emery needed to know what happened. This story was almost as important as the one about how her grandmother created vampires. This was the story of her magical heritage. The decisions made then had changed the trajectory of what should've been her life.

Lily opened her mouth to speak and a sob caught in her throat. She swallowed hard again. "I never planned to fall in love while trying to fulfil the prophecy. Sharing my life with someone who was destined to die wasn't something I'd considered. I didn't need the heartbreak, and there aren't many men who could handle the pressure of being with someone more powerful than them. Not to mention, consorts of the heir are too often assassinated."

Emery's heart broke for everything Lily had to endure. Love didn't consider what was fair and once it sunk its claws in, there was no denying it. Even if one could walk away, there would always be the gaping hole where it snared. But there was hope for Lily. The damned stars had given her a second chance.

"And what about now? Is love an option? Now that you know Malcolm's your mate?" She knew how insensitive she was being. Lily had loved Kipton, but Emery had a soft spot when it came to the oldest royal. Malcolm deserved his mate and so much more after all the bullshit he'd put up with at the hands of her sister. And so did Lily. "What I mean... is you can't possibly still want to be alone. You're not the heir any longer and Malcolm is also immortal. Even if you were still the heir, Malcolm knows what it takes to be royalty."

Lily frowned. "I'll always be the heir. I didn't abdicate, I was shunned."

Emery reached over and slid her hand into Lily's. "So take back your rightful title."

"Don't you mean your title?"

"I don't want it." She'd never spoken the words out loud, but Emery meant them. "I may be a witch, but my only stake in their politics is how they pertain to my daughter. If that means that I need to be the priestess, I'll wear that crown, but I think there are others better suited than me." She gave Lily a pointed look.

Lily choked out a laugh and patted Emery's hand, then released it. "I don't want it either. Kipton taught me that when you have a title, you either become the job or realize the job isn't worth the title. There is no in between. He was the best of all of us. He wanted peace for his people and wasn't afraid to stand up for what was right. "

"What happened to Kipton?" Emery whispered, knowing there wasn't a happy ending to the story.

"When my mother found out I'd fallen for the vampire prince, she was livid. She planned an attack on the castle. Used the schematics I'd sent her my first week there." A tear rolled down Lily's face. "It was a massacre of my own doing. Both sides lost so many lives that day, but ultimately I lost my chance at love and failed the supernatural world all in one day."

"I'm so sorry, Lily." There was nothing she could say to take away the pain in Lily's eyes, but damn she wished she could.

"Kipton died at the hands of my mother. His last words to

me were 'don't give up.' But how could I not? How could I come back from losing him? When I found the King mortally wounded I offered to save him, because I was broken, and I knew he'd demand retribution for my mother's actions. I wanted him to ruin her. To demolish the coven that stole my future from me. The King told me he'd pay whatever the price was to save him." Lily lowered her gaze and her voice fell to barely a whisper. "I'm not proud of what I did, Emery."

The darkness in her swelled, and Emery didn't need to ask what the price was, but did so to urge Lily on.

"The price for that type of magic is another source of life, and the only one near him was his wife." Lily sobbed, bringing her hands to her face, and Emery had to turn away to hide the shock on her face.

She knew Lily had performed dark magic, but she never guessed she was a murderer. It didn't fit. This was the woman who fought to keep her alive. Who saved her daughter. She didn't think Lily would be capable of the darkness that it would take to perform that sort of magic.

Then again, rage and loss corrupted even those with the most light.

I'm the perfect example.

Emery grabbed a piece of chocolate and offered it to Lily. They hadn't used magic, but sometimes chocolate just made things a bit easier.

Lily took it, and Emery offered her a smile. "That's how you knew about the darkness consuming you. You used dark magic to save the King."

"Aye. I no longer cared. A life debt is one that is not easily repaid, and I had that of the Vampire King of the Americas. Which is how I came to stay with his family. After I was officially shunned, where they went, I went. His protection extended to me as long as I didn't interfere with his kingdom."

"You were banished not only for loving Kipton, but for saving the king." The same thing that would happen to her if she chose Augustine or he chose her. There was no option for a happy ending.

"My mother sent my sister to curse me after I didn't return home. She knew I'd let my twin near, that I wouldn't suspect her to be the snake I now know she is. Vishna wasn't powerful enough to bind me, but she bound any witch sired from my womb. I am sorry you have had to pay for my transgressions, lass."

"It hasn't been all bad." Emery laughed, because it totally had been, but she wasn't about to rub it in Lily's face. She unwrapped and ate another piece of chocolate. "It's so crazy to think you are my great, great, great, great, add a few more in there, grandmother."

Lily chuckled and it was good to hear that after everything, she could still laugh. "It's not that crazy when you're immortal, but thank you for making me feel older than dirt."

"If it makes you feel any better, I don't see you that way." Emery shrugged as she tried to find the words for how she felt about Lily. From the moment they'd been thrust into each other's lives, she'd felt connected to her, but it was only here in this moment that she realized they shared a bond through so much of what they'd experienced. "You're like the older sister I always wanted. The one who has my back but also sort of scares the shit out of me."

Lily's smile grew wider. "I like that notion. It's been a long time since I've had family I actually liked."

"Me too. So, what happened next? How did Vishna come to be the priestess?"

"Not long after I'd been banished, Vishna killed our mother and took the coven for herself." Lily narrowed her gaze. "Take note of that. I fear it's a running theme for immortals. You must trust no one."

"So after you were banished and started following around the king and his family..." Emery tipped her head and smirked with a wiggle of her eyebrows. "How did I come about?"

"Not that it's any of your business, but I was lonely. I was away from the coven and it's not like the king welcomed me with open arms. There have been many suitors over the years. One may have left me with more than just a weekend of good memories. I had the baby but gave her up for adoption. I couldn't raise her under the nose of the vampires and I figured she'd be safe since she wouldn't have any magic. I didn't know Vishna would find out and track down her line later. She has kept close tabs on every witch who could threaten her reign."

"Is that why Montgomery women don't live long?" Emery's rage simmered and her palms heated. One more fucking reason to hate Vishna.

"I suspect it might be," Lily said with sorrow in her eyes.

Emery's anger abated as she stared silently at the woman in front of her. Lily had been dealt shit hand after shit hand, and she still managed to have an air of grace and hope about her that Emery could only wish to emulate someday. She rubbed her belly and whispered the question that burned within her.

"What was her name?"

"Colette."

Emery weighed the name in her mind, allowing it to roll around on her tongue. "That's a beautiful name."

"Thank you."

"Thank *you*. For sharing your story with me. For finding

hope when honestly no one would have blamed you for giving up. But you didn't answer one thing."

Lily glanced up from her lap and furrowed her brow. "What's that, lass?"

"What comes next?"

She chewed her lip, a habit Emery was beginning to think was hereditary. "I truly don't know."

"Malcolm—?"

"I don't know if I can," Lily interrupted, her hands twisting in front of her nervously. "It's not that I don't want to. It's just… Kipton was the love of my life. If you had asked me then, I would have told you he was my mate. There was no way I could have known what the mate bond would actually feel like, but what we had was real. What's worse, my body has no problem betraying what my mind knows it felt for Kipton." A sigh escaped Lily and she paused, looking toward the sky. "With Kipton it was gradual and always exciting. Never knowing if we were going to get caught or if we'd succeed on our quest, but as long as we were together it didn't matter. But with Malcolm...with Malcolm, it hit me like a ton of bricks. The moment I saw him, there was no one else in the room, he captivated me down to my very bones. But I can't reconcile that he's not the only one in my heart."

Lily was downright poetic with how she described the mate bond. It took over a person's life and there was no arguing with it. But it was also a beautiful thing at its core, or at least it should be. Emery sighed, wishing she had a simple answer, and knowing she was the last person who should give any advice on mates. "I know you love Kipton. You always will. But giving Malcolm a piece of you isn't going to make your love for Kipton mean anything less. This is why you haven't accepted him as your mate, isn't it?"

"That and I can't fathom being as miserable as you."

Emery winced. "My situation is not yours. August and I… we can't seem to fit. Not yet at least."

"It doesn't matter." Lily shook her head and stared off into the rustling trees. "I can't be Malcolm's any more than you can be August's. At least not as the world stands at the moment. We've always been a part of their world, from the moment our ancestors created vampires. Separate but connected. Always fighting. You're my hope for a happy ending. Maybe someday it'll be in the cards for me and Malcolm. But before there can be an us, there needs to be a you. You and August need to mend what has been broken."

"I'm not sure happily ever after is in our cards. It's possible you're right and there are too many ghosts that haunt our past for us to ever grasp what's rightfully ours. But I promise you we will fulfill the prophecy. If it's the last thing I do, I will ensure the stars align for my little girl, and there is peace for our people."

"I have no doubt you will. I'll be by your side every step of the way." Lily tossed a playful spurt of magic. It rose cheerfully into the air before falling back down and hitting Emery in the leg. "Okay, enough blubbering. Stand up and let's get you comfortable with the elements."

Emery groaned playfully, but the truth was that talking with Lily had restored a bit of hope in her. And reminded her that Lily was a badass witch who was not to be fucked with. She better do as she was told.

Chapter Twenty Two

AUGUSTINE

Something akin to regret pricked Augustine as he pressed his hand against the wall of the shower. It was the first moment he'd had alone since arriving back at the castle, and he was beginning to think he'd rather spend the day with Jessi than face the shitshow inside his head.

We both know that's a stretch.

Augustine chuckled. August was right, no one wanted to spend time with Jessi. Still, keeping busy had been his best option thus far.

His first stop had been to see Thea and update his Mother and brother on the vision so that he could enlist them to help prepare his sister to be moved to Scotland. The hope in the Queen's eyes ripped him apart. She pulled him into a hug and thanked him profusely, but it wasn't thanks he deserved. Emery had done all the work, he'd only facilitated when it looked like she would fall where she stood. Ultimately she had the vision and would need to master her magic to save Thea… if they could even find the flower. Malcolm was practically bouncing with confidence, inspiring smiles from their ragtag band of rebels, but Augustine wasn't so sure.

There was too much that had to go right, and infinitely more things that could go wrong.

Things were already getting complicated. Leaving Scotland had been harder than he anticipated. He tasted the hint of a lie in his thoughts before August had the chance to berate him and amended them. Leaving the country was nothing; leaving Emery was what gutted him in a way he wasn't prepared for. She'd called him out and left him questioning everything he'd known to be true about himself and the only life he'd ever known. No one did that. He didn't allow it. But for her he'd all but rolled over and taken it with a few idle threats he wasn't even sure he'd follow through on.

Except the eye rolls. He'd enjoy punishing her for those.

Augustine leaned against the cool tile as the stream of water hitting his chest went cold. He exhaled a frustrated sigh. Emery wasn't supposed to have this kind of power over him. The mate bond wasn't supposed to affect him as it did August. But it did. And he bloody fucking hated it.

He should continue to deny the pull he felt toward the little witch. Ignore the way his heart nearly stopped when she'd fallen to the ground. Or the way he wanted to burst with pride when she clung to his wrist and took his blood willingly as if he was the only one in the world who could save her.

But it wasn't only the physical reactions that plagued him. Not anymore. No, the little minx didn't only grab the mate bond and jerk it till his cock was at attention, she was charming her way into his heart with her intelligence and resilience. In the last few months she'd found a strength within her that even she hadn't known existed. She may think herself broken, but there was a fire in her that had only just been ignited. All it would take was a gentle breeze—a tiny push in the right direction—and he had no doubts Emery would accomplish all she set out to do, and then some. Which only left Augustine to wonder where he would stand when she did.

Do you even know where you want to stand?

A warning growl rumbled from deep within him at the obnoxious trapped half of himself. Even though his question wasn't unfounded.

It had been so simple before Scotland. She was his enemy. A tricky little witch who needed to be destroyed. Things were black and white. Now he stood in the shower, his fully erect dick mocking him, and considering what August had with Emery. It didn't make sense to him. It defied everything he thought he believed. His heart was something he'd given sparingly and never outside those he deemed his family. He never felt the need to. It was beneath him. A woman was meant to provide his heir and stand by his side looking pretty for pictures, as it had been for every royal vampire that came before him.

But then he had tasted it. Raw, unbridled love. He felt it in varying degrees through August's night with Emery and then again when she looked at him and unknowingly let it slip down the bond.

It was intoxicating.

The kind of feeling that made a man's cock stand at attention and demanded he consider selling his soul to attain it.

But that was not who Augustine was. That wasn't his role in the grand scheme of things. He was the protector. The monster who ensured those he cared for were taken care of. He didn't need or deserve the love of a woman, especially that woman.

The thought gave him pause.

Emery didn't owe them anything. Hell, she'd be well

within her rights to give the supernatural world her middle finger and walk away.

But she wouldn't. She wasn't like the majority of the supernatural community. Egocentric and single-minded.

She was better than that. Better than him.

Augustine sighed, and gripped the base of his shaft.

Every time he thought of her, he ended up in the same place. With a hard-on he could do little about. Even if he did jack-off to the thought of her, it wouldn't satisfy him. Nothing short of her sweet body would ever satisfy him again. That and he didn't have the time to take care of it, considering he had a meeting with his father in just under a half hour.

He stood under the cold water and willed his dick to get with the program.

If it hadn't been for Emery's vision, he may have stayed in Scotland and gone toe-to-toe with his little witch just to test the depth of his reckless feelings.

His little witch.

His feelings.

Augustine scoffed. Emery was destroying every bit of him piece by piece and forcing him to become more like August.

I'm really not that bad.

"Shut the bloody hell up." His dormant half had been unusually silent while Augustine worked though his feelings, and he wasn't sure if that was a good thing or a sign he was losing an uphill battle.

He turned off the water and wrapped a towel around himself. He needed to get his head on straight. They had five days to find the flower that would save Thea's life and he had to ensure the King remained in the dark on everything going on in Scotland. If that wasn't enough, he had to keep his emotions in check when it came to his father. He had to be careful not to think too hard about the lies the king had been spewing, or how he had kept August in the dark about the political climate of their kingdom... or his involvement in Sloane's death.

Bloody fucking hell.

He'd barely been able to give Flora's revelation any thought before Emery had suckerpunched him and fell into her vision. It only made sense that his father had learned Sloane was a witch, but that didn't explain why he would lie to August, or why he would bring Emery to the castle. He could've used Sloane and Emery to start the war he'd always wanted with the witches, but he didn't, and Augustine needed to know why.

August would be better suited for the meeting, but there was no way in hell Augustine was going to let him out.

I'm still here, you know. All you have to do is listen to me.

"Oh now you're offering to help? Didn't have a single useful thing to say during my existential crisis in the shower just now?"

Not until your head is firmly out of your ass. And without evidence, it will get shoved back in. I'll gladly take the lead if it keeps our daughter safe, and gets Thea to Scotland. I'll even return to my place in the backseat if you need.

"What's the catch?"

All you have to do is admit that Emery is our mate.

There it was. August's push to further his cause. Ever the diplomat.

"You know she is," he growled darkly.

I do. I'm pretty sure I fucked her and cemented that fact. The issue is you aren't willing to accept her despite everything in you that tells you she was made for us.

"I'm never going to accept her." It was something he wasn't sure he could budge on. "She may be my mate, but she can't be my queen. She is still a witch, August, and we are still the crown prince of vampires." It couldn't matter that she was everything August said and more. There was no happy ending for them.

She is a witch. But we will be king. We can change the course of history with her at our side. What if what Rex said is true? Our kingdom will accept her.

We? Our? When had they joined the same side?

"I'm not you."

But you are. You told Emery yourself.

"Damn it," Augustine muttered.

He wasn't ready to deal with this. He needed to focus on the meeting ahead. Pushing August into the background—which he protested quite loudly—Augustine quickly donned his favorite suit. He picked up the file Malcolm had given him, detailing what he was supposedly doing while he was in Scotland.

Augustine flipped through the pages and found documents in Rex's handwriting. He grunted with approval. If Rex wrote it, that meant the intel was solid. The vamp who killed Miles in Los Angeles had been spotted and traced back to Chicago. That's where the trail to the Mistress went cold, but there'd been five more cannibal attacks since he went to New Orleans. Thirty deaths total in addition to the fifty they'd lost after the wards fell. Thirty-seven more in the last four days, all from attacks on smaller strongholds.

Bloody fucking hell.

A knock distracted him, and he glanced toward the door. "Come in."

He expected Clovis, but it was Yessenia who entered. Augustine hadn't seen her since he'd sent the rest of the Culling women away, and her presence now couldn't mean anything good.

"Your Highness," she curtseyed, extending a three-ring

binder in his direction. "I need your approval on a few things for the wedding."

Augustine's jaw tightened. He bit back every curse he wanted to hurl at Yessenia. There was no doubt Jessi had put her up to this, knowing he would take her head if she'd shown up. He'd all but forgotten about his pending nuptials.

He kept his hands behind his back and looked down at the binder then up to Yessenia. "I trust your expert opinion, Yessenia. Please let my fiance know that sending you is no better than sending herself. Should she interrupt me again with trivial wedding decisions, I'll follow through on every promise I've already made to her."

"Yes, your highness. It's just…" Yessenia swallowed hard. "These were items from the king."

His stomach sank. If his father was involved, there were ulterior motives at play, none that would bode well for him.

"Ah, I see." Augustine took the binder from her, the symbol of the King's reach over him. "I'll speak with my father then. Thank you."

Yessenia gave a quick curtsey and scurried from the room, likely worried he'd take out his anger on her.

He flipped through the binder, breathing an irritated sigh. It was filled with things that could be handled by Yessenia and Jessi. There was nothing he needed to approve, but still his father didn't flex his power without reason. He read through the details of the ceremony, noting that they had been altered to include facets of the hunt.

When he reached the passage that should contain his predetermined vows, he stopped. His grip tightened on the pages, and he saw red.

They'd been changed to the vows he spoke to Emery. Or rather, the vows August spoke. He needed to remember the distinction. The problem was it didn't matter to the mate bond. They were one in the same. As he read the words, the bond tightened in his chest until he could scarcely think.

Forever in my heart. Forever in my veins. Forever on my lips.

Fuck.

Augustine threw the binder across the room before hurling his fist into the stone wall, cracking one of the bricks. He shook out his hand and paced the length of his room to try and dissipate the misplaced anger he felt.

They were just words. They didn't mean anything to him. The ache in his chest was just the mate bond, not an unprecedented sentimental side to himself he couldn't control. It wasn't the side of him that questioned every single interaction with Emery since she'd come back into his life. He could speak the words to Jessi. He'd never mean them. Never would he bind himself to another in that way. Not that he could do so again. They were just words. They meant nothing.

Keep telling yourself that.

"Shut the fuck up, August. You are the reason I'm in this mess."

Just admit she's ours.

"No."

Augustine threw the door open and stormed down the hall. He pulled out his phone and tapped a message to Malcolm, telling him to have his sister and mother ready to go. The minute he was done dealing with his father, they were going to Scotland, and then he was going to war. At the very least, killing witches would distract him from the emotions he refused to acknowledge.

Augustine's spirits raised slightly when he saw his father was waiting for him in the War Room alone. He had little desire to get sucked into a debate with his father's advisors. They were as bad as the King. Bunch of brown-nosing yes men who did whatever his father said. That likely included killing Sloane.

"Ah son, come join me." The King moved around the map table and poured the two of them glasses of blood. "I got your report. Nicely done closing in on the Mistress. I assume you'll find her soon and eliminate her."

Augustine's stomach rolled as he took the glass. The last thing he wanted was stale, room-temperature blood, but he'd drink it to keep up appearances. "Yes, of course. Consider it done." He didn't know how they were going to do that, but he trusted Rex's intel.

He ran his fingers over the detailed map his father had set out, studying where the suspected coven hideouts were located. They were spread far and wide over the territory, and his father had already hit the ones they knew about closest to New Orleans. It was smart. Most of the witches would try to remain close to their homes in the hopes they'd be able to return to the place so ingrained with their magical history.

"What're your next steps?" he asked. "Have you located the priestess and the members of the inner circle?" Augustine swallowed the rage that threatened to rise as he thought about Vishna. His personal vendetta with the priestess over the death of his son was not something he would put aside. She had known what she was doing… just as he would when he drove a knife through her immortal heart.

That would make Emery priestess, August chimed in. *Intended heirs, Augustine.*

He pushed August's thought from his head. He wasn't going to let him ruin this. Emery wanted Vishna's head on a spike, and he intended to give it to her.

Think about this, Augustine. You need to play this correctly. She needs to be ours first before you kill the priestess. If she is the priestess before you claim her as your own, there's no hope for us.

Ever the diplomat, Augustine thought grimly. Of course August had already thought through the ramifications of what it would take to make Emery his. Neither side would accept them if either of them were already rulers.

It was a good thing Augustine hadn't fully committed to the notion of claiming her.

August pushed his frustration to the forefront but he ignored it.

His father pointed to the purple points on the map in North Carolina, Maine, Washington, and New Mexico. "These are the strongest coven strongholds. We've got eyes on them all, and we'll know if they are setting up anything like the compound in New Orleans by next week. Then we'll bomb them all simultaneously. Before your wedding day, we'll be free of the witches."

Augustine should be elated, but dread coursed through him. He scrubbed his chin with his palm. His father's plan was ludacris. Some of the strongholds were in major cities. The casualties alone would be catastrophic. "What about the humans in the area? Isn't the goal to keep a low profile? We already executed a major event in New Orleans, we shouldn't be attacking on a full scale again so soon. And what of our people? Are we giving the heads up to our people in the area to get out?"

"Humans are the least of my worries. The media will spin it to be some sort of domestic terror attack, and they'll move on. As for our people, they shouldn't be living near strongholds to begin with."

Augustine looked down at the map again. "Humans are our primary food source, with blood banks supplementing the rest of our population. Of course our people live near there.

We can't just leave them to die or live in the aftermath where they could be at risk of exposure."

The King scoffed lightly and sipped his drink. "Casualties are part of war."

Augustine stared at him wide-eyed, wondering when his father's logic went out the window. "Yes, witch casualties are expected, but it's our job to protect our people and stay under the radar. We'll be hunted next if we're not careful. It's happened throughout history. We get too cocky and the humans follow the breadcrumbs."

Without warning, the King slammed his goblet down on the table, blood splashing across the maps. "You're my heir not my equal!" he yelled, a twinkle of crazy in his eye. "I'm not interested in your opinions on my war tactics. This is my war, which makes it my call."

Augustine stood deathly still, not giving in but not retreating. His father may not have ever truly trusted him, but he'd never shut him out from discussing strategy. Augustine was a master tactician, honed in the art of war. This...this felt personal.

"Father we can't—"

He was interrupted when Dorian bolted through the door, not bothering to knock. "Your majesty. Your highness." His tawny brown hair was disheveled and eyes were wide, darting between them. Augustine might not have worried, but the grief on his pale face twisted his gut.

Augustine threw his hands up and turned away, pinching the bridge of his nose. What the hell was Rex getting at sending a sentinel as green as Dorian to brief his father?

"What the hell do you think you're doing, sentinel?" his father boomed. "I am your king, your superior should have taught you better."

"He's dead, your majesty." Tears misted Dorian's eyes and he whipped his head to Augustine. "They're all dead."

No.

His chest constricted and Augustine struggled to suck in a breath.

No. His eyes narrowed on Dorian, searching for a hint of a lie.

No. Not this on top of everything else.

He swallowed the lump in his throat and managed to speak. "What do you mean they're all dead?"

"The team, your highness." Dorian choked and his eyes went glassy. "We went on the mission as the king ordered, infiltrating a warehouse on the outskirts of town. There were too many of them. Rex… he tried to get everyone out, but those magicked vamps picked them off one by one. I've never seen anything like it. In all my years, I've never… He died so I could get out. He died for me." The young sentinel's voice echoed his disbelief as his eyes dropped and he extended his arms toward Augustine, holding a length of wrapped leather. "He gave me this."

The instant Dorian placed the cloth in his hands, Augustine knew what it contained. He unwrapped the worn leather and revealed the blade he'd given to Rex on their first mission together. The hilt was covered in blood. His blood.

Augustine grasped the hilt of the sword tightly, his shaking hand the only part of him that gave any indication to the rage that consumed him. He spun on his father, only barely stifling the need to press him up against the wall and hold the blade at his throat. "What the hell were my men doing on a mission without me?"

The king shrugged and sipped his blood, as if Dorian hadn't just told him their most elite squad of sentinels had been killed. "They've been without you for years, Augustine."

"Not like this." His voice betrayed him, shaking through his snarling lips. "Not when we are at war. We had an agreement. Those were my men. They could do your bidding unless we were at war. Then they'd be by my side, and my side only."

"I needed them. They're the best we've got... well, they *were* the best we had. I wanted to get a jump on finding the Mistress. You were busy with your witch and bastard child, and they were already in the area, so I sent them in."

"They were my men," Augustine growled. His grip on control faltered further as he realized what his father had said.

He knew.

The king knew about Emery and his daughter.

Augustine heard once that rage was not far off from peace: they flexed the same muscles within. A man who was on the edge of rage often found peace in his anger. He'd never understood it until this moment.

He stilled and tightened his grip on the hilt of Rex's sword, praying his father would give him a reason to use it.

His father swirled the last of the blood in his cup and gave Augustine a pointed look over its rim. "Did you really think you could keep your child's existence a secret from me? The witches we captured were all too willing to sing about their pregnant heir before we slit their throats. It's not hard to put two and two together."

"Get out, Dorian."

The sentinel gave Augustine a long glance before stepping out the door. At least he would have plausible deniability if asked later what happened.

The moment Dorian was gone, Augustine's voice dropped to a deadly octave and each word he spoke was a pointed threat. "You will leave my mate and heir out of this."

"Mate?" the king mocked, "She's a royal witch and that

child will have her blood. They're both better off dead. No witch will be recognized as an heir to my kingdom. You'd be better off ridding yourself of them now. They make you too soft."

All cognizant thoughts went out the window the moment the King threatened his child. Augustine moved with the speed of a warrior. Pulling Rex's sword from its sheath, he rammed into his father, pressing the older man into the wall, blade to his throat. "You will leave my mate and heir out of this," he repeated.

The King's lips twisted up in a sardonic grin. "Kill me, and I promise you when my men find where they're hiding, they'll kill them and leave nothing but their entrails for you to find. They're closing in, and Scotland isn't that big."

Augustine growled and even though he was relieved his father didn't have eyes on Emery, he pressed the blade harder, drawing a drop of blood at its tip.

"You want to test me," the King goaded, "but you won't if it risks the life of your child. You're a disappointment, and I've already invested too much in you. Do what you must, but know my reach is far and wide, Augustine. You won't win against me."

End him Augustine. We'll get there before him. We'll keep them safe.

But what if they couldn't?

He couldn't guarantee that, not when he was being pulled in a million different directions. He wasn't supposed to care about them. His father was a mad man, the malice in his eyes only confirmed he'd been two steps ahead the entire time. Augustine wasn't ready to lose his heir or his mate. He still wasn't sure where Emery fit in his life, but he knew that he needed her to live.

"What do you want from me in order to call off your hunt?"

"For now, you are going to do as I say and bring me the Mistress' head. Then you're going to marry Jessi in three weeks and give me a rightful heir to my throne."

"And you'll leave Emery alone?"

The King shrugged. "For now, yes."

He's lying. He always lies.

Augustine chewed the inside of his cheek and inhaled a sharp breath. "Fine. I'll do it." He lowered the blade and took a step back. "On one condition."

August was right, and he didn't believe for a second his father would keep his word, but playing his game would possibly give him some time and work in their favor.

The king adjusted his shirt and ran his fingers across his neck where a single drop of blood still remained. "I don't think you are really in a place to be making demands, but I'll humor your gumption."

"I'll do as you want, but I get to lead my own team to hunt the Mistress, and you'll let me do whatever it takes to save Thea."

"That's two conditions, but fine." The King waved his hand nonchalantly as he crossed the war room and rang the bell to alert the feeders that their presence was required. "But don't think to undermine me, Augustine. I may not want to start over, but accidents happen, and it wouldn't be the first time I had to cull a new woman."

Augustine's mouth parted, but he quickly shut it to hide his shock. His father was casually threatening to end his life and host a Culling of his own to produce himself a new heir as if it were no big deal.

"I'll keep that in mind," Augustine ground out before he

gave his father his back and stormed out of the war room, slamming the door behind him.

His chest heaved in time with his erratic heartbeat, and his mind raced.

We need to tell them.

Augustine was about to agree when he noticed Dorian slumped against the wall, his head hanging to his chest.

The young sentinel scrambled to attention and blinked away the tears in his eyes. "Your majesty, what do you need from me?"

Augustine's rage lessened, if only slightly. "It's Your Highness, and you can return to the sentinels." They'd help him adjust after the loss of his team.

"If it's all the same to you, Rex insisted you were Your Majesty and I won't dishonor him. Also," Dorian paused and held his chin high, a glimmer of something Augustine would attribute to pride in his eyes. "I won't be returning to the sentinels. You are my commander and where you go, I go."

Great. Just what he needed, a damn puppy of a sentinel on top of everything else. Then again, he may need to have eyes in Scotland and the castle at the same time, and Dorian might be the answer to that problem.

"Fine. Keep up, and if you repeat a thing to anyone about what you see, I'll kill you myself."

Dorian nodded and followed silently behind him as he weaved through the castle. A plan was forming in Augustine's mind—one that would ideally keep all those he cared about safe, but he needed to act quickly if it was going to work.

Augustine shot a message telling Malcolm where to meet him and then another to Lily letting her know they would need a portal in fifteen minutes and to gather everyone, including the wolves.

The forest was quiet when Malcolm showed up carrying

Thea. She looked so small and frail in his brother's arms. She'd lost more weight and even though he didn't think it was possible, her eyes had recessed further. The queen kept pace with Malcolm, her gaze darting from the path to Thea every few seconds. She looked worse as well. Her skin was hollow against her cheeks and her hair was a rat's nest on top of her head.

Augustine balled his fists at his sides. He'd never seen his mother portray anything other than an image of perfection. She was the one who rallied them under the tyranny of his father and held them to a higher standard. The witches had reduced his mother to little more than skin and bones. He'd kill them for that, too.

"Were you followed?" Augustine's eyes scanned the forest, and he opened his senses to any thing that didn't belong.

Malcolm shook his head. "No. I don't think so. I took them out the hidden passageway by the stables."

"Good. Not that it matters entirely. The king knows about Emery and the baby. He's closing in on Scotland."

"Fuck." Malcolm sighed and shook his head. "Have you told Callum?"

"They're gathering everyone and I'll inform them when I get there. The king gave me his word he'd leave them alone for now and allow me to do whatever it takes to save Thea. As long as I cooperate and help him achieve his plans."

Malcolm's eyes narrowed, and Augustine braced for the lecture he was about to receive. "But that means marrying Jessi and being his lackey."

"If that's what it takes to keep my child safe then I'll do it." He'd do it a thousand times if it meant keeping his daughter safe and alive. If that was the only way to have his flesh and blood, his first born, then he would make it work.

"What about Emery?"

"What about her, Malcolm?" Augustine gritted out. "It doesn't matter that we're mates if the moment she steps foot out of the little bubble she's in, she's killed. As it is, I don't know how long the King will let her live. And that's assuming Callum's father doesn't come after them as well. Which is exactly what I'd do if I was our father, and I was looking for a loophole to the deal I'd just made. I am not king yet and until I am, I have to play by our father's rules or lose the only things that mean anything to me in this world."

Malcolm opened his mouth, but closed it again, apparently thinking better of whatever he was going to say.

Good. He was learning to pick his battles.

Augustine raked a hand through his hair as he debated if he wanted to divulge what he'd learned in Scotland to his brother. "There's one more thing I have to tell you."

"Why do I get the feeling I'm going to hate the next words to come out of your mouth?"

"Because you are." He winced. "The King had Flora kill Sloane on his orders. He compelled her to do it."

Malcolm's face twisted in agony, and he cast his gaze to the floor.

Augustine couldn't imagine what his brother was feeling. While Sloane had turned out to be a royal bitch and treated his brother like shit, it didn't change the fact that Malcolm had loved her with everything he had.

"Why?" Malcolm whispered, his voice hoarse.

"I don't know," Augustine said, beating himself up for letting his rage get the best of him in the war room. "I didn't get the chance to question him between finding out he knew about Emery and learning my entire team had been killed."

"Shit. I'm sorry, brother."

"Our father has ensured we get knocked down everytime

we try to stand on our own. He'll pay for what he's done. Not today, but I swear he won't get away with this."

"It's probably better you didn't let on that you know about his involvement in Sloane's death. Let him think he's two steps ahead."

Augustine nodded.

Behind him magic crackled and a portal opened. Emery stood on the other side, Lily at her shoulder. Both women gasped when they saw Thea, and Lily placed an arm on Emery's elbow to stop her from running toward them.

The bond in Augustine's chest tightened and dread coursed through him. He'd only just begun to come to terms with whatever the hell it was he felt for Emery, and even though he'd continued to deny it at every turn, the thought of losing her forever was something he could no longer fathom. She was his, and he'd realized it too late. He'd have to continue pushing her away to keep her and his child safe.

"Here, take her." Malcolm nudged Augustine's shoulder and gestured for him to take Thea.

Augustine's face contorted, his brow furrowing. "Aren't you coming with us?"

"No. I have a lead on Octavian. I'm heading to Romania to see if it's solid and then I'll circle back to Scotland."

"Lily will portal you, I'm sure."

Malcolm looked over his shoulder at his mate and lowered his voice so only Augustine could hear him. "She's not ready to see me. Not yet. I'll be there soon though."

Burned by Sloane and now by Lily. His brother was a damn saint for putting up with the Montgomery women. Augustine saw the heartache in Malcolm's eyes, but under it he also saw the fire when he spoke about Lily. Gods help that woman when Malcolm decided he was done playing her game.

Augustine wrapped his arms under Thea's small frame, and pulled her tight to his chest. Then he turned to his mother. "Let's go."

The Queen stepped forward and placed a kiss on Thea's forehead. "I'm not coming either."

"The hell you aren't!" His gaze met his mother's and he silently pleaded with her to not argue with him. "The king is on a rampage, I am not leaving you to be his punching bag. Step through the damn portal."

She placed her hand lovingly on his upper arm and gave it a squeeze. "I know how to handle your father. He'll leave me alone so long as he thinks I'm useful to him, which means remaining close to keep up appearances. Also, I can keep Jessi off your back so you can do the things you need to end this destructive campaign he's on."

Augustine gritted his teeth. This isn't how it was supposed to go. Nothing about his trip to the castle had gone according to plan.

"Augustine," the queen cupped her hand on his cheek. "You are doing an amazing job, my son, but you need to stop shutting everyone out and let them help you fight. You can't do it all, and wanting to has blinded you to the things that really matter." She patted his cheek and stepped back. "Take care of Thea. I'll keep researching here to see if I can find anything on the flower."

"She's going to survive this," Augustine declared, holding his mother's tired gaze.

Her lips tipped up into a weak smile. "I know. I love you."

"Love you too, Mom." Augustine nodded to Malcolm and magic tingled over his skin as he stepped through the portal with Thea.

Instantly, he was transported to a crisp evening in the Highlands. The chilled air carried Emery's scent, sweet and intoxicating. It hit him like a wave crashing on a rocky shore. His chest constricted and he wanted to pull her close, to give into the mate bond that was pressing on his chest, demanding he claim her.

With a pang, Augustine realized that this might be the last time he saw her without a wife in tow—a wife who wouldn't be her.

Emery raced to them and ran her head over Thea's hair. Her brow was wrinkled with worry. "Is she okay?"

"If you find the antidote, she will be." His words were harsh, but they had to be. He couldn't let her in this time. If he did, he wouldn't be able to turn his back on her again. And walking away was their best chance to keep her safe. "Is everyone gathered?"

Emery flinched at his cold tone and backed away from him. "Not yet," she replied, her eyes lowered. "Lily still needs to portal in Flora and Draven." She looked past him to where Malcolm stood on the other side of the portal. His eyes were trained on Lily. "Malcolm's not coming?"

"If you'd like that brother, too, you're going to have to get in line, he's spoken for."

Her lips turned up into a cute little sneer, and she scoffed at him.

Augustine bit back his smile and walked past her toward the cottage. The little witch shocked him at every turn, forcing him to want and feel things he'd promised he'd never allow himself to crave. He had no idea what came next for them, only that he must do everything in his power to protect her and his daughter.

And that meant keeping Emery and her decadent lips away from his heart. And everything else.

Chapter Twenty-Three

EMERY

Emery's heart was breaking. The sweet little girl with bouncy gold ringlets and a love of music lay on her death bed because of the unending vendetta between witches and vampires. Thea was an innocent kid. She was too good for a world where the pure became pawns and the villains played on a scale of gray. No one was safe from their motives. Not even a child.

Emery stared out into the Highlands sunset, mostly to distract herself from the darkness churning within her. The sun and clouds mocked her with their beauty. A storm would be much more befitting of the turmoil inside her.

They needed a win. Even a small one would fuel the hope she tried to maintain for the future of her child and the supernatural world. Her lesson with Lily had done the job, but the moment she'd seen Thea in Augustine's arms, that hope had faltered, and Lily's warning to stave off the dark was growing less effective by the minute. Especially when they had enemies on every front with more joining in the fight against them.

It didn't surprise her that the king wanted her and her daughter dead—that was to be expected. Terror filled her, though, when she considered how close he was to finding them. He knew they were in Scotland and even though he'd agreed to stop looking in exchange for Augustine's cooperation, she didn't believe the king would stand by his word.

Also, she hated the idea of Augustine doing anything his prick of a father suggested. The King was a vile creature who only cared about his own vendetta. And though Emery would love nothing more than to portal herself to the castle and shove a stake through his heart herself, when she'd suggested it aloud, she was met with dagger-like glares from Augustine and a bullshit diplomatic response from Callum.

"Emery, are you paying attention?"

Her head snapped up toward Lily, who stood with her hands on her hips at the nightstand beside Thea. "Huh?"

Behind Lily, Augustine leaned against the wall, his head tilted to the side as he eyed her with a curious stare.

She glared at him, and sent a stab of hatred down the bond, knowing it would only hit the barrier he'd erected, but he'd still feel its intent.

His jaw tightened and a growl of warning filled the room.

She almost stuck her tongue out at him, but settled for ignoring his display of dominance.

He made it clear where they stood when he'd left for the castle, and even though his words conveyed every bit of hatred, his actions spoke differently. If he really didn't care, there wouldn't have been fear in his eyes when she woke from her vision, nor would he have given her his blood to help her feel better when her energy was depleted. Still, there was a lot of room between don't-want-you-to-die and I'm-your-forever-mate, and Emery had no idea where he fell on that spectrum. He was a damn enigma of twisted actions.

She ran her tongue over her teeth as she remembered his

blood on her lips. She shouldn't want to taste him again, but she did. Every bit of him was a reckless temptation to her, but his blood was an itch she almost couldn't deny scratching. It fed the darkness within her and invigorated her in ways she didn't think possible through magic she didn't understand. Maybe it was the inherent magic that kept him alive, or maybe it was the simple fact they were mates. All she knew was his blood connected her to him and everything in her wanted more of it, despite knowing it was a terrible fucking idea.

Because at the end of the day it didn't matter.

She was just the little witch bitch to him and he was willing to throw away whatever he felt without a second thought. What was worse was she understood why he'd agreed to his father's terms. She'd have done the same thing if he was any other man and it meant keeping their daughter safe.

But she was his mate. The love of her fucking life as dictated by the stars. Stars she didn't even want to worship or believe in, but because of who and what she was, she'd been thrust into their purview and forced to do their bidding. Free will played a part, but fate always seemed to win. Basically, every living being was meant to bend over and take whatever the stars handed them, and there wasn't a damn thing anyone could do about it.

Still, even if they were nothing more than star-crossed lovers, Augustine owed her a conversation if he was planning to actually marry her fucking nemesis.

Lily picked up a notebook from the nightstand and studied the words, ignoring the silent showdown between her and Augustine. "I've narrowed it down to two possible types, and one is more likely than the other. The Enchanted Amaryllis flower has healing properties but also a magic of its own. It's a living thing just as any other, but it is said to have been the home of nymphs before they fled the mortal world back to the land of the fae. Its magic is rumored to negate other forms of magic, thereby protecting the nymphs from those who sought to attack them. It hasn't been seen in centuries, but I think we might benefit from looking near the cottage. "

"You think there's a chance it's close? Why can't we go to where it was last seen?" Augustine pushed off the wall and looked over Lily's shoulder at the text. "You can portal us there."

Lily shook her head. "I can't do that. I can only portal safely to somewhere I've been before. If I haven't seen the place in person, there's a chance you won't make it through to the other side."

Augustine shifted his stance away from Lily and ran a hand through his tousled hair. "For Thea, I'm willing to take that risk."

"Of course you are," Emery grumbled under her breath. He could take all the risks and make all the life-changing decisions on a whim.

Augustine's turbulent eyes trained on her and she raised a brow, uncaring that he heard her. Served the asshole right.

He kept his face passive, and his eyes glued to her. "What makes you think we should look near the cottage?"

Emery made a show of rolling her eyes and focused her attention on Lily.

A low growl filled the room and Emery had to press her lips together to hold back the satisfied laugh that bubbled in her chest. That was three eyerolls. She was really racking them up nicely.

Lily's eyes narrowed on Augustine with a look that could kill, and it almost pushed Emery into uncontrollable laughter. She closed the book and leaned in to check Thea's temperature with the back of her hand. "If it was seen in Emery's vision, the odds of us finding it close by are high. I don't believe the stars would send us on a wild goose chase. Still, we need to ensure the vision comes true—free will is still a major part of our destiny. Which means searching high and low where we can."

Lily might be more experienced in studying magic, but Emery wasn't convinced the stars wouldn't fuck them over just as quickly as they guided them. As it was, they had a sick sense of humor given all that had happened so far. "So we're all going for an after-dinner stroll through the woods?"

"Aye."

Emery opened her mouth to argue but then closed it again. She was exhausted and as much as she didn't want to spend the evening traversing the woods, she'd do it for Thea. She could only hope Augustine would be gone by then.

Her brow furrowed and then Lily turned back to the book and wrote something down. "Good, now that's settled, I need to work out a few more components, and the tension between you two is unbearable. Emery, why don't you go help Callum prepare dinner and let the others know the plan, and Augustine, stick around for a few minutes, I have something I need to run by you. "

The tone of Lily's voice reminded her of a teacher ordering a student to the principal's office. Emery snorted, picturing Augustine with his hands held out and Lily swatting them with a cane. He turned his signature stick-up-his-ass glare on her, and she stifled her laugh and shrugged. "What? I'm just amazed that Callum cooks more than just breakfast and cookies."

The heat in his gaze grew exponentially, and Emery knew he'd tasted her lie.

Lily didn't look up from her work, but chuckled. "Aye, he might as well be a world renowned chef with how good his meals have been. I've preferred to let him cook in my time with him. Now go."

Emery ignored the promise of retribution behind Augustine's death stare, a vow they would have words before he left. She would rather forgo his attempts to put her in her place. He believed he was her savior, but once again, her needs and wants had gotten lost in translation.

When she entered the kitchen, Callum was standing at the island prepping the meat in a chef's apron. He had already put Flora to work chopping veggies. Ansel, Draven, and Dorian were at the table pouring over a map of the area, likely discussing the security of the cottage. Lily assured them she'd been able to use illusions to hide the cottage behind the wards, but the men were on edge with the King closing in.

After she relayed Lily's message, Callum assigned her the menial task of peeling potatoes and Emery fell into a rhythm beside her best friend. The mind-numbing work allowed herself to focus on anything other than Augustine or the situation at hand.

"How are you doing?" Flora whispered, breaking the silence between them.

Emery gave a halfhearted chuckle. "If I told you I was fine, would you believe me?"

Flora paused and waited for Emery to look up at her. When she did, her best friend arched a brow. "Not a chance in hell."

Her lips tipped up into a half smile, and Emery leaned in and bumped Flora's shoulder. "I've missed you."

"I missed you too. I'm sorry I didn't find you sooner. After Chelsea…" Flora didn't need to say that their best friend's death had broken her. Emery felt every bit of the same ache in her heart, and it was only magnified by the fact she still didn't know what really happened to their friend. Only that she was the primary suspect. Flora shook her head. "I'd already been assigned to Callum's court, and I wasn't allowed to see you."

"I didn't kill her."

Flora nodded and gave Emery a reassuring smile. "I know. You loved her like I did. We were the sisters none of us had."

Except Emery did have a sister. One who was killed by Flora's hand at the order of the king. She didn't blame Flora. The king was solely responsible for Sloane's death. But the sting of all those lost deepened with each passing day. It also left Emery questioning the King's endgame. He knew about her daughter. He knew Emery was alive and in Scotland. It was only a matter of time until she had to face the reality that she couldn't hide forever. There was a very good chance that she might be the next one being mourned.

"Do you know who killed her?" Flora's voice echoed the question Emery had asked herself a million times.

She shook her head, wishing she had a better answer. "No. It's among the things on my 'What The Fuck Happened?' list."

"Things really have changed since we last saw each other," Flora admitted, her voice trailing off. Emery watched as her friend replayed events in her mind.

It was true. Everything had changed since they were last together at the ball. She'd been happily in love with August, and Flora and Chelsea were going to be living their best lives as vampires by her side.

Then everything went sideways.

"That's an understatement." Emery stopped peeling and looked down at her rounded stomach. "I'm pregnant, and you're a wolf and a vampire. No one, not even the stars, could have predicted we'd be here."

Flora stopped chopping and raised a brow. "You going to tell me how that all went down?"

Callum snorted behind them. "Well Flora, when a man and a woman love each other..."

"Mind your own business, Callum," Flora waved the knife in her hand toward where Callum stood at the stove. "You're just as much to blame for this. I hear you're the one who pushed them together."

"I regret nothing," Callum called over his shoulder. With a flourish, he pinched some salt from the well and added it to the stew he was stirring. "But if you're going to blame me, next time at least let me participate. I'll gladly take responsibility for the next baby. I might even teach you a few new things you could do with Augustine."

Emery laughed despite herself, and threw a dish towel at his head.

Callum caught it one-handed and continued to stir as if she hadn't interrupted him. "Also, if you two are going to keep chatting, you need to remember you are in a house full of wolves and vampires. No conversation is sacred with our ears."

"Nothing is sacred in general with you nosey parkers around," Emery mumbled under her breath. Callum still hadn't let her forget that he'd heard every gut-wrenching moan from the night she had spent with August.

"You love us," Ansel chimed in from the table, before returning to a clearly engrossing conversation with Dorian.

Draven listened in with an aloof expression, but Emery hadn't missed the way he watched Flora. He exhibited the same kind of protective nature as Augustine, which meant he was absolutely listening to every word they said.

Possessive asshole men.

She looked at Flora and sighed. "Here's the short version. I got knocked up, August found out I was a witch and split his personality and became Augustine ninety-percent of the time.

Augustine wants his daughter, but also wants me dead… at least, that was the plan until a few hours ago. It seems as if he's maybe changed his mind on that, but also he has a stick shoved so far up his ass he can't see reason. So we're at a bit of an impasse."

Flora's mouth dropped open, but it only took a second before it widened into a full smile. "It's a girl?"

Her smile was contagious. Emery's lips formed one of her own, and she nodded.

"I am so excited for you, Em." Flora turned back and began chopping the last of her carrots. "Do you have any names picked out?"

"Not yet." She'd considered a few, but none of them felt right. She was perfectly fine with calling the baby her little urchin until she was born. "I sort of wanted August to be a part of the process, but seeing as he's not around at the moment, I'll hold off on any decisions."

"Do you think he'll come back?"

Emery nibbled on her bottom lip. Did she think he would come back? The answer was complicated. Emery needed August to come back, but she also needed Augustine. They were two sides of the same fucked-up coin and she needed them both. Although as it stood, she was about to lose them both to the King's ultimatum. She swallowed hard past the lump in her throat, and gave an answer that protected her heart. "I hope he becomes what he's meant to be."

"Aye lass, he will," Callum reassured her. He took the cutting boards that held the potatoes and carrots and tossed them into the pot.

Flora nodded and wrapped an arm around Emery. "We'll do whatever we can to help."

"Thank you." She blinked back the tears that threatened to fall.

The chairs and tables creaked in the dining room. Flora and Emery looked over to see Dorian, Ansel, and Draven headed for the door.

"Where the hell are you lads going?" Callum boomed from the stove. "Dinner's almost done."

The three looked like deer caught in the headlights, but it was Draven who spoke up, his southern accent making him sound almost innocent. "Dorian seems to think he could best a wolf in a fight. Challenged Ansel here to a sparring match, and I'm not going to miss this ass kicking."

"Did he now?" Callum turned to where Flora and Emery stood. "Can you lasses keep an eye on the stew? Only needs to be stirred every five minutes or so."

"Absolutely." "Yeah." Emery and Flora answered at the same time.

A mischievous grin grew on Callum's face as he took off his apron and headed for the door. "In that case, fifty bucks says Dorian takes Ansel down."

Draven threw his head back and laughed. "Oh you're on, brother."

"Brother?" Emery turned to Flora. "Did I miss something?"

Draven waited for Callum at the door before flashing a fang filled smile at Flora. "Be good, Bubbles."

"Bubbles?" Emery snorted and raised a brow at Flora.

"Don't ask." Flora rolled her eyes at the nickname and waited until the men were outside. "And to answer your previous question, Draven is Callum's half brother. It's how he's both a vampire and a wolf."

Emery's mouth dropped open, and she was at a loss for words.

"I know," Flora laughed. "I was shocked too. But it makes

sense. Somehow Callum has his hand in everything, why should that be any different?"

"Right?" Emery tilted her head to the side as her hands found her hips. For the first time in a long time she felt like herself. Gossiping with her best friend about life is exactly what she needed. "He is literally the most shady person I know. And yet I can't help but kinda like the guy."

"I know," Flora scoffed. "It's an annoyingly accurate description of how I think we all feel about him. He's a parasite you kinda start to love despite the fact he'd kill you if it served him."

"So Draven is Callum's half brother. I'm assuming there's a story there?"

"There is, but it's not mine to tell. And I'm not sure Draven is ready for everyone to know the details yet."

"I can respect that. So, on to the next question of about a million that I'm dying to ask." Emery moved toward the stove and lifted the lid from the stew to give it a stir. A fragrant steam rose to greet her, and her mouth started watering instantly. "You were sired by Draven and you're his mate. You literally drink blood now. How is that?"

Heat filled Flora's cheeks as she nodded, but her eyes were filled with uncertainty.

"The blood isn't so bad. I don't need it as often as most vampires since I am also half wolf. That's a trip. My first shift was a shit show, but now I feel more grounded in myself than I ever have. Like I somehow always knew I'd need my wolf, but didn't realize exactly what I was missing. And Draven... He's something. I absolutely love him despite his brutish, controlling perfectionist nature, but it's still complicated."

"Amen, sister." It was almost exactly how she felt about August and Augustine. Hell, they were the same person to her now; she just wasn't sure what to call them. Somehow she didn't think Asshole Vampire was something he'd accept. "How did we both end up with such complicated love lives in the span of a few months?"

"Speak for yourself," Flora laughed and opened the fridge, pulling out a bag of blood. "My love life has been both complicated and non-existent my whole life. Now that I actually have one, it's both amazing and terrifying."

"How so?" Emery reached up and grabbed a glass from the cupboard and placed it on the island.

Flora sighed and poured the blood into the glass. Instead of sipping it, she fingered the white pendant at her throat. "I didn't ask for this life. I never wanted to be a queen. A mate. I knew I'd never be chosen by August, so all I had to do was avoid getting sent home. Which I did. I was a member of Callum's court for all of twenty-four hours. Then he sent me to the wolves. One reckless adventure later, I fell right into the arms of Draven and the pack snagged my heart right along with him."

"The whole mate thing is sort of crazy, isn't it?"

"Right? Like how is it possible to be so drawn to someone and still want to run the opposite direction screaming? Draven infuriates me most days, but one heated look from his stupid big green eyes, and I'm a fucking puddle."

"You love him, don't you?" Emery knew the answer before she asked. She could see it in the way Flora's face lit up when she talked about Draven. The way they were aware of each other's every move, even from across the room. They were what mates were supposed to look like.

She was happy for Flora, but Emery's heart ached when she realized it was something she may never have.

"Irrevocably. And I hate that I do. This was never the plan. I can't be the mate to the future alpha of the pack. I'm a girl from podunk nowhere Canada who grew up in a vampire's castle and hadn't even flown on a plane before two months ago. Not to mention the plethora of shit we faced hunting down the moonstone. If you'd told me this would be my life, I'd laugh you right out of town. And that's saying something, considering I've known about the supernatural world since I was four. I'm not queen material, which is essentially what the mate to the alpha is." Flora moved across the kitchen, pacing the length of the island, her hands knotted in front of her. "I'd come to terms with the fact I wasn't made to be royal. I was okay being a member of Callum's court, but now I'm mated to Draven and basically a princess. I love the pack, they are mine as much as you are, but I don't know if I can do this."

"Take a breath, *Chelsea*," Emery teased, remembering the way their friend often rambled seemingly without breathing. She placed a hand on Flora's shoulder and pulled her into a hug.

Flora hiccuped a sob against her. "I love him, though. I just… I don't know if that's enough."

"It will be." Emery pushed her back and took Flora's hands in hers. "I knew from the moment we met, and you pointed that damn dagger at me and declared you'd protect Malcolm and August that you had a fire in you. You're my best friend. You listen with unwavering patience and call me on my shit when I don't want to deal with it. Callum told me it was you who restored the moonstone. I imagine that's no small feat. I have no doubts you're going to make an amazing wolf queen. And if they can't see that, well… fuck them. You can come be a member of my court."

Flora smiled and wiped away a stray tear. "Are you saying you'll have a court for me to be a part of?"

Emery chewed her lip. Is that what she was saying? The words had just slipped out. At one point, she'd assumed she and August would end up together, but more and more she wasn't sure they'd ever get that opportunity.

She inhaled deep and for the first time spoke words from the heart instead of what would have been the answer everyone wanted to hear. "I don't know that it will be August's court. I love him. He's my mate. Even Augustine too, impossible as he is. He's still a part of the bond, and I don't know that I could survive without them. But I'm not sure there's anything left for us anymore. Not if he goes through with marrying Jessi." Emery blinked away fresh tears caused by the pain in her chest as the mate bond protested her words. "But I'll have my own court. A court in which my daughter and all hybrids will be welcome, celebrated even. A sanctuary for the supernatural community. No matter what happens, I'm a royal witch, and I'll protect what's mine."

"Wow." Flora's eyes widened. "That's incredible, Emery. What does August think about that?"

"He'll protect what's his." Augustine's signature gravely voice filled the kitchen.

Flora and Emery's heads snapped to where Augustine stood at the base of the stairs, his arms crossed at his chest. Heat filled Emery's cheeks as his gaze locked on her, stormy seas that gave away nothing, leaving her to wonder what he'd heard.

Damnit. She should have known better. Callum warned her the house wasn't a safe space to talk openly.

Augustine strode toward the back door, his eyes never leaving Emery's. "I'm going to check the perimeter. Tell Lily I'll be back when she's ready to portal me."

"But dinner's almost done." Flora's statement was meant to be sweet but Augustine's eyes darkened, and his lip curled into a sneer.

"You aren't serving anything I want." He stepped through

and the door frame shook as he slammed the door behind him.

"Damn." Flora whistled a falling note. "You weren't kidding when you said you broke him."

Emery stared at the door, torn between going after him and demanding an honest conversation and asking Lily to ward him out of the house completely. "It doesn't matter what happens between us. As long as he protects our daughter, I'll survive."

"That's no way to live. He's your mate. I don't know what that means for vampires and witches, but for wolves it's not something you can walk away from. I couldn't imagine Draven hating me."

"You're right," Emery said softly, her eyes trained on the door Augustine had just slammed. "It's no way to live."

Chapter Twenty Four

EMERY

She was either brilliant or a damn idiot, but with fists clenched at her side and her spine steeled, Emery darted out the back door after Augustine.

He stood in the clearing before the woods with his head tilted back, staring up at the starry sky. Emery matched his stance, only instead of standing idly, she gave each of the constellations above a big middle finger. She didn't understand their need to fuck everything up so royally for them.

When her gaze fell back to Augustine, he hadn't moved. To anyone else, he might seem like a normal man admiring a beautiful night, but Emery knew better. His shoulders were tense, carrying the weight of the world. At least by Augustine's standards. If only the damn fool would let her in, he'd see she was damn capable of sharing the load.

"Hey," she snapped, keeping a steady stride toward him. "You don't get to just walk out on us. On me."

Augustine closed his eyes and released a sigh. "Don't, Emery." It came out as a plea, the anger that had been in his voice inside now laced with desperation.

"What, Augustine? You can dish out orders but you can't take them?"

His hands balled into fists, and he turned his gaze, which was as dark as the sky above, to meet hers. "Tonight is not the night, little witch."

Emery stopped short of where he stood, hands on her hips and fury on her tongue. "Give me one good reason why not. Because I didn't think tonight would be the night I find out my mate would rather marry the wicked bitch of the castle than fight for what's right, yet here we are."

A manic laugh bubbled in from him, a clear attempt to hide the fracture in his always stoic facade. "You mean fight for you. *That's* what you want. You want me to fight for you, to come crawling to you on my knees and beg for you to allow me into your life and between those perfect legs of yours, and it's not something I'm going to do. I'm going to protect what's mine by any means necessary. And before you deny it, yes little witch, you are mine. So if that means I have to take a bride who's not my mate, you bet your sweet ass I'm going to. But that's not why you need to turn around and march back into that house. No, you need to go because I'm on the edge and the darkness won't care that you scream no. Any other night I'd fight with you 'til daybreak, but I'm barely keeping the monster at bay and with you standing there, your blood smelling so fucking sweet... I don't know if I can hold on. You want to see the monster? Keep pushing me."

Her eyes narrowed, trying to see through the cracks in his words, and her heart raced. Did she want to see the monster? The tingle down her spine said yes, even if her brain warned against it.

"What really happened at the castle?" she pushed.

"I told you," he tisked like it was no big deal. "The king gave me an ultimatum and I took it."

She didn't need to be a vampire to know his words dripped with lies. "Now give me the truth."

"You want the truth?" Augustine stepped toward her, and his glare pinned her in place. "My men are dead because I was too busy saving your damn life. And after that blow to the chest was delivered, the king..." he hesitated, his eyes finding the ground and his jaw tense. When he spoke again his voice was low, but held so much anger that Emery nearly lost her nerve. "I lost control and attacked him. Not because he's on the verge of attempting an all-out massacre of the supernatural community. No. I held a knife to his throat with every intention of ending his life because he was threatening my mate and daughter. It fueled my darkest rage, begging me to take his life. And I wanted to. Fucking hell I wanted to, Emery." He took another step toward her, every muscle on him tense. "And now you're here, pushing me, for gods knows what reason, probably some noble attempt to goad me into slipping and admitting how much you affect me. But I'm a fucking monster and this won't end well for you, little witch. Just being near you is too much. Your delicious form taunting me, making my cock hard with need, while the bond reminds me every moment of every day just how perfect you are for me. You're the light to my darkness and every fiber of me wants to cling to you. You, standing there, in all your glory with a pulse that beats in time with mine with blood that calms the storm within me. The blood of my enemy. So excuse the bloody hell out of me if I need a moment that isn't plagued with your suffocating presence."

Emery's lips parted, and his gaze zeroed in on them, causing her to press them shut. She didn't know what to say. Where to start. So she took a page out of Augustine's book when the words were harder to speak than the actions their body demanded.

She took a step forward, her eyes firmly on his chest so she wouldn't lose her nerve, or see how he still looked at her like his enemy. She couldn't bear to see him look at her like that, not after everything he just said. When she stood chest-to-chest with him, Emery went up on her tiptoes and slowly, steeling each vertebrae as she did, lifted her chin so her eyes met his midnight depths.

Augustine sucked in a breath, and his lips brushed hers as he did, sending a flood of electricity through her.

Gotcha.

That was it, that one simple touch was all it took to push him over the edge.

He crushed his lips against hers, and his tongue swept against them, demanding entrance. He kissed her like he was starved, with the knowledge that one bite could ruin him. But Augustine didn't give a damn and neither did she. His hands gripped her shoulders, and he stepped toward her, pushing her back while his lips devoured her.

Emery's magic flared within her. Her wind danced around them, pushing them together. They went to war against each other, a tangle of limbs, clawing at one another, demanding dominance, though neither would submit.

Her back hit the rough bark of one of the pine trees that lined the forest with a hard thump and Augustine's hand moved to encase her jaw, angling it where he wanted so he could demand more. His fangs elongated against her lips, and Emery traced each point with her tongue, earning her a panty dropping growl from deep within his chest.

She smiled against him, but her victory was short-lived as Augustine pulled her lip between the very fangs she'd teased and bit down. His chest heaved against hers, their hearts racing in time.

When he pulled away, it wasn't the blood on his lips that

drew her eyes, but the way he ran his tongue over every inch in a desperate attempt to ensure every bit of her life force was consumed.

"You said my blood calms you," she whispered through her pants.

"Yes." Augustine winced as if the word physically hurt him to admit. He closed his eyes, the tick in his jaw pulsing, and Emery didn't hate the way his admission made her feel. "Your blood not only sates my blood lust, but calms the storm that rages inside me. One of the fantastic side effects of our mate bond I suspect."

"Then use me."

The words slipped from her mouth without a second thought ,and she wasn't sure if it was the heat of the moment or her own desire to reclaim the mate she'd lost, but there was a confidence in her words she felt to her core.

"What?" he whispered, stepping back. She missed him instantly, the heat of his body replaced by the cool summer night air. His eyes widened, and his Adam's apple bobbed hard as he swallowed.

"When was the last time you fed?" His jaw tightened like he was ready to argue, but Emery wasn't about to allow it. Her hands found her hips and she pressed. "Answer me."

"It's not your concern." He tipped his head back to look toward the sky, and she suspected he was trying to find a way to reconstruct the walls she'd broken through with her kiss.

"Isn't it? You're my mate. I don't want you to suffer, even if I do loathe your narcissistic ass most days."

His eyes whipped to hers, and a possessive smile tugged at his lips like a cat who'd caught his prey. "The dripping arousal between your legs says otherwise."

Heat filled her cheeks, and Emery started to roll her eyes,

but stopped herself remembering how much he hated it when she did.

If he realized what she'd been about to do he didn't say, but instead openly ran his tongue over his elongated fangs.

Emery sucked in her bottom lip and reached up to pull her hair from her neck, not missing the way Augustine's eyes zeroed on her beating pulse. "Use me. Take what you need."

An animalistic snarl tore from him and the glimpse of his darkness shot a pang of longing through her. This was as much for her as it was for him. She needed the connection to him as much as he did her.

"I can't." His words were barely a whisper.

"Can't or won't?" She knew the answer, but she wanted to hear him say it. He was the one denying them what they both wanted, not her. She knew they were bound to go round and round on the fucked-up carousel of their mate bond, but she was willing to make the sacrifice.

A sensuous warning that made heat instantly pool in her belly fell from his lips. "You don't know what you're offering me. If I give into this now, if you give me what I crave so fucking bad it hurts, it will be only you I seek. Up until now, it's been August who has fed from you. But I am not him, little witch."

"No you're not. As you've said, you're a monster. But if you could pull your head out of your ass for five minutes, you'd see you're *my* monster. We're shackled together whether we like it or not." Emery reached out and tangled her hand in the front of his shirt and pulled him toward her.

He took a reluctant step toward her, trapping her between his legs. She pulled him down so her cheek pressed against his and whispered in his ear, echoing the words that she'd told August at the ball. "Bite me. Only me."

Time crawled, and her words hung between them, a desperate plea and a daring proclamation.

Emery let him go and stepped away, though she kept her eyes trained on him. The indecision in his eyes stung, but everything in her knew they were supposed to do this. She was supposed to be his light, as he was her dark. Not because the stars said so, but because they were two halves of a whole. Just as the day met the night, starting and ending with spectacular arrays painted across the sky, they were meant to bleed together and be the spark of something incredible.

She just didn't know how to make him see that.

Augustine's mouth hitched upward, and he closed the distance between them, pressing his chest against hers.

She took another step back, unsure if his smile was one of malice or mischief, and he closed the distance again, the tree's bark digging further into her back.

He leaned in and pressed his nose to her hair, inhaling her scent before trailing his breath down the side of her face. When it tickled the curve of her ear, she inhaled sharply and a soft growl vibrated through her. "When I bite you, there's no turning back, little witch. You will be mine. This isn't temporary. My body will crave you and I will hunt you till the bloody fucking ends of the earth to satisfy that craving."

"And you'll be mine." Her hands gripped his hips and she pulled him so his arousal ground into her core, the bark of the tree biting into her back.

"That's not how this works," he breathed, trailing his lips and nipping at the lobe of her ear.

"For now," she whispered. Her magic was coiled too tight and her needs too great to back down now, but the argument wasn't over. Not by a long shot. It wouldn't be until he came to terms with what the hell they were to one another.

"Emery, I'm serious."

The use of her given name instead of his beloved little witch gave her pause, but only for a moment. She knew the gravity of the situation, and she was all in. Even if Augustine wasn't yet. She could be certain for the both of them. It would likely break her when he walked away, but he'd come back. He'd always come back and that was something she could work with.

"It almost sounds like you care about how I feel, Augustine. Are you sure August hasn't rubbed off on you?" Emery taunted as she tilted her head to the side, exposing the length of her neck to him. "Do it."

She half expected him to continue arguing with her, but this time, Augustine didn't hesitate. His mouth pressed to the curve of her neck and his fangs pierced her skin. A shiver racked through her, pebbling her nipples against his chest and landing straight in her clit. A breathy moan fell from her lips and she arched her back with need.

It shouldn't have been a downright sexual experience, but every inch of Emery felt as though she would burn from the inside out. It wasn't like the heat of her magical fire, fueled by her rage. No, this fire was a pure aching hunger, a want that thrummed with the pulse of her veins, refusing to be ignored.

This man. This vampire. Her mate.

He would be the death of her and she would welcome it with open arms if it meant she could keep him for her own.

That was her last coherent thought before his venom flooded her system, and Emery fell into the depth of their shared desires.

Chapter Twenty Five

AUGUSTINE

Emery moaned.

She fucking moaned, and it was the most beautiful sound he'd ever heard.

His hands snaked inside her sweater, seeking to claim every inch of her soft flesh.

He planned his intent to be something innocent. Something platonic, something to draw the line between them as nothing more than a means to an end, but being so close to her, he should've known his body would allow nothing less than what the bond between them demanded. Lust surrounded them and it took everything inside him to keep from running his hands lower to the sweet arousal between her legs.

This was supposed to be a simple feeding, but nothing was simple with Emery. With each pull of her life force, her body writhed against him, and his responded in kind. A seductive dance of their bodies used to convey the words neither would dare to speak.

Words *he* wouldn't speak.

But with every pull of her blood, every touch of her body, Augustine's rage simmered, and his concern for the rest of the world melted away. There was only Emery. Only this magnetic force between them. This was a mistake, but it was a mistake he'd make over and over again in order to feel nothing and everything in the same moment.

"Augustine." The breathy way his name fell like a plea from her lips was nearly his undoing. She reached her hand up and tangled it in his hair, pulling him tighter against her neck.

His head spun with satisfaction. Her blood and her body were his, if only for this brief moment. It should be enough, but it wasn't. A taste would never be enough when it came to Emery. The bond ensured she was the air he breathed and his venom fueled every wicked desire. She was rooted in the core of his soul and the deep seated fire within him needed more. He needed her. All of her.

Augustine pulled his fangs from her taut flesh, but didn't bother to lick the wounds closed. Not yet. He pressed his arms into the tree on either side of her head and whispered against her tousled hair. "What do you want, little witch?"

He needed her to say it. For her to be the one to initiate what he so badly wanted to give.

"You. I want you, Augustine." Emery's gaze locked with his, and he savored every bit of truth in her words. Her tongue darted out and wet her lips, and in that moment Augustine would give her anything she wanted. "Take me over the edge. I don't want to feel anything but this."

Anything but you, the bond seemed to whisper the sentiment she left hanging between them.

He was only too willing to comply. He dropped his hands from the tree and traced them down the curves of her soft form. "You are fucking perfect," he growled.

When he reached the hem of her shorts, he traced it with his knuckle before using a flick of his fingers to unfasten them.

He turned her around so she was facing the tree and laced her fingers in his, lifting them to rest on the bark above her head. "Don't move them from this spot."

"And if I do?" She purred her obstinance.

"Your punishment grows," he growled, nipping her shoulder. "You still owe me for those eye rolls."

Augustine didn't miss the way she shuddered at his promise.

His hands gripped her hips, and he dug his fingers under the waistband of her shorts, gently pulling them down. He lived for the quiet thud they made when they hit the ground at her feet.

A gasp fell from his lips when Emery arched her back and pressed her bare ass against the hardened cock trapped in his jeans. "No panties," he mused, "you really are a dirty little witch."

"I didn't want panty lines," she shrugged, but he could hear the wicked grin in her words.

He splayed his fingers over the rounded globe and gave it a squeeze. She wiggled against him, and a moment later he reared his hand and gave her supple flesh a hard smack. "Or you wanted to tease me with this perfect ass of yours."

Emery jumped, but he didn't miss the soft moan that accompanied it. "I guess you'll never know."

"Oh, sweet girl," He rubbed the heated flesh of her ass, loving the soft pink mark she wore. "I'll always know. If your intentions aren't plainly written on your face, then the bond we share, the one you refuse to close, lets me know every wicked thought that crosses your mind."

"And yet, this is the first time you've touched me because you wanted to and not out of obligation to your fucked up moral code." Her voice was playful, but the subtle dejection radiating through their bond pierced him..

"My venom has a mind of its own when it comes to you, and my dick has been hard since before I took your neck. How do I know it isn't you who's enchanted me the way you did August in the garden?"

Emery snorted, and Augustine could almost hear her roll her eyes. "It would've been hard anyway. You want this as much as I do."

He gave her ass another hard smack.

"Ouch." She jumped and whipped her head around. "What the hell was that for?"

"You rolled your eyes at me...again." He shrugged, uncaring that she was angry at him. He'd love every moment of demanding her respect. "You know how I feel about that."

"How could you possibly have seen that?" she scoffed, although the way heat filled her cheeks and arousal dripped from her pussy, he'd bet his little witch liked a bit of pain with her pleasure. He could work with that.

Augustine worked his hands over the rounded flesh of her ass, kneading the fiery flesh. Emery fell silent as he trailed them over the flare of her hips. Her body molded to his as he traced the swell of her belly. The evidence that she was his, that they'd shared something so pure once.

"I'll only ask you once more, what exactly do you want, little witch?"

"I want you." Her breathless reply radiated through him... straight to his dick. He'd never tire of hearing those three words fall from her lips.

A soft moan escaped her as Augustine dug his fingers into her hips, dancing along the edges of where he'd marked her. "Be specific."

"Fine," she huffed, an air of annoyance in her voice. But she couldn't fool him. She dripped for him and loved when he gave her an excuse to use her smart mouth. Coming into her own had allowed her to embrace the darker side of herself, and she was just as filthy as he was. "I want your darkness. I want to feel you stretch me as only you can. I want you to drive your cock into me until I forget the world around me. I want to take you over the edge with me and fall into the place where it's only you and me."

Fuck, she was incredible.

In one quick motion he tore open his jeans and freed his cock. He gripped it at the base and notched the tip at her entrance.

Bloody hell.

He sucked on his bottom lip, stifling the moan that threatened to escape when he found her drenched and ready for him. All his carefully laid plans went out the window.

Augustine leaned forward and whispered against her ear. "You are mine, little witch. This dripping, tight cunt belongs to me."

"Yes. Now fucking move," she growled, and her body trembled against him, pushing him past the brink of need.

Augustine didn't hesitate, thrusting up, impaling her until her ass met the base of his shaft.

Her tight channel clamped down hungrily on his cock, and she chanted his name. Augustine pulled her against him and took a step back, bending her over so only her hands remained on the tree and she was forced to take him deeper.

Emery met his pistoning cock with enthusiasm. Using the tree as leverage, she rocked her hips, taking everything he had to give and demanding more.

She was Heaven and Hell. She was his calm and he was her fire. Two pieces that were always meant to be one.

Her moans grew louder, as she took her pleasure, and he wished she could see how sexy she looked as she met his thrusts with her greedy pussy. She was bloody magnificent.

"Play with yourself, little witch." Augustine instructed. "Take what's yours."

One of her hands dropped from the tree and reached between her legs. He knew the moment Emery traced her clit because she clenched around his cock like a damn vise.

"That's it. Take what you need. Bring yourself to the edge, but don't you dare come. You come with me. Only me."

The moment he said the words he wished he could take them back, but she felt so damn good. So bloody fucking right he couldn't fathom anything else. He could blame the venom. Could even blame the mate bond. But once again he'd only be fooling himself. She was the drug he never should've tasted, but now that he had, every second his cock wasn't buried balls-deep in her pained him.

"I'm close." Emery spoke between deep pants. "I'm so fucking close, Augustine."

The bond tightened in his chest, he was close too, and he wanted nothing more than to follow her into oblivion, but he also wanted to push her. To sear his body into her memory so completely that even after he left she'd never come and not think of him.

"Not yet, little witch," he ground out. "You come when I say you come, with only my name on your lips."

"Please, Augustine." His name was like a prayer, filled with reverence and a hint of despair.

He rocked his hips, picking up his pace as he chased his own climax. His balls tightened and though he shouldn't give any more of himself to the little minx, he wanted to. He needed to be on her lips, in her veins, filling her with the darkness she craved. He bit his wrist and in one swift motion pulled her up so her back was against his chest. He slipped his free hand into her camisole and twisted her nipple between his thumb and forefinger.

When Emery cried out, he pressed his wrist to her lips, stifling the sound as he pushed her over the edge. Her channel tightened around him and he bit into the fleshy part of her neck. The sound that left her throat and vibrated around his wrist was every bit the chorus of pleasure he needed to snap the last bit of control he possessed.

His legs shook, and Augustine held her close as he spilled his seed into her, cresting with her into the waves of pleasure that coursed through them both.

The magic of the bond swelled, and he opened his end, taking every bit of radiance Emery felt and releasing his own darkness. She quivered against him, sucking at his wrist as if it was the only thing keeping her alive.

Augustine groaned against her skin, savoring each moan-filled breath and searing the picture of the way she fit perfectly against him into his memory. She was his, and at the same time she wasn't. He didn't know that there was a world in which they'd ever truly belong to one another. Not so long as his father was king and she was heir to the witches. He'd have to keep her close for their daughter's sake, but even when he was king, there was a chance his people wouldn't accept her.

But he did.

He wasn't ready to voice it out loud, because that would make it real. But in his heart Emery was already his. From the moment he'd laid eyes on her in his club. She'd always been his.

His source of life.

His mate.

About bloody fucking time you admit it.

Augustine ignored August's jab and licked the wounds at Emery's neck. The moment he slipped his cock from her she collapsed against him. He spun her and held her in his arms, resting her back against the tree and pressing his forehead to hers.

Emery looked up at him, her doe eyes glassy. Her skin held a subtle magic glow, a glow of pure bliss. He wished he could bottle it and keep it for when the dark days were on the verge of winning.

Augustine pressed his lips against hers, stealing a kiss that was chaste in comparison to what they just shared. He basked in what he knew would be a stolen moment he'd cherish forever. A snippet in time that was only for them.

"You think they heard us?" Emery's eyes glanced to where he knew the cottage sat behind him. They weren't against the first row of trees, but they were within eyesight and most certainly within the hearing range of a supernatural being.

Augustine chuckled, leave it to Emery to ruin the moment so perfectly. "Oh, I'm sure of it."

She snorted a laugh and buried her face in his chest. Augustine pressed his lips to the top of her head.

Emery tensed against him and softly pushed him back, the sigh that fell from her lips no longer playful, effectively breaking the fragile bubble that surrounded them. She lifted her eyes to his and he wished he could freeze time to stop what he knew came next. "What are we doing here, Augustine?"

But the stars weren't on his side. He didn't even know when he started believing the witches' stars dictated their lives. He never had before. Then again, he'd never experienced magic like he had with Emery.

Augustine trapped her hands against his chest, needing the connection between them to remain, even as he prepared to distance himself.

He was a selfish bastard.

"We're allowing ourselves to take what we need." He spoke as if it was so simple. It was anything but.

"And when we walk away from here?"

Even though her words were steady, the bond quivered on her end, and Augustine almost broke. He almost told her. Emery deserved to know his heart was hers as much as he suspected hers belonged to him. But he worked in logic and strategy, neither of which provided a future where they got their happy ending. Not yet. Not as long as Emery and his daughter would be hunted for what they were. It was possible that someday change would infiltrate his kingdom, but he couldn't live on hope alone. He wouldn't survive if anything happened to them.

"I'll go back to the castle and do what I must for my people." The words tasted foul and he struggled against the need to take them back.

You're an idiot.

The hope fell from Emery's eyes, and she dropped her head. "That's what I thought."

"It's not personal, Emery." But it was. It was as personal as it got. He was doing this to save her. To save their daughter from a king who was well on his way to becoming a tyrant and a kingdom that wasn't ready for her brilliance.

"Of course it isn't. It's just what we are, right? The job." She huffed a manic laugh and her words dripped with sarcasm. "We're the job. You're the prince and I'm the savior of Callum's prophecy come to life."

Augustine ran a hand through his hair, needing to keep his hands busy so he didn't grab her and never let go. "If that's how you want to look at it."

She pressed her lips together and nodded, "And the next time one of us has needs?"

He hated that he could see her holding back tears. Tears he

put there. It was for their own good. He couldn't put them in danger.

He shrugged his shoulders in an attempt to distract from the way his throat bobbed, masking his own emotions. "That's up to you, little witch. I will crave you till my dying breath, no other blood will satisfy me the way you do. I can't be your prince, but I will always protect you and our daughter. Can you take what I'm offering?"

Please, say yes.

He wasn't sure if it was his own pleading or August's, but they held the same sentiment.

Emery hesitated and Augustine held his breath, preparing for her refusal. Even though he'd just told her he couldn't be her prince, she'd always be his princess, his solace in the world. He may have to marry Jessi, but she was the means to an end. Not Emery. Emery was his reason to live.

Which made him every bit the monster he told her he was.

When she nodded, Augustine let out a sigh of relief and placed a kiss on her forehead. "Are you sure you're okay with this?"

"No," she answered, her voice a hoarse whisper as the last bit of her vulnerability slipped away.

He sucked in his lower lip and bit down, blood pooling at the tip of his fangs. He couldn't blame her, but that didn't mean it didn't rip his heart in two any less.

Emery straightened her spine and relaxed her shoulders, as if putting on invisible armor and preparing for battle. When her eyes met his again, they were hardened pools of amber. "Nothing about this is okay, but it's the cards we've been dealt. You can tell yourself that you are doing this to keep us safe, that Jessi is the lesser of two evils. But we're not helpless, Augustine. The king will come for us. You're an idiot if you think he won't because he gave you his word. He killed my sister. One day you are going to get your head out of your ass and realize it's you and me against the world. Not only for the sake of our daughter but all supernaturals. I can only hope that day is sooner rather than later, because at some point I'll move on, and you'll be left with a kingdom in ruins and a bitch by your side. I won't run. I'll be your blood but that's where it ends. I refuse to be your unhappy leftovers just because I'm shackled to you by magic."

"You're mine, little witch," he growled.

Emery ignored him and placed her hands on his chest, forcing him to take a step back. She pulled up her shorts and walked toward the house.

She stopped and his heart tightened when she turned around and whispered. "For what it's worth, I'm sorry about your men. You've already lost more than anyone should. Even in war."

His mouth formed a grim line and he nodded. "Thank you."

Emery's eyes searched his, though he wasn't sure what she was looking for. There was nothing left for her to grasp. She expected him to fight for her, for them, but she couldn't see that's exactly what he was doing. There was a game to be played, royal politics in motion. He couldn't just go against his father and expect the kingdom to fall in line. It didn't matter that he agreed with her. His father needed to be dealt with, or no one would be safe. Strategy won wars, not love and hope.

She shook her head and turned back toward the house, and he let her keep walking.

Hope is the foundation of change. You need to fix this, Augustine.

"There's nothing to fix. Boundaries are what's going to save us all from heart break later."

You're a naive bastard if you believe that.

He was. There was no doubt he and Emery would combust in a blaze brighter than the depths of hell, but at least he knew what he was fighting for. He had a plan, and he only prayed she could still look upon his face when all was said and done.

Chapter Twenty Six

EMERY

A crown adorned the head attached to the midnight eyes that captured hers.

Augustine smiled at her and growled. "Mine."

Heat filled Emery's cheeks as she nodded, ignoring the full hall of people hanging on their every move. She lifted up on tipped toes so she could press a kiss to her king's lips. "Forever."

Tears pricked her eyes as the vision dissipated and another took its place.

She stood alone, her vision blurred by tears as she held her daughter and looked down on the funeral pyre. The body was draped in white, a dozen black dahlias held together by a leather thong with the Nicholson crest etched in gold resting on top of a broadsword.

A sob caught in her throat as sentinels pushed the pyre into the darkness of the lake.

"I'm sorry," she whispered and called her fire to her palms, lobbing the heated globes to land on the pyre.

The flames caught and Emery tipped her eyes to the stars, cursing their existence.

The night went dark and Emery blinked her eyes, barely keeping tears from falling. Ansel and Dorian stood before her, their heads cocked to the side.

Fucking visions.

She hated the damn stars.

Ever since Augustine had left three days prior, they'd found the most inopportune moments to gift her with visions. As if the dreams of war growing more gruesome each night weren't enough, her days were filled with images of her and Augustine living happily ever after or dying tragically.

She tried desperately to block them out, but the more she fought them, the more violently the stars pressed them upon her.

After days of seeing the same possibilities, the images were branded on the inside of her skull. The loving smiles and moaned I love yous between panted breaths, followed by unimaginable sorrow. It was fucking torture.

But visions weren't absolute, no path set in stone, and as long as Augustine remained a stubborn overgrown asshole, there would be no hope of any of the happy ones coming true. Which only left tragedy.

Emery shook her head as she reached up and pulled her top knot tighter. "Let's go again." She plastered a smile on her face and nodded at Ansel and Dorian who sat side by side in the heather filled field.

Sweat poured down their faces and she didn't miss the way they sighed at her command. They'd been helping her hone her elemental skills for the better part of the afternoon, only stopping when she got the tug of a vision or she needed to ingest copious amounts of chocolate to keep up with her magic.

They pushed themselves and her, but never so far as to chance hurting herself or the baby. Which Emery was grateful for. It was the perfect distraction from both her inability to master her magic and the vampire she tried her best to forget.

Especially when he played a starring role in her visions.

"Are you sure?" Ansel arched a brow, ever the protective guard dog. "Was it another vision? Should I get Lily?"

The last person she wanted to talk to about it was Lily. As much as she loved the woman, it was difficult to be around her right now. Lily wanted Emery to write down every instant of every vision and consider what it meant. There was no question that Lily meant well, but more often than not, Emery felt like the older witch was more fascinated by the fact Emery was star touched than by what the vision was actually doing to her psyche. She blamed it on the fact Lily had been alone for so many years.

The truth was, these visions were breaking her.

One. Fucking. Vision. At. A. Time.

Emery narrowed her gaze on Ansel. "I don't want to talk about it. Now get set or I'll tell Dorian all about your nightly beauty routine."

"As if I don't already know, Your Majesty." Dorian huffed. "You know he convinced me to bring back his laundry list of products when I checked in with Augustine at the castle yesterday?" Dorian snorted, and though it was meant to be with disgust, Emery could almost see the hint of a smile at his lips.

Emery stifled a laugh as Ansel turned beet red, ignoring the way Augustine's name sent a flutter of butterflies through her stomach. She was more interested in why her wolf was blushing. "It's Emery. We've been over this, Dorian."

The sentinel gave her a pointed look like it didn't matter how many times she told him, he'd still use the title he felt she deserved. He was an interesting vampire, unlike the ones she'd met at the castle. They'd all had a cunning and confident aire about them, but Dorian was quiet. He picked and chose when he interjected, but when he did, it was meaningful, and sometimes extremely funny. He matched the norm for masculinity, never turning down a fight, but he was still somehow softer than the castle vampires... though no less deadly.

Ansel reached out and punched Dorian playfully in the arm. "The real joke is on you guys. When you get old and wrinkled I'll still have fresh, beautiful skin."

Dorian's eyes slowly raked over every inch of Ansel, and even Emery could feel the heat in his gaze. "Immortal being, sweetcheeks. I'm going to look this good until the day I die."

"Oh my gosh. Did you just make a joke, Dorian?"

"I'm more hung up on the fact that he just called me sweetcheeks," Ansel muttered.

Dorian shrugged. "I stand by it. Besides, I'm more than just a good looking face. Despite my lack of moisturizer."

Emery and Ansel tipped their heads back and laughed, and she couldn't help but swoon over the smile on Ansel's face. Happy looked good on him. Not that he hadn't had moments while they were in New Orleans, but there always seemed to be something holding him back. It disappeared when he was around Dorian. Anyone could see the wolf was smitten for the rogue sentinel.

"Well immortal or not, I need to hone down these elements so get your ass moving, or I'll settle for a stationary target."

"Yes ma'am." Ansel gave Emery a mock salute and took off across the field they'd claimed for practicing.

Emery waited until Ansel was out of earshot and glanced at Dorian, "Don't tell Augustine about the visions, please. I know you report every move I make. I just...he's made his decision. He can't come back here anyway. He doesn't need to know about this."

"I can see how much they're affecting you. The way your face slackens and your eyes rim with tears. He's your mate."

Dorian inhaled a slow breath as if questioning his decision to say anything at all.

"I know, and if they were important, I'd tell him. But as it is, the majority of them I have no desire to ever see again."

"But are they what you need to see?"

Emery hesitated, mulling over his question in her mind. Why would the stars show her a happy ending that wasn't attainable? Or plague her with tragedy that would break her? She knew visions were only possible outcomes, and free will was a bitch of a factor that made them borderline useless, but each of them felt so incredibly real and it was impossible to know what choices would lead to them happening.

"I've found that if you work with the stars the stars will work for you. There's a reason they're showing you these visions, I can't imagine it's to be cruel. The stars are fickle, but they are only a divine entity working beyond and within the balance of good and evil. They punish as they see fit, but they also reward, and I imagine they want you to succeed."

"You're pretty insightful for a sentinel. I thought vampires didn't believe in the stars."

Dorian turned his eyes to the hills and a disheartened look crossed his face. "When you've lived as long as I have, you realize you're no one but a humble servant to something bigger than yourself, whether it be the gods, the stars, or some unknown to be discovered. The only question that remains is what will you do with the life you've been given?" His lips flattened into a hardened line and he glanced at Emery. "As long as they don't put you in danger, your secret's safe with me, your majesty."

His words brought her a slight comfort, though they didn't bring her any sort of closure. It wasn't the time to dive deep into her emotions concerning the stars, but there was no doubt that she needed to make the time to do so.

"Thank you, Dorian." He nodded and Emery's lips pulled up into a devilish grin. "Now run."

He laughed as he took off after Ansel. He caught up in moments—super vampire speed—and tripped the wolf as he passed. His laughter carried across the field along with Ansel's curses.

Emery smiled and shook her head. She was lucky to have them. When they weren't spending their time searching for the damn purple flower, they'd insisted she learn battle magic since she couldn't learn to kick ass physically so long as she was pregnant. That didn't stop them from teaching her how to throw a punch though.

Magic was a lot more practical at the moment, and Lily urged her to try and learn every use of her elements. At the compound, there was no use for throwing wind or forming a fireball. Most elementals used their magic to aid in day-to-day life and nothing more. Warming water for tea, drying off after a shower or rainstorm, growing food, all very domestic and easily hidden. Modern magical warfare had become nonexistent. Only a handful of the royal witches were old enough to even remember the elemental warriors of centuries past.

Lily had found a few old scrolls on their tactics in Callum's expansive library, and as she read them, Emery couldn't deny she was impressed. Elemental warriors were badass and the backbone of any witch army with their abilities to shape the battlefield as they wanted and call upon the elements for offensive and defensive attacks.

Even if she only had access to two elements at the moment, she was determined to master them.

Emery's magic rose within her as she called on the wind of the Highlands to aid her, using the memory of what she and Augustine did under its breeze to fuel it. Passion was easy to pull from. She'd had plenty of it in the last week and even though it ultimately left her confused as hell, she found comfort in it, making air the easiest element to manipulate.

She brought her hands together, circling them as if she was forming a snowball. The air spun around her and when she was confident she'd gathered enough, she thrust the ball of air toward Ansel and Dorian, who darted across the field like balls in a pinball machine.

Ansel, who'd been watching her, dodged her first attempt, but he wasn't as lucky when she fired another, more confident in her technique.

The air hit him square in the gut and he doubled over, his laugh knocked out of him.

"Nice hit," Dorian called. "Let's see if you can do three in a row and catch me at vampire speed."

Emery inhaled a deep breath, trying to locate the stores of magic in the world around her. She'd barely tapped the well of her magic to fire those two shots, but she was afraid with three rapids she'd start to deplete herself. Magic wells grew as the witch continued to hone their skills and unfortunately that meant hers were still miniscule compared to those who had used magic their entire lives. She'd peter out long before they did.

She really needed to learn to replenish her magic from the stores located in the world around her. It was like learning to circular breathe. To inhale and exhale at the same time. She couldn't even do that with breathing let alone with her magic.

Emery reached in her pocket and pulled out a piece of chocolate. She looked down at it and sighed. The sickly sweet cocoa used to bring her such joy; now it might as well have been a cough drop.

Fuck magic for taking away a joy she didn't know she'd miss until it was gone.

Until she learned how to circulate magic, she'd be stuck popping chocolate or sucking veins. But seeing as her main source of blood was absent, and he'd all but threatened anyone who offered to help, she and her hips were stuck with chocolate.

After the sweets kicked in, she circled her hands once more and nodded to Dorian, who took off using his vampire speed. Emery quickened her movements and shot three blasts of air at her moving target, aiming ahead of him and hoping that was the right tactic.

All three missed.

Emery's jaw tightened, and she had to tamper her rage to avoid tapping into her fire. She thrust her hands out, pouring every last bit of magic she had into calling the air to her aid. She aimed for just ahead of Dorian and instead of a ball meant to hit him, she erected a wall in front of him.

None the wiser, Dorian ran full speed into the barrier. He tumbled back to the ground, and she half expected him to yell at her, but savored his gruff laugh as he staggered from the ground. "That was incredible!" He rubbed his jaw as he started walking back toward Emery. "That air barrier packs a punch. Did you mean to do that?"

Emery punched her fists in the air in celebration. "Sort of. I just wanted to stop you."

"Well, mission accomplished."

"You okay, fang boy?" Ansel asked, trotting up next to Dorian.

Dorian growled and glared at the wolf, and Emery hid her smile behind her hand. Ansel was going to give Dorian a run for his money.

The two of them walked in silence toward Emery. By the time they'd reached her she'd finished another small piece of chocolate and the lightheadedness from using her magic had subsided. "Shall we try with fire now? Maybe pure magic?" Emery channeled her ever present rage into a fireball in her palm.

"I've seen you with fire. I'd like to keep my life if that's okay with you," Ansel joked.

"How about earth or water?" Dorian suggested, shaking out his muscles. "Still not quite grasping those yet?"

"Not really. Water is hit and miss, and earth is non-existent." Her heart was not ready to cooperate and give her something to work with, and her dreams were just as finicky.

Lily constantly reminded her that once she tapped into them, she wouldn't have to flex as much of herself and the core drive of the elements to cast them. Basically it was like riding a bike. She had to keep trying and failing until one day it would click, and she'd be able to take off. Until then though, she was stuck figuring it out on her own with Lily riding her ass around every turn and a flirtatious wolf and vampire as her only allies.

"It's getting late, and I'm starving," Ansel complained.

"You're always hungry," Emery chuckled.

"Guilty." He wrapped an arm around Dorian with a wolfish grin. Emery didn't miss the way the sentinel leaned into Ansel, and the faint blush that marred his cheeks before he startled and shrugged him off.

Ansel would never admit it but he was missing his pack. Even though they'd all become like family at the cottage, she was beginning to see how the wolves filled a role within the pack even if all that meant was providing a warm body to snuggle up next to. Even as a mostly lone wolf, the impact of being secluded with a bunch of vampires and witches was taking its toll on Ansel.

He brushed up against Dorian, ignoring his rejection. "Want to fuck with Callum while he cooks?"

Dorian stepped away from Ansel's clingy wolf touch, but a smile crept up his lips. "You know I'm in. He just *loves* when I move his shit around the kitchen without him noticing. You in, Emery?"

Damn they were cute together.

Emery shook her head, wanting them to bond a little, even if it was at Callum's expense. Callum would never admit it, but he was as romantic as Malcolm, even if he wouldn't let anyone see it. "I think I'm going to take a nap before dinner, but you guys have fun."

"See you at dinner." They waved and took off toward the cottage.

Emery followed the path from the field down to the lake and sat on the boulder where she'd reconnected with August. The memories made her clench her thighs. Drunk bees took flight in her stomach.

She missed him.

Missed Augustine.

They were the same and yet they were still so very, very different.

The eastern sky caught her gaze as the first and brightest stars appeared in the evening sky, taunting her. Life would be so much easier if they could talk to her and tell her what the hell she was supposed to do instead of sending her visions that filled her with both dread and hope in a single breath.

Maybe Dorian had been right, and she needed to open up to their will. She listened and regurgitated everything they'd told her thus far, but deep in her heart, she held doubts that she could do what they asked of her.

Her motivations were driven by her wants, needs, and insecurities. Letting go would mean facing the fact that she may not end up where she believed she needed to be.

Could she be okay with that?

She searched within her, feeling magic bubble in her chest, and her hands roamed over the swell of her belly. As long as her daughter was safe, she could do anything.

Even lose the only man who ever made her feel.

She tipped her head to the sky and inhaled the fresh Highland air. Her magic excited, a frenzied mess within her chest.

The world tilted, the trees and water blurring away.

Damnit.

Emery closed her eyes but instead of the darkness she'd come to associate with slipping into a vision, light burst behind her eyes and something cracked within her.

"Daughter of the light, welcome to your sight."

Snippets flashed before her eyes like a flip book of happenings she didn't understand.

Augustine standing toe-to-toe with his father. Midnight ringed eyes. Twin bassinets being swung in the cottage. Blood flowing down marble stairs. A circular tree in a dense forest. Fire, so much fire. Hands dipped in ink. Pyres. Poppies. Waves. Letters. Magic. A sword, etched with the constellations of the stars.

Over and over they played in her mind, until Emery blinked and returned to consciousness, tears flowing freely down her face.

Her body sagged, and she pulled out a piece of chocolate, not caring that it tasted bland on her tongue as it replenished the depleted feeling in her body. It was all too much to process. She reached in her back pocket for the notebook Lily insisted she carry and jotted down as many of the snippets she could remember.

These visions had been different, they felt solid and yet fleeting and none of them directly tied to her in that moment. She looked back up at the sky, her mind swirling with the possibilities of what they were trying to tell her.

Keep going. Your future is written among us, they whispered with the breeze.

Emery shook her head and read her notes again, still in awe of all she'd seen. She didn't understand a damn thing the stars wanted from her, but she felt a confidence in them that hadn't been there before.

They believed in her, and she prayed they wouldn't lead her astray.

Chapter Twenty Seven

AUGUSTINE

There wasn't anything he hated more than dressing up for court.

At least when there isn't a fuckable little minx guaranteed to make things interesting.

Augustine growled as he viewed the memories of Emery August pushed forward of the last time he'd been dressed in a royal getup. She'd most certainly made that night worth it. At least that event allowed for a tartan. Where a tartan, or even a suit could make a man feel powerful, the high-necked tailcoat and ruffled shirt his father insisted he wear to preside over court did the exact opposite.

He should be thrilled his father wanted him to preside over court—it was the first time he'd ever given Augustine the reins and allowed him to preside over anything political. The King's advisors spent the last three days prepping him and boasting about how this was a step in the right direction to prepare Augustine for his own rule.

Perhaps it shouldn't have surprised him that it was a shit show.

The first day, he'd pushed back against everything they'd suggested, and he'd received a threatening letter from his father with a map that had major areas of Scotland crossed off. The fucking bastard had no issues hitting below the belt to keep him in line. After that, Augustine smiled and nodded through their lessons, which resulted in the utmost praise of the advisors. They suddenly believed he'd make a fine king. They didn't see the dog and pony show for what it was. Another attempt by his father to keep him and the rest of the kingdom in line.

Augustine let out a deep sigh and left his chambers, headed toward the queen's wing. It had been three days since he left Scotland, and he was already sick of life at the castle. That wasn't true. It wasn't the castle, or even the fact that he had to play the political game that irritated him. He was made for those things. It was the incessant ache of the mate bond that made life miserable. Every night he stared at his phone, Lily's phone number on the screen. All he had to do was call her, and he could be in Scotland in minutes. He could give the mate bond what it wanted. Who it wanted.

He snorted as he thought of the way August used to sit outside Emery's door at the castle and how pathetic he thought it was. Now he was contemplating doing the same damn thing to appease the clawing need in his chest. Hell, he'd gone so far as unburying the damn dragon stuffed animal from the pile of things he'd stored as evidence against her all those months ago and clinging to it each night as her scent washed over him.

And you said I was pathetic.

"Shut the fuck up," Augustine growled as he rounded the hallway to his mother's wing.

The Queen stood in the hallway waiting for him with a weak smile on her face. She'd attempted to get back to her duties since he'd taken Thea to Scotland, but anyone with eyes could see she was struggling through the motions.

She pulled him into a hug when he reached her. "Any word on the flower?" she whispered softly.

Augustine shook his head. He'd spent any free moment of his days that wasn't preordained by his father searching the libraries of the castle for any hint of the Enchanted Amaryllis to no avail. He was exhausted. They all were. Lily was doing everything she could to keep Thea comfortable, and Callum was leading a search of the grounds within the wards while Flora and Draven split their time searching through the wolves' archives and roaming outside the wards in Scotland. None of them had found a single thing, and they were running out of time. The full moon would rise in two days' time, and he feared Thea wouldn't make it to the next one. She'd been so frail and weak when he left her.

His mother stepped away and weaved her arm through his, leading him down the hallway. "You look nice today."

"I look like a gods damned monkey ready to jump through hoops."

She gave his arm a loving squeeze. "But a very handsome monkey."

Augustine chuckled. "You have to say that, but thank you."

"How's Emery?"

Wasn't that the million dollar question. Just the mention of her name had his heart racing. He needed to get a grip if he was going to survive being away from her for any extended period of time. Which is exactly what he planned to do.

Augustine's eyes zeroed in on the floor in front of him, and he kept his face passive as he ground out, "She's fine."

"My sweet boy." His mother tugged on his arm, pulling him to a stop. She searched his face with her soft gaze. "I've spent my fair share of time with Jessi the last few months, and while she isn't ideal, she's not the worst."

A snort escaped him, but he didn't speak, allowing his mother to continue. She clearly hadn't been spending time with the same wicked bitch he had for the entirety of his Culling and the months following.

"Still I can see that despite all she may be, she's not who you love. I can see that every time you're around her, and even when you're not. Even more so now. You wince at her touch and your eyes are vacant when she attempts to engage with you. I think you've finally accepted what Emery is to you. I hope you won't let that slip away."

Augustine shook his head, shielding himself against the hope in his mother's words. There wasn't room for that any more. "It doesn't matter, Mother. She's the heir to the witches, and I'm the crown prince. If my father doesn't kill her, it's likely my subjects will."

"Don't be a stubborn ass, Augustine," his mother snapped, her eyes narrowing in the way only a mother's could. "You're not your father. His brand of corruption doesn't suit you. Your darkness is pure, a blackhole that swallows light, but you don't consume it, you let it radiate through you. You're the future. You and your mate."

He allowed his hands to drop and took the queen's in his. "Her light may be the only thing keeping me going, but as much as she's my mate, she cannot be my queen."

His mother scoffed, and he half expected her to smack him upside the head. "Excuse me son, but you're a selfish idiot."

"You're not the first one to tell me that," he muttered. August reminded him of every chance he'd gotten since leaving Scotland.

And I will continue to every moment until you rectify the situation.

Lucky him.

"I hope you know what you are doing, Augustine. Yours is not the only fate that hangs in the balance."

As if he needed the reminder. But he couldn't let his mother see how much that fact shook him to his core. It seemed everything he did these days was for the benefit of everyone else, and though it was out of character for him to care beyond his own needs and that of his kingdom, he found he didn't mind. Though he wasn't about to examine any further what that meant.

He stepped forward and placed a gentle kiss on his mother's cheek. "I do."

Augustine stepped toward the door where he was to collect his future bride for an afternoon spent listening to the grievances of his people. The first step, according to his father, in becoming a ruler fit to take over their kingdom. For Augustine, it was the first step in his own plan to find out where his subjects stood. To see if there was any truth in Rex's words.

A pang of grief struck his heart at the loss of his comrade, and Augustine vowed once more to avenge his death and right the wrongs of his father.

The fighting had only gotten worse. The King sent out his sentinels nightly to search out smaller compounds of witches and eradicate them. His plans to attack the largest cities were nearly complete, and Augustine needed to know if it was the right move. If he allowed his father to proceed, the loss would be catastrophic on all sides and the repercussions could affect generations of supernaturals to come.

He didn't bother knocking on the door to the common room and entered only to wish he'd knocked. Jessi stood on a pedestal in front of a mirror surrounded by Scarlett, Amelia, and Jenni, members of his Culling who'd come back to the castle to help her prepare for their wedding. She was draped in white tuling with the royal seamstress pinning it to her and for a split second he was transported back to a similar scene months before.

Augustine had been in the recesses of August's mind, but he would never forget the way Emery looked that day, prepping for the ball with her friends. She was stunning in a moment of almost carefree bliss until she turned and saw them. August was prepared to give her the ultimatum, stay or go, but seeing her like that… it made them want to demand she stay. She hadn't been innocent, but even then, both August and Augustine had known she was it for them.

And yet you're staring at your future bride, and it's not Emery.

His jaw tightened, and he coughed loudly into his fist to call attention to himself instead of dignifying August with a response.

The women all whipped their gaze toward him, and the three Culling women jumped in front of Jessi who tried to cover herself.

"Augustine, you aren't allowed to see me in my gown," Jessi complained, but her coy tone told him she'd planned this. She'd known he was coming to get her to hold court, and she ensured she'd have the opportunity to remind him of their pending nuptials. It was the only thing she talked about. She lived and breathed becoming his queen.

He almost rolled his eyes but stopped himself, and a smile crept onto his face as he imagined his favorite witch doing the same. Augustine let out a chuckle and gave the women his back. "It's Your Highness, and I'm sorry for the intrusion, but you are supposed to be ready to go hear the grievances of my people."

"Don't you mean our people?" He could almost hear the pout on her lips.

"No. They are my people until we are married, but my father insists you attend."

"Oh." Her hurt response slipped out.

He'd hurt her feelings but he couldn't bring himself to care. She'd been on a sweet and sour kick the last few days. One moment she was sweet and he could almost tolerate her, the next she was a manipulative bitch on a quest for power as his wife.

She bounced back and a loving, if fake smile, returned to her face. "I'll be just a moment."

The click of her heels filled the room as Jessi retreated into an adjoining room to change.

"You can turn around now, Your Highness," Jenni informed him.

The Culling women stood around a small table, glasses of blood in hand. They'd all chosen to be turned and assigned to an embassy within his court. From what he'd heard, Jenni and Amelia were thriving in the south and west coast respectively. Scarlett was adjusting in Toronto, but she still harbored some resentment that Jessi had been chosen to be his wife.

Jenni extended a glass in his direction. "Would you like a glass? O positive."

He swallowed hard and shook his head. "No, thank you."

The truth was he wanted the glass. Emery's blood was beginning to slip from his veins and the bloodlust was creeping back into the recesses of his mind. He would need to return to Scotland soon, if only to feed, but he wanted to do so sparingly. There was no way he'd risk his father finding out where they were.

Sure, let's go with that. It's definitely not because you're worried you won't come back if you see her again.

A growl rattled through his chest. August was becoming a bold thorn in his fucking side.

Then stop denying yourself.

He didn't respond. Augustine knew why he was making the choices he was, and he stood by them. It didn't matter what August thought. Not when Augustine had every intention of proving he was making the right decision.

He tapped his fingers behind his back as an awkward silence fell over the room. What the hell was he supposed to say to these women? They weren't in his Culling anymore, they were his subjects, but still it didn't feel right to treat them as mere courtiers.

"Your Highness?" Amelia wrung her hands in front of her. "May I speak freely?"

"Yes, absolutely." Anything to break the silence. "Is there a problem?"

"Yes. No. I'm not sure. It's just… I'm trying to understand this war with the witches. I've always known there was animosity between the factions, but it seems counterproductive. Why can't we all live in peace? The humans have figured it out somehow, why can't we?"

Her face held so much confusion, and Augustine wished he could bottle her naivety and bathe in it when the pressure of his world got to be too much. With age came knowledge, but it was a damn curse to understand the complexities of life.

He spoke evenly, trying to explain their world in the simplest way possible. "The humans still have war. It was only in the last century that equal rights became a popular idea. The hatred between vampires and witches goes back a hell of a lot further and you have to remember, vampires and royal witches are immortal. Our memories are long and we aren't known for our forgiving natures."

"But so many are dying." Her plea mirrored that of others, but it would always fall on deaf ears. Death was a part of life when you lived as long as they did.

Still, he tried to find his humanity. "Did you lose someone, Amelia?"

She nodded, her heart raced and tears rimming her eyes. "My sire."

Bloody hell. She was barely a fledgling. Losing a sire would be like losing a limb.

He stepped forward and pulled Amelia into a hug. She may not technically be a member of his Culling any longer, but he would always take care of these women as if they were. "What can I do to help?"

"Nothing," she sobbed into his chest. "Just make sure this war is worth it. I don't wish this pain on anyone."

Augustine ran his hand down the back of her head, trying to soothe her. He didn't know what to tell her. Nothing he said would bring back her sire or fill the hole ripped through her chest. Only time, and maybe a taste of vengeance would do that. This war would wage on regardless of her wishes, or even his own. It was centuries in the making and he knew it would be worth it for their world.

"What's going on here?" Jessi's shrill voice filled the common room.

Amelia untangled herself from his grasp and wiped her tears from her eyes.

"Calm down, Jessi," Scarlett snapped. "Augustine was offering his condolences on the loss of her sire."

Jessi's lips twisted into a sneer. "He could do so without his hands on her."

Augustine growled and strode across the room until he was towering over his fiancee. "I can do whatever I damn well please with my hands. Now if you're done making a fool of yourself, we're going to be late." He offered Jessi his arm and turned toward Amelia. "Again. I'm very sorry for your loss, Amelia. If there's anything I can do, please let me know."

"Thank you." She curtsied and nodded.

They barely made it to the throne room in time, and by the glare in his father's eyes, Augustine was sure he'd hear about it later.

His throne had been placed in front of the dais with a secondary throne that would become Jessi's when they married. Above them was a skylight and Augustine couldn't help tighten his lips at the two bright stars that shone through, despite the light in the hall. He prayed they weren't there to mock him but rather do something right for a change and aid his cause.

The King presided over them from the upper level of the dais, a feeder draped across his lap. Along each side of the room were the nobles of their court who lived nearby and frequented the castle to line his father's pockets with money. In the center of the room a path has been left clear for those who had traveled for the quarterly opportunity to meet with the reigning monarch and air any grievances. It was a whole to do, one he heard his father complain about often.

Augustine found he didn't mind it so much. Sure, he'd much rather be out hunting the Mistress, but hearing the needs of his subjects surprisingly filled him with a sense of pride. Even if being on his throne stung as if he was sitting on tacks. But that was something he'd rectify as soon as he was king.

Although many of his subjects' issues were trivial in the grand scheme of things, in just a few hours he felt as if he had actually made a difference for the first time in ages. He'd set a plan to establish blood banks in a few of the up-and-coming vampire communities within their borders and heard the cry of his people for fledgling education when sires were absent. That particular one felt good, and he'd make sure to pass the information along to Amelia. For the first time he could see why August cared so much about doing work for his people. While Augustine had always stood by his vow to protect his kingdom, it was too often in the capacity of brute strength. This was different. It wasn't a one-time fix or the stroke of a blade. Instead, he was building something—something that would feed his people for years to come.

There is so much more for you to learn about being king. Dare I say you might even like the diplomatic bullshit you have fought against tooth and nail.

Augustine smiled to himself and turned his attention toward the man walking through the archway of the throne room. The man was small in stature, but built like a wall which was only enhanced by the determination set in his jaw.

Jessi shifted beside him, reaching out and placing her hand on top of his where it sat on the armrest of this throne. His instinct was to react and pull it away, but before he could, his peripheral vision caught the tightening of one of his advisor's jaws. Forcing himself to stay calm, he gave Jessi's hand a reassuring squeeze.

His advisor relaxed and gave him a nod.

Bloody hell, he hated playing this damn game.

"Bellamy Cormac," the footman announced and Augustine concentrated once more on the task at hand.

"Your Majesty." Bellamy bowed to the King and then gave Augustine a deep nod. "Your Highness."

"Bellamy," Augustine nodded.

Bellamy nodded. "It's Bell, please, Your Highness."

At these words, Augustine could have sworn the stars shone brighter through the skylight above him. He blinked to ensure he wasn't crazy, but the light remained, and he wondered if he was the only one seeing it. "What can I help you with?"

"The war against the witches."

Augustine's spine straightened, and he narrowed his gaze on the vampire before him. Every subject prior to Bell had danced around the subject of the witches. There was an undertone that told him that the war was what they all wanted to discuss, but no one had the balls to broach it. Until Bell.

Augustine nodded, wanting to know more about the man who thought to question his family in front of the entire court. "Where are you from, Bell?"

"Santa Fe."

"And what of the war did you want to discuss?"

"It's an injustice to your people, Your Highness." Bell raised his voice, passion fueling his outburst. "It's broken our way of life in the Southwest."

"I suggest you lower your voice. We're merely having a conversation." Augustine attempted to diffuse the situation, even if he wanted to agree with Bell. So much of what his father had ordered so far was an injustice. "How has the eradication of witches affected you?"

"We didn't want them eradicated," Bell ground out, his eyes locked on Augustine and his hands fisted like he was prepared to fight.

Augustine nodded, trying to remain impartial and fair as he heard Bell's plea, but something deep within him was stirring, and with every moment, playing the game was becoming more of a nuisance. "Witches and vampires have been enemies for many millennia. What concern is it of yours if they live or die? They would sooner see you burn in the sun."

"Maybe the witches of New Orleans and the vampires who frequent your court feel that way, but our community isn't like that. We live in harmony with the witches in Santa Fe. They provide us with tonics and enchantments, and we protect them through the night. They may have been our enemy at one time, but it's a misconception that they are evil. They're people, just as we are. Were. They see our souls, not our bloodlust."

"Blasphemy!" the king cried out, and Augustine heard the shriek of his feeder and a heavy thud.

He turned around to see his father's feeder on the floor, and the King standing to his full height, fury in his eyes.

His father stepped down from the dais, each word spoken in time to emphasize his point. "The witches are our enemy, and it's treasonous for you to be fraternizing with them."

"They aren't our enemy, Your Majesty," Bell pleaded. "We need them as much as they need us. And your war is killing not only witches but vampires as well. A fourth of our small community was killed in your last raid, and I know ours is not the only community suffering."

"They shouldn't have been where the witches were. If they had been at home, they wouldn't have been killed," the King spat and there were a few cheers from courtiers in the room in agreement.

Bell's mouth dropped. "You would defend the deaths of innocents?"

The King moved in a blur and before Bellamy could react, his head was separated from his body.

Jessi screamed and buried her face in Augustine's shoulder and for the first time, he offered her genuine comfort in the form of an arm around her.

His father held up Bell's severed head and boasted. "They weren't innocent if they were with our enemy. They were traitors."

Fury rose in Augustine, and he stood from his throne, his lips twisted into a sneer. "Does that make me a traitor, Father?"

"You've seen the error in your ways and returned to where you belong." The king's eyes narrowed and a wicked smile stretched across his face.

Nothing good ever came from that expression, and Augustine could only wait for the punishment to come for his outburst. Not that he regretted it. His father was out of line.

"What does that mean?" Jessi whispered from behind them, and though he shouldn't care, the hurt in her voice made him wince.

"Oh, he didn't tell you." The King laughed and dropped Bell's head at Augustine's feet as he moved to get a better view of Jessi. "You know you really should confide in the woman who is going to be your future bride, Augustine."

"Tell me what?" Her gaze darted between Augustine and his father.

"Nothing." Augustine ground out, and his gaze softened toward Jessi, silently pleading she drop it. When she nodded, he returned his hardened facade and met his father's smug visage. "Is this going to be our strategy moving forward? Kill those who oppose your war? I thought this was about listening to our subjects, about doing what's best for the kingdom."

"It is." He chuckled and opened his arms to those who dared to remain and watch the argument between heir and monarch. "What *I* believe is best."

"You can't just kill those who disagree with you."

"That's a bit hypocritical don't you think? Your hands are the furthest thing from clean, Augustine."

"I am not the king."

"You're right. You aren't. So sit your ass down where it belongs: at my feet."

Augustine's jaw tightened, and he glanced around the room. Some of the courtiers had snuck out, but the majority were waiting to see what happened, to see where the chips fell. This would be the moment they remembered that either solidified Augustine's future as king or turned them against him. His eyes trailed back to his father's glare. And for the first time, Augustine didn't give a shit about anything other than doing what was right for his people.

There was no way he could back down.

He stood from his throne and moved to where his father stood. "I will return to your feet, Father. But heed my warning, you may be the king, but I am the future, and I will fight for the needs and wants of my people. I will usher them into a new era if that's what they crave."

The king bared his teeth, but Augustine didn't give him a moment to retort. He turned and stormed from the throne room. He didn't stop until he was outside. He tipped his head toward the sky and yell tore through his body at the stars that shone down on him.

His chest heaved after he'd released every ounce of pent up emotion. Augustine righted himself and set his shoulders back, his gaze drifting over the castle he called home.

For the first time he felt truly royal. Like he was meant to be king.

Chapter Twenty Eight

EMERY

Flames licked Emery's hand, dancing along her fingers to the music of the wind. They didn't burn, but instead created more of a buzz that tickled her skin with its warmth. She closed her hand and the flames extinguished, some of them jumping back into the bonfire and others dissipating in the night air. When she opened it again and willed her magic, they erupted once more.

"You're getting pretty good at that," Ansel commented beside her as he smashed a marshmallow against a piece of chocolate between two graham crackers.

He'd been so engrossed with his s'more, Emery hadn't realized he'd been watching. Ansel had thrown a hissy fit when he found out she'd never had a s'more before. It wasn't something Ada ever deemed necessary when she was growing up. Not that Emery hadn't asked for or wished for normal human experiences, she had. She'd seen people enjoying s'mores on the beach or bike rides with their families, but it wasn't till she was older that she decided to learn things on her own. S'mores just never topped the list.

Ansel planned to rectify that situation.

He handed her the s'more, practically bouncing in his seat,

and Emery couldn't help but laugh. "With the way you, Lily, and Dorian have ridden my ass the last three days, I'm glad I'm finally starting to see some improvement." She'd spent nearly every waking moment practicing some sort of magic. She was growing stronger, but not much had changed. Wind and fire still came to her easiest. Water was still a fickle element between its three states, and earth was stubborn as fuck, refusing to bend to her will.

"And now you have a reward." Ansel looked from her to the sticky sack in her hands, waiting for her to eat it.

Emery shook her head and took a bite. The marshmallow and chocolate squeezed out the sides, and she giggled as she tried and failed to keep it from going all over her face. It was every bit as delicious as Ansel described. Crunchy, yet soft and sweet. "I think this is my new favorite dessert," she spoke through full cheeks.

"I told you it would be." He licked his own fingers and set up another marshmallow on his stick. It was a wonder how Ansel kept any sort of muscle on him considering his love of all things sweet. He stuck the pillowy snack over the fire and nudged her with his shoulder. "How are you doing?"

She looked up and met her protector's easy smile. The cottage had fallen into a routine and whoever was currently residing there fell in line and played their part. But when it came to Emery, almost everyone at the cottage walked on eggshells. And she didn't blame them. Between the loss of her son which she refused to dwell on, Augustine's constant rejection, and the swell of her hormones, she was a ticking time bomb and no one could tell when she would blow.

Not even herself.

One minute she'd be happily practicing her magic and the next an image of Augustine in the castle with Jessi's grimy hands all over him would play through her mind, highlighting how she'd be left to raise their child alone while they played house. Which was usually followed by rage, and her setting something on fire.

She pulled a piece of stray marshmallow from her cheek and shrugged. "I'm fine."

Ansel raised a brow and smirked. "The fact that we've been through two fire extinguishers in the last two days says otherwise."

"I'm managing," she lied through her teeth knowing any vampire in hearing range could taste it. Thank goodness Dorian and Callum were inside, and Draven and Flora were off cannoodling somewhere doing wolfy things. They were a damn cute couple, and while she was so happy for her best friend, a part of her hated seeing them together. It only reminded her of what she'd lost.

The truth was Emery was barely keeping it together. The few times she'd set things on fire had been when she'd lost control of her emotions, but there were plenty of times she was on the edge and successfully reigned them in. Logically she knew she should be allowed to grieve and feel every bit of the cards the stars had dealt her. In the last week, she'd lost her son, seen a vision of how to save Thea with magic she had no idea how to use, given Augustine permission to use her as his personal blood bag, and then watched him walk away and choose to protect her alone instead of trusting they were stronger together. Not to mention the endless visions of futures she couldn't fathom. Sorting them was an artform all on its own and there was no one to guide her but the dusty old books Lily kept dropping in her room. None of which were all that helpful.

The average person could end up in a mental ward after experiencing what she had in such a short time. But Emery wasn't average. She wasn't allowed to be. She was the heir to the witches and the mate to the crown prince of vampires. She was hand picked by the stars to usher in a new era for supernaturals. Saviors didn't get to break down. They didn't get to fall apart.

Ansel reached out and wrapped his hand around hers. "You don't have to face everything alone, Emery."

"I know, and I appreciate all the help everyone here has put in..." Her voice trailed off and all she could do was give his large hand a squeeze. There was a hole inside her where the one person who should be sitting by her was, and though she loved her little family, it wasn't the same.

"But we aren't him," Ansel finished the thought that she wouldn't dare put out into the world.

Emery sighed and side-eyed Ansel, a weak smile tipping her lips. "No, you're not, but you are my family, and I'm sorry if I'm making you feel like you aren't good enough."

"Pshhhh. I know you love me." He leaned over and bumped her shoulder, and Emery chuckled. "He's an idiot. He'll be back, he won't be able to stay away."

Emery's laugh morphed into a choked sob, a sudden wave of sadness washing over her. "You're right. He'll be back, but it will only be to feed, or to see his daughter. He's not interested in me beyond that."

Fucking hormones. She couldn't help the waves when they hit. One minute she was holding it together, and the next she was a blubbering mess.

Ansel's brows reached toward his hairline. He reached out and wiped the tears that stained her cheeks. "Is that what you call coming out of the woods with his come dripping down your legs?"

"Really, Ansel?" Emery fisted her hand and hit his shoulder.

Ansel roared laughing and play fell back as if she'd wounded him.

"Does everyone know?" she asked, her cheeks feeling hot all of a sudden.

"The entirety of Scotland could smell your entangled fluids."

"You really are crass. Why didn't anyone say anything?"

"Well I for one was ready to kill the bastard, but Dorian convinced me it would be my life that likely became forfeit, not to mention no one knows what to make of the two of you. You're mates. I know what that feels like. It's the most incredible feeling in the world…" Ansel grew quiet and his eyes distant. Emery knew his thoughts had drifted to Sebastian as they so often did. "The thing is, you are a witch and he is a vampire. There is no precedence for what that means. We don't understand it, but those of us who are gathered here know the importance of your union. That doesn't mean he gets to treat you like shit though, Emery. You deserve better, you have to know that."

"I know, and August is better. You'd like him. But Augustine is who will get us through this war with the witches and ultimately help me secure a future for our daughter in the supernatural world."

Augustine also lit a fire within her that had yet to be doused four days later. She may hate his stubborn facade, but deep down he was one of the good guys. His motives were aimed at protecting those around him, even when his attitude said otherwise. She only needed to figure out how to convince him she could hold her own in his world. Everything within her told her they were meant to take on these challenges together. Not only that, but every bit of information she'd been given from the stars revolved around the two of them.

"You aren't alone in that fight, Your Majesty," Dorian interjected.

Emery had been so engrossed in her conversation with Ansel she hadn't noticed he'd joined them across the circle, followed by Draven and Flora.

Ansel shifted beside her and not for the first time since Dorian's arrival to the cottage, her wolf protector blushed in his presence.

"How many times do I have to tell you, Dorian, just call me Emery, please. I'm not a queen."

Dorian reached for s'more fixings and proceeded to stab the marshmallow with his stick. "You're the mate of my future king, that makes you a future queen."

Unwarranted rage flared in her belly. "Actually, I'm told that honor belongs to a bitch named Jessi, but that's not the point. Here at the cottage, please call me, Emery."

Dorian's eyes narrowed, and as always he wouldn't concede. "As I was saying, you and Augustine are not alone in your fight. The tides are changing within the kingdom, and the majority are not happy with King Leywn's reign of fear. Many of the vampires want to embrace the future, to finally find peace in the supernatural realm. There are plenty of places where witches and vampires live in harmony. There is still tension of course, as bad blood is hard to dilute, but overall they tolerate each other and in some cases even work together."

"They do?" If it was true, it must have been a recent development. In all her time at the castle it was only ever taught that vampires and witches hated each other.

"He's right, Emery." Draven spoke up from across the fire. The quiet alpha rarely interjected, and only when it mattered most. "The supernatural world is changing. A century ago the wolves wouldn't have accepted me as their future alpha because of my hybrid blood. Now though," he draped his arm around Flora at his side, "they welcome me and my mate as their future. That's not to say there won't be those who oppose. We've had a few, but overall the acceptance has been widespread. I believe if you give your people a chance, they will welcome your daughter and your mateship."

Tears pricked her eyes and Emery nodded, taking his words to heart. They were a nice sentiment, but they weren't as reassuring as she was sure Draven meant them to be. "They aren't my people, but you are right that they will have to decide. I will not force my daughter upon the witches or the vampires as their princess, but I will create a place for her in our world."

"That's where you're wrong, princess." Draven said, the term not as a patronizing nickname but rather as what she was. "You are the heir to the witches, and whether you and your mate believe it or not, the princess of vampires through your mate. These are your people and they will look to you to lead despite whether you are ready or not."

"And it may be sooner than you think," Dorian added softly, almost as if it were an afterthought he'd meant to keep silent.

Emery's gaze zeroed in on the sentinel. "What do you mean sooner than I think? Did something happen?"

Dorian shook his head and fixed his eyes on the fire in front of him as he fidgeted with the stick in his hands. "Not yet, but there are whispers in the ranks."

Emery leaned in, scooting to the edge of the long where she sat. "What whispers?"

"I shouldn't speak out of turn."

"Dorian," Ansel ground out beside her. "If it involves Emery, I suggest you speak and soon."

The same magic Emery had seen flare in Dorian's eyes

before lit for a split second before he closed them. "It doesn't directly, but it will affect his majesty." He pressed his lips together and chewed on his bottom lip as if weighing the consequences of telling them what he knew before releasing a heavy sigh. "I've stayed in contact with some of my brothers in order to keep tabs on what's going on at the castle. Yesterday, Augustine made a stand against his father."

Emery sucked in a breath and her heart leapt in her chest. "He did?"

She didn't need him to answer. She'd seen it. One of the snippets the stars had gifted her. It was that moment. The feeling in her gut told her she was right.

Dorian nodded. "The king killed a subject during the airing of grievances. Someone who opposed a war against the witches. Augustine publicly disagreed with the death and chastised his father."

"Is Augustine okay?" Emery's chest constricted as she waited for his answer. She'd know if something happened to him. There is no way the bond wouldn't react, but that didn't mean he was safe in the castle.

"He's been laying low and my sources tell me he has since reconciled with his father, but it started movement in the underbelly of the castle. Rumors are flying. Those who would stand behind the prince think he should make a move for the throne. People want change. They are tired of the oppression at the hands of a king who would force his people into a war they do not want. Life at the castle or an embassy is not an accurate representation of the vampire kingdom. The king has put so much effort into planning a war with the witches that he's neglected his people. The people want a ruler who will help them. They want peace, your majesty."

Emery narrowed her eyes at the use of the false title. She really wished he'd stop using it.

"Emery," he amended, as if ready to plead his case for why she should believe him. "Hope is a fickle thing, but it has the ability to set ablaze a rebellion, and I think that's what your mate has done."

Hope was all she had left. Something she had in common with the people of Augustine's kingdom. Her kingdom, too, according to Dorian. She understood how they felt. The witches had neglected her at every turn. What she would have given for someone to care enough to stand up for her and demand she was worth fighting for.

"I don't know what everyone expects me to do," Emery whispered for the first time. It felt like a weight was lifted from her as she trusted those who placed their trust in her.

Dorian's eyes locked on her. "I suspect you will do what is right and fight for your people."

She cast her gaze around the fire, meeting the eyes of Flora, Draven, and Ansel as they all nodded in agreement.

"You aren't alone, Emery," Flora reiterated.

Tears pricked at her eyes, but before she could answer the call and agree to their promises, Callum tore from the house and down the steps to where they sat, a wild look in his eyes. "Lily is portaling Malcolm here. He found her grandfather and with him, the fae flower we need."

"Really?" Dorian and Emery said in unison.

"Yes." Callum's gaze locked on Emery. "Lily wants you to meet her upstairs. You're going to help her save Thea."

No pressure.

Chapter Twenty Nine

AUGUSTINE

Augustine sipped the top shelf whiskey and rested his head on the soft cushion of the seat back. He shouldn't be drinking with the goal of getting drunk, but that's what he was doing. If he was drunk, even if it only lasted a short time, he wouldn't have to consider the fact it was the full moon and they were no closer to healing Thea, that his father was days away from launching attacks that would further cripple his people, or that he was going absolutely insane staying away from Emery. He tipped back his glass and savored the burn of his third glass of whiskey. Two more and he might achieve a buzz. At least for fifteen minutes.

It had been months since he'd been back to the club. Nothing had changed. The music that spoke to his soul still pumped from every speaker, and the top shelf liquor never ran dry. He paid his elite staff to ensure it ran smoothly in his absence. The problem was, he had changed.

Getting lost for a night in the music didn't hold the allure it once did. Not alone at least. With each melody belted out on stage, each sultry undertone expertly woven through the lyrics, Augustine only yearned to share the moment with one person.

The pink-haired little witch who consumed his every thought.

His bloodlust was growing stronger by the minute. It had reached the point where every other thought was of piercing his favorite spot on Emery's delectable neck. So much so, he had to actively try to keep his fangs from elongating permanently. As much as he hated to admit it, he was absolutely failing in his attempt to stay away from her. The bond grew tighter with every second away, and he wasn't sure how much longer he could keep fighting against the inevitable.

"What was your number tonight?" Damian yell-whispered over the music to Jonah in the booth beside him.

Bloody fucking rookies. Augustine clenched his fists. He didn't mind that the sentinels had taken to drinking at the club after their missions. Nor did he care that they sampled the locals. But openly discussing their kills where any human could hear them was where he drew the line.

Genocide of his people had been perpetrated for less throughout history.

Rex would have never allowed the men in his battalion to be so careless.

"Seven," Jonah boasted. "You?"

"Ten." Damien tipped back his beer and took a long pull. "Looks like you're buying again."

Augustine set his drink down, and rolled up his sleeves. They probably had no idea he sat in the shadows beside them, but they would remember their place and the rules set forth for them before the night was through.

Before he could lay into the sentinels with all the pent-up rage he should have channeled elsewhere, one of his newer commanders stepped forward and slammed his fists onto the young sentinels' table.

"Who the fuck do you think you two are?"

The rookie sentinel's eyes widened and a knowing smile stretched across Augustine's lips. These two were about to get their asses handed to them, and as much as he would have loved to deliver them himself, he'd enjoy every minute of watching it happen.

"I...we...no one sir." The two of them stumbled over their words. "We were just discussing our night."

"Where everyone could hear you," the commander hissed, and Augustine wished he could remember his name. "Get back to the barracks. You're on duty until the two of you can get your heads out of your asses and remember that while we have a mission, the code comes first always. That means keeping your fucking mouths shut. While you're at it, why don't you let Johnson know you'll be on latrine duty until further notice. I hear he's got some mighty fine toothbrushes that fit in the grooves of the tiles just right."

The two of them groaned, but with one stern look from the commander, they nodded and scurried from the booth at what humans would perceive as impossibly fast.

The commander straightened his shirt and turned to where Augustine sat watching.

Augustine nodded and extended his hand, welcoming the commander to join him. He then waved to the bar and gestured for two whiskeys to be brought to the table.

"Thank you, Your Highness."

"It is I who should be thanking you. Those two got off easy under your punishment, Commander..."

"Braxton." He gave a small bow toward Augustine. "Shall I steepen the penalty, Your Highness?"

"For a first offense, no. Should they repeat though, send them my way. I'd love the chance to remind them why we have a code."

"Yes, Sir."

The waitress brought over their drinks, and Augustine nodded toward Braxton before bringing the smoky whiskey to his lips.

The commander swirled his glass and studied the liquid before setting his glass down.

Augustine cocked his brow and rested his hands on the table in front of him. "It's not customary to turn down a drink with your prince."

"I'm sorry, your highness. It's not the drink. It's just… may I speak freely?"

Augustine raised a brow. What was it with everyone and coming to him with that request? Did he have a sign stamped to his forehead that said 'Tell Me Your Problems.'? Still, he was intrigued by the commander's request and gave him a slight nod.

Braxton shifted in his seat and chuckled. "Maybe I will have that drink." He grabbed the glass and nervously tipped it back, downing its contents entirely.

Does he know that's a hundred year old scotch?

"Better?" Augustine asked, suspicious of what the commander had to be nervous about.

"Yes, Sir." He settled back against the highback booth and inhaled a steady breath. "You may or may not know, but your stand against your father has sparked hope within the castle. Within the vampire community."

He had heard something of the sort in the underbelly of the castle, but he'd paid it no mind. The King would not allow there to be anything other than obedience. It didn't matter that their rumblings confirmed what Rex had shared, or that somewhere deep inside him his own hope had been sparked that he could have everything he ever wanted if he fed the rising dissonance.

"I've heard the rumors, but I'm not sure what good bringing them up will do. I'm not the King, and I still have to play my part."

Braxton chewed his bottom lip, clearly mulling over Augustine's statement. When he'd come to his conclusion, he looked up with determination in his eyes though his voice was barely a whisper. "And what if your part was to lead an army of your own?"

"Sounds like treason." He tipped his glass in unison with his brow and took a sip of his whiskey, savoring the taste on his tongue and wishing it was Emery.

"It's only treason if you don't succeed, sir." Braxton retorted, catching Augustine off guard.

He quickly reigned in his surprise at Braxton's treacherous suggestion. He couldn't reveal how much the idea appealed to the darkness that fueled him. "And what would the success of my army look like?"

"What the people want. You on the throne, bringing light to the future of our kingdom. One where we aren't neglected. One where peace prospers, and we are free to work with other supernaturals." He spoke as if it was such a simple answer. As if sentinels and subjects alike wouldn't have to die to achieve that goal, even more so if they were up against his father.

"I should kill you for even speaking of this," Augustine hissed through his teeth. He didn't know Braxton any more than he knew any other of his father's commanders. Rex was his man, and he was gone. Nothing about Braxton indicated he was putting up a front. The fact his heart beat steadily spoke to the truth in his words.

His phone vibrated in his pocket and he reached down and silenced it through his jeans. Whoever it was could wait until after his conversation with Braxton. A conversation, it seemed, that could change everything.

"You should kill me, but you won't."

Augustine nodded, urging him on and hoping he had something to back up his treasonous plan. He needed an indication that this wasn't a trap set by his father to confirm Augustine's loyalty to the crown. It didn't matter that he had considered many of the same things over the last twenty four hours.

"I saw you in the throne room yesterday, Your Highness. It wasn't just the way you stood up to your father for taking Bell's life. It was the fire in your eyes, the recognition of the tragedy that is taking place across our kingdom. There are many who would side with you, even in our own ranks. You only need to take the helm."

Bell, not Bellamy. Pieces began to fall into place in Augustine's mind, and they lended to Braxton's motives. "You knew Bellamy, didn't you?"

Braxton sighed and inclined his head. "I did, Your Highness. We grew up together. I tried to tell him it wasn't the right time, but he insisted. It cost him his life."

"It will cost many more to achieve your end goal." Augustine's eyes narrowed as he waited for Braxton's response.

"I know, but I can't let Bell's death be in vain," he whispered, his head bowed. Braxton looked up at Augustine and he could see the fire in the commander's eyes. "But it's not only for Bell. Our people deserve to be free of the tyranny of this crown. They deserve the right to choose their future without repercussions."

Braxton stoked the fire in Augustine's chest, and he found himself nodding along with him.

Augustine's phone went off again, and this time he was thankful for the interruption, if only because he was about to jump in the fight with both feet, consequences be damned.

Which was something he couldn't afford to do. Not when so many relied on his protection.

Lily's name flashed across the front of his screen and panic caught in his throat as he quickly swiped to answer. "Is everything okay?"

"Can you be ready to portal in five minutes?" Her words came out quick and jumbled, only adding to Augustine's panic.

He turned away from Braxton and lowered his voice even though he knew the vampire could hear every damn word he said. "I'm in the city, why, what's wrong?"

"She needs you."

"Who? Thea?" Fuck, if anything happened to her he didn't know what he would do. "What happened?"

"No, Emery." What he had perceived as panic in Lily's voice, he now realized was annoyance. "She needs to let go in order to make the flower grow as we need. She can't shut her damn brain off and tap into her magic."

"Wait, what? You have the flower? What the bloody hell, how come no one let me know?" He was both relieved and fucking furious. Thea likely wouldn't have made it through to the next full moon, and now there was hope she would if Emery could save her.

"Fucking Callum," Lily cursed, adding a few in her native tongue for good measure. "He was supposed to call you. Malcolm arrived with Octavian and the flower. But we're running out of time, and Emery needs you."

Augustine sucked in a breath and bit the inside of his cheek. "I'm not sure I'm the solution."

He really wasn't. He would likely attack her neck the moment he saw her, and they hadn't exactly left on amazing terms. In fact he could almost guarantee he was the last person she wanted to see after his spectacular rejection of her claim that they were better off fighting together.

"I don't care about your noble cause, Augustine," Lily yelled, and he could have sworn he saw Braxton wince. "You are her gods damned mate, start acting like it."

"Fine," Augustine growled out, sensing there was no way out of this, especially considering he would do damn near anything to save Thea. He wouldn't dare mention to Lily that he wasn't the only mate not meeting the standard that was expected of them. "Where do you want me to meet you?"

Lily told him the exact location of a nearby park where he could meet her, and he hung up the phone.

"Fuck," he sighed.

"Woman trouble?" Braxton quirked a brow at him.

"You have no idea." Augustine tipped back the rest of his whiskey and slid from the booth. He signaled for another round to be brought to the commander before meeting his gaze. "I will consider your proposition. For now this stays between us though. All of it."

"Yes, Your Majesty," Braxton nodded.

Augustine chuckled at the improper title. "You've been talking to Dorian, haven't you?"

"He may have reached out," the commander said with a sly smile.

He'd have words with Dorian after he dealt with the Emery situation.

"Good luck with your problem," Braxton called out as Augustine headed across the bar and into the muggy Chicago evening.

Luck was the last thing he needed if he was going to face Emery. More like a damn miracle.

Chapter Thirty

AUGUSTINE

Everyone was crowded in the living area when Augustine arrived at the cottage. Callum paced in front of the hearth, an outward sign of the nerves that permeated the room. Flora and Draven cuddled together on the love seat, while Ansel taught Dorian to play chess at the dining room table. The former made him sick with their outward display of love, and the latter had no idea they were each stealing longing glances while the other made their move. Mostly he was jealous he didn't have what they did, though he'd never admit it out loud. He'd walked away from Emery, and he couldn't regret it. Ultimately it's what was going to keep her and their child safe. Even if the most recent revelations could possibly change all that. He couldn't let himself hope. Not with the number of uncertainties still in play.

Lily turned around and threw her hands up. "Wait right here while I go prepare Emery for you."

Augustine's lips pulled into a line as the weight of his stare bore down on the witch. "You didn't tell her you were going to get me, did you?"

Lily winced and gave a minor shrug. "Not exactly."

Malcolm snorted and stood from his seat on the edge of

the armchair where Lily's grandfather Octavian sat mumbling to himself. Augustine could only make out every other word, but they were the ramblings of a crazy man. In one breath it was something about the fairies coming back to earth to take the babies and the next he was going on about how when the time was right things would fall into place under the dark sun.

His brother stepped in front of him and pulled Augustine into a half hug, patting him on the back. When they separated, Augustine nodded to the stairs. "Any notion how it's going up there?"

"And how would I know? I've been here with the love birds and crazy pants since Lily banished us from Thea's room and then left to get you."

"You know we can all hear you, asshole," Flora piped up from the loveseat.

"Oh I'm aware." Malcolm muttered and tipped his head to Ansel and Dorian. "At least those two are oblivious."

"Not to your musings we aren't. And I don't appreciate your assumptions, your highness," Dorian snapped, never taking his eyes off the chessboard.

Augustine shook his head. The tension in the room was almost unbearable. It was a miracle no one had lost any limbs. He swiveled back to Malcolm, "Lily hasn't said anything to you?"

His brother's jaw tightened and he shook his head. "Not unless you count barking to get out of her way when I tried to help."

Augustine chuckled. That sounded exactly like Lily. For as powerful as she was, there was no doubt she'd spent the better half of her life alone at the cottage in the woods. If anyone other than Callum or Emery stepped out of line or didn't do things the way she envisioned them, she'd bite their head off, even if they were trying to help.

"Can't you feel Emery through the bond?" Malcolm asked. "I honestly figured you would have been storming through our door sooner."

"It doesn't work that way." It did work that way, though now that he mentioned it, the bond had been quiet more often than not since their tryst in the woods.

Augustine reached down the mate bond and found she'd closed it off to him. He wasn't sure how he felt about that. She'd never shut him out before. Not for any extended period of time at least. She'd made it clear she wanted to accept him for the sake of their daughter. He'd grown accustomed to the warmth it provided, the silent reminder he wasn't alone in the battle for their safety. Even if he hadn't offered the same in return, which he knew made him a complete asshole, but he couldn't bear to feel her while he attempted to stay away.

"How does it work?" Malcolm pulled him back to the present, though it was hard for Augustine to focus on anything other than the silent bond.

"How does what work?" He leaned on the banister and glanced up the stairs for any indication he could approach, the sudden urge to go to Emery growing within him.

"The mate bond. Being mates." Malcolm followed his gaze and frowned.

Augustine huffed a laughed. "You are asking the wrong person. I may be Emery's mate, but we are the furthest thing from a picture-perfect coupling. You and Callum have this presumption that being mated is the greatest thing, but it's brought nothing but hell to Emery and me."

"It brings hell because you let it. Both of you are so damn stubborn," Malcolm retorted, but his words were filled with an uncharacteristic venom.

Augustine's harsh gaze landed on his brother, and he snarled. "And I suppose you and Lily have it all figured out?"

"No. Where do you think Emery gets her stubbornness from? It's a family trait and Lily must have invented it. She's avoided me at every turn. Every opportunity we've had to address this godforsaken longing tearing through us, she's hiding behind Callum or working on 'the cause' as they call it. At least I am trying to address everything despite it leaving my mind a damn mess."

"What do you mean?" Augustine snapped, every protective bone in his body swelling. "Did she hurt you?"

Sloane had done a number on his brother. He'd been healing slowly with Emery's help during her time at the castle, and Augustine thought he was doing better, but maybe he'd misread the signs. If Lily thought she could hurt Malcolm under his watch, she was greatly mistaken.

"No, she hasn't done anything and the problem with that is I both want her to and dread the idea of giving my heart to another woman. I both loathe her and love her and I hate myself for it, but at least I'm fucking trying to figure this damn thing out so we aren't left pining for each other for all of eternity. She has been running from the moment we realized what we were to one another. I thought I was ready, but the more she runs, the more I question if this is even what I want. How can a woman have so much damn control over me when we haven't even spoken more than a handful of words to one another? I am at my wits end, Augustine. When's it my turn to get the not-shitty end of the stick?" Malcolm ran a hand through his hair and turned away from Augustine.

Fuck. He was such an asshole.

He'd one-hundred percent misread Malcolm's headspace. Augustine had been so caught up in his own bullshit that he hadn't seen the signs his brother was struggling with all this.

At the same time, what could he say? He wasn't lying when he said he and Emery were a terrible example of what mates should be. He fought the bond tooth and nail, even right then, he was doing the exact opposite of what it demanded of him.

"Fuck. I'm sorry." Malcolm scrubbed his face and retreated back within himself. "You don't need my sorry ass on top of everything else you're dealing with."

Augustine reached for him and pulled him into a hug. "You're my brother, Malcolm. I'll always be here for your sorry ass. I'm sorry I haven't been there for you lately. I don't have an excuse."

Malcolm's chuckle vibrated against his chest. "You can make it up to me when all this bullshit is over."

The two of them pulled apart, and Augustine patted his brother's shoulder. "So what are you going to do about it?"

"My instincts are telling me to take her over my knee and force the lass to listen, but I somehow don't think that's the right answer."

Augustine snorted. "And that's saying something coming from you. You're supposed to be the kind one." He'd pay good money to see that go down. He might even place a bet on Lily.

"We both know my kindness only goes so far. It won't be long before I give into a darkness of my own, hunt her down and demand her attention." He rubbed his wrists as if he was trying to keep himself from running up the stairs and taking what he wanted. It was a feeling Augustine knew well, being at the whim of his little witch. "It was easier being in another country, but I've been in this house for all of two hours and I'm going insane with the need to hold her. I don't know how you did it for so long with Emery in the castle. How you continue to do it. As much as loving her scares the shit out of me, I'm ready to give in if it ends the torture."

"How do you know I haven't taken what I need?" Augustine said with a sly smile. "I'm not a saint, Malcolm, and Emery is far from pure."

Malcolm arched a brow. "So you two have finally admitted what you are?"

"Admitted, yes. Accepted no." Augustine's eyes found the ground and the bond tightened in his chest, protesting his words. "I can't accept her. I am the crown prince and so long as my kingdom is under attack by witches, and our father has put a price on her life, I can't make her my queen."

Even he could hear the defeat in his words, but that's just the way it had to be. At least Malcolm wasn't bound by the same constrictions. He could walk away from it all for Lily if he wanted to. Not that he would. The stubborn fool.

Seems to be a trait we all share.

Augustine snorted, and Malcolm's brows furrowed in suspicion.

"But you want to accept her."

Augustine waved him off, shaking his head. "It doesn't matter what I want."

"Brother, you need to realize you are the crown prince, but before that you are a man, and a man needs his mate at his side. You were literally made for one another. I know because I feel it when I think of Lily. Stop being such a stubborn ass, and put yourself first for once."

Pot, meet kettle.

"No shit," Augustine muttered under his breath.

"What?" Malcolm looked at him like he was crazy, and maybe he was. Talking to another half of him inside his head.

"Nothing." He wasn't about to get into it with his brother. Not only because he didn't need to know about August, but because mates were complicated as shit and no two were the same. He would have to figure it out with Lily.

"It sounds like you gave yourself the advice you needed to hear."

"If only it were that fucking easy."

"Ain't that the truth?" Augustine nodded toward where Octavian sat on the sofa. "What does he think of the whole mate bit? That's why we found him, right? He was a mate?"

Malcolm shrugged. "Is a mate, was a mate, I have no idea. I've had maybe one lucid conversation with him since finding him. And even that was questionable. The moment I mentioned mates he was eager to leave with me. Packed his bag in less than five minutes."

"He's been like this the whole time? What the hell happened to him?"

"Your guess is as good as mine. I'm not sure how much help he's going to be, but we've got him, and he had the flower."

Great. The only lead they had on mate history was certifiably crazy, and they were essentially back to square one in figuring out the parameters of the bond.

"Augustine?" Lily stood at the top of the stairs, sweat on her brow, and her hair pulled up in a mess on top of her head. "We're ready for you."

"Wish me luck." He gave his brother a mock salute.

Malcolm nodded at him, and Augustine walked up the stairs, dread filling his chest while excitement fluttered through the bond. He had no idea how the hell he was going to help Emery, but he was damn well going to try.

When he reached the top of the stairs, he turned toward the bedroom, but Lily stopped him with a touch on his arm. "Remember the other day when I told you she needed you as much as you needed her?"

Augustine nodded silently, wondering where she was going with her question.

"This is one of those moments. She doesn't believe she can do what needs to be done."

"I'm still confused as to what you think that has to do with me?"

"She needs to tap into her earth magic, and coax the flower to bloom. If she can't do it, I can't gather the magic from within. You are her other half, her mate. Just as you were needed to heal her when she accepted her magic, I suspect if she has you on her side, she'll be able to open herself to the magic she needs to channel."

"She hates me as much as I hate her." A lie if he'd ever told one, but thankfully Lily wasn't a vampire.

"Which is not at all." Lily cracked a smile, basking in the knowledge she could see through him. "We've all seen the way you two are together. All words and teeth until the other is in danger. Do this for her. And if not for her, for Thea."

"Okay, but on one condition." He was already committed to helping, even before this little conversation, but that didn't mean he wouldn't use it to his advantage. "You need to talk to Malcolm."

Lily's mouth formed a line as she silently contemplated his words.

"You are breaking him, Lilyana. He's the most hopeful romantic I know, but between Sloane's bullshit and now you running away from him and the bond he feels so deeply, you are going to ruin the best thing that has ever happened to you. So as you told me recently, get your head out of your ass and don't hurt him or I'll kill you."

Lily's brows raised clear to her forehead, and Augustine half expected her to fight with him, but she reluctantly nodded. "Fine."

"Good." He patted her shoulder gently.

She gave him a narrow-eyed look, and nodded toward the

doorway. "Go then," she said with a sigh. "I have to talk to your brother."

The bedroom was dark aside from the light radiating from the two lamps on the nightstands. While it looked exactly like it had in the vision, it felt different being there. Like a weird sort of deja vu where he knew what would happen and yet so much could have changed because of free will that he wasn't sure he should feel any sort of confidence.

Thea remained where she'd been since she'd arrived. Her skin had grown more ashen and her hair fell flat around her, the curls Augustine loved losing their bounce.

Emery sat cross-legged in the middle of the chaise by the window with a pot in her lap, tears streaming down her face. A stark difference from the confident woman he'd seen in the vision, and he couldn't help but wonder what had changed that they'd ended up here instead.

He wasn't sure what he could do to help her. Their situation was beyond fucked up, but if Lily thought his presence would help her do what she needed to do to save Thea, he'd give it everything he had. As a bonus, his participation would push Lily toward Malcolm, which they both desperately needed. As for Emery and him, Augustine didn't know what his actions might do for them. He wasn't even sure what he wanted them to do, only that he would likely savor every moment spent with her come morning. He and Emery were two ships lost at sea, searching for a place of solitude but destined to end up on their own remote islands.

Emery didn't move when he approached and sat behind her. Her eyes remained trained on the flower, her grip tight on the pot in her hands.

The Enchanted Amaryllis was smaller than he remembered, its purple petals folded up, overlapping with a hint of a pink glimmer at its edges. It was alluring in a way that spoke of its magic, demanding his attention.

"Em."

Emery slackened into him, her chin falling to her chest as she released a defeated breath. "Have you come to shove in my face how much I need to do this? How it's all on me to save Thea? I know all that."

His chest tightened. He'd never heard Emery sound so defeated. Not even when their son was torn from them. She was supposed to be the hope in the dark, and she was so damn lost in it.

Augustine placed a soft kiss behind her ear, ignoring the way her thumping pulse raced so damn close to his mouth he could practically taste her. Now wasn't the time. "No, little witch," he whispered, "I'm here to remind you that you are the future queen of the witches, and as such you have more power running through your veins than any other. You have the ability to do this."

"I can't." She choked on a desperate sob. "August, I can't."

I'm here, princess. Augustine, do something. For fuckssake.

August was right. As was Lily. Emery was lost.

Augustine slid so she sat between his legs. He ran his hands down her arms until his covered hers, her back rested against his chest and her ass pressed against his growing arousal.

Not the fucking time, he chastised his dick, but there was no way he could be this close to his mate and not be turned on.

He breathed against her ear, loving the way she shivered against him. Augustine searched his heart, trying to find the words that were buried deep. The words that he knew would guide Emery but would leave him with an open wound—a wound he wasn't sure would heal if he carved it from his heart.

For Thea, he reminded himself, though he knew it was for so much more.

Augustine inhaled and breathed against her. "Emery, you are the most incredible and infuriating being I have met in my long life. You drive me insane with your need to make the world right, but I'd be lying if I didn't say I admire your tenacity. Your hope is a wildfire spreading, your will is the fuel that will lead your people." A*nd mine*, he added silently. "You are the future queen of the witches, and you know how I feel about witches."

Emery huffed a laugh, and its warmth radiated through him.

"But Princess, you aren't like the other witches. You are a force unlike anything I have ever encountered. Self-assured in yourself and your cause, and yet completely selfless. You constantly put others before yourself. You have everything it takes to be an amazing leader."

She turned her head, nuzzling herself against his face. "I know what you're trying to do, Augustine, but while your words are pretty, they aren't true. I can't even conjure the simplest earth magic to make this damn flower bloom."

She was broken. All the training in the world wouldn't help Emery, and neither would his empty words. Not if she didn't believe it herself.

Something he overheard her telling Flora about magic popped in his head, and he knew the best course of action. It was risky, but what he was doing wasn't helping.

"You're right," he scoffed, dropping his hands from hers and leaning back. "You can't do it. I don't know why I thought you could."

Emery dropped the plant between her legs and spun on him. "So all those things you said were lies?"

There she was. His fighter. The spark in her eyes fueled him. "I meant them when I said them, but I can see I was wrong. You can't do a damn thing for Thea. Maybe I should call Vishna. She's an elemental, correct? She could probably open a bloody flower."

"You would go to the witch who killed our son?" Rage flooded their bond, and Emery opened her palm, allowing her fire to dance across her skin. "How fucking dare you even suggest that? I'd rather die than trust that wicked bitch—"

Augustine crashed his lips against hers, stealing her words from her.

The fire in her palms disappeared, and the moment he tangled his hand in her hair she opened for him, deepening the kiss. She gripped his shirt, pulling him closer. She breathed him in as if he was her last fucking breath, and he'd give her all of his if it meant she wouldn't let go.

The window beside them flew open and a cold wind whipped around them, tangling the pink hair he loved so much all around them.

Emery shivered and pushed him away. "What the hell, Augustine?"

A smug smile painted his lips. "I was proving a point."

"And what exactly was that?" She shifted back from him and he grabbed her hands, needing to keep her close.

He wasn't letting her go. Not then. Maybe not ever.

Augustine gripped her forearms and held her as he spoke, hoping she'd relax into him again. "You told Flora your elemental magic is driven by different parts of you. Fire by your rage, wind by your desire."

Emery cocked a brow. "And? I don't need a magic lesson from you, vampire."

"Humor me." He reached up and tucked her hair behind her ear, his hand lingering a fraction too long on her pulse. "Water is driven by…"

"Dreams." She huffed, clearly annoyed. "They change constantly like water does."

"And I suspect you struggle with it because your dreams, like water, are constantly evolving, contingent on so much that is out of your control."

Emery nodded.

He reached up and tucked the hair on the opposite side behind her ear, this time cupping her face after he'd done so. "And earth? What is it driven by?"

"Heart..." she whispered, and Augustine didn't miss the way her voice fell off. "It's driven by heart."

He tipped her face up, so her amber eyes met his midnight ones. "And what does your heart want, Emery?"

She closed her eyes and attempted to look away, but Augustine caught her chin between his fingers. "I asked you a question, little witch."

She opened her eyes, and the fire within them had diminished. "I don't know."

"I suspect that's part of your problem here."

Emery scoffed. "This isn't some joke. Believe me, I wish I had an answer for you, but you're the reason I don't know. You're the reason my heart is fractured, the reason I can't save your sister. I want nothing more than to save that little girl. She was one of the few lights in my life while I was at the castle, but I can't because the only part of my heart I'm sure of is the part that carries my eternal love for our children. Unfortunately, that's not enough. Earth demands my whole heart, and I can't give that, because I no longer hold its entirety. Thanks to this damn mate bond, you will forever hold a piece of my heart and as long as I don't have yours to fill the hole, I'm downright fucked."

Augustine's mouth fell open ready to bite back, but he closed it. "You're right."

"What was that? I don't think I heard you, Your Highness."

"I said you're right, Em." His gaze locked with hers, the amber of her eyes swirled with darkness or magic, he wasn't sure which. "I haven't given you my heart. I can't."

Because you are a damn fool. And we both know that's not true. You just fucking won't admit it, which is basically just a lie, which is a construct. Let's face it Augustine, she damn near owns you.

August wasn't wrong. But saying it out loud made it real, and for the safety of Emery and his daughter, he couldn't do that. It was fine if everyone in the cottage knew, but he'd already seen what would happen if his father found out. The threats on their lives. He imagined it would be worse if the kingdom found out. Until the war was over and he knew where they all stood, he couldn't chance an uprising that would target them.

"Not even for Thea?" she asked desperately.

Fucking hell she was going to break him.

He swallowed hard and shook his head. "Not even then. Giving you my heart means giving you August back. It means forsaking my kingdom and bedding the enemy. There will be war."

He lied through his teeth, forcing every obscene reason he could into the space between them. He wanted to run, coming here had been a mistake.

Emery was shaking her head. "I need you just as much as I need August. War has already arrived and it's so close to touching me I can fucking taste it. The stars love to remind me. When they aren't sending me dreams of you through the bond, they send me dreams of blood and destruction. And if it's not dreams, it's visions of every amazing and terrible thing that could happen in our long lives. But the hope that keeps me going is our daughter. She's the reason I give you my heart, Augustine. Not because you've been a stellar mate, because frankly you're the worst. She is the reason I—" Emery dropped her head and her hands roamed over her belly. A smile tugged at her lips and she looked up at him with a wonder he hadn't seen since her days at the castle.

"You what?" She couldn't just leave him hanging like that. He needed to know what his daughter was responsible for. He needed to know every painstaking emotion Emery felt for him if only so he could torture himself later when he played them on repeat through his mind.

She didn't respond but instead grabbed his hands and pressed them to her stomach.

A few seconds passed, and Augustine was beginning to think she was crazy when something rolled across his hand from under her skin.

Augustine sucked in a sharp breath and snatched his hand away. His eyes dropped to her stomach, then up at Emery. "Was that?"

A genuine smile, the kind that reached her eyes, stretched across Emery's face. "Yes. That was our daughter."

"But..." Holy shit, that was their daughter. A smile took over his face. "How long has she been kicking?"

Emery giggled, and it was the most beautiful sound. "That's the first time I've felt more than a flutter."

He reached out to touch her again, but pulled his hands back. "May I?"

Emery's smile stretched wider and she nodded.

He placed his hands on either side of her swollen belly and waited. "Come on, sweet girl. Kick for me again."

As if responding to his voice, two little jabs hit his left hand. And then another one moments later hit his right.

Our daughter.

Augustine wasn't sure if August meant him and Emery or the collective two of them inhabiting their body, but he gave a quiet. "Yes."

"You talk to yourself a lot, you know that? It wasn't something I ever noticed before."

I didn't always have a smartass living in my head, he thought to himself.

You were the smartass, asshole. Give me my body back, August huffed.

"Our body," Augustine corrected as she waited for another kick.

Emery jerked back from him. "What the hell does that mean? My body is mine."

"It's cute you think that, but I wasn't talking to you," he murmured, his sole focus on feeling his daughters movements. "I'm talking to August."

"Really?"

"Yes. He's in awe of our daughter, and he thinks I'm an asshole."

"I mean he's not wrong," she joked and Augustine's face split into a grin. "I didn't know he was able to communicate with you."

He didn't mind being the asshole. It was a necessity. "It's a new thing. I was never able to communicate with him before when he was in the forefront. This time around the fracture was much deeper. We are two in a shared body."

"And always will be?" She rubbed her belly, but the sadness in her voice was evident.

"I don't know," he whispered, resting his hands over hers on her belly. There wasn't really an answer he could give her.

These were the cards they'd been dealt, and he wasn't about to give up his place in the world to return to the depths.

"I need you both," she breathed out quietly, the words locking in her throat. "You're my mate as much as he is."

"You have us both," he replied, attempting to placate her by running his thumb over hers.

"Do I?"

His lips twitched, and he wanted to beg her not to ask him to do something he couldn't. Not yet anyway. "For now. I can't make any promises for the future."

She shook her head, and his heart threatened to stop in his chest. "I can't accept that."

"Emery, I—"

"No Augustine. I deserve to have all of my mate."

The bond between them went cold as it had for all those months she'd been in New Orleans. The difference was this time, he didn't need the emptiness to survive. When he'd hated her, it was easy to thrive on the emptiness. Now it taunted him. He couldn't stand being shut out. What a bloody hypocrite he was. He'd been shutting her out all along, and she'd still done everything to be what he needed.

"You deserve all of me and more, little witch." He leaned in and whispered against her ear, the words he kept hidden in the shadows clinging to her light. "I hope someday I'll be able to give you all you desire, but until that day, please just be mine as much as you can."

Emery searched his eyes for a fraction of a moment and looked away. Augustine was about to pull back, unsure what the look meant, when she surprised him and snuggled into his chest. She stilled and slowly opened their bond, flooding it with every ounce of confidence and love she'd stolen from him.

She reached for the flower she'd cast aside and placed her

hands on either side of the pot. A soft golden glow emanated from her hands, forming thin tendrils that weaved their way around the stem of the flower. When they reached the flower, they fought against the pink shimmering petals, pushing against them with ease. On a quick inhale, Emery grunted and her hands grew brighter. More tendrils exploded from her hands, but this time they dug into the roots of the flower.

Augustine knew the moment the flower accepted Emery's magic, because the flower began to glow the brightest pink and from its glow it began to bloom. Each of the petals opened slowly, revealing an inner layer of petals. The inner layer swirled open and revealed a golden center filled with tiny seeds.

"Go get Lily, there isn't much time." Emery swayed against him, and Augustine was momentarily torn. "Go, Augustine."

He tore from the room to the hall where Lily waited. "She did it."

Lily ran into the room and took the flower from Emery, quickly working against the short time frame she had to extract the components she needed.

Augustine scooped Emery up and pulled her against his chest. She slouched against him, limp in his arms, her breaths shallow. Panic filled him. "Lily, what's wrong with her?"

"She's exhausted. Give her some of your blood and let her sleep. She did her part, now let me do mine." Lily was extracting the golden seeds, which were losing their glow as soon as they were plucked from the flower. She was quickly adding them to the mixture she'd already prepared.

He knew all that. He'd seen it in a vision before. But it didn't do a damn thing to settle the distressed feeling in his chest at seeing Emery slackened against him.

"I'll send Malcolm up to help."

Lily glared at him through her incantation but didn't object.

Augustine carried Emery to his room and laid her on the bed before heading down to inform Malcolm of his new job helping Lily.

When he turned, he found Emery just where he had left her, looking pale and small on the bed. He pressed his wrist to Emery's lips, and she opened softly, moaning around his flesh when his essence hit her tongue.

"Thank you," she whispered after she'd taken her fill, and rolled over before curling into a ball.

He grabbed a blanket and tucked her in, pressing a kiss to her forehead. She was magnificent.

Emery grabbed his hand. "Please don't go. My emotions are frayed, and my magic is depleted. I don't want to be alone right now."

"Sleep, little witch. I'll stay."

Augustine kicked off his shoes and undressed, tugging on a pair of sweatpants. Emery's breathing was even when he slid onto the bed beside her. Before he had the opportunity to situate himself, she rolled over and curled up against his side.

She fit perfectly.

He wrapped his arm around her and placed a kiss on the top of her head.

They were beyond fucked up, and he didn't deserve anything she had to offer, but he wasn't a saint and he'd enjoy every stolen moment with her.

Chapter Thirty One

EMERY

No.

No no no. Emery searched for an escape, a way out of the battle that threatened to claim the cottage. Her family.

They can't be here.

Her hands drifted to her swollen midsection.

My baby.

Bronwyn marched forward, trampling the morning dew that clung to the morning grass, an army of witches behind her.

No.

Emery shot up from her nightmare, her hair plastered to her face, drenched in sweat. Her chest rose and fell with quick shallow breaths, and her eyes darted around the room, looking for anything, anyone to cling to.

There was no one. Panic gripped her spine as the images of her dream haunted her even awake, and she cursed that there wasn't anything she could see to tell her when this vision would take place.

Soft kicks from her daughter against her belly distracted her, both calming and fueling Emery's panic. She needed to protect her, and she silently prayed her dream wouldn't come to fruition.

But she knew in her gut it would. It was too vivid. Where some of the others had been cloudy on the fringes and felt more dreamlike, this one was clear as reality.

Emery swallowed hard, her throat hoarse as if she'd been screaming, which she had in her dream. She reached for the glass of water she kept on the nightstand, but it wasn't there. She searched the room only to find none of her meager possessions filled any of their usual spots.

Shit.

The door clicked open and Augustine walked in holding a tray. His eyes raked over her and widened slightly on where her hands gripped her stomach. He set down the tray on the bureau and raced to her side. "What's wrong? Is it the baby?"

"No." She could barely speak, the image of Bronwyn's hardened gaze haunting her. "I had a dream. A vision."

"Here," Augustine left to grab the glass of water and tea from the tray. "Drink whichever will help your throat."

Emery took the water and drank half the glass while Augustine set the tea on the nightstand. "What time is it?"

"It's still early." He stood and moved to the window, opening the curtains to reveal the faint outline of light over the hills to the east. "I just wanted to make sure you had something to eat when you woke up."

Emery narrowed her eyes on him. Who the hell was the nice guy doting on her and what had he done with Augustine?

"August?" she questioned, more hope than necessary in her voice. While she craved Augustine, August would know how to comfort her. He'd know the right thing to say to calm her and stars knew that's what she needed.

The man before her growled, sending a bolt of pleasure through her. She scoffed at her body's impeccable timing. All it took was one growl, hell, one look and the bond ensured she was ready for her mate. It didn't matter that their world continued to fall apart.

"No, little witch. It's still your favorite mate." Augustine's lips curled into a mocking smile as he sat beside her. "Now tell me what you saw."

Emery shook her head. "Gather everyone. I'll tell you all together."

Every muscle on Augustine tensed like he wanted to argue, and though he looked like he was ready to punch something, he nodded.

Augustine made quick action of gathering up those currently at the cottage to inform them of her dream while Emery showered.

They had barely made it down the stairs when Emery was swept up into strong arms and spun in a circle. She giggled against Malcolm's chest and the overprotective asshole who'd followed her down the stairs growled at his brother.

"I've missed you, replacement twin," Malcolm said with a smile as he set her down in front of him.

Emery rested her hands on his chest and beamed up at him. "I missed you too, your royal doucheness."

Augustine and Lily glared daggers at the two of them. Dorian, Ansel, Flora, and Draven sat at the dining room table engrossed in what was happening, but pretending not to be.

"I don't think our mates like our closeness," she whispered playfully, untangling herself from his arms. She'd missed the hell out of Malcolm. He'd been her confidant at the castle, and even though she'd found other compatriots along the way, Malcolm would forever hold a special place in her heart.

He released a growl that sounded a lot like a laugh. "Given their attitudes, I think our mates can suck it."

She was inclined to agree, but before she could say so, or tell him she'd seen a snippet of him and Lily together in her visions, Malcolm cut her off. "I got you something in honor of coming into your powers and as a thank you for saving my sister."

"Oh, did you?" Emery was torn between a swoon and a scoff. Malcolm wasn't the sweet romantic type, not with her. Which usually meant he was up to no good.

Malcolm smiled mischievously and pulled out a tube which looked a hell of a lot like a container that held an expensive bottle of alcohol.

"I swear to gods Malcolm, you better not be teasing my pregnant ass with my favorite top shelf whiskey." Though she secretly hoped it was, because after this pregnancy she couldn't wait to roll the smoky sweet flavors over her tongue.

"It's better." He barely kept his smile hidden behind pursed lips as he handed the tube to Emery.

She examined the soft velvet that lined the outside of the tube before popping the lid off, and Augustine stepped up behind her to glance over her shoulder to see what was inside.

It was a rolled up bit of black fabric.

Her eyes traced to Malcolm and raised a brow, but his smirk gave away nothing more than that he was clearly up to something. She tugged out the fabric and unrolled it.

The instant she realized what it was, Emery snorted and threw her head back, roaring with laughter.

"Is that what I think it is?" Callum cackled from the kitchen where he prepped breakfast.

Emery shook out the black cotton and snapped the brim. The bastard got her a witch's hat. An honest-to-gods witch's hat, complete with a pointed top that stood straight up.

She slipped it on and spread her arms wide while spinning in front of everyone. "What do you think?"

"*Now* you're a witch," Malcolm teased and pulled her in for another hug. "I'm glad you're okay." he whispered against her hair.

"Thank you so much." She wrapped her arms around him and held him tight as her chest constricted and tears threatened to fall.

These people had become her family. It was a fucked up family in so many ways, but it was all she had, and she wouldn't trade it for the world. She looked over Malcolm's shoulder at each of their members, each of them special to her. Even Draven and Dorian had slid right in and made themselves at home. Her eyes finally landed on where Augustine had moved to stand beside them.

His midnight eyes raked over her, still tangled in Malcolm's arms, and his expression was unreadable. She wanted to exchange his brother's arms for his, to bridge the chasm that continued to separate them, but she couldn't bring herself to move. Not when she didn't know where they stood. Every time they drew boundaries, one of them overstepped. They couldn't help it. It was like telling the sea it couldn't cross onto the dry sand, an inevitable need to keep the world turning.

They had to figure their shit out. The safety and future of everyone in the room depended on it, especially with the witches arriving at their doorstep.

As if reading her mind, Augustine's eyes narrowed and he gave her a small nod.

Emery inhaled a shaky breath and untangled herself from Malcolm once more. She stepped to his side so she could address everyone in the room. "I need to tell you all something."

"*That* doesn't sound promising," Ansel piped up, speaking what everyone else's expressions were conveying.

"It's not." She shook her head. "The witches are coming to Scotland."

Chapter Thirty-Two

EMERY

Worried eyes marred every member of their little group.

They sat around the dining room table, excluding Octavian and Thea who were still sleeping. Augustine and Malcolm were catching everyone up on the intel they had on the Mistress. If the witches were coming, it was no doubt on her order.

The Mistress was the epitome of why vampires hated witches. She fueled the hatred between their people when she broke the relative peace they'd had for nearly a century. She was the reason Augustine struggled to see Emery as more than his enemy. They'd made some strides considering he was willing to fuck her against a tree, but he still held back, and she had no doubt it was in part because she was a witch, just like the bitch who was killing his people. The same bitch who, if aligned with the witches of New Orleans, would likely be hunting their daughter as well.

Just another enemy to add to the list.

"We need to find her and end her," Augustine argued, running his hand through his tousled hair. He had no business looking so damn delicious that early in the morning while discussing the murder of her ancestors, but Emery couldn't help the flip-flops her stomach was doing, staring at him. It probably didn't help that he'd been a complete gentleman the majority of the morning, and she had no clue what the hell to do with that other than enjoy every minute of it. The other shoe would drop eventually, and he'd be back to his assholish tendencies.

"You're not wrong," Malcolm argued, "but it's clear we need a different approach. Everything we've tried so far has only led to the death of our men."

"Malcolm's right, Augustine." Callum picked up his glass and took a sip of crimson liquid.

Augustine's throat bobbed beside her, his eyes locked on Callum's glass. Emery narrowed her eyes in concern. He hadn't been back to feed since their night in the forest, and even though royal vampires could sustain themselves longer, Augustine's bloodlust wouldn't allow for it. It was clearly taking its toll.

Draven raised his hand to interject, ever the quiet Southern gentleman. "I find it interesting that she's been two steps ahead of y'all all this time. Seems possible that she has someone on the inside feeding her information. Might I suggest we do our own recon using sources outside the castle?"

It wouldn't be the first time the witches utilized spies. Emery, Dahlia, and Sloane had lived at the castle over the span of twenty-five years with no one being the wiser. Well, until the end. The king did have Sloane killed, and they still didn't know exactly why.

Emery shifted in her seat, and Augustine swallowed hard again, his lengthened fangs poking out from his lips as he did.

Stubborn idiot.

She leaned over and placed her wrist in front of him. "Drink."

He glared at her and shook his head, even though she couldn't miss the longing in his eyes. "You're still recovering."

Fucking hell. What was with the nice guy routine?

"I'm fine. But it's clear you aren't. Just bite me," she hissed, trying to keep her voice down but failing considering everyone at the table was of the supernatural variety.

Callum slammed his hands down on the table and whipped his head toward them. "Just bloody take her wrist, Augustine. You are cranky, and gods know you don't have it in you to think strategically when the lust takes over."

Augustine narrowed his eyes on Callum and his lips twisted into a snarl as if this wasn't the first time they'd had this argument, but he didn't protest. "Fine."

Emery stilled when he reached for her wrist. This wasn't the first time he'd fed from her, but it was the first time he'd done it publicly since the ball. Plus, that had been August, and they'd still been tucked away in a blissful bubble that had yet to burst.

This was Augustine, and as much as he was her mate, he saw her as a means to an end. Or so she told herself. She repeated the mantra as he brought her wrist to his lips and kissed the spot. She couldn't think about what had transpired the night before. The way he'd manipulated her to get her to use her magic, the way he softly caressed her belly and smiled as their daughter kicked, or his barely there declaration to just be his. Every time she thought she'd figure out how best to move forward—how to get past her love from him—he shocked the hell out of her.

Augustine's eyes drifted to hers, pinning her in place. His lips parted and he spoke softly. "What do you want to feel?"

Emery's brows rose. He'd never asked her that before. He'd always given her what he thought she wanted, which more often than not was loosely related to the fact they were having sex when he fed from her.

"Um, clarity?" Her voice was unsteady, but then she said more confidently. "I don't want you to alter me."

Augustine nodded and bit into her wrist.

She clamped her eyes shut and sucked in her bottom lip to stifle the moan that settled in the back of her throat. Callum started talking again, but Emery could hardly pay attention. Not with Augustine's lips on her skin. She fought hard against the mate bond's call, which screamed for her to climb into his lap. They needed the separation. She meant what she said the night before when she demanded all of her mate. ...At least, her brain meant it. Against her wishes, her heart was lost to the man beside her.

His venom seeped into her, and Emery welcomed its calming effects. The drugged feeling she expected never came. Instead she felt as though she'd had an incredible night's rest, risen and had the perfect espresso and was ready to face the day.

Why hadn't she asked him for this before? It was better than any cup of coffee. She imagined what it would feel like to have this clarity coupled with a mind-blowing orgasm. *That* would be the way to start her day.

Emery clenched her thighs and shook her head, trying to hide the struck-stupid smile on her face. She couldn't start thinking about Augustine in that manner, not with a room full of vampires who'd know the second she was turned on. She closed her eyes to block out the room. Really, she shouldn't be thinking of him in any way, but imagining waking up beside him, experiencing blissful orgasms by his hand… it wasn't helpful.

Augustine smiled against her wrist as he continued to pull from her, and she felt a hint of something more seep through her. It wrapped around her heart, not in a constricting way but in a manner that warmed her from the inside out. She couldn't place the emotion. Or maybe she didn't dare name it. It felt almost like a loving embrace.

Her eyes shot open, and she raised a brow as Augustine finished, lapping his tongue across her wrist to close her wounds.

He gave her a pointed look as she waited for him to say something. Anything. But he turned his attention back to the conversation at the table, ignoring her completely. Not even a thank you for the relief she knew he was feeling.

Emery's hands heated, and she considered burning a hole through his designer jeans.

Fucking prick.

If she were being reasonable, she would have recognized that he'd done exactly what she'd asked him to do, but she didn't want to be reasonable. Not when it came to him.

She pulled her magic into her hand, willing it to smolder over her skin and just as she was about to place it on the high-priced denim, Augustine reached out and placed his hand on her bare thigh.

Emery smothered her magic and sucked in a breath as she tried to contain the butterflies that took flight low in her belly. She craned her neck to look up at Augustine, but he didn't return the courtesy. He just kept his hand firmly on her, stroking her with his thumb.

"So it's decided. Malcolm will stay and help with Thea and Octavian. Dorian and Ansel are going trade off working with Augustine to track the Mistress and will report back as needed. Flora and Draven will return to the wolves and see if they are willing to fight beside us. Emery, you will continue working with Lily on your magic."

"Huh? I mean... I'm going to... what?" How the hell was

she supposed to concentrate on what anyone said with Augustine's hand precariously close to the arousal she was trying to ignore.

"You're going to stay here, little witch, and learn your magic," Augustine repeated, his voice dripping with condescension as he inched his hand up her thigh, just close enough to her pussy to make her clench with need, but far enough that it did little to relieve her wants.

Emery scowled and smacked his hand away.

A smug smile stretched across Augustine's face, and she struggled to figure out what the hell had gotten into him.

Emery turned to look at Lily, who had her arms crossed over her chest and a scowl on her lips. It was a sentiment she shared. She suspected Lily wasn't happy Malcolm would be a permanent resident at the cottage.

At least the cottage would be entertaining. Once Augustine left, of course.

"What about the witches coming?" Emery interjected as a way to distract herself from the vampire beside her. "Shouldn't we be preparing for that?"

Callum nodded. "Lily assures me the wards will keep them out, but even if they should attack, this isn't the only stronghold we have established. You and Lily will be able to portal us away should we need to."

Emery raised a brow but didn't remind him she could scarcely control her gifted magic, let alone cast a portal. "Retreat. That's our plan?"

"For now. We have no idea what we are up against. We've got no intel from the supernatural world. We're living in a bubble, and until we find out more from each of the factions and are ready to make our stand, we will run. Not only for our safety but the safety of your child. Remember, Emery, you are holding the future of our cause."

Callum spoke with no hesitations, and for the first time Emery saw the diplomatic crown prince he'd trained his whole life to be. She'd grown so used to the laid-back, self-serving prick he chose to be ninety-nine percent of the time, that it was almost easy to forget he was a future king as well.

That didn't mean she agreed with him.

"Your cause." Emery threw up her hands and looked around the table. "And what exactly is your cause, Callum? What are any of our causes? We are a cluster fuck of individuals who have no idea what comes next. I don't know what you want, and you have never bothered to ask me what I want."

"Mates." A gravelly voice interrupted from across the room. "Mates are the cause and mates are the answer. They are the past, the present, and the future."

The table went silent, and everyone turned to see Lily's grandfather standing at the bottom of the stairs holding a still-sleepy Thea in his arms. He was significantly older than the rest of the group, not only in age but appearance as well. His hair was silvered, and his beard nearly white. His blue eyes were piercing, yet kind. Almost as if they'd seen too much in his long life.

Octavian tilted his head toward Thea. "I found this little one bouncing along the upper deck. She could use some breakfast."

Malcolm stood and quickly strode to the older man and took Thea from his arms. "You can speak outside of riddles?"

Octavian chuckled and moved to one of the open seats at the table. "Yes, Malcolm. Although I am regretfully crazed the majority of the time these days, I do have my lucid moments. I will say you should make use of them while you can. I fear that there is a time coming when nothing I say will make sense."

"Join us then." Callum gestured for Octavian to sit in the empty chair at the opposite end of the table next to Lily.

Tears welled in Lily's eyes, and her lips quivered as her grandfather dropped into the seat beside her. "Hello, my sweets."

Lily launched into his arms, wrapping her own around him. "I thought I'd lost you," she sobbed against his chest.

Emery clasped her hands at her chest and tears rimmed her own eyes as she watched the heartfelt reunion between Lily and Octavian. She couldn't imagine what that felt like. Everyone in her family was gone for good. There would be no lucid moments to savor. No magical transformation to bring happy tears to her eyes. Lily was the closest thing she had to family, and when she'd found out she wasn't alone, Emery had been filled with every emotion under the sun.

Octavian ran his hand over the back of Lily's head. "Crazy most days, but not lost." He reached his hand across the table toward Emery and opened it to her. "And you must be my great granddaughter."

"Add a few more greats in there, and you've got it." She placed her hand in his, a rogue tear rolling down her cheek. "I'm Emery."

Octavian gave her hand a gentle squeeze. "It's nice to meet you, darling girl."

Malcolm set Thea down so he could put together a plate of the waffles Callum had made for her. As soon as she was placed in the chair, Thea jumped up and ran into Emery's arms. Her eyes widened when she saw Emery's swollen belly.

Baby? Thea signed, bouncing in place.

"Yes. You are going to be an Auntie," Emery signed in return.

If possible, Thea's eyes grew wider than they already were.

She smiled with all the light inside her and hugged Emery. For one blissful moment, all was right in Emery's world.

Thea pulled away and looked up, her tiny eyes filled with life. *Thank you for saving me.*

Always, sweet girl.

Thea settled in on Emery's lap and silently ate the waffles, fruit, and bacon Malcolm placed in front of her. Emery savored the closeness, dropping her nose to Thea's hair and breathing in her child-like scent. She wrapped her arms tightly around Thea, smiling to herself.

"You're going to make an excellent mother," Octavian said, watching her, a glint in his eye. "Although I must say your choice of hat is baffling. You do know the witches didn't actually wear hats like that? I should know, I was married to the first."

Emery tipped her head back and laughed. "I suspected as much, but a good friend presented it to me as a gift, and even if he meant to be a sarcastic ass, I'll cherish it till the day I die."

"You'll make a good mate as well." Octavian beamed and heat filled Emery's cheeks.

"Thank you." She nodded and stole one of Thea's blueberries. "If you don't mind me cutting to the chase, what did you mean mates are the past, present, and future?"

"Oh my dear, humor an old man and tell me how you met your mate? I must admit, it is fascinating to me—a vampire and a witch. Aside from my own fate blessed pairing, it's never happened in all my years. The stars must believe you are something special."

Emery looked up at Augustine and though his mouth was painted into a tight line, he nodded, urging her to tell their story. "I was a member of his Culling. I took my sister's place after she was murdered by his father."

Octavian's brows arched and his eyes widened. "And after all that, you love him?"

"Damn," Ansel chuckled. "He's more ruthless than the lot of us."

Emery swallowed hard, not daring to look at Augustine beside her. She could feel his stare boring into the side of her head, waiting for her answer. The truth was she did love him, but she wasn't about to put herself out there and get rejected by him in front of everyone. She'd had enough of that in private.

"He's my mate," she said with a shrug of her shoulders.

Thea finished eating her breakfast and slid from Emery's lap to go play in the living room with a few toys Malcolm had remembered to bring for her in the hopes she'd wake up.

Emery smiled as her eyes followed the bouncing curls of the youngest royal, but her smile fell when she returned her gaze to Octavian.

"Ah, but that's not what I asked, dear," Octavian tisked. "You see, a mate bond is something incredible. It spans across species. Wolves have mates. Fae have their Bonded. Even the angels on high have their counterparts. But a witch-vampire bond is special. It was forged from love with love and yet, it's somehow beyond love. It's two souls so in sync with one another that they quite literally beat in time. While one can exist without the other, the one left behind will be forever lost, struggling against the grief of not being whole."

"What you're saying is that unrequited emotions between mates can drive us insane," Malcolm snapped, and Lily's eyes whipped to where he sat. It was lucky she'd already put away her knife from breakfast because Emery wouldn't doubt it might find Malcolm's chest at that point.

Those two were going to have a long road ahead of them if the visions Emery had seen were ever going to be reality. But she hoped they would, because there were no two beings that deserved happiness more than them.

"Something like that," Octavian mused. "But it's not impossible to survive."

"Is that what happened to you?" Augustine questioned, his eyes locked on Octavian. Emery studied his profile, but she couldn't get a read on him. His side of the bond was still closed to her and his moods and actions had been all over the place that morning. It was impossible to tell what he was thinking.

"No, Augustine. I'm a special case. My soul is no longer my own. It was lost when my wife, my mate, was killed."

Emery winced at the same time Flora gasped, and Augustine bowed his head and offered his condolences. She'd known his mate had died, and it was likely at the hands of another witch. That didn't make it any less tragic for Octavian.

"Oh young prince, she was a royal bitch," Octavian chuckled and Lily snorted beside him nodding in agreement. "Celeste wasn't made to be my mate. Our bonding was a happy accident. Well, at least for me it was. She hated me for my part in keeping her abominations alive, and when our bond snapped into place, she fought it for a long time before accepting we had to make it work."

"And did you?" Malcolm questioned, his eyes pinned on Lily though she was trying to pretend to ignore him completely.

"For a time." Octavian sighed. "You see, Celeste had her own agenda as the leader of the coven. By then she'd hidden her connection to vampires, convinced the supernatural world that the Culling was the only way to continue royal vampire lines, and fueled the hatred of our species. Toward the end of her life, Celeste began to question her decisions. It was actually Lily who made her question it."

"She did?" Lily piped up, a mix of awe and hurt in her voice.

Octavian nodded, with a sad half smile. "Your need to explore the prophecy and willingness to see past the hatred ingrained into witches gave her pause. Soon after, she was gifted a vision from the stars and set a plan into motion. One that would fix what she'd broken. That was when Vishna made her first attempt on Celeste's life."

Lily gasped. "My sister?"

Emery wasn't surprised in the slightest. It sounded exactly like something Vishna would do. There was no way her son was the first blood on Vishna's hands. That woman would do whatever it took to achieve her goals, which clearly included taking her throne by means of assasination. Poor Lily though believed it was her mother, not the twin she'd loved. At least until Vishna banished her after Kipton's death.

"Yes, my sweets," Octavian confirmed, taking Lily's hand in his own. "Your sister did not like the direction your grandmother was taking the coven. She first garnered your mothers help to successfully assassinate your grandmother, and then arranged for your mother's disappearance. With you out of the line of succession, she could do what was necessary to become the high priestess."

"She wanted to keep building the hatred between vampires and witches," Emery surmised.

Octavian nodded and his eyes trailed down to the table. "She did. Celeste knew her days were numbered, the stars had told her as much." He paused and the room was silent, everyone hanging on Octavian's words. He lifted his head and turned toward Callum. "She was the one who sent you the ancient texts, Callum. And she ensured you'd meet someone and continue your line, Lily."

Lily's eyes widened and her mouth parted. "Adam?"

Malcolm growled and Lily turned her head briefly to give him a mean scowl.

Emery leaned forward, ready to lay into Lily, but Augustine's hand on her shoulder pulled her back. She turned and glared daggers at him.

Who the hell did he think he was to stop her, especially when Malcolm was well within his rights to feel as he did? Sure, it was in the past, but Emery would be lying if she didn't recognize that she hated every bitch who came before her in Augustine's life. And she knew there were many. Hell, she'd felt every ounce of jealousy when August was pursuing the other women of the Culling, and that was just dating. Lily had a child with this other man. He was the reason Emery was alive. That didn't mean she liked the guy. Out of loyalty to Malcolm, she fucking hated him.

Mate-in-laws had to stick together.

Octavian glanced between each set of mates and a deep chuckle rumbled in his chest, but he didn't acknowledge the rising tension between them. "I don't think she picked him specifically. Your grandmother worked in mysterious ways and her magic was greater than any I've met thus far. She's the only witch I've known to have three concentrations." Octavian winked at Emery. "That is until you, dear."

Emery furrowed her brow and considered his words. "I don't have three concentrations. Only two."

"For now." He wiggled his eyebrows and a playful smirk tipped his lips.

Holy hell. She could barely handle the two concentrations she'd already learned about so far, how the hell was she supposed to add a third. And how could he possibly know about a third? He was a vampire, he couldn't be star gifted.

Emery raised a brow, her eyes transfixed on Octavian. "So

what will be my other concentration?" she said, with more sass than necessary.

"That I don't know, dear." Octavian answered with a shit-eating grin. "You'll have to wait and see, I suppose. I only know what my role is in the grand scheme of things. Even then, the stars can't account for free will as you know."

She didn't believe him, not for a damn second. Octavian came out of nowhere, spouting all these truths according to himself, and everyone at the table was eating it up as if it were law. Of course, there were aspects of his words she wanted to be true, but it all seemed too convenient to her. The stars hadn't been kind to her, why would they start now?

"And what is your part in all this?" Annoyance clouded Augustine's voice, matching Emery's own. For as much as Octavian had been forthcoming with them, he was still a code to be cracked.

"My penance for my role in our creation was, when the time came, to deliver the flower and usher in the future of the supernatural world. You all," his eyes scanned the table, "are the future of our world. Each faction represented by mates who are destined to rule with love and compassion. It won't be simple, and I fear there will be war before there is peace, but you will shift the tides and bring order not only for us, but all supernatural beings."

"No pressure." Draven let out a heavy sigh.

"I know." Malcolm snorted. "Has he met Augustine?"

The entire table burst into laughter, save for Augustine who wore a defiant scowl.

"So what comes next?" Emery asked. She didn't think she could take any more of his convoluted information. As it was she could take a week and still not digest everything Octavian had shared.

His eyes dilated and shifted nervously around the room. "The place where the nymphs and berserkers play."

"What?" A few at the table said in unison.

They all turned and looked at Octavian who wore the same silly smile he had when he arrived with Malcolm the night before.

"Grandfather?" Lily placed a hand on his shoulder.

"Oh sweets, love and change are the beauty of life, like where the heavens meet hell and poppies grow wild."

The back door opened, and Dorian walked in from his perimeter search. His eyes locked with Octavian and his smile faltered. "What did I miss?"

"Ooooooh," Octavian cooed. "You're not one of mine, a lion in the grass."

Dorian's eyes widened and he searched the room for any indication of what was going on.

Emery laughed, a bit of relief flowing through her. "I think we've officially lost him."

Chapter Thirty Three

AUGUSTINE

Sweat stuck to every inch of their skin as Augustine and Ansel waited for the signal from Draven to enter the warehouse. They were merely there as backup—a technicality he hated. He despised waiting, especially when the Mistress was involved, but this was the wolf's mission, He'd only been called in as a courtesy.

One he appreciated.

Augustine counted the minutes to keep his mind from straying to everything Octavian had shared with them. If he hadn't already been questioning his ability to stay away from Emery after feeling their daughters' sweet little kicks, Octavian's description of mates may have done the trick. As it was, feeding from Emery had left his body begging for more. His bloodlust hadn't returned, but her essence running through his veins was like being struck by lightning, only lightning may have been more kind. Each time he consumed more of her, she lingered longer like an electric current running through his veins, creating the most pleasurable torture known to man. She managed to weasle her way into every waking moment, to the point that all he could think about was returning to her side.

"Hey, stop day-dreaming." Ansel rubbed his hand down Augustine's bicep lingering just a moment too long.

"Stop being all touchy feely," he snapped, thankful vampires weren't pack beings. It was clear Ansel was feeling the withdrawals from pack life, but that didn't mean Augustine wanted to be his personal snuggler while out on missions.

"Sorry, I can't help it. You're practically pack now. My wolf just wants the connection."

Augustine gave him an offended look. He was not practically pack. There was nothing about that life that appealed to him. Just the idea of being in anyone else's personal space beside Emery's made him want to vomit. He huffed and turned back to the door they were waiting for Draven's team to breach. "Well go find someone else to snuggle."

"I'll just ask Emery when I get back to Scotland," Ansel muttered. Augustine could practically hear the smug smile that accompanied it.

Augustine growled and brought his forearm to Ansel's throat, pressing him into the wall of the warehouse. "I swear to gods, wolf pup, if you lay a fucking hand on her..."

"Whoa, whoa," Ansel threw up his hands in surrender. "We've been over this, Dracula, I'm not interested in Emery in that way. She's the closest thing that I've ever had to a best friend since Sebastian died. She's pretty much the farthest thing from my type, but she gets me and I get her. Plus you've made it clear you aren't interested in anything beyond a superficial mate bond. Don't you think that's kinda shitty of you to hold it against her if she wants to snuggle with her big cuddly wolf friend?"

"She's mine," he managed to grit out through the rage that consumed him. This wolf had a bloody death wish if he thought Augustine was going to let anyone cuddle Emery, platonic or not.

Ansel raised a brow and tightened his lips as if to say he wasn't sure of that. "Well, you better make sure she knows that. My big strong arms aren't the only ones in that cottage, you know."

Augustine said nothing for several long seconds trying to decipher Ansel's words. Which got him nowhere except more upset. "Did something happen that I should know about?"

"No way, that girl only has eyes for you… right now. But we've all heard her crying when she thinks she's alone. Sometimes it's for the son she lost, other times it's for the mate she's unsure of. The first I can understand, but the second is because you are a total dipshit."

Augustine growled again, which triggered Ansel's arms right back into a surrender.

"All I'm saying is this: a girl like that won't wait around forever. You better decide if you're willing to watch her walk away." Ansel pushed off the warehouse wall and stepped around him to flank the other side of the door.

Augustine didn't have time to process Ansel's words because just then, the door slid open and Flora poked her head out.

"It's clear. She's not here."

"Fuck," Augustine exhaled at the same time Ansel yelled and kicked the sheet metal wall.

"Damn it all to hell." Ansel shifted toward the door. "I'll kill her if she hurts those pups."

A growl rumbled in Augustine's chest in agreement. "I'll leave enough of her for your wolf to gnaw on the bones."

"You're assuming I'm not going to grind her bones into dust before that." Flora grinned and Augustine was taken back by the fire in her eyes.

"Damn, little wolf," Ansel praised, looking Flora over. "You got teeth."

Augustine's brow furrowed as he realized something. "What the hell are you doing here, Flora?"

She didn't back down, holding the door open and ushering them in. "I'm not the pampered princess you remember, Your Highness."

He could most definitely see that. Not that he'd approve of her being a part of any sort of mission. Hell he didn't even want Emery anywhere near the war. Augustine inclined his head as he walked through the door, stopping in front of Flora. "I'm also not your prince any longer, and as mate to your pack alpha, you will soon be a royal in your own right, so it's Augustine."

Flora nodded and opened the door all the way, ushering them inside.

The moment Augustine stepped through the door, he gagged.

"Sorry," Flora winced. "I probably should have warned you, it's downright rancid in here."

Blood coated every surface. Splatters on boxes. Puddles in the middle of walkways. Even the ceiling dripped with it. But it didn't smell like ordinary blood. No, it almost reminded him of Emery's but where hers was sweet with a hint of spice, this blood was pungent with the smell of rotting death.

The warehouse was set up exactly as every other of the Mistress' abandoned hideouts. Boxes piled high in every corner concealing the centermost area where she conducted her business. Sometimes it was the corpses that lead the way through the maze to the center, other times it was residual magic. This was the worst of them all.

Augustine ran his fingers through the sticky crimson on

the nearest box. It shimmered in an unnatural way, almost as if it had purple glitter in it.

Magic. And a lot of it.

"Is it wolf blood?" The shake in Ansel's voice betrayed his worry.

"No." Augustine splayed his fingers, the blood dripping between them. "It's human and laced with a shit-ton of magic."

He wished he'd worn a suit and had a handkerchief on hand, but Ansel insisted he stop being a pretentious asshole on missions, so he had to settle for wiping his fingers on his jeans. "Where's Draven?"

"He's in the center, going through what was left behind."

"Were the pups there?" Ansel asked cautiously, almost sounding as if he were afraid to find out the answer.

That's why they were there. The Mistress had moved on from only killing and turning vampires into her cannibal army to kidnapping young wolves who had only barely awoken, many of them between the ages of eleven and fifteen.

"No." Flora choked on a sob. "There's no sign of them that we saw."

She wiped her eyes and abruptly turned and stalked off through the maze of boxes, leaving them to follow.

Augustine turned to Ansel. "Did I miss something?"

"One of the pups taken was a young boy named James. He took a liking to Flora during her time with the pack. She feels personally responsible since she and Draven have been spending so much time in Scotland and weren't there to protect them."

Bloody hell. "Weren't the kids taken when they were out on a nightly run?"

Ansel's jaw tightened along with his fists as he nodded. "They were, but that was something Flora liked to do with them. She is just finding her wolf as many of these pups were. She felt a connection with them."

Damn. Augustine ran a hand through his hair. He couldn't imagine if Thea was taken. At least when the witches attempted to take her, they'd only managed to spell her. He would move heaven and hell for that little girl. Flora seemed to feel the same about these young pups.

He followed Ansel through the boxes as images of his own little girl ran through his mind. She'd be a target too, so long as the Mistress remained at large, and even maybe afterwards, if the supernatural world didn't accept hybrids. The wolves had accepted with Draven and Flora, but that would be a big ask of the vampires. There was no way for Augustine to know which way it would go, only that he would protect his child at all cost.

Which meant being there for Emery, too.

When they reached the center, Draven was directing a team of three wolves, processing the area. A table sat in the center, lifted on pallets. The entire thing dripped with blood, shimmering the same as what he found at the entrance. There were five chairs placed strategically around it with paint on the ground between each of them, forming a star. A salt circle linked each of the chairs on the outside. It looked like something out of a horror movie, but Augustine knew they were dealing with a very real monster.

"Have you seen this before?" Draven asked as he came to stand beside him.

"No. Nothing like this. It almost seems like there was some sort of ritual that took place here. Take photos and send them to Lily. Ask her if she recognizes it."

"Kade." Draven called over the taller of the three wolves and handed him his phone. With his sandy blond hair tied low at the nape of his neck, he looked nothing like a soldier.

Draven apparently was lax with his enforcers appearance. "Take photos of the scene and send them to Lily and ask her if she's seen anything like this."

"On it, boss."

Draven huffed through a smile and handed Kade the phone. He shook his head and followed Augustine around the circle, giving instructions to his other enforcers as he did. One of the dark haired enforcers disappeared down an adjacent hallway, while the other helped Kade with the photos and cataloging the scene.

Augustine's eyes darted over every surface, cataloging what he was seeing. "Most of the warehouses we've raided thus far held the bodies of vampires the Mistress had attempted to turn. We've been working under the assumption she has some sort of dark magic she uses to turn them, but Lily has never seen anything like this, so we're really flying blind."

"We found something," The wolf who'd one of the wolves hollered from the distance.

Augustine, Draven, Flora, and Ansel started toward the wolf. Flora led the way, and Augustine could scarcely make out the soft prayer she sent out that they wouldn't find the body of one of the pups. When she rounded the last corner before the rest of them, and let out a loud gasp, Augustine feared the worst.

Thankfully, it wasn't one of the pups.

It was a witch. Her head was cocked at an impossible angle, and her eyes were completely void of life. Blood ran from her eyes, ears, nose, and mouth and pooled around her head.

"What the hell happened to her, Mateo?" Ansel approached the body and knelt near the head.

"How am I supposed to know, I just find the bodies?"

Mateo shrugged, covering his nose to lessen the nauseating smell. "You're the one who hangs out with witches."

"Don't touch her!" Augustine bellowed, and Ansel threw up his hands. "You don't want to touch any residual magic on the body."

"But sniffing the glittering blood is okay?" Ansel retorted, his brow raised.

Augustine wasn't going to give him the satisfaction of knowing he had a fair point, but gestured for Ansel to continue his search of the body.

Flora shivered next to him, her arms crossed in front of her and eyes locked on the body. "I fucking hate the Mistress. They are barely old enough to shift, Draven."

Draven took a step toward his mate and moved to place his arm around her, but Flora shrugged him off.

"No. Don't try to placate me, Draven. I'm not broken. I'm fucking pissed. I could kill your brother for bringing the wolves into this war. She's taken our children. I'd put money she was behind the attack on Thea and she's killing Augustine's people. They may not be mine anymore, but I was raised in the castle, they welcomed me as a Culling woman. I was a member of Callum's court. They are as much mine as I am theirs."

"Brother?" Augustine thought he misheard Flora, but the way their eyes widened told him that he hadn't. His gaze darted between them, and his brows rose in anticipation of their answer.

Draven's throat bobbed, and he winced slightly. "Callum and Emery didn't tell you?"

"Didn't tell me what?" It seemed Callum enjoyed letting him find things out the hard way—a subject he'd make sure he brought up with his cousin the next time he was graced with his presence.

"Well this is awkward," Flora said, wiping away her tears.

Draven pressed a kiss to Flora's forehead, smiling. "Callum is my half brother. His father raped my mother, mistaking her for a human at the hunt. It's how I am both vampire and wolf."

Bloody hell. Didn't see that coming, August murmured inside him.

Neither did Augustine. He had so many questions, many of them not suited to be asked at that moment, but maybe after a glass of whiskey. Or three.

"So you're my cousin."

Draven shrugged, but then pulled his shoulders back and smiled. "Technically, yes. Not that I'm expecting anything from your family, or Callum's. I've got everything I need with the wolves."

"Huh," Augustine huffed and that slowly turned into a slow maniacal laugh. He extended his hand toward his newest cousin. "Welcome to the family, Draven. We're a bit of a clusterfuck."

Draven chuckled and gripped his hand, shaking it. "So I'm gathering."

Augustine glanced at everyone else in the room. "Anyone else want to drop some random family secrets on me? Maybe reveal they are my other long lost mate that shouldn't exist? Or maybe they are a god and all this has been one giant experiment on the supernatural world we can opt out of now?" He'd reached his breaking point. It shouldn't have been as funny as he found it, but he couldn't stop the laugh bubbling in his throat. There was no way he could have guessed Draven being his long lost cousin would send him spiraling but it did.

He raised his hands and questioned again. "No one?" Another laugh escaped him. His whole life was one big joke. There wasn't a plan of his that hadn't been turned upside-down on him, and he was fucking sick of being blindsided. By Callum. By the Mistress. By his father. But most of all by Emery.

That damn little witch had dug under his skin and every time he turned around she was wrapping herself around him and fucked him sideways, and not in the good kind of way. She fucked him every time she opened her pretty little mouth and spoke straight to his damn heart where the bond connected them. And then Octavian had asked her flat-out if she loved him, and he hadn't breathed deeply since.

Flora stepped out from beside Augustine and after giving her mate a reassuring nod, wrapped her arms around him. "You aren't alone in any of this, Augustine. We've got you."

"We've got you."

Augustine stiffened as her words sunk in. Fight or flight instincts danced on the edges of his mind.

"You're her best friend," he whispered, feeling as though this was wrong. Flora couldn't possibly want to be there for him. Not when her loyalties lay with his mate.

I know you want to do everything on your own Augustine, but we aren't meant to live this life as solitary beings. We need them just as much as they need us. It's okay to let go. They are family.

"She may be my best friend, but we're friends too, more than friends. We're family." Flora echoed August's words. "Get your head out of your ass, and let us help you too."

Augustine's chest rumbled, but he then sagged into her touch, for the first time appreciating a connection maybe as much as Ansel. But this was different. It wasn't a visceral need or all-consuming lust like his connection with Emery. It wasn't physical, or wholly emotional, but it was something he hadn't realized he needed.

All his life he'd lived within the confines of the castle. He had never relied on anyone, choosing to be the one everyone else leaned on. Malcolm. Rex. His men. They all relied on him, but when it came down to it, Augustine's willingness to allow anyone to be there for him only went so far.

August was the one who trusted. He was the one who played the diplomatic game and forged relationships with any sort of meaning. Augustine had always condemned him for it, but maybe the bastard had the right idea.

About time you gave me some credit.

Ansel stepped up beside them and wrapped his arms around Augustine and Flora. Draven stepped forward and gripped his shoulder tightly. As much as he hated the thought of it, he found comfort in their embrace. They weren't his blood—well, except Draven—but somehow they were exactly what he needed in that moment.

Emery was his future and his daughter was his heart, but Draven, Flora, and even Ansel were his chosen family, and they'd accepted him despite all his flaws. He knew Lily and Dorian also fell into the category, even if they weren't there.

"Thank you," he whispered as he untangled himself from them. "I…"

"Don't choke up now, bloodsucker. Just because we're family doesn't mean I like you." Ansel punched his arm, and Augustine couldn't help but laugh.

"The feeling is mutual, guard dog." His eyes met all of theirs. "Thank you for reminding me to get my head out of my ass. I appreciate having you at my side."

"You better not forget it," Flora threatened, though the smile on her face did little to enforce her menacing words.

"I'm going to make a phone call, I'll meet you at the tarmac, Ansel?"

"Sure thing," the wolf nodded.

Augustine left the warehouse and ran through the deserted packing district, only stopping when he reached the city limits. He pushed himself to keep going, the wind, reminiscent of Emery's magic, freeing him of the last reservations he held.

In the last six months, his whole world had changed. He'd fought it every step of the way. The thing was, the more he fought against what the stars had apparently determined as his destiny, the more he wanted it. With each day, he was left questioning everything he'd ever known, and he was tired of living this way. Not when there was too much he could hold on to. He may lose it, in this war, but as the old saying went, he'd rather have loved and lost than never loved at all.

He'd found his chosen family.

He declared himself ready to fight for his kingdom.

And now he was ready to fight for the woman who belonged at his side.

Chapter Thirty Four

EMERY

Portals fucking sucked.

Emery stared down at her hands. She had the incantation memorized and the hand movements were simple, but she still hadn't been able to conjure the circle that would take her to the front of the cottage where Dorian waited for her, probably making a flower crown for Thea. That little girl had all the big bad vampires and wolves wrapped around her little finger.

Lily sighed beside her, but didn't look up from the book she was reading. "You have to focus. Don't just see the place you want to go, feel it. That's why it's best to only portal to places you've been before, it's the ties to that place that make your ability stronger."

"I have to be able to make my magic cooperate before I can do that," Emery rolled her eyes, feeling a pang of disappointment that Augustine wasn't there to chastise her.

"Incantations are the same as elements at their core," Lily said in a tired voice. "They stem from your core but are fueled by your mind."

Emery whipped around and glared at Lily, her own frustration bubbling over. "Maybe for you, that's your concentration. For me it's a whole new aspect of magic I've never used."

Lily's eyes narrowed over the spine of her book first at her and then to where Malcolm sat on the back porch, having a tea party with Thea and Callum. "It's the same thing. Just feel it in your core and focus." Annoyance laced her voice, but Emery suspected it had nothing to do with her inability to master the portal incantation and everything to do with Malcolm becoming a permanent fixture at the cottage.

The older vampire prince tipped his sun hat at Lily with a sardonic smirk and threw one side of his pink feathered boa over his shoulder.

Emery pressed her lips together, holding back a laugh. She had enjoyed every moment of having Malcolm around. Between him, Dorian, and Ansel coming and going, she hadn't had much time to dwell on the witches' arrival or the fact Augustine hadn't returned for the last week. He hadn't closed his end of the bond since Octavian's arrival and she found comfort in that, but it also left her questioning where the hell they stood with each other. He may be off hunting the Mistress and playing fiance to Jessi, but there was no denying there had been a shift in their dynamic after they'd saved Thea.

Of course, neither of them had addressed it, save for a few questionable emotions shared through the bond in the dark of night.

Emery turned to Lily, some of her own mate frustrations fueling her outburst. "Will you just fuck him already? I can recommend a tree just inside the forest line as a romantic spot, but please put the rest of us out of our misery and do something about the ungodly tension between the two of you."

Lily's mouth dropped open and her cheeks flushed. She

swallowed hard and squared her shoulders with feigned confidence. "How do you know we haven't already?"

Emery arched a brow and pursed her lips in question. "Have you?"

"A lady doesn't kiss and tell," Lily said pointedly and brought her book up so she could no longer see Emery, effectively ending the conversation.

Fat fucking chance Emery was letting it go, though. Lily and Malcolm had made the cottage downright miserable any time they were thrown into any sort of forced proximity with each other, aside from their morning walks together in the garden. Emery didn't know what sort of deal they had going on that called for the daily cease fire, but she was tired of walking on eggshells with the two of them the other twenty two hours of the day.

She looked over her shoulder and shouted toward the house, for Lily's benefit, knowing the vampires would hear her even if she whispered. "Callum, have they fucked?"

He snorted. "They absolutely have."

Malcolm snorted tea from his nose and struggled to wipe his face. "I'll kill you, Callum."

Callum shrugged and sipped his tea, pinky pointed straight to the sky. "You know the drill. When living with vampires, if it's not thick or soundproof, we know."

Malcolm scrubbed his face and then mouthed *I'm sorry* at Lily.

Emery frowned and knelt on the opposite side of the blanket where Lily sat. "So you slept with him, but you haven't sealed the bond?" she whispered, even though she knew the guys could still hear her.

"How did you—? "

Emery tipped her head to the side. If there was anyone who would know if they'd sealed their bond it was Emery.

"You'd be struggling to fight the bond if you had, and I don't see Malcolm letting you do that. The fighting between you would look completely different if you were avoiding him afterward."

"More like you and Augustine?"

"Yup, exactly like that." Emery grimaced as she grabbed the book from Lily's hand and set it down. She then called her magic and threw up a wall of wind between them and the boys, hoping it would muffle their voices.

Lily smiled as she tested the wall with her own magic. "A wind wall, very impressive."

Emery shrugged like it was no big deal, though on the inside she was fist bumping herself and jumping for joy that she'd managed to cast it correctly. "It was in one of the books you gave me as a way to muffle sounds."

"You could just cast a silencing veil." Lily waved her hand and magic shimmered around them, blocking out all of the sounds of the Highland afternoon.

"Show off," Emery huffed with a smile. "You know I can't cast incantations."

"Yet. You will someday."

Emery reached for the small satchel and pulled out a piece of chocolate, popping it in her mouth. "So, now that we're alone, are you going to tell me why you haven't sealed the bond with Malcolm despite sleeping with him?"

Lily abruptly tried to change the subject. "You're still not pulling enough from the world around you to sustain your magic consistently?"

The chocolate melted on her tongue, and Emery suppressed a satisfied groan. "If you must know, I'm getting there but it hasn't exactly been easy going. Now that that's settled, answer the damn question."

Lily pulled the discarded book into her lap and fingered

the edges, her gaze firmly fixated on the blanket. "I just...I'm not ready."

"Kipton?" Emery's heart ached for Lily almost as much as it did for Malcolm. ...Well, maybe not quite as much considering Lily's actions toward her debatably favorite prince, but Lily had been through a lot too, and love after loss was a damn hard thing to accept.

"No. I'm just scared." The last three words were barely spoken.

Emery sighed, knowing exactly how she felt. Fear was a hell of a bitch. Her own fear of trusting August was what landed them as enemies. In another world, she would have grown a pair and told him about who she was. They would have discussed it, and he would have accepted her because of her honesty. That may be her truth, but it didn't have to be Lily's.

"He loves you, Lily. I know it seems impossible, but the bond isn't wrong in its choosing. And Malcolm, while a total douche canoe sometimes, is also one of the most loyal, caring men I have ever met. Don't let what Augustine and I have become taint what is supposed to be a beautiful thing. Look at Flora and Draven. You need each other. Don't waste time fighting it, or you might lose him."

"We're stuck together." Lily scoffed, stealing her own piece of chocolate.

"Yes, but you can lose someone even when they're sitting right next to you." Emery's mind drifted to her own darkness, where she'd resolved to live as the blood bag and baby momma to Augustine for the rest of her life. While she had no doubts the bond would ensure she loved him through it, her resentment would only grow and eventually, she'd just be dead inside.

I can't live like that.

Except she could. She would. For her daughter she'd endure it.

A bitter flavor filled her mouth, the sweetness of the chocolate suddenly gone. With a small sigh, Emery pushed away her thoughts. She could examine her feelings later, right then she needed to get Malcolm and Lily on the same damn page and not in the chapter her and Augustine currently occupied.

Lily raised her tear-rimmed eyes and a half smile tipped her lips.

"Go." Emery urged, nodding her head toward the cottage. "You both need this. I can keep practicing alone."

"Are you sure?" Lily hesitated, her eyes narrowing on Emery, looking for an excuse to not go to her mate.

Emery smiled and insisted, "Yes."

Lily gathered up her book and satchel, leaving a few pieces of chocolate for Emery. Just as she raised her hand to drop the silencing veil she stopped and whispered. "Their blood?"

Emery tipped her head back and laughed. She wished she'd had someone to warn her about that little part of sealing the bond. "It doesn't taste bad. Perk of the bond."

"Okay." She dropped the veil and started toward the house where Malcolm eyed her skeptically.

"Just, don't do it in the house right now," Emery hollered, giving Malcolm a heads up as to what to come. "Save Callum and Dorian's poor ears."

Callum snorted and she could have sworn Malcolm's cheeks grew a shade redder.

Lily turned around and shot a playful bit of magic at Emery, who hopped out of the way just in time to avoid being zapped.

A genuine smile tipped her lips. At least one set of the only known vampire witch mates had a chance at a happily ever after.

After the two of them left, Callum took Thea inside to start prepping dinner, and Emery tried to refocus on the task at hand.

Fucking portals.

Too bad after her little talk with Lily all she could think about was the mate who left her.

Her heart longed to see him. Not because the bond demanded it or because she believed they were meant to be together. The truth of it was she missed him. She missed the unwavering comfort he provided, even when he was being a complete asshat. For everything Augustine wasn't, there was so much he still was. The way his face lit up when he felt their little urchin kick hit her right in the ovaries—it was a magic Emery wished she could bottle. He was going to be an amazing father. Then there was the new tone of his voice, the way it broke when he asked her to just be his. He was as desperate as she was to give into the love they shared. Because that's what it was. Pure, unbridled, knock-you-on-your-ass, kick-you-when-you're-down, love. And only in the depths of her soul could she admit she wanted every bit of it.

But he didn't. Or nine times out of ten he didn't, and once he left her side he solidly forgot about her until he needed a top off to survive.

A single tear fell down her cheek, and she wiped it away. There was no use crying over it all. She needed to let it go.

She turned around, needing to focus on anything other than Augustine. Even though it would likely prove impossible, she pulled her magic deep from her chest and willed it to her hands. When the two glowed with bright golden spheres, she closed her eyes and simultaneously circled her hands while whispering the incantation from memory.

Another tear fell down her cheek, and she choked on a sob. "Little witch?"

Emery's eyes snapped open and her mouth dropped, a soft gasp falling from her lips.

A golden circle of her magic had formed in front of her and in the center stood Augustine. A very naked Augustine. His brows were arched, and Emery squirmed as his midnight stare worked her over.

Not that she wasn't wearing the same expression, doing the exact same thing. How could she not when tiny droplets of water rolled over his bare chest, caressing every ripple and curve. She sucked her bottom lip into her mouth and her eyes zeroed in on his cock, which stood straight toward his belly, the tip slick with his arousal.

By the time her eyes locked with his again, they were smoldering. "If you keep staring at me like that, I'm going to pull you through that portal and reenact everything I just fantasized about during my shower."

Emery choked out a cough, caught off guard by his words. "You fantasized about me?"

A wicked smile tugged at Augustine's very kissable lips. "Every damn day, little witch."

Heat pooled in her belly, and she knew she should stop there. She should close the portal and walk away from the heartache she'd inevitably feel later after asking the question burning on her tongue. But she didn't. "And what exactly were we doing that resulted in you leaving the shower so, with your cock standing straight and glistening?"

The sound as Augustine tipped his head back and laughed zipped through her like electricity, landing directly on her clit.

It was hands down one of her top five favorite sounds and she was jonesing to find a way to make him do it again.

"There's one thing August has done that I haven't had the privilege to enjoy myself, and I live for the moment I do." He dropped the towel that was in his hand and took a step toward the portal. "We were in the music room, in the castle. I know it's one of your favorite places to escape to, but we weren't making music. We were composing a bloody fucking symphony."

A shiver tore through her and Emery fought against the need he'd sparked and the way her nipples tightened at his words.

Augustine's eyes never left hers as he reached down and fisted his cock in his hand. "You were tied to the top of the grand piano, legs spread open, bared completely to me. At my mercy."

Fuck, did she want to be exactly there.

Emery pressed her thighs together, the friction of her jean shorts doing little to alleviate the fire he'd stoked between them.

Augustine's eyes flicked to her core, zeroing in on her movement and a sinful grin tipped his lips. "Should I keep going?"

Words failed her, but she had to know what happened next, even if it was only so she could fuel her own fantasies later. She nodded slowly. It didn't matter that it was a terrible fucking idea, she was entranced by every word that fell from his capable lips.

He gave his cock a leisurely stroke, making a show of rubbing his arousal down his lengthened shaft. "The way your pussy weeped for me made me hard on sight, so hard I had to restrain myself from forgoing my plans and taking you hard and fast. Even in my fantasies you are able to wreck me, little witch."

Emery chewed her lip so hard it was a miracle she hadn't drawn blood. She fisted her hands at her sides in an attempt to keep them from trailing across her body and into her shorts where she wanted them.

Augustine's timbre dropped to downright sexy. "You like the idea of me taking you hard and fast don't you?"

Anything she said to deny it would be a lie, and he would know it. His roughness was one of Augustine's best traits, as far as Emery was concerned. Where August was a more gentle lover, taking what he needed but only at the consideration of her, Augustine was a damn mercenary, pushing her to the edge and dropping her down the damn cliff, knowing her pleasure and his own waited for them at the bottom of the chasm.

"I thought so, but in this fantasy it was about my pleasure. The absolute need I have to taste every inch of you. The desire to devour your sweet pussy as you come under my expert tongue. And let me tell you, Emery, in my fantasy you are the sweetest fucking thing." He picked up the speed of his hand, his words spoken on panted breaths. "The way your slick folds welcomed me as I parted them with my finger. The feel of your clit, hard and plump as I sucked on it with elongated fangs. You became my favorite dessert in one solitary moment."

"Augustine, please." Emery's hands drifted involuntarily over the skin of her thighs just below the hem of her shorts, toward her apex.

Her eyes widened as she realized how close she was to losing it. Losing control of her emotions. Losing in the constant battle to keep her wits against Augustine. Losing the slight grip she had on her magic that kept the portal open.

Maybe it would be okay if she lost that. It would force her to walk away.

"Please what, little witch?"

"You know damn well what."

Augustine chuckled. "You're the one who opened a portal to my private chambers without invitation. I was getting ready for the wedding rehearsal and poof there you are. Not that I'm upset by the intrusion. I'd take you over Jessi anyday."

She'd heard the part about taking her over Jessi, but all her brain could focus on was he was dressing for his wedding rehearsal. His wedding to Jessi at the hunt. Two days and he'd be a married man.

And she'd be nothing. Well… his mate and baby momma, but not his wife. Not his chosen partner.

Emery blinked and heat no longer ran through her, despite Augustine's perfect form still rubbing one out for her.

It was like she'd been doused with a bucket of cold water.

She eyed the kilt and jacket that were so much like the one August had worn at the Scottish Delegation Gala. He'd looked downright fuckable that night. Emery shook her head as her emotions got the better of her. "I should let you go."

She kept her voice steady despite the lump in her throat. There was no way she was going to let him see how much it all affected her. He made his choice, she told herself over and over as she turned away.

"Should you?"

The weight of his question hit her like a ton of bricks. It was more complicated than just his simple question. Emery looked over her shoulder to find Augustine standing there, hands at his sides, sorrow and pain in his eyes that she couldn't decipher.

What he was really asking was: Do you want me to go? Do

you want me to marry her? Please say something to stop this madness.

He opened his mouth then closed it again like a fish out of water, but no words came out.

They never did when she needed them most.

Emery sighed, her resolve restored. If he wanted her, he needed to choose her.

Movement at the top of the hill where she'd met Drave and Flora caught her eye. The moment she focused on it, her heart sank, and her face paled.

"Emery?" Augustine prompted, but when she didn't answer, panic filled his voice. "Emery, what's wrong?"

"The witches are here."

Chapter Thirty-Five

EMERY

The note was signed by Bronwyn and delivered on the wind. It said they wanted to talk and nothing more.

Thirty minutes had passed since then, and though they hadn't attacked, Emery still wasn't sure she trusted them enough to talk about anything. Or maybe it was that she didn't trust herself not to exact every bit of revenge she was owed. One thing she knew for sure was she was not about to allow her newfound family to face them alone. Much to Augustine's dismay.

He'd thrown on a suit faster than she'd believed was possible and charged through the portal to Scotland, forgetting all about the rehearsal for his pending nuptials. The ones he insisted on going through with for his kingdom and her protection despite her protests. Then he'd forced her to drink from him to replenish her magic, even though she'd insisted she was fine.

Admittedly, she felt better afterward, since her magic was almost depleted after keeping the portal open so long, but she was infuriated by the constant whiplash she received from him. One moment he was pulling away and getting married, the next he was having fantasies about her and charging headlong into battle to save her.

After gathering everyone—including a very irritated-looking Lily and Malcolm—they decided it would be best for Dorian to go with Thea to a second secure location while the rest of them spoke with the witches. Lily would portal them away if it seemed as though the witches were going to attack, but ultimately they needed to know what they wanted and if they could provide them any useful information.

Emery's hopes were high that it wouldn't end in bloodshed, but of course every time she needed a vision from the stars on an outcome of future events, they were silent. She was beginning to think it was a useless fucking gift.

The evening Highland sun had begun to dip below the hill where Bronwyn stood outside the wards with two other witches at her side, exactly as they had in her vision. She knew when their group reached its crest, the rest of their army would be visible. Hundreds of witches, clad in barely enough to be considered descent, with enough magic to decimate the countryside should they unleash it. Beyond that, Emery had nothing to go on. She didn't know how the confrontation would end.

Everyone was silent for a solid minute when they reached the top of the hill, each eying the other trying to determine what would happen next.

When the silence became too much, Emery stepped forward, and Augustine flanked her, the heat of his body radiating at her back. She didn't need the bond to know he meant to protect her, but she was surprised he let her take the lead.

Bronwyn stood before her, head held high as she glanced over Emery, clearly sizing up what she'd become. Her eyes didn't hold any malice, but that didn't mean she wouldn't smite Emery right off the damn hillside if it suited her. The witches were nothing if not selfish, hateful beings, and Emery wasn't about to let them dictate her life any longer.

Neither Callum nor Lily said a word about Emery's break from the plan to let them take the lead. She couldn't have prepared herself for the change of heart once she was faced with the witch who'd abandoned her. Who'd played a complacent role in the death of her son. She couldn't stand down. This was her fight to be won. Callum had his cause, and Augustine had his kingdom. She was the intended heir of the witches, a role she prayed Lily would take from her, but until that day, she had every intention of holding her faction responsible for their actions.

"Bronwyn," Emery nodded in greeting. Her magic vibrated in her chest and of its own volition snaked down her arms in beautiful golden tendrils.

"Emery." Bronwyn's voice was barely more than a whisper, the exact opposite of what Emery expected of the inner circle member. Her eyes traced down Emery's arms and her mouth dropped. "You have access to your magic."

Emery's face twisted in disgust. "No thanks to you and your priestess."

Bronwy's shoulders sagged, the brave-leader facade she'd worn faltering. "Emery I didn't know."

"Bullshit," Emery spat, taking a step forward. "You were part of the inner circle. You shunned me the moment you found out I carried Augustine's child."

"What was I supposed to do?"

The fucking audacity.

"What were you supposed to do?" Emery's voice rose with her rage, along with every bit of emotion she'd suppressed since the moment she'd lost her son. Magic danced in her chest, tugging against the leash Emery attempted to keep it on. "You were supposed to listen to me. You were supposed to be the scholar you claimed to be. At the very least, you were supposed to be a decent fucking human being and give a shit about me and my children. At the very least you were supposed to be my gods damned friend."

Emery stepped forward until she stood toe to toe with the green magic of the ward and something swelled within her, growing in tandem with her anger. It posed like her magic, but this was something new. Something malevolent and sinister, and Emery welcomed it with every fiber of her being.

And then she snapped.

Darkness clouded her eyes until she was drowning in it.

These witches had broken her in ways that were unforgivable. Their blind trust in a coven made them just as guilty as Bronwyn and the inner circle.

A cruel grin twisted at Emery's lips, and she lowered her gaze to watch as the physical manifestation of the darkness within her swirled down her arms, melding with her golden magic in a beautiful array of dark and light. When she lifted her eyes to Bronwyn once more, she knew they no longer held amber irises.

She'd been consumed, and fuck if it wasn't exhilerating. Every bit of her pent-up sorrow caught in her chest, but instead of pushing it back down and telling herself to 'just deal with it for the sake of everyone else' she allowed it to fester. To morph into a fury she could unleash on the world.

"Your eyes," Bronwyn gasped.

"Do you know what the witches have done to me?" Emery asked, her voice no longer her own, replaced by a gravely seductress of darkness. "I could almost forgive them for abandoning me my entire life, but I will never forgive them for taking the life of my child."

Bronwyn's eyes trailed to Emery's midsection and back up

to her eyes. Horror etched on her face. "W-what do you mean?"

Rage flared within her and flames danced along her arms, but it wasn't Emery's fire that took action. These flames flickered black and they sought to destroy. "Don't act like you didn't know."

Dark tendrils struck from her open palms like lightning from a cloud and collided with Bronwyn.

A scream tore from Bronwyn's lips and the witches who surrounded her. She took a step forward, and held her hands up to stop them from interfering in what was clearly between her and Emery.

How mistaken she was. Bronwyn was just the start of the vengeance the darkest parts of her soul demanded.

"Emery, please." Bronwyn's words came out gargled. "We. Here. Surren…"

Emery heard her name, but it didn't register. She wasn't the levelheaded witch who thrived on logic and heart. No, that girl was gone. In the face of her enemy, she'd been consumed by the darkness that plagued the depths of her mind and soul, and this new version of herself reveled in it.

The darkness poured through her veins, feeding her in a way nothing else had. A bewitching chaos that freed her from the constraints of right and wrong until there was only what burned in the darkest parts of her soul.

Magic and power crashed around her like an oncoming storm. Her entire body vibrated with the weight of it, and it fueled her rage. She refused to back down from its turbulence, not when with it she'd be able to take back control. Of her life. Of the pain that threatened to swallow her every moment of every day. To demand retribution from the witches that left her, throat bared to the unforgiving supernatural world.

Bronwyn's face twisted in pain as thick crimson began to

drip from her eyes and nose. She coughed and blood sputtered from her lips, spraying Emery's front, her eyes widening as she registered what was happening. "Blood. Magic," she gargled at the same moment Lily's soft voice tried to cut through, calling her back.

But Emery couldn't bring herself to care. All she saw was blood, and all she felt was frenzied wrath. "Your priestess released my powers, in order to flood my system knowing it would kill my children. I should kill every single one of you for following her."

"But you won't."

Emery froze.

That voice. The sultry voice of a man beckoning her to stand down.

Her mate.

Lost in her vengeance, Emery barely recognised Augustine as he stepped in front of her, blocking her view of Bronwyn.

She traced the hard lines of his body through his crisp button down, the need to run her hands down them niggling in the back of her mind. She shook away the thought, lifting her gaze until she reached his midnight orbs. They matched hers. Pools of black with barely any light. This man, this perfect specimen of passion and indignation, was her prince of darkness.

Her tongue darted out, and she licked her lips, ready to ride into the throes of revenge with him at her side.

"This isn't you, little witch." His words spoke of contradiction, but the way his chest rose and fell with panting breaths told her he was just as turned on by the idea as she was.

"You wouldn't kill my people for following my father."

"If he killed my son I might. Then again," a manic chuckle

escaped her, "he killed my sister, so maybe I will demand retribution."

"Emery," he warned, sliding his arms around her waist and pulling her so the planes of his chest pressed against her.

"What, my prince?" She tipped her head to the side and gave him a seductive pout. "You don't like me when I'm powerful like you?"

"You are a fucking magnificient sight to behold, but no," he bit out, his unforgiving glare challenging her.

Emery searched his eyes, and she shrugged. "Well I think I might. The darkness feels incredible."

If he wasn't with her, he was against her.

Augustine reached up and traced his hand down the side of her face until he cupped it. "You aren't meant for the shadows, Emery." Augustine ran his thumb over her bottom lip and despite him trying to deter her, she shivered under his touch. "I need you to be my light, little witch. You and our daughter are the only shining ray of hope I have left. Please."

His plea was almost her undoing. This man. Her mate. He needed her. Her daughter needed her. Her magic wavered slightly, but didn't retreat from Bronwyn completely.

Emery focused on his midnight depths, trying to discern the truth in his words. She shook them from her mind. They were just words. He didn't mean them. He couldn't. Not when he'd continuously turned her away and made it clear everything and everyone else held more weight in his world than she did. All he had to do was accept her. To stand by her side and fight with her, but he didn't. And so his words meant nothing.

She shook her head, pushing him from her mind and refocused her magic on the witches who took everything from her.

Inky black magic exploded from her palms like lightning

across the sunset sky. It seeped into each of the witches who stood behind Bronwyn. One by one they opened their mouths to scream as her wrath consumed them, but all that came out were bloody gurgles.

Augustine growled and tangled his hand in her hair, craning her neck until she was forced to tear her gaze from her beautiful vengeance and stare into his eyes once more. He dipped his head, and Emery sucked a breath, savoring that she could almost taste his lips against hers.

"Don't make me end you, little witch," he pleaded, his voice filled with the turmoil that swirled in his eyes.

The shadows instantly took notice of his threat and flared within her, recoiling from Bronwyn and the witches, recognizing Augustine as the more immediate enemy that stood in its way.

Her tendrils wrapped around him, weaving their way over his skin in a way that she could almost taste the sandalwood and pine that were so uniquely him. It sparked the bond in her chest to life and Emery's vision grew cloudy as images of August flitted through her mind. Him cupping her cheek and brushing his thumb over lips. His hands trailing over her as they danced at Scarlett's party. The way he looked at her as he spoke his promise to love her forever at the gala. His cock claiming her as his.

Rage morphed into lust and vengeance, fueling the darkness in her blood's need to claim Augustine in the same way. To meld their darkness and satisfy the bond. She'd make it so he couldn't walk away or pose a threat to her need to end the witches.

She leaned into him, rolling her body over his and wrapping her hands around his torso.

A delicious moan escaped Augustine as his fangs elongated and he traced them along her cheek to her ear, nipping the sensitive flesh. "That's it, my little witch. Be here with me. I'll take every bit of your darkness. And when it becomes too much, I'll let you have your fill of my own. Use me, take what you need, but don't be like me."

"No," she growled against his cheek, as blood poured from his tear ducts. Her tongue darted out and tasted his essence. It danced on her tongue and her magic rose, rooting itself in him. She writhed against him, the darkness calling her back to its depths.

"Yes, Emery. I need you. Beside me. Guiding me to the light when I falter. Please, princess…" He wrapped his hands on either side of her belly, and his voice fell to little more than a breath on the wind. "I'm begging you to be my light."

The little urchin in her belly kicked where Augustine caressed, her own light pressing outward from deep in Emery's womb.

A sob caught in Emery's throat, his plea and their daughter's light breaking the hold of her dark magic.

Emery sagged in Augustine's arms, pain filling her as each dark-filled tendril recoiled its way back into her. She looked up at Augustine to see streaks of blood down his sharp cheekbones. She inhaled a sharp breath and panic coursed through her. She reached up and with shaky fingers brushed away the evidence of her darkness.

"Look at me," he commanded, and Emery's eyes darted to his, her breathing evening out as she focused on him. "Stay with me. Just you and me, right now."

"I….I hurt you. I…I'm sorry. Fuck, Augustine. I didn't mean…What the hell happened to me?"

"It's okay Em, I've got you." He pulled her into his arms, and Emery melted against him, a soft moan escaping her.

The air around them seemed to hum and buzz with the magic she'd expelled, and she wished she could take it all back. The pain had been too much, filling her every moment of every day since she'd arrived in Scotland. The arrival of the witches tipped the scales, and there was no stopping it.

Bronwyn and the witches deserved to be held accountable for their actions, yes, but giving into the darkness wasn't the way. Still, she understood why Augustine dwelled there. She could get lost in the heady magic forever. It fulfilled something in her desires she didn't know she had, and that scared the ever loving shit out of her.

She'd felt invincible. Like nothing could touch her.

Augustine's hands trailed up her back, and he sent streams of calming energy down their bond. Emery leaned into him, not allowing herself to question the change in his demeanor.

He wasn't supposed to care, but if he didn't, she'd have been lost, and there would be an army of dead witches at her feet.

Guilt ripped through her chest, not because she'd tapped into whatever dark magic possessed her, but because she should feel even an ounce of regret, and she didn't.

What the hell have I become?

"That's incredible," Bronwyn whispered, awe in her voice. "You have blood magic and elemental magic. Dark and light. And he just brought you back from the throes of darkness."

Never mind the fact that Emery had just tried to kill her, and borderline still wished she'd succeeded, of course Bronwyn was more interested in the fact she was a freak and manifested dark magic.

Emery untangled herself from Augustine's arms so she could face the witches. He allowed her to, but pulled her against his side, his hand firmly planted on her hip.

"She's also star touched," Lily piped up from behind her, and Emery whipped around, glaring daggers. Their enemy didn't need to know all her secrets.

"Three?" Bronwyn gasped. "But no one since Celeste has had three concentrations."

Lily nodded and stepped forward to stand beside Emery.

Bronwyn wiped away the blood from her cheeks and rose her brows at Lily. "And you are?"

Shit. Emery's lips parted realizing these two didn't know each other. Lily was banished long before Bronwyn was born, and she was wearing the same face she'd worn at the castle as a precaution.

Lily dropped the illusion she'd worn, her face becoming that of her twin, the former leader of the New Orleans coven. "I'm Liliana."

Bronwyn's mouth fell open, then closed and opened again. She blinked a few times as if Lily would somehow change into someone else each time she opened them instead of mirroring her twin, the priestess. "You're supposed to be dead."

It's incredible how it was so easy for Emery to forget they were twins. She didn't see Vishna when she looked at Lily. They were nothing alike. Just as her and Sloane weren't.

"I'm sure Vishna wanted you to believe I was dead. But no, I was exiled for loving a vampire."

A spark of hope filled Bronwyn's voice and piqued Emery's interest. "Your mate?"

Emery rolled her eyes. Of course that's the only thing Bronwyn took away from that statement.

Augustine pinched her side. "I saw that," he whispered against her hair.

"Good for you," Emery snapped, the pounding in her head growing to a roaring stampede.

He pinched her chin between his thumb and forefinger and dragged her gaze from Bronwyn to meet his. "Are you okay?"

Emery jerked away, swaying on her feet before he caught

her again. "I'm fine," she lied through gritted teeth. The truth was she could barely stand. The darkness hadn't funneled any magic from the world around her; it had only taken from within. That left Emery feeling cold and exhausted. She felt rather like she'd been hit by a train.

"You're not fine." Augustine pulled her against him so her back was to his chest and bit into his wrist. He pressed it to her lips and demanded she drink, not taking no for an answer.

She couldn't have fought him off even if she wanted to—there was no fight left in her. She resigned to sit back and listen to the conversation that had continued while she drank the only thing that would bring her back and dampen the hold of the darkness that even now was nipping at her from the depths of her soul.

"How do you know about mates?" Callum interjected. He'd remained unusually quiet thus far.

"More importantly, why the bloody hell are you here?" Augustine growled.

Bronwyn's eyes widened as they landed on Emery, and she comprehended what she was doing. She sighed and straightened her shoulders, stepping into the role of leader once more. "To answer your question, Your Highness, we are here to ask for forgiveness, and to surrender to your command. As for how I know about mates, after Emery left, I was intrigued by the things she shared. I couldn't sleep until I knew if there was any truth in her words."

Emery snorted against Augustine's wrist and rolled her eyes again. Bronwyn never could ignore the lure of information. Augustine gave a small pinch to her waist, an unspoken indication that he knew what she'd just done, promising retribution for the small indiscretion.

Emery looked up, heat in her eyes as she pinned a glare at him. "What? It wasn't even directed at you that time."

"But I do so love punishing you," he whispered against her ear.

Emery shuddered, clenching her thighs tighter. Augustine pulled her tighter against him, bringing his wrist back to her lips. She shook her head, feeling the effects of their bond taking hold and chasing the effects of her magic away.

Augustine arched one dark brow and frowned. "You need more."

"I'm fine. I'll take more if I need it."

"Why would you surrender?" Callum asked sharply.

"After the attacks left the New Orleans compound decimated, the inner circle was split among the covens to ensure order. This book showed up where I was sent." She reached in her satchel and pulled out a weathered brown book.

Emery bit back a laugh. It was the twin to the book Callum had stored back at the cottage. Augustine, Lily, and Emery all looked at him expectantly, waiting for him to fess up to sending it.

"It wasn't me," Callum growled though his eyes never left the book in Bronwyn's hand. "I suspect our crazy old vampire friend had something to do with it, considering he is how I received my copy. I'm assuming that's also how you found us?"

"So it's all true, isn't it?" Bronwyn choked out, seeming to piece everything together. "Our history is not what we were told. We are meant to be one supernatural entity, not factions at war."

"Aye lass," Callum nodded. "But that still doesn't tell us why you are here."

Bronwyn looked over her shoulder at the witches who stood behind her, waiting for her to give them direction. When her gaze fell back on the group of them, a frown painted her face. "We have nowhere else to go."

Lily and Emery sucked in a breath simultaneously. She'd known the coven in New Orleans had fallen, but there were so many spread throughout the United States. She figured there would be plenty of places for them to go. This was the last place they needed to be. Especially since she wasn't exactly feeling any sort of warm and cuddly feelings and had proven —even if it was without any planning on her part— that she could end them with one outburst of darkness.

"What do you mean?" Malcolm interjected from Lily's side.

"The coven has fallen. Vishna is dead and a woman by the name of the Mistress has named herself the new priestess. She's killed anyone who chose to oppose her and is building her own army."

"Bloody fucking hell," Augustine breathed.

Emery tried to shrug out of his grasp, her body shaking with rage as the stars ripped her dreams of vengeance out of her hands.

Augustine's grip tightened on her waist and he spun her against him so her head buried against him. She raised her hands and splayed them on his chest pushing away. The darkest part of her magic swelled in her chest, and when she looked up she didn't need to see Augustine's tightened jaw to know her eyes were black as night.

"Emery."

"Don't, Augustine. All I wanted was to smite her evil ass off the face of this earth. But now that has been taken from me. I won't be able to look her in the eye and watch the light fade from her eyes, taking her life as she took our son's."

Augustine's brow raised and he tucked a piece of her hair behind her ear. "You're vicious, little witch."

Her lips twisted into a wicked grin. "You have no fucking clue."

"But killing Vishna wouldn't have brought you peace. It wouldn't bring our son back and it won't create the world our daughter deserves."

Emery released a deep sigh. "But it would feel good."

She hated that he was right. Her magic hated that he was right. Killing her wouldn't change anything except there would be one less evil witch to contend with. But Vishna wasn't the root of their problems, just the current manifestation.

He cupped her face and lowered his head so his lips brushed against her ear as he whispered. "It would, and I will personally ensure you will get retribution for all the wrongs perpetrated against you. There is still more war left to fight."

She nodded, savoring the way her face brushed against the rough stubble on his jawline.

Emery swallowed hard, and turned in his arms, hating the way everyone was staring at them with pity in their eyes. There was no doubt they saw her as unstable and maybe she was. She'd pushed her grief so far down it had fed the darkness, but now it was free and she wasn't going to force it back into the box.

That didn't mean she was going to dwell in it. Emery straightened her spine and looked beyond Bronwyn, avoiding the gaze of her little family. She searched for anyone she knew. It should have been the first thing she'd done. None of the faces she wanted to see stood out in the crowd, and a pit formed in Emery's stomach. "What happened to Wren?"

Bronwyn winced and shook her head. "She fell in line as the Mistress's third."

No. She shook her head back and forth. So much for not plummeting into the darkness.

"And Agatha? Dahlia?"

Augustine's grip on her tightened as he offered her strength through the bond, coaxing the darkness into submission. She didn't want it. She wanted to feel despair, to fall into it. It was so much easier to live there, but he wouldn't let her. Where the hell was this commitment when she actually needed him?

Bronwyn looked down and continued shaking her head. "I don't know."

Emery's chest tightened as she considered all the other witches at the compound. She was torn between the need to kill them all herself and the notion that none of them deserved to die because they disagreed with a murderous bitch like the Mistress.

You were almost the same murderous bitch, she reminded herself.

She was. But even if she didn't want to actually kill them, that didn't mean she was willing to welcome every stranded witch to her tiny slice of heaven. Especially the witch standing in front of her. "What made you think you would have a place with us? You were just as bad as the rest of them, Bronwyn. Worse even, because you knew what you were doing."

Augustine leaned down and growled in her ear. "You are their heir, little witch. Act like it."

She pulled away from him, solidly shocked by his words. Not that he wasn't right—he was more right than he had any business being—but more so because he'd acknowledged who she was and still had her ensnared in his arms.

"You are our future, Emery. And you, Lily, once everyone realizes you're alive. The Mistress aims to wipe vampires out of existence with her abominations. She seeks power and cares little for those whose opinions differ from our own. We…" she gestured to the witches behind her, "We don't want to fight any longer. We wish to find our mates. To have what you have. What I just witnessed between you and Augustine was incredible—I've never heard of someone being pulled out of the darkness when they're in the throes of magic. It's something that differentiates the dark from the light. The dark pulls every essence of your being into its grips when being cast. It steals who you are. And if what I read is true, there is someone out there for each of us. Someone to be our light in the darkness. We want to explore that. We're tired of having our lives dictated by a witch who cursed us. We want to have families. To calm the insatiable need within us. You have created the perfect little family, Emery. We want to fight for that. For you. For us."

Emery looked up at her mate, afraid of the expression she expected to see on his face. She assumed he would be ashamed by what he'd had to say to pull her out from the darkness; ashamed of everything he'd said since. They were far from perfect. A clusterfuck of epic proportions was more like it. But when she did lock eyes with him, she found a softness to his midnight depths she'd only seen when he felt their daughter kick for the first time. This time, it was directed at her. He didn't have to say anything, she could feel it in the bond. A turning point. A warmth between them, that had only previously existed in stolen moments, flooded her.

A light in the darkness. Was it possible they could be that for each other?

Augustine broke the trance and turned to face Bronwyn. "We might not be the best example, but mates are very real, and everyone should be so lucky to find theirs."

Emery did her best to hide her shock but there was no way Augustine didn't feel it down the bond.

His only response was to pull her tighter against him.

Bronwyn's eyes glistened with real tears. As they fell, they washed away the rest of the blood that marred her face. Emery still didn't trust her, or the witches she'd brought with her, but there was no denying the genuine hope in Bronwyn's eyes at the prospect of finding her own mate.

"Do you know who the Mistress is?" Emery asked, hoping this was the major break they needed in finding her.

"No." Bronwyn sniffed and wiped her face. "She wears a mask and hides behind her army of vampires. All I can tell you is she has a powerful blood witch on her side, much like you, Emery. That's the only way she'd be able to create an army of magic vampires.

"A blood witch? That's what I am now?" So the darkness had a name.

"Octavian did say you had a third concentration," Lily chimed in. "Now we know what it is."

"What does that mean?" Emery asked curiously, the remnants of her dark magic pulsing under her skin, calling her to invite it back out to play.

"I have no clue, lass." Lily took Emery's hand in hers and gave it a squeeze. "Blood magic is a dark magic, one not blessed by the stars. Our magic pulls from the world around us and is fed by our being, our intent. Blood magic is starved of natural beauty. It drains both the witch and the inflicted of their being. Their soul."

Emery's eyes darted to Bronwyn. "I'm so sorry." She may not trust or even remotely like Bronwyn at the moment, but she didn't want to drain her soul. Not really.

"It's okay. You didn't know."

But the darkness had. It had wanted to rip her in two for its own twisted pleasure, and Emery was ready to allow it that vengeance. She had *liked* it. She had felt satisfied by the idea of letting it twist inside Bronwyn. Suddenly Emery felt very cold indeed.

Unaware of her internal debate, Bronwyn continued, "I know you have no reason to believe us, but I assure you we will earn your trust. And I want to start by telling you that your castle is not safe, Augustine. The Mistress has spies within, and she plans to attack after the hunt, during your nuptials."

Fuck.

Emery shifted her weight, and her little urchin moved toward her lower back. A shooting pain ripped through the bottom of her abdomen. She cried out and grabbed her belly as her knees wobbled.

"Are you okay, Em?" Augustine gripped her elbow and pulled her against him to keep her steady.

"Don't call me that," she snapped, hating that he used August's nicknames for her. "And yes, I'm fine. She just moved against a nerve."

Augustine gave her a pointed look, but didn't retort. He turned his attention to the group. "Shall we take this conversion inside where Emery can sit?"

"Yes." Lily stepped forward and touched the wards, opening them so Bronwyn and her witches could walk through. "I'm afraid we don't have accommodations for all of you, though."

"Don't worry about that. We'll handle it. We just need a space to set up."

Lily huffed a laugh. "Like the old days."

Emery made a note to ask her what that meant.

"Yes, but with a few modern twists." Bronwyn turned and gave instructions to the two witches who must be her second and third.

"Behind the cottage there is an open field, you can set up there." Callum said, pointing toward the area he'd described. "Let us know if there's anything else you need."

"Thank you." Bronwyn gave him a deep nod.

"Don't thank me yet, witch. If you do one thing to harm our family, I will be the least of your problems. Mostly because you won't be breathing."

"Understood."

"Also, please tell your witches to keep their clothes on." Emery's eyes roamed over the scantily clad army of witches. "If I have to see any more cocks and boobs, I might throw up."

"Deal. I'll let everyone know." Bronwyn smirked, and nodded in agreement before turning and delegating jobs.

Emery squeaked when all of a sudden her feet were no longer touching the ground, and she was pressed against Augustine's chest.

"I can walk, you know," she protested, squirming in his arms.

"I know." He licked his lips, knowing it would distract Emery from her protests.

Too bad she wasn't about to give this one up. The witches already thought she was some crazy anomaly, she didn't need them also thinking she couldn't do things for herself.

She planted her hands on his chest and pushed herself away. "Then put me down."

"I don't think I will."

She wiggled against him, trying to loosen his grip, and he pinched her thigh in return.

"Ow," she squealed. "Don't you know it's not kind to hurt a pregnant woman?"

He pulled her up higher against him and nuzzled his nose against the pulse in her neck. He exhaled a heavy breath. "You scared me back there, little witch."

Emery stilled. Those were the last words she expected him to say. "I did?"

Nothing about how he was acting made sense. From the

moment she'd accidentally opened the portal to his room in the castle, he'd treated her as if she was something special to him. Something he couldn't lose, and yet the last time they'd spoken, he'd made it damn clear they were nothing more than starcrossed mates destined to only do what was best for their daughter.

Augustine nodded, as he placed soft kisses on her jaw. "I thought…It doesn't matter what I thought, but I meant what I said. I need you to be my light."

Emery opened her mouth to press him but stopped. She didn't want to argue with him. In the span of one almost catastrophic afternoon, they'd grown closer. It was like they were building something; something more than what they had been in the past… Something she desperately wanted to cling to.

So she did.

Laying her head on his chest, Emery closed her eyes and drifted to a world where this was the beginning of their happily ever after, where the sound of their hearts beating in tandem was the only thing that mattered.

Chapter Thirty Six

AUGUSTINE

He'd officially missed the rehearsal for his wedding, but it had been worth it.

He could have done without the whole almost-losing-Emery-to-her-dark-magic thing, but it had led to her being wrapped up in his arms, so even that was almost worth it.

As a result though, there would no doubt be a shit show to deal with when he returned to the castle. It wasn't so much the wedding or Jessi that he was nervous about. It wasn't as if he was going to actually go through with the wedding anyways. Emery was the only woman who would stand at his side. Even if he'd yet to tell her as much.

The issue was he still needed to play the game. Despite how much it irritated Emery. He'd piss her off time and time again if it kept her safe. Plus, when she let her fire shine through it made his cock stand to attention. A fact he struggled to keep hidden.

The bigger problem was his father would no doubt take issue with his absence. He was likely organizing his troops at that very moment to storm the Scottish countryside in search of Emery. Thankfully, the majority of the troops were loyal to him and not his father, courtesy of Braxton. It was how he knew the King's attacks on the covens were all mysteriously going to go wrong.

That didn't mean Emery was safe. She wouldn't be until his father wasn't a threat and the Mistress was handled. It didn't matter that there was an army of questionably loyal witches at her back or that Emery had access to some scary-as-hell blood magic.

Scary and incredibly intoxicating.

He'd meant every word he said to her. Augustine needed her to be his light, but he couldn't deny the allure of her darkness. The way it seeped through their bond and melded with his own. She could be his dark queen. They could rule the supernatural world together, and all would bow before them.

But that's not who she is. That's not who we are.

No. It's who he was. And who he was becoming was still too much of a mystery for him to sway one way or the other. All he knew was he needed Emery by his side in some capacity, and he'd take down anyone who tried to stop them.

Even if that someone was the darkness that resided in his little witch.

Emery slammed her palms on the table, pulling him from his thoughts. Her movement made the map of the castle flutter against the makeshift war room table the witches had erected in their tent city. There was fury in her eyes. Fury that he longed to stoke into passion.

"Why the hell can't I go?" she asked.

Augustine's eyes dipped downward. The way Emery's arms pressed on either side of her breasts pushing them together left him distracted. Which was fine with him, considering she wasn't going to win this battle no matter how well she argued.

"Malcolm's letting Lily go," she complained, when he didn't respond.

"Hey," Malcolm threw his hands up in surrender and stepped away from the table. "Leave me out of this. Malcolm doesn't think she should go either, but he knows better than to argue with his mate."

"At least one of the Nicholson brothers is smart," Emery muttered under her breath as she glared daggers at him.

"Ha!" Lily laughed wryly, firmly on Team Emery. "No he just knows I'm older, wiser, and could magic his arse out of existence."

"Amen," Bronwyn chimed in with an easy smile on her face.

Augustine suppressed a snarl at the comradery that was already forming between the three witches. He never would have agreed to their fragile alliance if he knew they were going to consistently side with Lily and Emery and gang up on him.

"It's not about letting you go," Callum protested. He'd been playing both sides of the argument, and Augustine was about to tell him to pick a damn side. "Emery, our plan hinges on you. You have to be in Scotland to open the portal to the castle so the witches can come to our aid when the Mistress attacks."

Augustine suppressed a triumphant smile. Emery couldn't argue with that logic. Their plan would live or die by Emery's damn portal. She was the only one besides Lily who could do it, and Lily would be busy portaling in Flora and Draven along with their army of wolves from Tennessee. They'd need all the help they could get to ensure the Mistress didn't take the castle, while also protecting his kingdom and the people attending the hunt and his fake wedding.

"That's all fine and dandy, Callum, but if you expect me to stay here after the fact and let you all fight the Mistress, you have another thing coming," Emery said, folding her arms over her chest.

Augustine growled for the umpteenth time since the argument broke out. "I'm not going to have my pregnant mate show up while I'm hunting and marrying a woman who is not her."

Emery's eyes flared, and there was a hissing sound from the other women in the room.

Oooohhh, you fucked up buddy, August whispered.

Shit. August was right. He regretted the words the instant they flew out of his mouth, but they hit the mark he'd intended them to.

Emery winced, but she didn't back down. No, while she remained silent to the rest of the room, she assaulted him through the bond with every bit of rage and hatred she possessed in her beautiful body, and he could feel the darkness that tainted its edges.

He bit back the feeling of guilt that threatened to overwhelm him. Usually he flung his words carelessly, especially when he knew he was right. Emery thought he was trying to cage her, to hurt her. But this wasn't about that, not this time. Augustine only needed to keep her safe, and if that meant she hated him for the next two days while they killed the Mistress, he'd gladly take whatever she decided to throw at him.

Her eyes began to glow a soft golden color with black lighting throughout, and he braced himself for a painful magical attack. But Emery didn't dignify him with any sort of response. Instead her face twisted into a sneer, and she stormed from the tent.

Augustine stared at the flap of the tent waving in the night air, wafting the traces of lavender and spice. He wished there was a better way to make her understand where he was coming from. It wasn't that she couldn't hold her own in battle. Hell, she had more gumption and fire than many of the sentinels under his command, not to mention magic that could bring any man to his knees. She'd almost succeeded in bending him to her command, and she was still untrained. It wasn't even about controlling her, though he was sure she thought he enjoyed that.

In fact, it was that he couldn't lose her. Not after he'd just pulled his head out of his ass and realized how much he needed her.

Not that he'd told her any of that. It was on the list of things to address that night after they'd solidified their army's plans for the hunt... which overall wasn't looking good for him.

"You better go after her." Flora's words were less encouragement and more a thinly veiled threat.

"I know," Augustine whispered.

She cocked a brow at him from across the table. "You do?"

Augustine sighed, repositioning a few of the figurines to reflect the changes they'd made. "I'm a lot of things, Flora. An idiot is not one of them."

"Could have fooled me," Malcolm snorted and wrapped an arm around Lily, effectively rubbing in that he and Lily were on better terms.

Must be nice.

You could fix this.

He growled at both Malcolm and August. "I trust you to

finalize everyone's positions and ensure everyone knows the plan."

Malcolm nodded. "I may not be the brilliant strategist you are, brother, but I know how war works."

"Thank you." Augustine nodded and rounded the table toward the exit.

"Don't thank me. I've got the easy task. You've got a pissed-off witch with blood magic to deal with."

Flora gave him a weak smile, and Lily and Bronwyn nodded reassuringly.

Augustine stepped out of the tent and started toward the cottage, only to stop when Emery's scent didn't linger in that direction.

"Damn it," he cursed to no one and everyone at the same time. She'd headed deeper into the witches encampment, toward the woods.

Suck it up, cupcake, you have to fix this.

"I will," he muttered.

He made his way through the rows of tents that looked exactly the same as the one he'd just exited, though he knew better than to assume they all looked the same on the interior. Illusion magic was an incredible thing. The inside could be anything the witches deemed necessary, regardless of the size of the tent from the outside. And thank goodness they were sound proof.

Ansel had mentioned what life in the compound had been like during their week of working together, and while he's seen a great many things in his long life and visited many brothels, even he could do without the constant sound of flesh hitting flesh that echoed through the camp.

Not all of the camp was bad. It reminded him of the wars of centuries past. Living out on the land, away from cities relying on campfires and fur blankets to make it through.

There was a certain magic to a camp—the camaraderie of its army and the stories that could only be made within its borders.

Witches traveled from tent to tent laughing and carrying on as if they weren't misplaced refugees. As he passed, they eyed him not with the hatred he expected, but with an almost reverence. They whispered revelations about mates and how they wished to find their own, even if it meant consorting with a vampire. His personal favorite was the in-depth description of his iron clad ass that they'd love to take a bite out of.

A young girl who had to be no more than four ran from her mothers side and stopped in front of him. She had unruly jet black hair and stunning eyes the color of a Caribbean sea. When she craned her neck and looked straight up at him, Augustine was rewarded with a toothy grin. "You're a vampire."

He chuckled and knelt down so he was at her level. "I am. And who are you?"

"I'm Haven." The little girl extended her hand to hand him a heather blossom. "Here, I picked this for you."

He took the flower and brought it to his nose and gave it a sniff. "Thank you, Haven."

Haven tipped her head to the side and furrowed her tiny brow. "Are you going to save us?"

Augustine managed to keep his jaw from dropping although the question dumbfounded him. This little girl, who no doubt was taught from birth to hate him and his kind, wanted him to save her. To save her people. And she believed he had the capacity to do so.

"I hope so," he replied, and was surprised to find he meant it. Saving these witches from the Mistress meant saving his own people. It meant saving Emery's people. It meant saving his daughter from a future where she would likely be hunted for what she was. His goals were all woven together and for the first time, he felt like he had what it took to accomplish them.

"Me too." Haven wrapped her arms around his neck and gave him a quick hug before she turned and skipped off, back to where her mother sat sorting herbs and watching their interaction with a nervous smile on her face.

Augustine gave her a friendly smile and a nod, hoping it would ease her nerves some.

The witches Bronwyn had brought with her were nothing like he expected. The last time he'd clashed with the witches was over a hundred and fifty years prior. They'd been prudish and heathenistic, set in the old ways of the coven.

Not that he'd been any different. It was another time, and their differences seemed far greater.

But these witches were not like those he'd encountered back then. They weren't even like what Emery had described of the coven. These men and women were like those Bellamy had spoken of. They truly wanted a future where all the factions lived in harmony, and they were willing to fight for it.

So are we.

"You've been mighty quiet lately. I figured you'd have a ton of diplomatic bullshit to add with the witches arriving, but instead all I'm getting is snark and attitude."

Took you long enough to notice.

His response gave Augustine pause, something wasn't right. "Are you okay?"

You can't tell?

Bloody hell, he didn't need one more thing to contend with. He shook his head as if his inner self could see it. "No, is something wrong?"

Augustine, you're becoming me and I'm becoming you. You're finding your light and I'm embracing my darkness. I don't know when it started, but every time you choose the light, a piece of us is mended. We are reforming.

"We are?" he whispered, the idea of being mended gripping him to his core. It should be what he wanted, but mending meant losing himself. What did a mended August and Augustine even look like? Would he still be him? Or would August take the forefront?

Aye. And to answer your question, I have no idea.

Fear coursed through him, and Augustine wasn't sure if it was August's or his own. There was too much that had to be done for him to fade away.

August remained silent as they reached the edge of the witches camp and entered the dark woods. Augustine latched onto Emery's scent again and took off at full speed in her direction. She'd had enough time to sulk, and he needed to fix the things he'd broken.

All of them.

They might not be the perfect mates, but she was his intended and would forever be. They were the hope for so many and it was time they started acting like it.

He stopped outside the clearing where she sat and watched her bathed in moonlight. There was no way she could have known the place where she sat was considered holy ground. It was one of his favorite places in all of Scotland. Somewhere that wasn't of this realm. The place carried a magic all of its own.

He hadn't been there in ages, easily a hundred years, but aside from where the forest grew rampant, claiming what rightfully belonged to it, the secluded pools hadn't changed. The water from the nearby lake still spilled over in steady falls into the waiting pools beneath. The rock from the base of the mountain hid them from view, and unless one knew which path to take, it was impossible to find the hidden oasis.

But of course, Emery had known. Augustine guessed that without realizing it, she had communed with the magic of this place.

She sat by the water's edge and twirled her finger in the still pool, steam rising from where she touched. Augustine admired the innocence of the moment. If he didn't know any better, he'd just as soon assume she was a girl drawn to the magic of the pools, daydreaming about her future. He knew better, though—she wasn't daydreaming, more like plotting how she would kill him in his sleep.

"I know you're standing there." Emery didn't look up from the water, but reached out to him through their bond. "I can feel you."

Augustine stepped into the clearing, stopping far enough away that she wouldn't feel like he was encroaching on her moment. "And what do you feel?"

She licked her lips drawing his gaze there as she exhaled. "Nervousness. Lust. Peace."

"Sounds about right."

Her gaze flitted to him, and she tilted her head in a curious manner. "Surprisingly no anger, which I've come to expect as a staple from you."

Augustine sighed and lifted his foot to take another step toward her, but stopped himself. "I'm not here to fight with you, little witch."

"But you aren't here to relent either." Her voice fell, defeated as if she already knew the answer. She looked away from him and back to the water that twirled beneath her fingers.

A silence fell between them like a chasm, expanding deep and wide. He didn't know how to fix this. As much as he wanted to run to her and make her understand he wasn't going to marry Jessi, that she was it for him, he couldn't. It killed him that they never seemed to be on the same page. Hell, he wasn't even sure they were in the same book anymore. What was worse, most of this shit was his fault for taking too damn long to see what was right in front of him.

He ran a hand through his hair and sighed. "You know, this is one of my favorite places."

"You've been here before? I only found this place last week while searching for that damn flower." She didn't look up at him, so he couldn't see the curiosity in her eyes. Her lust for knowledge was one of her shining attributes, and he loved piquing her interest.

"Aye. Malcolm and I would come out here in the summer months, back before there were roads and cars to get you the majority of the way here. Before settlers claimed the land for their clans. We'd camp under the stars and, if we were feeling brave, skinny dip in the pools."

Emery lifted her gaze and cocked a brow. "Brave?"

His lips pulled back into a genuine smile, and he shrugged. "Shrinkage."

Emery threw her head back and laughed, and bloody hell if it wasn't the most beautiful thing he'd ever heard. "That's a real thing?"

"You have no idea." He gestured to the pool where her hands still roamed. "That water is all snow."

"Shall we give it a try?" Her demeanor had changed to that of the playful woman she'd been at the castle all those months ago. The woman who challenged him and wasn't one for backing down.

Augustine stalked toward where she sat, only veering off at the last second to sit on a boulder across from her. "Are you so willing to kill off any future heirs?" he teased.

She shrugged and ran her hands over her belly. "I've already collected on that front."

"Legend has it these are the pools of the fae."

She pulled her hand back from the water and looked at him. "What?"

He chuckled. "They won't harm you." As if to show her, he leaned over and placed his palm to the water's glassy surface. "It is said that the pools heal the body, mind, and spirit. Humans would bathe in them in order to be cleansed for when they offer themselves to the fae on the altar behind the falls."

"And do you believe that?"

"My sister was saved by a fae flower not of our realm, and our world contains vampires and wolves, why shouldn't the fae have lived here? Not that I've met any." He wasn't sure he wanted to, either. The same legends told stories of terrible beings that tricked humans into servitude and killed without mercy leaving nothing but the remnants of crushed bones in their wake.

"No, I mean do you think the water heals?" Her voice dropped to barely a whisper, and Augustine wasn't sure if she meant for him to hear her next words. "Could it heal us?"

He stilled, and inhaled a deep breath that was meant to calm him but did little to slow his racing heart. The air in the clearing seemed to hang on her every word, the playful banter they shared replaced once again by reality.

They were already on their way to healed, but she didn't know that yet, and he didn't know if she'd accept him. Her question led him to believe the odds were in his favor though.

A truly terrible plan popped in his head and before he could give it too much thought, a smile split his face and he went for it.

"There's only one way to find out," he taunted, before

shooting to where she sat, scooping her up and with her tucked against his chest, jumped into the pool.

Emery sucked in a sharp breath and released a string of curses.

It really was a terrible plan.

When he broke the surface of the water and stood, the water fell to his waist, his balls retreated into his body, and Emery sucked in a gasp and smacked his chest. "What the fuck, Augustine?" She squirmed against him, pressing her pebbled nipples against his chest and even though it was colder than a witch's titty, his cock found the will to stand at attention.

"We're attempting to see if the water works." He shook out his hair and gave her a playful grin.

Emery scoffed and mumbled under her breath. "The only thing it's doing is giving me frostbite."

"So fix it," he dared, as his eyes trailed down her wet body and he inhaled her sweet, intoxicating scent.

Emery stilled against him, her eyes lighting the moment she realized she held the power to remedy the situation.

Gods she was fucking beautiful.

As much as it pained him to do so, he slid her down his body until her feet rested on the sand below. Emery didn't step away as she placed her hands in the water. A soft golden glow radiated from her fingertips and filled the water around them, penetrating the depths of the pool. It rippled away from them until it touched every corner of the small lagoon. When it reached the waterfalls on the opposite side, it churned with the crashing waves, and the golden light reflected off every surface in the small clearing.

Slowly, the water around them grew warmer, and within minutes steam rose from every inch of the glassy surface.

Emery looked up at him and the smile she wore gave way

to a soft chuckle. "I didn't realize this was something I could do."

His breath hitched, and he was speechless. She was stunning. Her face bathed in the residual glow of her magic and light of the moon between the trees. She was easily the most beautiful creature he'd ever seen, enhanced only by the scenery of his beloved Highlands. She scrunched her nose as Augustine placed a kiss on her forehead. "You are incredible, little witch."

"Augustine, I…"

He cut her off, pressing a finger to her lips. "I know. But I'm done fighting with you."

"I'm capable of helping," she countered, her voice begging for him to see reason. "I could take you down right here with my magic if that would help you see me as more than just a liability. And don't smirk at me like that, I absolutely could."

"I highly doubt that, little witch."

Emery stepped back and waved her hands, and her wind whipped up around them, causing a cyclone of warm water to advance on him. He watched her closely, afraid that the use of her magic, coupled with her anger, would send her reaching for the darkness again, but he detected none in the bond or in her eyes. Satisfied with his assessment, Augustine attempted to shoot from the water toward the shore, but he wasn't quick enough. The wall of circling water surrounded him, thickening as it tightened, making it impossible for him to pass through.

Augustine narrowed his eyes on Emery as she continued to close the water around him. "Stop this."

"No." She closed her hands into a fist and tightened the water around him even more, to the point he was being lifted into the cyclone. If she accomplished that, there was no stopping her from closing him in. And there was no way he was about to let her take him down.

She'd had her fun, now he would have his.

Augustine bent his knees and using every bit of strength he possessed, jumped straight up and out the top of the cyclone.

Emery's mouth fell open, and he savored the fact he'd surprised the shit out of her. She recovered quickly and aimed her attention at his falling form, throwing shots of pure air at him and only missing because he arched his body out of the way.

He landed behind her and instantly wrapped his arms round her, pulling her hands to her side. "Very impressive, little witch," he breathed against her ear. "I can see you've been learning the old ways of the warrior witches."

"Mages. And yes I have."

Augustine trailed his fingers down her arms and laced them with hers. She was more impressive than any mage he'd ever encountered. Maybe it was because she'd mastered so much of her magic in such a short time, or maybe it was because he was so damned turned on by her tenacity and determination. Either way, lost in that moment, he was inclined to give her anything she wanted.

She tightened her hold on his hands and snuggled into him, bringing them to rest on her swollen belly. Augustine sucked in a breath against her ear at the stark reminder of exactly who they were fighting for. The reason he couldn't give Emery what she wanted.

Emery shuddered against him and it took everything in him not to grind his growing erection against her ass. "I am sure you would slay on the battlefield, my ferocious little mage, and I would love nothing more than to ride into battle with you at my side, but Emery…" He shifted his weight and turned her so she was facing him, her eyes locked on his. "I am only a man, and you can't ask me to risk the only things in this world I truly love."

The word slipped out without thought, and though he had intended on telling her in some grand gesture like August would, this seemed to fit better. A slip of the tongue, the same way she'd slipped into his heart against his will.

She blinked up at him and whispered, "You love me?"

"With all of my being," he replied, his voice cracking slightly with the weight of his emotion. Augustine leaned in and pressed his forehead to hers as his hands drifted to rest on the sides of her belly. "Emery, you are everything I'm supposed to hate. You infuriate me beyond belief and make me question everything I'm supposed to be."

Emery chuckled. "Not really selling the whole I love you thing."

No he really wasn't. Augustine reached up and tucked a flyaway hair behind her ear, allowing his fingers to trail down her chin. He captured it between his forefingers and tipped her gaze to meet his own. "You may be the bane of my existence most days, little witch, but you are also the only thing that keeps my heart beating. I can't lose you. You and our daughter are not only the future of our peoples, but you are the only future I can picture for myself. Even if our worlds fall apart tomorrow, I'll survive knowing I have you still at my side. You are my home more than any castle. More than any kingdom. You are my everything."

Emery smirked and pressed her hands to his chest, running up and locking them around his neck. "A simple 'I love you more than winning' would have sufficed, but I'll take it."

"You are more important than any war, Emery."

She lifted herself onto tipped toes and pressed her lips to his. "I love you too."

"I know," he smiled against her lips, his heart flipping in his chest. This was their moment. Their first step at mending everything he'd broken between them. She loved him, and he would do everything he could to honor that love.

"And how are you so sure, Your Highness?"

A grin played around the corners of his mouth as her breath panted against his lips. "I told you, you are shit at hiding your feelings."

"Fucking bond."

"Fucking bond is right. But I'd much rather be fucking you." He ran his hands down the wet curves of her body, grazing the sides of her breasts with each of his fingers.

A shiver tore through her, and he'd bet it wasn't from the cool night air.

"Would you like that, my little witch?" He fingered the hem of her wet sweater and slowly he slid his hands beneath, running his fingertips over her soft skin. Following the swell of her belly with both hands, he skimmed over her ribs and squeezed her full breasts before trailing his thumbs over her pebbled nipples. He loved the sharp hitch in her breath, loved how her body reacted to his touch, and even more, loved how she moaned his name. "Would you let me claim you under the moon, and then fuck you on the altar of the fae, demanding they bless our union?"

"Yes," she whimpered, gripping the front of his shirt and pulling him closer.

He stepped back and loosened her hold on him. "Then strip for me. Show me what belongs to me."

Chapter Thirty Seven

EMERY

The warmth of the water around her held nothing against the heat in Augustine's eyes.

He loved her.

His words. Not the made up fantasies in her head of their never-in-a-million-years-happily-ever-after. It was real. She'd felt snippets of his love in the past weeks only to have it doused by his damned mind. This was so much better than anything she could have imagined. She'd fight him with everything she had if it meant they'd end up together, because as much as it hurt her to argue with him, it hurt more to think of her life without this feeling. Without his love surrounding and filling her so wholly.

Emery turned and sauntered away, leaving him to watch as she swayed her hips with every step. If he wanted a strip tease, that's what he was going to get.

Water dripped from her clothes as she reached the shallows. With trembling fingers, Emery gripped the bottom of her sweater and lifted it over her head before tossing it onto the shore. She smiled shyly as she looked over her shoulder, holding his gaze, as she reached between her shoulder blades and unsnapped the clasp of her bra. Sliding it from her body, she tossed it on top of her sweater. She loved the effect she had on him, the harsh swallow that bobbed at Augustine's throat, his tight jaw, his clenched fists.

"You're trying to kill me." A wicked smile filled his mouth.

"You'd die happy, " she whispered, lust thick in her tone.

"Indeed I would."

Emery broke his gaze and hooked her thumbs in the waist of her soaked shorts. Ever so slowly, inch by inch, she leaned forward, peeling them down her legs along with her panties, and exposed her bare flesh.

Augustine growled, a low guttural growl that should scare her but only fed the lust in her veins. Water rippled toward her, breaking against the backs of her calves, and she knew he stalked toward her.

Just as she straightened, he gripped her hips in a painful hold and spun her. He tore her shorts from her hand and flung them past her sweater and into the woods while his midnight eyes searched hers. Emery gasped and her lips parted, her heart hammering in her chest.

His grip on her hips tightened as he lowered his head and sucked her bottom lip between his, scraping his fangs on the soft interior before pulling back. "You sure you're ready to be mine? I won't let you go again, little witch."

"I want this," she whispered, her hands sliding up the wet fabric clinging to his muscular chest. She fingered the top button of his shirt, unfastening it and moving down to the next. When she unbuttoned the last one, she looked up at him and lifted her hands, cradling his face in her palms. "I'm not afraid of being yours, Augustine. I've always been yours. Even when I hated you. Even when we were separated by thousands of miles. I was yours."

"Bloody hell, Emery," Augustine growled. He tangled his

fingers in the hair at the nape of her neck and crashed his mouth against hers.

Emery moaned against his lips, her core clenching with need. Augustine didn't kiss— he possessed, forcing her jaw open and demanding her obedience. One of his hands lowered, gripping her ass and pulling her against him. His cock was rock hard, and she longed for it to fill her, to pound into her until they both got the release they needed. "Up." His voice was thick with gravel.

Emery wrapped her arms around his neck, and he lifted her up to wrap her legs around his hips. His mouth never left hers as he waded them through the pools toward the crashing sound of the falls. With each step, Emery tightened her legs, grinding herself against his trapped cock. She needed this. She needed him.

She didn't realize the falls were so close, and she gasped when Augustine walked through them. She started to pull away but his hold on her only tightened. Augustine swallowed her fear and forced his breath into her lungs, helping her breathe through the water.

When they made it to the other side, Emery pulled back and inhaled a deep breath as magic washed over her.

Augustine's devilish smirk sent heat through her core, and her magic flared within her, humming beneath her skin. "I believe I promised to fuck you on an altar."

She looked over her shoulder expecting a stone altar in a dark cave, but instead found an ethereal place brimming with the magic that trickled over her skin.

The alcove was bathed in a soft light, radiating from its center where a white crystal altar sat amongst the stone. It glowed with magic she could almost taste, leaving a mix of birch and citrus on her tongue. The magic welcomed her own, recognizing it as that of the earth.

"This place it's...it's beautiful." She craned her neck to take in as much of the sacred cave as she could.

"Not as beautiful as you will be, splayed for me in its glow."

Emery's breath hitched as her eyes locked on Augustine's smoldering midnight depths. Under the soft light of the altar, they almost glowed, reflecting the power radiating from it.

His promise had her nerves pooling in her belly, fueling the heat between her thighs.

Augustine set her on the edge of the rock and leaned in until his cheek touched hers. "Lie back and spread your legs. Show me how wet you are for me," he rasped against her ear, his lips grazing the curve of her lobe.

Emery leaned back, the cold stone biting into her elbows. She held Augustine's gaze as she allowed her knees to fall open, exposing her naked flesh.

He didn't move or even glance down at her soaked core clenching with need. She was aching. Desperate for his touch. Augustine remained stoic. The only indication he was affected by her display was the slight tightening of his jaw.

"I'm going to devour you."

"I hope it's everything you've fantasized about."

"Oh little witch, I have tasted every bit of that body of yours in my head. Multiple times. I've fucking destroyed your sweet pussy in my dreams." He closed the short distance between them and his fingers traced the inside of her thigh before sliding through her sleek folds and driving into her. He pulled out of her slowly, lifted his glistening fingers, and wrapped his lips around them. He did nothing to stifle his satisfying moan. "The real thing is fucking exquisite."

Augustine hooked his hands under her knees and pulled her ass flush with the edge of the rock. He pressed gentle kisses on one of her thighs and then the other. Emery shifted her hips, trying to force his mouth closer to where she really wanted it, but he pulled back and then gave her a teasing grin.

"Please, Augustine," she whispered breathlessly.

"Oh, I plan on taking my time with you. Tonight I make you mine. Every bit of you."

He lowered himself, dragging his lips down her inner thigh. Each brush of his mouth, every lick, every bite, tightened the coil within her, leaving her an aching mess. She squirmed, lifting her hips desperately, willing him to move to her pussy and take what she knew he wanted. What she wanted. She couldn't think with him this close to her, with the promise to wreck her fresh in her mind. She was wound so tight, it would've taken only the simplest of touches to send her over the edge.

"Needy little thing."

"Augustine, I swear—"

His mouth was suddenly on her. Licking along the length of her seam and sucking her clit between his teeth, sending her over the edge.

Emery cried out, his name on her lips followed by a string of praises she wasn't sure the gods deserved. It was the man between her legs who deserved every bit of her praise. She looked over the swell of her belly—the belly he created giving her a daughter—and somehow in that moment, she loved him even more.

Augustine didn't stop with her first orgasm, She got the feeling with him, one would never be enough. He devoured her cunt like it was his last meal, bringing her to the edge and forcing her into the depths of pleasure at his tongue. She came four more times with no breaks in between. Each orgasm was longer than the last, and Emery wasn't sure she'd survive. She struggled against the intensity, her thighs quivering, hugging his head as she gripped his hair.

Augustine only pressed harder, flicking her clit expertly like he was made to give her pleasure. He slid his hands around her thighs and pulled them open, his fingers digging into the soft flesh. She moaned at the mix of pain and pleasure and bucked against his face.

"It's too much. I need you..." she whimpered but Augustine didn't relent.

He growled against her pussy. "Beg me to fuck you, little witch. Fucking beg."

"Please. Please fuck me. I need you, Augustine. All of you," she purred.

"I'm not done tasting you yet. One more orgasm," he demanded, "and then I'm going to wreck this hungry little cunt. You are mine, Emery, from now until the end of time."

"Yours," she whispered, echoing his vow. "Always yours."

Emery tipped her head back, and a scream tore from her as his skilled tongue assaulted her again. He nipped and sucked until her stomach tightened, and she couldn't hold on any longer. The tell-tale tingle of her pleasure coursed through her, straight to her clit.

Augustine met her at the edge and when her core clenched with pleasure he slipped two fingers in her pussy, driving them in and out of her. He stroked the spot that was sure to send her falling, growling as he did. The vibrations tore through her as he traced his fangs over her clit, and Emery remembered the dark promise August had made her all those weeks ago.

As if reading her mind, Augustine sucked her clit hard and with his fangs, pierced the soft flesh of her mons.

"Augustine!" she screamed, coming as he synchronized the pull of her blood with the lapping of his tongue at her clit, and thrusts of his fingers. Her back arched, and stars and circles swam in her vision as she trembled, trapped in the endless waves of pleasure hitting her all at once.

Augustine emerged from between her legs panting, a wicked, fang-filled grin on lips that were coated with a mixture of her blood and arousal. "You come so damn beautifully, little witch."

His eyes raked over her naked flesh, and Emery's body reacted instantly, her flesh pebbled and her nipples tightened to impossibly hard points. But it wasn't only her need to ride this man into the next century, but the love she felt both from the bond and buried deep in his midnight depths. There in the cave, they were discovering each other as what they were meant to be. There was only them. Mates. Intended. Forever.

Augustine pulled her legs around him and lifted her up against his bare chest. Emery wrapped her arms around him, clinging to him as he climbed the steps and brought them deeper into the alcove where the altar sat.

He placed her on the cool crystal, and she fit perfectly as if it were made for her. Augustine circled her, his hungry eyes devouring every inch of his would-be sacrifice. He ran his fingers along the outline of her body on the altar, teasing her sensitive flesh.

Emery's gaze was locked on him until he disappeared over her shoulder. She arched her back and tipped her head back toward the edge of the table.

"Now isn't that a sight to see? Your back arched, breasts on display and that perfect mouth of yours parted. I hadn't planned to sample your mouth, but I think I'd like to see my cock between those pretty pink lips."

Without thinking, Emery wet her lips with her tongue, savoring the idea of taking him between them.

He reached for the button of his jeans and tore them open, his length springing forward. "Move to the edge."

Emery obeyed and scooted until her head hung off the edge, and she was face-to-face with the rounded head of Augustine's dick.

Gripping the base of his cock, he stepped forward and traced her lips with the glistening tip. "You're going to get me nice and wet for your sweet cunt. Not because you need to, because I can see you dripping from here, but because I want to claim the mouth that challenges me at every turn."

Emery parted her lips. Sliding her tongue over the tip, she savored the taste before he thrust down her throat without warning. She groaned around his cock, swirling her tongue around his pulsing shaft. Augustine might have thought he was punishing her mouth through his claim, but the joke was on him. She adored his cock down her throat. The memory of his moans the last time she'd taken him in the castle sent a needy shiver through her.

"Fuck, Emery." He stilled, allowing her to adjust then pulled out slowly. She hollowed her cheeks as he did, eliciting a pleasurable hiss from the usually in-control vampire.

Emery smiled around his cock, and he started to move faster, making her take him until he seated himself deep against the back of her throat and tears filled her eyes. Her hands gripped the sides of the altar as he slammed against her lips, taking his pleasure, and she could feel the moisture pooling between her thighs.

He swelled in her mouth and just when she thought he might come down her throat, Augustine pulled out, panting. She looked up at him and smiled. The midnight color of his eyes was gone, replaced by huge black pools.

Augustine used his thumb to wipe the tears at Emery's eyes. He circled around the edge of the rectangle altar, his dark gaze raking over every inch of her. He leaned over and placed a gentle kiss to her lips, sucking her bottom lip as he pulled away. "Hear my offering," his voice dripped with a reverent sarcasm, and Emery wasn't sure who he was lifting up his prayer to, but if it included his continued worship of her body, she didn't care.

He ran the tip of his nose along her jaw and down her neck, to the valley of her breasts, and Emery arched her back, needing more than just the gentle caress. Pulling one nipple into his mouth, he tugged it between his teeth.

"Not to the fae," he whispered as he moved to the other and repeated the teasing pull, "But to the stars above."

He climbed up onto the altar and situated himself between her legs. He leaned forward, his hands cradling her belly and he kissed the evidence of their love. "To my mate, I pledge my life. My love."

She sucked in a breath, his words penetrating her soul as he notched the head of his cock at her entrance.

Augustine's eyes locked on hers and the bond flooded with a plea for love. A plea for acceptance. A need to worship. He pushed in slowly, and she gasped, not just at the impossible fullness, but at the words that fell from Augustine's lips.

"Gu bràth nam chridhe."

Forever in my heart.

He pulled out almost completely then entered again slowly, leaning forward to press his lips to her throat. He grazed his fangs against her racing pulse, his words uttered in reverence. "Gu bràth nam fhuil."

Forever in my veins.

Augustine pulled out and pressed his forehead to hers, and his lips brushed hers as he spoke. "Gu bràth air mo bhilean."

Forever on my lips.

Tears welled in her eyes at his reaffirmation of the

commitment August made to her all those months ago in a hall filled with his people. This time meant so much more—it was a promise made with eyes wide open, with all their cards on the table. He was hers as much as she was his.

"Gu bràth," she whispered back.

Forever.

She butchered his beautiful language, but he didn't care. He smiled against her lips then followed it with a kiss that could only be described as searing. It sealed their vows and lit a fire within them.

Augustine pulled back, and Emery tilted her hips, clenching down on his length. "Now fuck me like you promised. Remind me I'm yours."

A truly captivating grin spread across Augustine's face, and he raised a brow, accepting her challenge. "Gladly, my mate."

He braced himself on either side of her, growling as he reared his hips and pistoned into her, stretching her, filling her until she was a delirious mess.

Emery moaned and tangled one hand in the hair at the base of his neck, while the other dug into the muscles of his back, leaving half moon indents in the shape of her nails. Her body clamped around his, unable to ignore the way he felt like home between her legs. She whimpered his name, rolling her hips against the pleasure he created.

"You're close, little witch."

It was a statement more than a question. Augustine knew her body as well as she did, so in tune with the way her channel quivered around him and the way the bond shook with her magic before her release.

He reached up and bit into his wrist, offering what he knew would continue to solidify their bond. "Take what's yours."

Emery's eyes narrowed on where his blood flowed, her mouth watering, and in the depths of her chest, the darkness stirred. She'd never made the connection before, but when she took Augustine's blood, her darkness thrived. The only way she could accept this part of herself was through him. He was her darkness.

She gripped his wrist and brought it to her lips, falling into the pleasure only he could bring.

Moments later Augustine followed her over the edge, claiming her with his fangs at the crook of her neck.

Every wave of their pleasure was like a pulse of their souls converging on one another. It was as holy as the altar they fucked upon. They didn't need a royal wedding, or a blessing of the stars, because what they shared was more than that. It was a messy simplicity that no one else would understand, but they did.

Augustine gave a few last lazy thrusts, milking every last throb of their climax and raised himself from her neck and cupped her face. "Mine."

"Forever."

Chapter Thirty Eight

EMERY

Late the next morning, she woke alone, after a deep and peaceful sleep. For the first time since she'd last shared her bed with Augustine, she slept without the horrors of war filling her dreams.

Emery sat up and basked in the morning sun that filtered through the window. A knowing smile tipped her lips. The replay in her mind and the dull soreness between her legs were the only reminders of the claiming that took place the night before.

She'd portaled them back to Augustine's room from the fairy pools after he insisted she needed to rest, only to spend the night doing anything but. Thankfully, that time she'd remembered to throw up a windwall to muffle the sounds... at least during round two. After that she'd been magically tapped out, and even though Augustine had replenished her with his blood, she was far too engrossed with her mate when he instigated round three and four to remember to silence anything.

Mate.

A four-letter word she always knew would describe her prince, but she hadn't dared hope would embody him.

But it had.

Augustine had finally accepted her for what she was. He claimed her. Loved her. Wanted a future with her. And even though the world was turning to shit around them, she could allow herself one morning, one moment to bask in the glow of what they shared.

Her heart was full as she reread the letter from Augustine for the third time, the drunk bees in her belly warring for space with her daughter's kicks.

Little Witch,

As much as it pains me to do so, I must return to the castle to deal with the shit show that is my wedding. Rest assured, I will not be giving myself to anyone other than you, least of all the wicked bitch of the castle as you so lovingly referred to my fiancee. She'll never hold a candle to you.

I've considered what you said, and while I don't want you anywhere near the war, my heart and my cock only want to hunt you.

Compromise my dear.

Lily and Malcolm will explain and help you get ready.

I'll see you tonight.

Yours,

Augustine

A knock at the door pulled her attention and Lily popped her head in. "Are you decent?"

She looked down at her clothes—Augustine's shirt and boxer briefs—positive that he had been the one to dress her before he left because she definitely was not wearing them when she'd fallen asleep tangled in his arms.

"For the most part." She popped a strawberry in her mouth and set the note back on the breakfast tray.

A smiling Lily entered the room, followed by a smug Malcolm who carried a large white box that looked suspiciously similar to the one that held her dress from the Scottish Gala.

Malcolm met her eyes, but either out of chivalry or respect for his mate, didn't take in the rest of her. "Did Augustine tell you why we're here?" He dropped the box on the opposite corner of the bed and retreated to the window seat.

Emery shook her head, as she continued to eat the decadent fruit Augustine had left her. "Not exactly. He said something about wanting to hunt me, and you and Lily helping me get ready."

The bed dipped where Lily sat, and she reached to steal a blueberry from the bowl. "I'd like to go on record as saying this is a terrible idea, but I also can appreciate the need to be with one's mate, which is the only reason I'm going along with it."

"Not that they weren't together the whole damn night." Malcolm muttered under his breath and Emery had to stifle a laugh when Lily glared daggers in his direction.

Her cheeks may have been flushing the hottest shade of pink at that moment, but she didn't care. The night had been worth it.

Emery's eyes darted between the two of them, and her heart swelled in her chest. "I'm so happy you two have finally accepted your bond." She could feel the happiness that radiated from the both of them. It was palpable, like magic hovering around them, protecting their love for one another. She wondered if it was the same for her and Augustine now that they'd accepted one another.

Lily flushed, and her lips pulled into a tight grin. "We should be saying the same to you."

"So it's okay when you give her a hard time but not when I do it?" Malcolm complained.

"I do it tastefully," Lily shrugged. "You're crass."

Emery rolled her eyes. They weren't going to let her live those sex noises down, and she made a note that the first order of business once it was safe was for her and Augustine to get their own place. Emery picked up the tea and brought it to her lips, touched that Augustine had picked her favorite flavor. "So what's this terrible idea?"

"You're going to attend the hunt as Augustine's prey," Malcolm said, with no regard for the fact she'd just taken another sip.

"What?" She nearly choked on her tea as she set the cup down, her eyes narrowed on Malcolm. "Is he crazy? Your father has all but put a bounty on my head. How the hell am I supposed to just waltz into the hunt in front of not only your father but the entire court?"

"With a little magic and posing as his fiancee, of course." Lily bounced on the end of the bed and waved her hand, changing her appearance to that of the woman she'd been when Emery first met her at the castle.

Emery looked between the two of them as she connected the dots of their plans. "No." She shook her head and raised her hands. "Absolutely fucking not."

How could they possibly think this was going to work? Emery rolled awkwardly from her spot on the bed—her stomach seemed to have grown overnight—and paced the length of the room. She shook her head as she tried to wrap her brain around their plan. "I am not going to the hunt wearing Jessi's skin."

It felt wrong for so many reasons, but mostly because she'd

have to pretend to be that wicked bitch, with her stringy blonde hair and oversized boobs.

"Fine," Malcolm shrugged nonchalantly.

Emery braced herself. She knew Malcolm well enough to know that whatever he would say next would be an attempt to goad her, and would likely set her off… Still, she wasn't prepared.

"Then he can hunt Jessi, and he'll be expected to fuck her as his prize when he catches her. Not that there will be an audience to ensure it happens, but other members of the hunt will be listening, and it's considered an honor to be the prey of the crown prince. Especially since she's to wed him after the hunt. They'll want to ensure he places an heir in her belly."

Fuck.

Flames erupted in her hands, scorching the down comforter on the bed.

Emery quickly dumped her tea on the smoldering fabric and tried to reign in her rage.

She'd forgotten all about that element of the hunt. She'd learned about the hunt when they were preparing for the Scottish delegation. It was a barbaric tradition in which the vampires hunted humans for sport. In the more recent years, they'd taken to hunting feeders or willing humans, but that didn't mean there wasn't the occasional human compelled to participate because a vampire couldn't resist.

She bit the inside of her cheek as anger and jealousy flooded her. Her magic continued to swirl in her chest, the darkness awakening. There was no way she was going to let Augustine hunt Jessi. It was no longer just August she loved, it was both of them, and just the thought of allowing anyone else to touch him made her want to murder any bitch who tried.

Lily winced, and Emery was certain her pupils had

grown to the dark pools that accompanied her gruesome blood magic. Lily turned to glare at Malcolm, silently chastising him for goading her. When she turned back, her gaze was steady and calm. "Breathe lass, what my mate was trying to say, albeit with less tact than his station provides him, is that Augustine asked us to come up with a plan to keep you safe, but also afford him the ability to honor his vow to you."

"He did?" she whispered, floored by Augustine's consideration. It sounded more like August, but she wouldn't complain if the darker half wanted to honor her.

"Aye, lass. He did."

She smiled and brought one hand to her chest while the other rested on her rounded belly. "So what does this entail?"

"You'll have to agree to the help of one more person to make it happen, and while I know she's not your favorite person, she's the best component weaver we've got."

Her rage bubbled again, and Emery focused on keeping her hands unlit. Lily didn't have to say anything else. She knew it was Bronwyn.

Of course the stars couldn't just give her this win. They'd given her Augustine, but it wouldn't be her life if they didn't continue to push her at every turn.

Emery searched Lily's eyes for any hint of hesitation. "You're asking me to entrust her with my life and the life of my unborn child."

"Augustine believed her when she said she would keep you safe, and he reminded her what was at stake. Something to the tune of ripping her apart limb by limb if she did anything to betray you again."

Just because Augustine is willing to put his trust in Bronwyn didn't mean Emery was. Then again, the alternative was leaving her mate to the clutches of Jessi which, to her heart, was debatably worse. It was a no-win situation where Bronwyn was the lesser of two evils.

Emery closed her eyes and inhaled an even breath. She could do this for her child. "Fine," she said through gritted teeth. "What do I have to do?"

Lily clapped her hands, and Emery could see the excitement in her eyes. "You just need to stand there in your dress and look pretty while we weave the illusion around you and tether it to an amulet which you will wear."

Emery's brows shot up. She must have misheard Lily. "Dress? I thought this was a hunt."

"Oh it is. And just as archaic as the practice are the traditions that go along with it. The humans are hunted in formal wear as if they were a prince or princess fleeing their captor. It's a sick and twisted game."

"It's also a lot of fun, for the record," Malcolm interjected before walking toward the bathroom.

"Maybe for you," Lilly hollered after him as the sound of running water filled the space. "You're not the one chased, fucked, and bled."

Emery snorted at the profanity falling from Lily's lips, but bit her tongue when the older witch pinned a glare in her direction.

Malcolm poked his head out from the bathroom and wiggled his eyebrows at his mate. "Oh I'll make it fun for you too, Tiger Lily."

Lily's cheeks flushed, and her eyes heated with a soft green glow. She picked up the nearest pillow and threw it at Malcolm, who barely dodged it, sticking his tongue out playfully.

Shaking her head, Emery pinched the bridge of her nose. "Okay, so dress, magic, amulet... anything else I need to know?"

"That's the jist of it," Malcolm said, as if it wasn't a big deal at all. "After the hunt, you'll pose as Jessi until the Mistress attacks, when you'll open the portal to Scotland as planned, and you'll bring your happy ass back to the cottage."

She swallowed her retort. There was no way in hell she was leaving, but she wasn't about to argue the point with Malcolm and Lily. Hell, she wouldn't even argue it with Augustine. Come hell or high water, she would be there to avenge the death of her son. To fight for her daughter's future.

"Where will Jessi be?" She shouldn't care, but the fact that the entire plan rested on her identity remaining a secret, it seemed like an important detail to know.

A wicked grin pulled at Malcolm's lips. "Don't worry about her. I'll make sure she's taken care of."

Emery wanted to push the issue, but she sort of liked the fucked up images that were filtering through her mind more than what Malcolm actually did with her.

She went over the plan two more times with Malcolm and Lily before they left her to the giant bath Malcolm had filled for her to prepare herself for the hunt. It really didn't matter what she looked like since she'd be wearing Jessi's face, but Augustine would be able to see her. Along with any witch present who specialized in illusions. To all the other vampires, she'd be Augustine's doting fiancee, playing her part in his family's tradition.

She studied her face as she applied the finishing touches on her makeup. The natural style suited her, though it was different from what she might have aimed for a year ago. Everything about the face that stared at her was different from where she was back then. The freckle above her lip was still there, along with the scar below her eyelid, but joining them were so many additional defining features that told her story

—a story that had evolved into more than she could ever have imagined.

There were the laugh lines at the corners of her eyes, courtesy of her late nights with Chelsea and Flora. The missing patch of her left eyebrow was a result of her fire magic licking her face while she practiced, and the dark circles around her irises marked her blood magic.

Emery inhaled a shaky breath and fingered her most prized change. The faint scars at her neck where repeated bites from her mate had left their mark. They would be insignificant to most, but to her they were a testament to the journey they'd been on. The bond was theirs to share, sacred between only her and Augustine, but the scars were an outward claim to any who would think to challenge their union.

It was only months ago the mark had shown up on her wrist, and she entered the castle an overly confident human with a hole in her heart where a family should be. Her hands drifted to the swell of her stomach and she smiled as a tear rolled down her cheek. "I've come a long way, my sweet urchin girl. I can't wait for you to meet the family that loves you."

"Hello? Emery?" Bronwyn called from the bedroom.

Emery wiped away stray tears and steadied herself. This was the only part of the plan she dreaded: placing her trust in Bronwyn. It didn't matter how many times she told herself that if Augustine could trust her, then so could she. Only time would heal the betrayal she felt. Unfortunately that wasn't a luxury they'd been granted.

She pulled on the dress Augustine had picked for her, finding it fit like a glove, hugging each of her curves, because of course it did. Augustine never did anything half-assed. She picked up the skirt and walked into the bedroom.

Bronwyn stood by the window alone with her back to

Emery, wearing her signature skin-tight crop top and ballooned joggers.

"Where's Lily?" Emery asked, annoyed that Lily would even think it appropriate to leave them alone.

Bronwyn turned, bowing her head in a sign of respect that was completely unwarranted. "She's on her way."

When she looked up, Emery appreciated for the first time how haggard Bronwyn looked. There were black circles under her eyes, and her cheeks were almost hollow. She wracked her brain trying to remember if she'd looked that way when she arrived in Scotland, or even at the meeting at the war room, and decided that she definitely would have remembered it.

"You look positively stunning." Bronwyn gave her a weak smile.

"Thank you." Emery nodded. She hesitated for a moment, and then asked, "Are you okay, Bronwyn?"

"I didn't have the strength to keep up the stream of magic into my own amulet if I was going to enchant yours." She walked to the window and lowered herself to the bench. "I'm just so tired. Every single one of those witches is looking to me to protect them. They have since we left New Orleans and we've lost so many along the way. Looking back, being a member of the inner circle was easy, Leading when you have no idea what the hell is coming for you next is a million times harder."

No shit, she wanted to say, but it wouldn't help the matter. Still, a bit of Emery's hatred for the woman lessened. Bronwyn was doing what Emery should have been doing all along, leading the witches who opposed Vishna and the Mistress. She hadn't known they existed until Dorian had informed her of the incident at the castle and even then she hadn't known to what extent.

There were so many who wanted what she did, and as much as she hated it, Bronwyn was included in that group.

Putting aside her anger, Emery crossed the room and sat next to Bronwyn. "You are doing the best you can with the cards you've been dealt. That's all we can do."

Bronwyn looked up at her, tears rimming her tired eyes. "I'm so sorry for what happened. I don't think you should ever forgive me, but please know I will never stop trying to repay you for the part I played in losing your son."

The words didn't sting as much as they once had, and though Emery hoped that didn't mean she was falling into complacency, she found comfort in that knowledge. Still, she wasn't ready to forget.

Emery folded her hands in her lap and searched for the words that would unite them, even if it was only for the sake of their people. "I know. And while I want to tell you that someday all will be forgiven, I just don't know that I can do that. But what I can do is promise to share the burden with you of protecting our people. You are no longer alone in this, Bronwyn. This place—this safe haven—is only the beginning. We will win this war, and we will ensure the safety of not only our people but all supernaturals."

Bronwyn smiled softly. "You're going to make an amazing queen."

"I wouldn't go that far," Emery chuckled. "But I'll definitely keep things interesting."

"Here." Bronwyn reached into her pocket and pulled out a small amulet, handing it to Emery. "We might as well get this started so Lily can secure the illusion to it when she arrives."

Emery fingered the amulet, examining the exquisite details. A purple stone sat in a silver inset that had an intricate swirl of vines etched into it. "It's beautiful," she whispered. "How does it work?"

"The amulet itself is fluorite, which in and of itself—like all crystals—can hold magic. That's what Lily will tether her spell to. But this particular crystal, when enchanted correctly, can provide protection to the wearer. It will grow cold when it perceives dangerous magic is near."

"Like dark magic?"

"It won't react to your own magic," Bronwyn assured her, easing Emery's fear.

"Well that's a relief."

Bronwyn tangled her fingers together in front of her, and nervous energy radiated from her. "Have you learned anything more about it?"

"Ever the scholar," Emery snorted. Bronwyn never could walk away from the allure of learning something new.

"Can't blame a girl for trying," she shrugged and leaned into Emery, and for a split moment it felt like nothing had changed between them since the compound.

"If I knew anything, I'd help, but I don't know anything about dark magic or why I have it." She turned and gave Bronwyn a genuine smile.

She blinked, and when she did, a snippet of a vision danced on the back of her eyelids. It was Bronwyn smiling as she sang to a bundled-up baby in her arms. Somehow Emery knew it was her daughter.

Tears pricked Emery's eyes as she opened them and stared wide-eyed at Bronwyn. "When all of this is over, I'd love to hear your scholarly opinion, since gods know I'm still learning about our world."

Bronwyn gave a small nod, accepting Emery's olive branch. "I'd be happy to help."

Emery glanced down at the amulet in her hand, painting her fingers over the stone and noticing for the first time that it held seeds and small flecks of what looked like some sort of metal, floating in its center. "What do each of the things inside the amulet do?"

"The seeds are from various plants and are blessed to promote growth in magic, the iron is from the daggers of the stars, meant for protection against evil and the flowers are just because it looks pretty and poppies remind me of you. A resilient wildflower that blooms wherever it is planted." Bronwyn held out her hand to Emery and arched a brow. "May I?"

Emery handed her the amulet and pulled her hair to the side so Bronwyn could clasp it around her neck. The moment she placed it around her neck, she felt its magic wash over her. It wasn't unpleasant as she expected. Instead it mingled happily with her own. She pushed her magic forward, welcoming the foriegn enchantment and embracing the warmth that radiated from where it sat on her chest.

She stood and did a twirl, the bottom of her dress flaring out in a plume of sparkles. "How do I look?"

"Ready for battle. Augustine isn't going to know what hit him."

She hoped that was the case. With each passing moment, her nerves coiled tighter, and Emery couldn't stop the hint of dread that grew within her. Not because of the hunt or because in a matter of moments she'd look like Jessi, but because it was as if the stars were paying full attention. She could almost swear they were casting a shadow on the night ahead, and nothing good could come from their darkness.

Chapter Thirty Nine

AUGUSTINE

Usually the exorbitant cost put into royal events bothered him, especially now that he knew his people suffered, but Augustine couldn't bring himself to despise the efforts put forth for the hunt. August had always hated the spectacle, but not him.

Augustine loved the hunt.

The back of the castle had been transformed into something straight out of a fairy tale. Twinkling lights were strung across the terrace, lighting the entrance to the hunt. Gold-and-jewel-threaded tapestries hung from the exterior of the castle, depicting the Nicholson family crest. Courtiers gathered beneath them and whispered the latest gossip about the crown prince missing his wedding rehearsal and who they thought would be the honored hunter at the end of the night.

At the edge of the terrace, two thrones, handcrafted with depictions of the hunt on the backs and sides, were set up for the King and Queen so they could look over the expanded dance floor where the hunt's festivities would begin and end. Torches lined the edge of the forest and castle, adding an ominous flicker of light that bounced off the trees and separated the hunters and prey from where the courtiers would gather to wait for the return of the hunters with their spoils.

Once every ten years, his people came together from all over the world to embrace their vampirism and celebrate their existence. Augustine was a little surprised to realize that knowing the true origin of vampires didn't change his love of the hunt. That witches had created them and then tried to eradicate them, only to be halted by the love of the first mate... if anything it fueled his need to participate in the celebration.

Because after all, he'd found his mate.

That night was an opportunity to let his most basic instincts out, to stalk his prey, hunt her, feel her fear as he closed in and then when she thought she'd escaped him, take what he wanted. Her life force. Her body. And this time he'd be taking what was rightfully his upon his creation.

Emery Montgomery.

His little witch.

His mate.

Augustine's cock twitched against his tartan, and any more thought of Emery would surely end with an obvious tenting of the fabric.

He shifted his weight and flexed his hands at his sides in an attempt to calm his arousal. He'd known the minute Emery arrived an hour ago, the bond between them alerting him. She would be taking her place with the prey, dressed as Jessi and safe from everyone except him. Just as he wanted it.

He never did ask what Malcolm and Lily had planned to do with the real Jessi, but ultimately he didn't care.

The King clapped his hand on Augustine's shoulder, bringing his attention back to their conversation with some of the more prominent nobles from other kingdoms around the world. "My son was attending a lead on the witches' Mistress, which is why he was absent at the rehearsal, but I assure you he is committed to his intended, and I have no doubt will conceive an heir this very night. Isn't that right, Augustine?"

So that was the lie they were perpetuating. He tightened his jaw and bit back the urge to tell his father where he could shove his wedding to Jessi. He'd already been chastised more than once over his absence, and his lack of remorse infuriated the King. They'd gone round for round in a verbal sparring match, but Augustine refused to regret protecting his daughter and his mate. His father remained unwilling to see reason on any front, forcing Augustine to play the game his father expected.

So though it hurt, he apologized to his father. The words grit like sandpaper on his tongue, but he promised to be the good lap dog the King expected him to be.

The king was testing him, and Augustine wasn't about to fail. He nodded confidently and gazed upon his father with the adoration expected of him. "Absolutely, Father."

Knowledge was power in most instances, and this was no different. Augustine only needed to bide his time. The majority of the king's army was no longer under his father's control, instead reporting to Augustine through his newest general, Braxton. They'd been making moves over the last week to assess the sentinels and advisors for loyalty. The advisors were primarily loyal to his father, but the sentinels wanted to see change. They wanted Augustine on the throne.

They were the reason they'd succeed when the Mistress attacked. Them and the army of wolves and witches that waited for his signal.

"And the search for the Mistress? How is the hunt going, Augustine?" The noble closest to Augustine pressed, a curious glint in his eye. The man's name was Graves, the newest royal to ascend to a throne in the kingdom that ruled over present-day Greece. From what Augustine could remember, Graves was younger than him, and though he was a crown prince, he tended to keep to himself and avoid social events. This was the first major event he'd attended as a monarch, and Augustine was surprised to learn he was participating in the hunt. A king didn't usually participate in the hunt.

The fact he pressed so hard about the Mistress had Augustine's alarms going off. He'd cautioned the king to be careful when discussing the state of their kingdom with foreign monarchs, but considering there were at least two more within earshot, his father clearly hadn't heeded his warning.

Augustine forced a politician's smirk. "We are closing in, Your Majesty. Any day now."

That night. They were going to end it that night, but he couldn't say that. Couldn't play his hand.

Graves nodded, his expression speculative. But he seemed to accept Augustine's words because he turned to make small talk with the King. Augustine allowed his gaze to drift to where Draven stood across the terrace, talking to one of his men. The wolves were there to protect the humans of the hunt, a job Draven took seriously considering what happened to his mother.

Thank the stars the Scottish King had been called home for an emergency, because Augustine wasn't sure Draven would be able to keep his cool around his biological father. Augustine suspected it was Callum's doing to keep the two separated, considering his cousin was conveniently absent for the event he loved nearly as much as Augustine.

Look at you, thanking the stars. I think our princess is wearing off on you.

Augustine rolled his eyes internally. August wasn't wrong, and while he might thank the stars, more and more he hated the damn things for the constant obstacles in his fate. It was one thing to have the typical trials of life, but the amount stacked against him and Emery had to be considered downright torture.

When Draven noticed Augustine he nodded, the signal everything was in place. The wolves were ready both at the castle and in Tennessee. The witches awaiting a portal from Scotland. And his men at the castle were on their guard, waiting for the Mistress to crash his wedding.

But first, he had a witch to hunt.

The bells tolled above them, signaling the start of the night's festivities. Excitement coursed through Augustine, which he sent through the bond, and a smile tipped at his lips when his mate returned her excitement laced with nervousness.

His elation was dashed when his father leaned over and whispered in his ear. "Don't cause a scene tonight, or I swear your mate will be dead by morning."

Augustine nodded, but didn't dignify him with a response. The King's words were a ploy to remain in control and nothing more. His mate was safe right under the nose of her enemies, with a legion of his army ready to protect her.

He followed his father down to the forest's edge, but instead of joining his mother on the dais with the King, he lined up with the other hunters on the opposite side of the dancefloor.

Malcolm appeared from the opposite direction and took up his place in the center by Augustine.

"Are you ready for this?" his brother murmured. The same excitement Augustine felt bounced in his voice and he wasn't sure if Malcolm was talking about claiming their mates in the hunt or taking down the Mistress.

"More than ready." For all of the above. "It's time."

Time to start his life with Emery and move past the trials

of the last year. Time to end the war between the factions. Time to create a world worthy of his daughter. Time to be the king he was always supposed to be.

The line of hunters shifted with nervous excitement on either side of them. Adrenaline permeated the night air so thick he could taste it as he would a lie.

His father stood before them, raised his hands to the sky, and looked over the crowd. "Welcome to The Hunt."

The gathered nobles, courtiers, subjects and hunters roared around him, lifting their glasses and voices in celebration. Augustine glanced around, taking in the carefree smiling faces of his court. They had no idea what was going to happen in a few hours. He wished he could tell them all to run fast and far from the impending battle, but any sort of preparation could tip off the Mistress' spies in the castle. He only prayed he could save as many of them as possible; that their plan would work and they'd head off the Mistress before she could attack fully.

"We come together to…"

Augustine tuned out his father's voice, having heard the same speech made by a different monarch every decade since he was able to participate in the hunt himself over a hundred years prior.

Yeah. Tonight feels different.

August's assessment was a sentiment he shared. It was part of the reason his lips kept reverting back to a struck-stupid smile. "You noticed it too?"

It feels monumental.

"That's because it is," he whispered, hoping none of the other hunters thought he was bat-shit for talking to himself.

Hell, even if they did, Augustine didn't care. They were going to put an end to the Mistress, and Emery would be at his side.

"...to celebrate the union of my son, Augustine Robert Finlay Nicholson to his chosen bride, Jessi Marie Reynolds whom he will be hunting and capturing tonight to bring to their wedding bed."

Chosen bride my arse.

Augustine bit back a snort. He stepped forward and waved to the congregated spectators on either side of the floor. When he stepped back in line with the rest of the hunters, the music started. It was the same song every Hunt: a ballad meant for lovers.

The prey entered. Most were women, though there was the occasional male. Augustine inhaled a shaky breath, waiting for his mate. He recognized a few of the women of his Culling, here as part of the wedding party. A smile tipped at his lips. Caroline, Lucinda, and Elle had each been assigned to an embassy within his kingdom, but had yet to be turned. It seems they'd opted to try their luck with other royal princes at the hunt to see if they could land themselves a spare to another throne.

Good for them. Even though none of them held a candle to his mate, they deserved to be happy in their eternal lives.

A flash of green caught his eye, and Augustine stopped breathing all together when Emery stepped onto the floor.

His heart jumped clear into his throat, and his cock took notice. She was fucking stunning. The emerald dress he'd chosen for her was beautiful on the hanger, but on her, it was a damn work of art. The flowers that decorated the bodice hugged her ample curves, begging for him to run his hands over them. They lined the deep V that accentuated her breasts, and a vision of Augustine ripping it the rest of the way down for easier access brought a seductive grin to his face. The skirt fell from her waist, mostly concealing the swell of her stomach, not that it mattered. No one was seeing her for her she truly was except him, and he loved every square inch of the womb that held his daughter.

Emery walked with such elegance, her back straightened and her neck elongated. She gave him a demure smile, but the heat in her eyes as they landed on him told him she was playing the game, but if she had it her way, she'd be wearing a shamelessly erotic grin meant only for him. In that moment, he was even more glad everyone else could only see Jessi's face because if they weren't, every vampire in the place would try to steal her after only one glimpse.

Everyone except Malcolm, who only had eyes for Lily standing next to Emery. To Augustine, she looked like a nameless human, but by the look of awe in his brother's face, he knew Malcolm was seeing the visage of his bonded mate. His love. And bloody hell did that man deserve it.

The music interlude changed to a staccatoed pulse and each of the hunters took a step toward their prey in time with the beats. It was purposeful. Calculated. Driven by the desire to claim.

Augustine drank in every inch of Emery's exposed flesh as he approached her and circled her poised body as tradition dictated.

"Welcome to the hunt, my love," he whispered against her ear as he rounded behind her.

"Thank you," she replied breathlessly, craning her neck so her gaze could follow him, exposing the length of her neck and pulsing vein to his aching fangs. "But we'll see who is hunting who when the night is done," she taunted, so low she knew only he would hear.

A possessive growl filled the space between them as he came to stand in front of her. Emery's scent wafted through the air, wild and untamed. Nostrils flared, Augustine swallowed the need raging throughout him. His gums ached, his heart raced, and his cock...his cock was so hard it was downright painful.

He arched a brow as he took a step forward, hiding the evidence of his arousal against the skirts of her dress. "Is that so?"

He offered his hand, and Emery delicately gave him hers.

Emery glanced up at him through hooded eyes, and he had to bite back a moan as the picture of what she would look like wearing that same expression as she knelt before him with his cock in her mouth. The thought threatened to make him come right then and there.

"It is, my prince," she whispered, ever the unassuming princess.

This woman was going to be the damn death of him.

She was breathtaking. Every bit the dignified queen she was meant to be. Unflappable to the world around them, and defiant to a fault. It only excited him more that he knew despite the pretty wrapping, she also concealed a darkness within her that rivaled his own.

As if to prove his point, exhilaration and lust coursed through the bond, and he could almost picture in his mind every dirty thought she was playing in her pretty little head.

Augustine barely managed to stifle his moan behind gritted teeth. "You'll pay for that," he growled.

Emery gave him the tiniest shrug and stepped forward into his arms, wrapping one around his neck while the other formed the perfect mirror to his own.

To hell with keeping the appropriate distance society dictated for the dance, he pulled her so close they practically melded as one. His court may not know it was Emery, but he hoped they could see how in love he was with his bride. Even with her growing belly between them, she fit perfectly, as if this was where she was always meant to be. And he'd fight to keep her there.

They twirled around the dancefloor, playing the game of coy lovers with the rest of the hunters and prey. As the final stanza of the waltz began to play, Augustine pulled Emery close and tangled one of his hands in her hair, demanding she look at him.

"You know the rules, little witch?"

She shivered against him but managed to nod. "Run as fast as I can, and don't get caught by anyone but you."

Augustine tensed and didn't bother to stifle the surge of overprotectiveness or the growl that accompanied it. "No one would think to touch you. But yes, and steer clear of the north woods."

"North woods, got it."

The music stopped with a loud crash, and Augustine pressed his mouth against Emery's, pushing his tongue against her lips and demanding entrance. He invaded her mouth, and she allowed him to take what was his, claiming her for the world to see.

When he broke the kiss, Emery clung to him, panting on wobbly legs. "Augustine," she murmured, her need hung in the air, as palpable as the arousal between her legs.

His lips turned up into a sinister smile, and he cupped her cheek and leaned in, giving her ear a tiny nip. "Run, little witch."

Chapter Forty

EMERY

Adrenaline fueled her as she flew through the trees. The forest growing denser as she moved. Emery's grip tightened on the skirts of her dress as she hiked them up and pumped her arms with each stride. She didn't know exactly where she was any longer, only that she had to keep running. Being pregnant wasn't exactly conducive to running through a damned forest, but somehow the promise of being caught was enough to convince her legs to continue pumping—one in front of the other.

The hunt surprised her. She had expected to hate it; the hedonistic spectacle of it. Instead, she found it shockingly… fun. It was a celebration of life, of vampyrism, and even of barbarism. Knowing that most of the prey were volunteers made it a little easier to forget that The Hunt had started as a rape, pillage, and bleeding of humans by vampires. But despite that, she could see everything it could be, especially from where she stood. She should be scared, as some of the women were. Mostly the ones who were coerced into participating —a fact she'd have Augustine rectify when he was king—but Emery wasn't afraid. She wanted to be there at the whim of her prince—her mate—celebrating his nature.

A laugh tore through her as she ran, the forest seeming to come alive, dancing beside her. She felt light as air, communing with the world around her as she ran for her life. It was borderline laughable to think she'd been forced to the castle all those months ago because of Sloane's death. How from something so incredibly tragic she'd found her new life. It hadn't been easy, but it was turning out to be a beautiful chaos she couldn't help but cling to. And it would be perfect once they outed the current tyrant on the throne and Augustine took the place he was always meant to.

The thought of her mate sent a spark straight through her.

If the thrill of the chase sent Augustine into a frenzy, it did double for her arousal. There was something about it all that made her chest tighten, and her entire core tingle. Augustine was tracking her. Only her. And when he found her, all bets were off. She'd wanted nothing more than to be claimed by him and now she would be in the most primal way possible.

There was no way she could have known she had a prey kink, but hell if she wasn't going to reenact this little fantasy over and over with her mate.

The forest was filled with the sounds of growling hunters and screaming prey, but none of it was shrill. None of the cries were from unwilling participants or the snarls of killers. One by one, the sounds of the hunt gave way to the spoils of capture. The release of moans, pleasure, and the slapping of skin followed by the unmistakable throws of venom-induced ecstasy.

With each step, her thighs clenched a little tighter. The tingling between her legs was only enhanced by the fact she had chosen not to wear any panties. Both a blessing and a curse, really. She couldn't wait to see Augustine's reaction when he discovered her deviance.

A swoosh of a black tail caught her eye, and Draven

stepped out from the bushes in his wolf form, a protector in the hunt. He looked over her shoulder and gave a nod before trotting off toward the sound of other couples. Only the nod wasn't for her.

Emery didn't need to turn around to know Augustine stood behind her. Her magic fluttered, and the bond pulled tight. Even without their connection she could feel him.

She turned around slowly, and her breath caught in her throat. Even though she'd just seen him moments before, he no longer resembled that man she'd danced with. Standing at the edge of the small clearing where she'd stopped, Augustine looked like someone lost in time. His hair was wild, barely contained by the circlet that adorned his head, and his eyes were wide with need.

He snarled, flashing his fangs.

There was no doubt he saw her as prey. His chest rattled under the shirt he'd unbuttoned to mid-chest, exposing the muscles Emery was intimately acquainted with. She sucked in her bottom lip and stifled a groan of her own as she longed to run her hands down them, leaving tracks from her nails in her wake, but there would be time for that later.

Her eyes trailed to his tartan, where his cock stood proudly against the material. She'd once teased him about wearing nothing under his kilt, and she was damn thankful he hadn't.

It seemed great minds thought alike.

Emery licked her dry lips and took a step back, her eyes never leaving her dark prince.

"You're mine, little witch." His voice was thick with a possessive lust.

Emery ran her arms down the curves of her sides, teasing him as she picked up the skirts of her dress. She raised them just high enough to give him a taste of her bare skin, but not quite high enough to reveal the prize he sought. Her lips spread into a bewitching smile. "You haven't caught me yet, Your Highness."

His eyes narrowed, and he stepped toward her. "Haven't I?"

For each step he took forward, she took one back. "I believe the term 'to capture' requires one to…possess."

Augustine arched a brow and graced her with one of his full smiles. The kind that made her go weak at the knees. He continued to stalk toward her, knowing damn well what that smile did to her. "And do I not possess you, princess? Have I not owned every inch of that sweet flesh?"

"You do," Emery scoffed playfully. "But I think the point of the hunt is to prove it?"

"Oh little witch, when I get my hands on you," he rasped, his voice strained as if his promise undid him as much as it did her.

She took one final step back and looked over her shoulder before pulling her lips into a tight smile.

"Don't you fucking dare."

But she did, and she loved every moment of daring him.

Emery turned and took off running, giggling like a damn school girl with every step.

As expected, Augustine was on her in seconds. Sweeping her up in his arms, he pulled her against his chest and nestled his nose in the hair behind her ear as he kept running. He nipped at her neck, dragging his fangs slowly over her sensitive flesh.

She didn't bother to stifle the moan he elicited with his touch. She squirmed against him, needing to get closer. "Where are you taking me?" Emery panted breathlessly.

"Where I can have you to myself. Where no one will hear you scream, or see your flesh as I take you in the moonlight." He stopped running and set her down at the edge of a small clearing where there was a blanket laid out with candles surrounding it.

"You did this for me?"

"Oh little witch, there isn't anything I wouldn't do for you."

He walked her to the blanket and set her down gently. This was not what she expected. It didn't seem like the kind of thing Augustine would do.

She looked up into his eyes and laughed. "Malcolm did this, didn't he?"

Emery's hands flew to her hips and she gave him a pointed look, a declaration she saw right through his bullshit.

"Okay fine. Yes, he did," Augustine chuckled. "I had fully intended on taking you hard and fast against whatever tree, bush, or boulder presented itself."

"Can I tell you a secret?" Emery asked, biting her lip.

"I would be honored to safeguard your skeletons, mate."

She raised herself on tipped toes and nibbled at his ear. "I was looking forward to you claiming me hard, fast, and against a tree."

His brows reached his hairline as he sucked in a harsh breath and exhaled a growl . "Were you now?"

She kept her heated gaze on him as she turned around and pressed her hips to his erection, and bent forward as she ground against him. "Or bent over a boulder."

Augustine sucked in his bottom lip and bit down, drawing a tiny drop of blood. She almost pounced and claimed it for herself, but she loved watching him come undone.

"I thought you might want me to… woo you."

The way he said 'woo' was fucking adorable, but it's not what she wanted from him.

"Malcolm woos a woman. You fuck them. You claim them and that's exactly what I want right now." She straightened herself and stepped forward until she was toe-to-toe with him. "You captured me, Augustine. Now you better damn well claim me."

He didn't need any more encouragement. His lips crashed against hers and his tongue instantly licked the seam of her lips, demanding entrance and sending a zap of electricity straight to her clit. No, actually it was the moan-wrapped growl that ripped from his throat that did it. It was the sexiest sound she'd ever heard in her life.

And he'd made it just for her.

Emery tangled her hands in his hair and pulled him closer so every inch of their bodies pressed together, and still it wasn't close enough. She wanted all of him. As much as he claimed her, she was claiming him right back under the moon and stars above.

Augustine's hands worked at the skirts of her dress, pulling them up to her hips. His fingers slipped between her thighs, and he made the delicious growl sound against her lips once more. "No panties again?"

"I figured you shouldn't be the only one going commando."

"How considerate of you." His fingers dug into her hips, and Emery whimpered against his lips. "Princess," he gritted out against her lips. "I am trying to be gentle. Trying to show you I care, but when you show up wearing nothing beneath this beautiful dress... it is hard for me to hold back."

"Hold back from what?" Emery asked breathlessly.

"I want nothing more than to shred this dress and take you as the prey you are."

There he was. There was her monster. The darkness she craved. She loved his newfound sweetness, his willingness to exude patience and consider her every want and need. But right then she didn't want the romantic side of her mate, she needed him to ravish her.

Emery sucked his bottom lip between her teeth and pulled back. When she released him, she looked up with a seductive grin. "Do it."

Augustine wasted no time, his lips captured her and he laid her down on the blanket at their feet. His hands didn't stop moving. Didn't stop touching and feeling, and it left Emery incoherent to anything but him and what their bodies demanded from them.

"I need you, Emery. I'm not going to be gentle the first time," he growled, still showing restraint, though she couldn't understand why.

She wanted this. Wanted him. His cock filling her. His fingers digging into her flesh.

"Take me," she pleaded, rolling her hips against the ridge of his erection.

He tangled one hand in her hair and the other traced the outside of her folds. "Are you wet for me?"

"Drenched," she whispered.

Augustine growled and pulled up his tartan, notching himself at her entrance.

"Bloody hell." His voice was hoarse, rough with need as he pushed into her, sinking until he was fully seated within her. "You were made for this cock. My cock."

"Augustine," Emery cried out as he rocked his hips, grinding against her clit as the fullness he created inside her drove her toward the pleasure she craved.

He didn't stop. Didn't slow even when she exploded around his cock the first time.

Emery was flying somewhere between orgasm two and three when Augustine flipped their position. He lay on the blanket with her over him, impaled on his cock.

The billows of her skirts surrounded them and she felt like the dirtiest little princess.

Augustine reached up and ripped the bodice of her dress, splitting the delicate flowers that held it together and bathing her breasts in moonlight.

He was absolutely going to regret that when they returned to the castle and there was little she could do to hide her bare flesh. She opened her mouth to say as much, but then his hands latched onto her breasts. Cupping them, he rolled her nipples between his thumbs and forefingers and tugged them with such ferocity the only thing that fell from her mouth was a curse-laden moan.

Her gaze fell to his and a wicked grin tipped his lips. "Ride me, little witch. Milk my dick with that glorious cunt of yours and take what's always belonged to you alone."

Emery basked in the control he was giving her. What should have been his hunt, he was sharing with her in the most intimate way possible.

His breaths came out in heavy pants and the desire in his eyes aimed only at her made her feel like she was on top of the world. Like nothing, not even the impending battle or the uncertainty of their world could touch her.

She rolled her hips and started to ride him. Slowly at first, but before long, the build up was too much and she fucked his cock like it was the only thing that could save her.

Augustine's hands slid up under her dress and dug into her hips, keeping her moving at a steady rhythm and driving them toward the pure bliss of release they both needed.

"Mine," he panted, over and over as he thrust up into her.

It was hard, rough and brutal. But with Augustine, she wouldn't have it any other way.

"Yours." Emery leaned forward and pressed her lips to his, whispering against them. "I'm so close, Augustine."

He growled and the rumble of his chest against hers sent Emery over the edge.

Augustine bit his lip and then captured hers, doing the same. The tangle of their essence and the passion of their kiss pushed him to follow her and for just that moment they fell into the bond they shared. They claimed each other with every thrust, every suck, every moan-filled movement.

In the middle of her hazy, sated state, Augustine pulled back, his nose brushing against hers. "I fucking love you."

Emery tangled her hands in his hair and placed a chaste kiss to his lips, sucking the remainder of his blood from them. "I love you too."

He raised a brow and gave her a seductive smirk. "Shall we go again?"

Emery shook her head and rolled off of him. Looking down at herself she realized just how much of a hot mess she was. Her dress was twisted and torn, and just by feeling her hair, she could tell she had a major case of sex knots.

"As much as I'd love to take you up on that offer, we can't go again. We have a fake wedding to attend and a battle to win."

Augustine propped himself up on his elbows and the confident look on his face told her she was about to get schooled. "Number one, I'm the crown prince. The world will wait on me if I decide I want to fuck my mate another twenty times before I fake-marry her. And number two, if you think I wouldn't ride into battle with you bouncing on my cock, you don't know me very well, little witch."

Emery cracked a smile, but before a witty retort could be spoken, a shockwave shook the forest, followed by a massive blanket of heat. The scent of smoke filled the air and shrill screams tore through the forest. Both of them whipped their heads toward the castle, and time stood still. Shrieks and howls continued to echo, and Augustine tipped his head as if trying to hear what was going on.

"They're attacking," he growled.

Emery swallowed hard. She didn't need to ask but still she did. "Who?"

"The witches." He shot to his feet and offered her a hand. "Get up, you're going back to Scotland."

"No." She shook her head defiantly and steeled her stance. "If you're staying, I'm staying."

"Please, Emery." Augustine ran a hand through his hair, shaking his head. When he looked up at her, he pleaded, using not only his words but the bond between them. "I can't lose you. I can't lose our daughter. Please don't ask me to choose between you and my kingdom."

"I'm not trying to do that. I just can't sit back and do nothing."

Silence hung between them, neither willing to back down, though Emery got the feeling Augustine wouldn't give her much choice. With each passing second, his gaze hardened, and she had no doubt he would tie her to a damn tree if he thought it would keep her safe. She prayed he made the right choice.

"Emery?" A soft voice from the opposite side of the clearing, interrupting their stalemate.

With a curse, Emery grabbed the blanket from the ground and pulled it around her shoulders, hiding where the front of her dress was ripped. When she was covered, she turned to face the voice that had called her name.

Instantly, tears welled in her eyes. She sucked in a breath and blinked three or four times, trying to discern if the image before her was even real.

It couldn't be.

A sob caught in her throat and she pushed past her mate

and walked toward the last person she ever expected to see again.

She was frail, wearing a long black shift that did little to hide the way her collarbones and ribs protruded. Her cheeks were hollow, and her chin pointed more than her own, but there was no denying her eyes. They were the same honey whiskey as Emery's.

Emery crossed the clearing, stopping just short of the figure she longed to pull into her arms and never let go of. She'd failed her too many times already, but if this was the stars granting her a second chance she'd willingly take it.

"Sloane?"

"Hello, sister mine."

Chapter Forty One

EMERY

The stars had to be smiling down on her. Sloane was standing in the same clearing as her, breathing the same air. Every memory of every shitty thing she'd ever done flew out the window. Her sister was alive.

Emery stepped forward and enveloped her sister in a hug, pulling her frail form against her. "Is it really you?" she whispered, afraid if she questioned it too loudly, Sloane might disappear.

"It is." Sloane gave her a weak smile and hiccuped as tears streamed down her face, matching Emery's.

"But you died?" Emery pulled back still gripping her sister's forearms. "The mark, and Flora said she killed you at the request of the King."

Sloane shrugged. "She did, but you should know us Montgomerys are hard to kill."

She clearly didn't know their family history. None of the women in their family survived. But maybe this was the dawn of something new. The coming of a new era for Mongomery women. Emery's hands drifted to her stomach. She hoped it was. She needed it to be.

Emery turned to Augustine, who had followed her and

stood a few steps behind her. His eyes were narrowed on Sloane and the muscles in his jaw ticked. "Go, your people need you. I'll stay with Sloane. I'll open the portal to Scotland for the witches and you can guide them to the castle."

"I'm not leaving you," Augustine snapped, but it was a borderline growl.

Startled, Emery stared at her mate in confusion. He had every right to hate Sloane for what she did to Malcolm, and the fact she was a spy in his castle. But could he not see that this was also a joyous moment? Sloane wasn't dead. The world around them was changing. Maybe there was some room for the family she'd always hoped for. Some measure of forgiveness they could reach.

She reached out a hand to him, but Augustine didn't move to take it. "The Mistress is attacking. Your kingdom needs you, Augustine. Go."

His eyes were firmly fixed on Sloane, and when she traced them to her sister, Sloane also wore a fixed glare."My men can handle it, and Lily is there to get the witches."

Sloane's eyes perked up at the mention of Lily, but that was her only reaction to Augustine's words. She dropped her gaze and zeroed in on Emery's belly, a half grin pulling at her lips. She brought her hands to cup either side and gently rubbed the swell. "You've certainly got a story to tell."

"You have no idea." Emery tipped her head and smiled, savoring these first moments with Sloane. "But first I want to hear how you ended up here. Why are you here?"

"There will be time for that later. Right now I am here to take you from this place," Sloane's eyes narrowed on Augustine, "from these monsters."

"Monsters?" Emery recoiled and blinked a few times, still processing that she'd heard her sister correctly. "Maybe the king, but Augustine is not like his father."

Sloane scoffed, her face twisting in disgust. "Isn't he? He killed Miles and has taken many innocent lives in his lifetime."

"He didn't kill Miles, the Mistress did. She is responsible for the current death and turmoil." Emery couldn't argue that Augustine hadn't taken the lives of innocents as well. It was in his nature, and while she didn't like it, she couldn't find it in herself to fault him for who he was before her. Who he was when he thought she was his enemy. He did what he thought was necessary. But that wasn't who he was anymore. Not completely. Also, she'd proven she could kick his ass for it moving forward if he tried to revert back.

"You want to stay with him? With these monsters that had me killed?" The disbelief written all over Sloane's face gutted Emery.

This wasn't how she anticipated this going. Then again, she'd never in a million years believed she'd ever have the opportunity to see her sister again. Her eyes lifted to Sloane's, and she grit her teeth. "I want the King's head on a spike for what he did to you."

"Why are you really here, Sloane?" Augustine spoke up, his voice low and deadly.

Emery whirled and glared daggers at him. It wasn't going to be easy to get these two to get along, but fuck if she wasn't going to try. Family was family, and Sloane was all she had left of her blood. Now wasn't the time, but if there was a way she could have her cake and eat it too, she damn well intended to try.

Sloane's features softened, but there was still an edge to her voice. "I'm here for Emery and to take the revenge owed to me for those who took my life."

Emery stepped forward and took Sloane's hands in her own, noticing with a niggling feeling that there was no spark between them as there was when Lily and her touched. "And I'm so happy you are here. I'll be right beside you as we dethrone the King who took everything from us. But the fact that you are alive is a miracle, and you'll see there is a whole new world waiting for us to form. We can do it together. Create the supernatural world we deserve."

"I'm only alive because of the witches who saved me. They knew the king would betray me, that he would try to eliminate me. So we took matters into our own hands. They saved me. They're the ones who taught me who I am and showed me what I could become. And they were right. I am so much more powerful than even they imagined. You are too, sister."

"That's what I'm saying." Emery's voice fell when she put together what Sloane had said. "Wait... you've been alive all this time and never thought to reach out to me?"

"I was so weak after they brought me back. I didn't know where you were or that the mark would transfer. By the time I was back from fighting my way to the land of the living, you were already deep in the Culling. We tried to find a way to get you out. We even killed that Culling girl thinking they would try to kill you, and we could use it as a chance to get you out."

"You killed Chelsea?" Emery staggered back, pulling her hands from Sloane.

Her sister shrugged as if Chelsea's life was no concern of hers. "She was a means to an end, and you can't tell me she wasn't annoying."

Emery's mouth dropped open, and she searched for words but they didn't immediately come. Her heart stumbled and she shook her head. "She was your best friend, Sloane. She was the first person to welcome me into the castle when I took your place. "

"Maybe when we were younger, but once I discovered what I was and who I was meant to be, everything changed."

"And who is that?" Emery snapped, rage bubbling deep in her chest. "Because from where I'm standing, you aren't any better than the King who tried to kill you."

"Oh sister," Sloane said, her voice a sinister purr. "You have finally asked the right question. Who am I? Your vampire knows. Or at least, he suspects."

"Emery, get away from her," Augustine commanded urgently.

Emery ignored him, still staring at Sloane. Something was wrong, Something was very, very wrong. Sloane's eyes were amber, yes, but there was a coldness there. Not darkness like she saw in Augustine. Not sadness or fear or even true anger. Her eyes were filled with… blankness. Emptiness.

"Tell me who you are, Sloane," she said softly.

Her eyes gleaming with that strange empty light, she leaned toward her twin. "I'm the Mistress," she cackled. She snapped her fingers, and Emery flinched back. "The one who will rule the supernatural with darkness and might."

The air was knocked clear from Emery's chest.

All the dreams Emery had formed in the short time of her sister's return were ripped away.

I'm the Mistress.

"You're...." The words caught in Emery's throat and her whole body shook with a mix of anger and despair. "You're the Mistress?"

"Emery, move back!" Augustine practically howled.

A black-hearted grin twisted at Sloane's lips. "In all her glory, dear sister. I have been waiting, biding my time. Dahlia tried to keep me under the thumb of the coven all those years, forcing me to do their bidding, but I was never meant to be an errand girl. They wouldn't even unbind my magic to let me do what needed to be done while I was in the castle. I even worked with that imbecil king in order to further my agenda. That was a mistake. He was never going to let me make the changes I wanted. He wanted to rule the witches himself, to keep us under his thumb."

Emery tried to reach for her magic, dark or light. It didn't matter as long as it would immobilize the woman in front of her. The one who claimed to be her sister, but was clearly a monstrosity. Her palms opened at her sides but nothing happened. Nothing came. No rush of magic. No tendrils. Even the rage she'd felt was lackluster in comparison to what she'd come to expect.

"Don't bother," Sloane taunted. "Your magic has been stripped. For now at least. You really should be careful who you accept drinks from, Emery. You never know what they could be laced with."

Panic shot through her as she retraced her steps of the night. The only drink she'd had the entire night was the water she'd requested before the hunt. The rest of the prey had poured their own wine in the staging area, many of them working up some liquid courage. Seeing as she was pregnant, she'd requested a substitute.

She'd done this to herself.

Sloane had stripped her magic, and Emery was now completely at her mercy.

Her eyes trailed Sloane as she walked past her to where Augustine stood, still as a statue. Unmoving, save for his eyes, which traced her sister as well. Of course. She would have had to immobilize Augustine. He would have grabbed her by now and raced out of the woods. She should have listened to him. Now he was caught. Trapped here. Because of her.

Emery clutched the blanket closer around her, but it did nothing to touch the coldness settling over her heart.

"What did you do to him?" Emery gritted out, trying to hide the panic in her voice and failing spectacularly. Nothing was going as it was supposed to. She only prayed Lily was able to get the wolves or the witches there to help whoever was attacking at the castle.

"He'll be fine. I still have use for him if he's willing to cooperate. But I couldn't have him vamping off with you or warning the others." She trailed her hand over his shoulder, her nails raking along the back of Augustine's neck, and Emery almost lunged out to stop her.

"When I heard all that bullshit about the heir intended and finding mates, I knew it wasn't for me. I hoped it wasn't for you either, but you went and got yourself knocked up, so clearly you drank the kool aid. I can't blame you though, Emery. I did too for a long time. But when I learned of dark magic, when I felt it course through me even before my magic was unbound— thank you for that, by the way. It was getting tiresome having to absorb magic and convert it to my own— When I felt the darkness for the first time though, I knew it was my calling. It was mine to manipulate. Mine to use and covet. I was meant to rule. Not only the coven, but all supernaturals. The coven who saved me saw my potential. They groomed me for the position, and we planned for years. You were supposed to be by my side, Emery."

Emery straightened her spine and lifted her chin. "I will never choose to kill innocents in the name of power."

It was clear to Emery that Sloane was certifiable. Whatever she might have been once was gone. Now, she was the darkness of the fall. The heir of the darkness who would gladly take everything and kill anyone in her way.

"Suit yourself," Sloane shrugged playfully, as if she'd already won. "I really only want the blood in your veins and the baby in your belly. A nasty side effect of coming back from the dead via dark magic, you can no longer procreate. Thank goodness I have a twin."

Sloane created a portal behind her with a wicked smirk. Without another word, she grabbed Emery's arm and pulled her through the portal. For as frail as Sloane looked, she had a deceiving amount of strength.

Strength or magic.

Emery was screwed. No magic. No strength of her own, considering she was trapped in a body she hadn't conditioned due to her growing belly.

Sloane growled against her ear. "Fight back and I'll kill you myself. As I said, I don't need you."

Emery nodded and allowed herself to be transported to what looked like the castle. She looked over her shoulder and gave Augustine a weak smile, mouthing the location she was being taken to and hoping he'd be released from whatever magic Sloane had him under soon.

When she turned to face the castle, bile rose in the back of her throat.

Nothing could have prepared her for the carnage she saw. Magic hummed through the air, and Emery couldn't decipher dark from light. Bodies of vampire royals and sentinels were strewn across the dancefloor and lawn with lakes of blood between them. Fires burned in patches, charring the ground and filling the air with dense smoke.

Emery craned her neck to look at the castle itself. Parts of it were missing, crumbled away from the witches' attack. The dais where the king and queen sat was demolished, the terrace covered in debris, and when she looked at the back wall of the castle, she could see straight through to the grand ballroom, the chandelier hanging by the last link of its chain.

Tears welled in her eyes. The spectators of the hunt never stood a chance. Anyone who'd been standing near the dais or lining the castle had been in the blast zone. Her eyes darted around, looking for the King and Queen but neither of them were visible in the carnage.

The Mistress had done this.

No, Sloane. She was the one who sanctioned this. She'd planned it out. Played them and made them believe it was the wedding she wanted to attack, but this had been her plan all along. Take out as much of the royal vampire upper echelon as she could.

The woman who held her captive wasn't the sister she remembered. She wasn't even the one who wrote all those terrible things about Emery in her journals. No, the woman before her was evil. She held no regard for life, only her quest for power.

All across the back of the castle, battles were being fought. Dorian and another vampire Emery didn't recognize fought alongside Ansel in wolf form, battling a group of the Mistress' magically enhanced vampires. They worked together to tear through one after another, but every time they finished one, another would join the fight.

They weren't going to be able to keep it up. She could see they were giving it all they had, but that could only take them so far.

Emery reached for her magic again, trying to see if she could feel anything, summon any sort of help for her friends, but nothing came.

Near the forest's edge, Draven and Flora worked as a team to tear the heads off unsuspecting dark vampires as they attacked Malcolm and a team of Augustine's sentinels. Lily and Bronwyn weren't far off from them. They stood back to back, casting both offensive and defensive magic to help those around them while fighting off dark vampires of their own.

Emery breathed a shaky sigh of relief that at the very least

Lily hadn't been stripped of her magic, and she'd been able to get both sets of back up to the castle. They weren't winning, but they weren't going down without a fight.

Another portal opened from the far side of the dais where she stood with Sloane, and Emery's heart sank when she saw more dark vampires walk through.

No.

There were too many of them. Even with powerful witches, vampires, and wolves on their side, they were ill-prepared for the battle that rang out across the castle. With each platoon of vampires that came through the portal, the hope in Emery's chest was further stripped away.

"They're magnificent, aren't they?" Sloane squealed, clapping her hands together like a sadistic seal. "Created from my blood and the bodies of vampires. They are compelled to listen to me, to do my bidding."

"You're taking away their free will."

"I'm giving them life after death," Sloane scoffed, like it somehow made up for stealing the eternal lives of those vampires.

"If that's what you have to tell yourself to sleep at night."

Augustine tore from the trees, his chest heaving and his eyes murderous. He took in the scene and his steps faltered ever so slightly. His jaw tightened and his eyes darted frantically until they landed on Emery at the base of the destruction with Sloane.

He raced to where they stood, but as he approached, Sloane flicked her hand out, freezing him once more.

Emery really needed to figure out how the hell she was doing that. It would be a useful skill to have and she'd love nothing more than to use it against Sloane as she slit her throat.

"Wren," Sloane hollered. "Let's get this over with, I'm

growing tired of playing this game. I've gotten what I came for."

Wren stepped through the portal, holding Agatha with a knife to her throat. The always kind cafe owner smiled at Emery over hollow cheekbones. "I'm so happy to see you dear, although I wish it was under different circumstances."

That is an understatement. What the hell is she doing there?

Emery's eyes softened and she took a step toward Agatha, the need to protect her rising in her chest.

Sloane stepped in front of Emery, halting her progress. "Enough of the pleasantries crone, you said you had a prophecy for my sister, and would only speak it to her."

Agatha's eyes locked on Emery and a soft smile tipped her lips. When she spoke it was directed only to Emery, as if they weren't standing in the carnage of the fall of the supernatural world. "The stars have gifted me with a reminder, my dear. The life you mourn is not gone. Your son is one with his sister, not in body but in spirit. They beat with each other, two halves of a whole. Do not let the darkness take you, Emery. Let it fuel you. Learn its ways so you may harness it and bring light. The lives you hold are truly the future. Don't let them slip away."

"You said you had a prophecy, you lying cow!" Sloane stepped forward and threw Agatha to the ground. "Not some cheap psycho babble bullshit."

Emery gasped and tried to step forward, but Sloane snapped her fingers, and Emery froze as solid as a statue.

"Did I say that?" Agatha giggled like she'd heard a joke only she was privy to. "I suppose I forgot I've already shared all the stars have willed me to share. This revelation was just a treat. There is no prophecy, just a reminder of truth to be shared before it's my time."

Sloane's jaw tightened and muttered a curse under her

breath. "It's no matter." She shook her head so her hair fell back over her shoulders, and straightened her dress. "The reminder might as well have fallen on deaf ears. Her babies are mine. The supernatural world is mine. And there isn't a damn thing my sister is going to do about it." She paused and gave a subtle nod to Wren. "We don't need her anymore. Kill her for her willingness to waste my time and bag me a wolf. We'll take what we need and be on our way."

"No!" Emery cried out, her eyes and mouth the only part of her Sloane had deemed worthy to remain functioning. "Wren, please. Don't kill her. Just let her go. This isn't you. You aren't a killer."

"You don't know me, Emery," Wren said. She shook her head sadly, as if Emery's faith in her was physically painful. "I'm not the friend you remember, and I don't want to live by the rules of the coven any longer. We are creating something bigger. Something better. A world where we all get along under the rule of the Mistress."

Emery's eyes landed on Sloane, and she pleaded with the sister she hoped was still buried deep in her. "I'll do whatever you want, just please don't kill innocent people."

"Innocence is relative," she mused, her eyes tracking something taking place on the battlefield out of Emery's view.

Agatha's eyes softened ,and she gave Emery a smile that told her she'd resigned to her fate. "Don't worry about me, dear girl, the stars have called my name, and I'm ready to dance among them. Keep your heart light, and your ear open to the plan the stars have for you. You'll soon see all as it was meant to be."

No. Emery couldn't just allow them to kill her. Agatha had done nothing but help her. But that in itself was the problem. She'd knowingly sacrificed her own life to try and bring Emery hope.

Still Emery didn't want to believe this was the end for her dear friend. It wasn't fair. How could the stars just allow her to die?

Emery's eyes darted between Sloane and Wren as she tried to decide which would be the more likely to consider her words.

She landed on Wren, and tried to appeal to the friend she'd loved. "How could you possibly think this is the answer? Please, don't do this. I'll do anything, Wren."

Her eyes narrowed, and for a moment Emery thought she'd reached her. But then her lips twitched and instead of a smile, a sneer cracked her face. "When there isn't anything left to call home, you choose the winning side."

Without a second thought, Wren reached up and with a flick of her wrist, broke Agatha's neck.

"No!" Emery cried out and thrashed against Sloane's hold. She spun and called her magic forward, but only sobs radiated from her constricted chest.

Sloane released her hold on Emery, and she crumbled to the ground. The night that had started so well had ended not only in battle but in the death of innocents. Not only Agatha, but all those that now lay on the battlefield.

"Let's go, sister," Sloane demanded. "We've wasted enough time here."

Emery stared at Agatha's body, lying on the ground just a few feet away. Something inside her broke open. She raised her head and turned to look at Augustine. He was frozen in place mid-stride, and his eyes were locked on her. *I'm so sorry,* she mouthed. She hoped he'd understand that she had to do what was best for the kingdom. That meant stopping Sloane.

Emery tore her eyes from the visage of her mate and looked up at Sloane through tear-stained eyes as she tried to tuck her feet under her to give her more leverage. "If you think I am going with you, that I am going to help you in any way shape or form after what you've done tonight, you are crazier than I thought."

"You don't have to agree," Sloane laughed. "That's the beauty of it."

Emery was about to launch herself at her sister, hands poised for her throat with only a prayer of hope to the stars on her lips when two bloodied hands wrapped around Emery and yanked her back. "Oh, but I do. Emery is a member of my court and my son's mate. I believe I *do* have a say."

The King tightened his grip on her hip and a knife dug into her throat. He leaned in and whispered in her ear. "I've got you now, Emery, save me here, and I might let your child live."

Sloane rolled her eyes and popped her hips like the king was only a minor annoyance. "What do you think you're doing, Lewyn?"

"That's 'Your Majesty' to you, witch. And I'm ensuring I make it out of here alive. We worked together once to fool the witches, let's strike a deal again. Your sister's life for mine. I'll allow you to rule the witches, but the vampires are mine, and you will stop killing my people. In return we will leave you to yours."

Emery huffed a silent laugh. Even she knew Sloane would never agree to that. She thought she was the ruler of the damned universe. She wasn't about to listen to this small man with his delusions of power.

On cue, Sloane tipped back her head and laughed. Her hands wrapped around her waist, clutching her stomach and she bent over as if what he'd said was the funniest thing in the world. She reached up and wiped a tear from her eye. "Your life was forfeit the moment you had me killed, *Your Majesty*. But I may still have use for you, so here are my terms. I need her blood, and a lot of it. Slit her throat and join me. Pledge allegiance to me, and I'll allow you to keep your life."

"Father, don't." Augustine's voice rang out above the battle still raging on all around them.

Emery glared at Sloane. Of course the manipulative bitch granted him the ability to talk when her life was on the line. She no doubt wanted him to plead with her and his father. To soak up every last bit of desperation on the lips of Emery's mate.

The king's body tensed as he weighed his options before he grit out. "I'll gladly kill her, the rest is non-negotiable."

"Ha!" Sloane elbowed Wren and raised a brow. Wren winced before joining in, laughing at the king's expense. When they finally quit, Sloane willed a ball of magic into her hand and tossed it up before catching it and pinning her gaze on the King. "If you think I give two shits about your negotiation, you're wrong. She's going to die regardless for choosing the wrong side. All you get to pick is whether you're going to fall with her or not."

The king swallowed hard. Clearly that wasn't what he expected her sister to say, though it hadn't surprised her one bit. Sloane was off her damn rocker—nothing and no one was going to stop her plans.

"So be it," said the king.

Three words sealed her fate.

Emery didn't feel the steel against her neck as it sliced through her. It was the blood that warmed her chest and the gurgling in her ears that let her know she was going to die.

There was no white light or flashes of life before her eyes.

As her body fell, she mouthed the three words that mattered most to her mate. His was the last face she would see. Emery could only pray he would save their daughter.

Not only so he wasn't alone, but for the sake of the world.

Chapter Forty-Two

AUGUSTINE

Augustine had been shot before. He'd been torn open gut to gullet on the battlefield. That was all before he'd emerged from the forest to find his home destroyed and his people burning and fighting for their lives. But none of that compared to the pain that ripped through his chest as he watched the light fade from Emery's eyes.

Time stood still as Augustine watched, powerless to help his love. Still held in Sloane's spell, his chest constricted with sobs that had no release. His rage had no outlet. He was fucking useless.

The Mistress stepped forward and swirled her fingers. Tendrils of dark purple magic formed a small container that sat in the palm of her hand and with the snap of her finger, Emery's blood began to rise from her wound and fill the container.

The scent of her essence called to him, and he fought against the magic that bound him with everything he had. The woman he loved was dying and there was nothing he could do to stop it. He searched for her heartbeat, locking in on its slowing beat.

No.

No, little witch, keep fighting.

He forced every bit of love and fight he could down their bond.

Her lack of response tore him apart from the inside out.

She wasn't allowed to give up.

She'd held them together for so long while he pulled his head out of his ass, she didn't get to give up now.

The woman Emery called Wren waved her hand behind the Mistress and muttered an incantation under her breath. Seconds later, an unconscious Ansel floated across the debris-filled dancefloor. His body hung limp as if only the air beneath him held him up.

A guttural roar erupted from Dorian's lips as he tried to fight his way to Ansel, tearing apart every vampire that moved in his direction, but there were too many of them. For every one he defeated, another took its place, preventing Dorian from breaking through.

Augustine could have sworn he saw Dorian glimmer slightly in the moonlight, but whatever he saw disappeared before he could study it.

Wren dropped Ansel beside Emery with a cold thud. Augustine extended his senses to Ansel's still form and though he struggled to find a heartbeat, it was there. Slow, but strong.

Nothing was going as planned. The darkness raged inside him alongside August, demanding Augustine do something—anything—but there was nothing he could do.

The Mistress looked him over as Emery's blood finished filling her container. "He's not royal, but he'll do. I saw him fight, and his body is delicious."

A growl rumbled from Augustine's chest, and the Mistress narrowed her eyes on him. "Fond of this one are you? Good. Remember I have him, because when I let you go, you'll have some choices to make, Augustine. You can bend a knee to me and save the life of your child, who will become my heir, or you can choose to be my enemy. In which case, this is only a taste of what your kingdom will endure. You choose."

His father snarled from where he stood above Emery's body. "It's my kingdom."

Augustine growled again. It was the only sound his vocal chords could manage, since they were locked along with every other aspect of his body. He was going to rip Sloane to shreds when he broke free, followed by his father.

The world thought he was dark before, but it was nothing compared to what he'd become to right the wrongs against his mate.

The Mistress snickered. "Oh I highly doubt that once he's done with you, Lewyn."

Augustine was growing tired of her flippant attitude. She'd played them all like a damn fiddle, and she knew it. There was no way they could have ever been prepared for this attack. They'd only barely begun to discover the level of dark magic she possessed. It was so much more than they'd anticipated.

His father's lip quivered, and his voice broke. His eyes darted back and forth between his son and the Mistress. "But I agreed to your terms."

Good. Augustine hoped he was scared, because if the Mistress didn't kill him, he would. The Mistress was right about one thing. His father wasn't leaving this place alive.

"And you also killed me. Payback is a bitch, Your Majesty." She snapped her finger, and the king was frozen with the rest of them.

The Mistress nodded to Wren, who whipped her hands in a circle, opening a portal behind them.

"Wait." A terrified female voice cried out and Augustine strained to see who it belonged to.

Augustine opened his senses and heard the same voice mumbling to herself. "Stupid fucking vampire. Lock me in a damn closet on my wedding night."

Jessi ran toward them from the dilapidated castle. Barefoot and disheveled, her designer dress was ripped and she was covered in ash from head to toe as she dodged bodies and debris.

A part of his heart constricted. He shouldn't care for Jessi, but she was still a member of his Culling. He may not be marrying her, but she didn't deserve to be thrown into the center of this war.

She stopped between Augustine and Sloane, panting as if she'd ran a marathon. Her eyes drifted to where Augustine and the King stood frozen, then down to Emery's bloodied body and a sinister smile took her face. "Take me with you, Sloane."

If Augustine's mouth could drop it would and he mentally took back every nice thing he ever thought about Jessi. The fucking bitch was about to switch sides.

Sloane tipped her head back and laughed. "Why the hell would I take you with me. You can rot in hell with the rest of them for all I care."

She'd definitely be rotting somewhere when he got free.

"You need me, that's why. I knew August was never going to forget his little witch bitch, so I took matters into my own hands. His father loves anything with a tight little body that will stroke his ego. I know everything he's put in place to fight against you, and everything he's hidden from Augustine. Take me with you and I'll share it all with you."

Sloane tipped her head to the side, considering Jessi's offer.

Augustine tried to break free of Sloane's hold, if only to rip

Jessi's head off himself. Emery called her the wicked bitch of the castle, but if you asked him that was too kind. This woman was as vile as the Mistress. Two pears cut from the same damn tree. Of course she had cozied up to his father. All she wanted was power and status, and when she figured out she would get neither from Augustine, she sought the only place left to find it. The joke was on her though. Even he knew there was no way Sloane would keep her alive for long. An informant was only useful as long as they had information, and he had no doubt Jessi's usefulness wouldn't last long.

"Fine." Sloane waved Jessi toward the portal and Jessi wasted no time scurrying through. "Don't make me regret this, Jessi."

Wren picked up Ansel and moved toward the portal, as Sloane followed and stepped through. She looked back, and her eyes connected with Augustine. "Emery's not dead… yet, but her soul is almost lost. Decide quickly if you'd like to have her by your side. I'll be in touch, Your Majesty."

Augustined tuned in once more to his mate's heart, finding it still beating in her chest, but only barely.

He was going to kill Sloane, and Jessi. Really he was going to kill every single one of the witches that served under her. But first he was going to end the man who did this to Emery.

The moment the portal closed, every single one of the dark vampires fell to the ground, dead. It was as if they'd never existed. Everyone stopped and looked around, confusion painted on their faces.

A gurgled cry rang out, and Dorian raced to where Ansel had vanished. "No. She can't have him." He turned his head to the heavens and bellowed a wordless roar.

And then, as if by magic he hadn't known Dorian possessed, the sentinel disappeared. Augustine blinked in surprise, staring at nothing. One moment Dorian was there, the next he was gone, vanished into thin air. No portal. No magic. Just gone.

It wasn't something he could puzzle out at the moment. The instant his own prison was broken, he rushed to Emery's side. Which was also coincidentally where his father stood.

The King wore a sinister smile, as if he'd already won the impending battle between them. Augustine wasn't going down without a fight.

...That was a lie. There would be no fight, because that would imply he was going to give his father the opportunity to live.

Augustine snarled, and his eyes fell to Emery.

This is for you, my love.

That moment's hesitation was all it took for August to push to the forefront.

Augustine fell back into the depths, an unwilling passenger in whatever happened next.

No, he cried out from the prison of their shared mind.

He clawed against August, trying to take back control. Emery was his mate as much as August's, and he demanded vengeance. If the bastard thought he was going to play the diplomatic prick, he had another thing coming. Their father had gone too far. No way was Augustine going to sit back and allow him to not suffer for what he'd just done.

He killed our fucking mate, August. Can you not smell her blood? She is bleeding out on the fucking ground, and you are standing there with your dick in your hand doing nothing.

Desperation filled his plea, but August just stood there. It had only been seconds but to Augutstine it was a lifetime. It was the difference between life and death.

"I need to do this," August ground out softly, agony filling his voice, and Augustine wasn't sure who he was trying to convince.

You better bloody fucking do something, or step aside because I am not letting her die, and I sure as hell am not bowing to the Mistress. And as for our father, there is no way he's leaving the castle alive.

The king raised a brow at August. "Ah, has my favorite son returned? You were always the more logical of the two of you."

Augustine held his breath, waiting for August to do something. Anything.

A few more painfully slow milliseconds passed. Augustine scratched and clawed at his prison, begging August to do something, *anything*.

And then August turned to face the king. He blinked once, twice, and took a deep breath before launching toward the king with a rage Augustine hadn't known his gentler side possessed.

The King realized what was about to happen seconds too late.

He should have run when he had the chance, but ever the prideful bastard, he hadn't, and it would be his demise.

Augustine smirked and retreated into the depths, offering whatever strength he could to his no-longer-weaker half as he pummeled their father to the ground.

This was a pivotal moment for August—one Augustine couldn't take from him no matter how much he wished he could be the darkness. They were almost one, with so little that differentiated them any more. This moment held weight behind it. It was their beginning and end. It would be the final nail in the coffin that imprisoned them for so long.

Augustine had always known this day would come. He was dying. With every blow to his father, August was freeing the darkness within himself. All he could do was pray when the moment was over he'd get to see her take another breath.

See her roll her eyes one more time and use that smart mouth of hers to drive him wild.

But it wasn't meant to be. He could feel himself being snuffed out.

Goodbye, Emery, he thought, as the darkness began to overwhelm him.

Chapter Forty-Three

AUGUSTINE

Blood coated his face, hands and torso, leaving him looking every bit like the monster he should feel like.

But he didn't feel monstrous.

The only emotion that coursed through him as he looked down at the headless body of the man who'd sired him was relief. His father's tyrant reign was over. He could no longer hurt his mother, or dictate what August or Malcolm did. He couldn't neglect their people's wants and needs. He couldn't murder his mate.

Fuck.

His mate.

Emery.

Fucking fix her.

August's chest constricted at Augustine's faint plea. He was still there, but only barely.

Augustine's darkness coursed through him, and he welcomed every tainted inch of it.

He dropped his father's head at his feet with a dull sound, and fell to his knees, pulling Emery's lifeless body into his arms.

Her limp form fell against him, and her head lolled back.

The beat of her heart was so slow he didn't think it was possible she could survive. Immediately he brought his lips to her neck and bit down, praying he wasn't too late.

He had to suck at her neck to bring any blood to the wound. Her heart was weak, nearly stopped. When the blood did come, it no longer sang of her as it washed over his tongue. August pushed his venom through her, willing it to spark something within her. Praying their bond would reignite her life.

Her vacant amber eyes gazed up at the heavens, as if she could still count the stars above. Still wrapped in the blanket from the forest picnic, she was so damn cold. He reached for the bond and found it lifeless. Her magic no longer hummed at the opposite end and every ounce of warmth he'd grown to associate with her was gone.

Sloane said her soul was almost lost. Without her soul who would she be? Emery's soul was the core of her very being— she used it to make the world brighter. The way she tried to see the best in everyone; the way she examined each situation with precision and logic; the way she rolled her eyes knowing damn well it would piss Augustine off... and the way she pulled Thea into her arms. Her soul made up all the best parts of her. If it was gone, she'd no longer be her. She'd be a shell and Emery wouldn't want that.

His only option was to give in to Sloane's demands. To bend a knee.

The thought made him sick, but what the bloody hell was there left for him to do?

We can't.

"What do you expect me to do, let her go?" August cried out, his voice breaking as he choked on the first of many sobs that lined his throat.

"No one expects you to let her go, Augustine." Lily placed a hand on his shoulder, and he leaned into her touch.

He didn't bother to correct his name. It didn't matter in the grand scheme of things. August, Augustine, either way they were losing their mate.

Lily gave him a gentle squeeze, and he glanced in her direction. Her eyes brimmed with tears as she took Emery's hand in hers. She gasped, and August knew she was feeling how cold Emery had become.

"Can you fix her?" He didn't want to allow himself to hope, but it was there in his voice. "Save her like you saved my father."

Lily hung her head and shook it slightly. "When I did that, I gave a life for a life. It was different. Emery's not dead. Not yet. Her soul is detached and waning. I can almost sense it hovering around us."

August lifted his head and searched the space around them, only finding the concerned faces of his chosen family and the stars above mocking him. If Emery's soul was there, he couldn't see her. He couldn't feel her. He was so fucking empty, and all he wanted to do was crawl within their bond and live where they were supposed to be one.

She wasn't supposed to leave him.

"I've never heard of such magic," Lily continued, "but I have no doubts it's tied to necromancy. Dark magic is a powerful thing, but it's beyond my purview. I can feel her drifting away. I fear once she's completely gone, there will be no getting her back, and I have no idea what that means for the bairn."

August bit the inside of his lip, refusing to believe this was the end. This couldn't be the only answer. He couldn't lose her and his daughter. Neither loss was acceptable. He shook his head as if somehow refusing to believe the situation would magically change the outcome.

He couldn't live without her.

But she could live. She needed to live.

He exhaled a sigh that only solidified his thoughts. He met Lily's gaze and with every ounce of confidence in his choice he made his request. "If she dies, I want you to take my life for hers."

Lily wiped away a tear, her mouth falling into a grim line as she shook her head. "I can't do that."

"Please, Lily. She needs to survive. For our child. For your children. She's the one who is meant to lead our people into the future. It's not me. It's always been her." He pleaded with her even though the desperation on her face told him there was nothing she could do.

"I don't know that my own soul would survive another use of dark magic."

"I can't lose her." August pulled Emery's body tighter against him. Burying his nose in her hair, he choked back a sob. She'd only been in whatever fucked-up stasis Sloane left her in for a handful of minutes, and already she was losing her scent.

"So save her." Octavian stood at the edge of the group, his head cocked upward as he spoke into the night sky.

August's eyes zeroed in on the original vampire. "Don't you think I would if I could? My venom didn't work," he spat.

"But your soul will, my boy." Octavian spoke as if it was the most simple solution in the world. As if they should know this was the only option.

August tilted his head at the old man, and his brows arched upward in utter confusion. The crazed old man almost never made sense, why should he pick this moment to start being logical?

"Did you all read nothing in the texts I sent?" Octavian sighed and crossed the space where not only his family and friends anxiously looked on, but also the surviving members of his court.

They would either shun him or accept him after this, and honestly August didn't give a damn so long as Emery was at his side. They'd have to bloody fucking deal with it.

Octavian took his time, dramatically stepping over the pools of blood and body parts. "She is your mate, August. Emery's soul will forever be tethered to yours as you are to her. You can pull her back from death."

"How?" August didn't dare to hope, but even he could hear the way his voice clung to his plea.

"A split of the soul."

August blinked at him and shook his head. "Are you crazy again?"

"No you, daft boy. You will need to split your soul. Give your mate a part of you that her soul can cling to. Even in death, your souls remain." Octavian's gaze bore into August, and his tone dropped, full of warning. "But this is a one-time deal, and there will be repercussions. You'll need to ensure your soul is whole. A soul divided can't be given."

Do it.

There was no hesitation from Augustine. No argument. No demand to allow him to take the forefront.

She's our future. Our everything. Ours. Together. It took us far too long to figure it out, but this is how it's supposed to be. Bring her back to us.

August started to nod in agreement but before he could bring his head back down, his chest tightened, and for the first time he felt whole again. It was like every part of him was in sync. No longer did he feel weak or like the darkness was too much to handle. He could breathe again.

And just like that, Augustine was gone.

...But not.

He was still there, in the rage that coursed through his veins and the lust that pooled deep within him.

August sucked in a breath and pressed his hand to his chest. He thought it would be some big to-do, becoming one with himself again, but it wasn't. He didn't know what he expected. Maybe fireworks or some grand realization as he and Augustine had become one in the same. It was an act of survival to split himself in the first place, but becoming whole was as simple as letting go and accepting every facet of himself. He'd never had a reason to before...

Before her.

His head fell and he locked on the woman who was the only thing that drove him to keep breathing. He'd gladly give up his soul again if it meant she was by his side to love and cherish. To raise their daughter and every other child he planned to put in her belly.

"Bite her, but instead of your venom alone, will your soul through your bond. Make sure to meter what you give. You only need to give enough to bring her back. If you give too much, you'll take her place, and while I know you'd give up your life for hers, you are both needed here."

August nodded.

No pressure.

He leaned in, and his lips hovering over his favorite spot. He licked her skin, lifted a prayer to the stars, and bit down.

Emery's soulless lackluster blood filled his mouth, and he fought the urge to gag. He swallowed hard and immediately sought the cold bond that tethered their souls. Panic flooded him as he realized there was nothing there. Where once her warmth and desire welcomed him, there was nothing but a barren grey desert void of any emotion.

August pushed harder, his lips sucking what was left of her essence into him while his mind searched the depths for his mate.

You are mine little witch. You don't get to leave me, he commanded, shoving every bit of himself down the bond in the hopes Emery was still there.

He wasn't about to give up. He would lose himself in her if that's what it took.

And then he saw it: the tiniest spark of gold, hidden in the deepest part of Emery's soul. Her magic cradled the spark as if it were a child in its womb, the last bit of her humanity that could save her from losing herself.

It recognized August immediately and began to pulse with need.

He ran towards it and latched onto it.

Emery's essence washed over him and somewhere deep within him, he knew what he needed to do.

Take what you need, he whispered.

And then he let go.

Chapter Forty Four

EMERY

Don't leave us.
You are mine.
Our children need you.
You cannot leave.
I need you.
Please, little witch.
You're my everything.
Come back to me.

August and Augustine beckoned her through the melodies she played. Their voices were commingled in a way that surprised her—dominance and caring together in one being. But Emery couldn't bring herself to leave the warmth and safety of where she was. Maybe it was a vision. Maybe she'd died and this was purgatory. It wouldn't have surprised her if that's where she'd ended up. But even though she wasn't entirely sure where she resided, she felt Augustine cocooning around her, protecting her, comforting her. She couldn't leave this place. She couldn't face what was beyond. This was where she belonged now. Small and hidden.

"You're not supposed to be here, granddaughter mine."

Emery glanced up from where her hands danced over the keys of a grand piano, entranced by the woman before her. She walked—no, it was more like she floated—with the grace of an angel toward the piano where Emery sat.

The woman wore a gown of silver that matched the expanding ballroom that surrounded her. The bright metallic color contrasted with her amber eyes.

Eyes Emery would know anywhere—they were the same ones that stared at her in the mirror day after day.

Emery didn't know how long she'd been in the ballroom, only that every time she placed her hands to the ivory keys of the magical piano, she fell into the music, lost in the emotion of her life as it played out before her in a perfect highlight reel of only the happiest moments.

A niggling in her mind told her she needed to embrace other moments, too—moments she'd all but forgotten. A voice whispered that the stars weren't done with her yet, but she pushed it away.

The stars could go fuck themselves.

Her soul was happy in this place where pain and heartache couldn't reach her.

"How do you know where I'm supposed to be?" Emery traced her fingers over the sleek black top of the piano.

"Because you are the final step in my greatest plans." The woman spoke in a layered voice, filled with wonder and awe, but still in a tone that was more declaration than suggestion.

Emery tilted her head and squinted her eyes, the woman's name popping into her head as if by divine intervention. "Celeste?"

"Emery," Celeste nodded, confirming her identity.

She wanted to hate the woman. Celeste was the one who had set in motion every bit of heartache and turmoil experienced by those Emery considered family. She was the reason Emery had never known true love until she'd found herself in the clutches of the enemies who should have never been her enemies to begin with. The dominoes from Celeste's actions set the precedent for the clusterfuck that was the supernatural community.

And despite all that, Emery couldn't find it in herself to loathe the woman. The exact opposite was true. She wanted to embrace Celeste as part of her long lost family. She wanted to seek her guidance. To understand why she was chosen by her and the stars to be the fulcrum of their plot.

But… how the hell was she here? Did that mean Emery did, in fact, die? And what the hell did she mean when she said Emery was the final step in her greatest plan?

Celeste clasped her hands together, somehow appearing even more ethereal than before. "Because you don't see the world in black and white. You see it in marvelous shades of grey and appreciate the flaws that make us. You are the beginning of the end and the light of the future."

"How did you—can you read my mind? And how do I learn to do that shit?" Emery could only imagine the fun she could have with that talent. The payback she could wield on Malcolm and Callum alone would make it worthwhile.

"You think too loudly, dear."

"I'm not even sure what that means, but to your point that I am the beginning and the end, I am pretty sure I can't do anything if I'm dead." The sadness that danced on the fringes of her absolute calm creeped in, reminding her of all she had left behind.

Dead. She was dead. "Fuck," Emery gritted out, knowing she was right.

Every bit of emotion Emery has successfully kept locked away came crashing down around her. Tears pricked her eyes, and Emery didn't try to stop them from coming. She sobbed at the thought of her daughter. She didn't even know if she lived or died. The perfect little girl with eyes of amber and ocean could be as lost to time as her mother. And Augustine. Another sob tore from her chest. Her mate would have lost his light the moment she ceased to be. Those two were her world, and she'd failed them, but not only them. The supernatural world relied on her and she'd failed them as well.

"I am not the answer. I could barely keep myself alive against my sister who has had magic the same amount of time I have. I didn't even notice I'd been stripped."

"Oh dear girl, you aren't dead. You are locked in the depths of your soul until you are ready to bloom. And as for your sister, Sloane's had a dark witch feeding her magic since long before her magic was unbound. Give yourself some grace, you've had magic for such a short time, and you came out unscathed."

"I wouldn't exactly call having my soul ripped away unscathed."

"No, but it was necessary. You are not the only one who has grown from this outcome. Everything is how it is intended to be."

Emery's brow pinched, anger pulsing in her chest. "No one asked me if I wanted to do this."

"And yet you would do it anyway. For your children. For your mate. For those who don't have a voice."

She stared at Celeste, trying to parse her emotions. She couldn't be everything to everyone, let alone whoever the hell it was she was supposed to be.

Emery slammed her hands down on the piano and the jumbled tones echoed through the room, echoing the turmoil of her soul. She hung her head and exhaled a shaky breath. "I'm just so damn tired."

Celeste floated closer and placed her hands on Emery's

sagged shoulders. "Even the greatest warriors need their solace. Find yours in your mate. He is ready for you."

Again with half answers laced with cryptic undertones.

Emery wiped away her tears and craned her neck to look up at Celeste. Her tone firm, she asked point blank, "What comes next?"

Celeste lips tipped up in a knowing smile. "I cannot say. The future is only for the stars to know, but I have seen glimpses, and if you stay true to your heart, you will end up where you are needed. Don't be afraid of the darkness, seek those who will help you love it and beware of those who seek to help too willingly."

Emery rolled her eyes and muttered, "It's no wonder Octavian was your mate, you both love to speak in open-ended riddles."

Celeste's smile widened, and Emery could have sworn she swooned ever so slightly. "Tell my mate I love him, and he can let go already."

Emery nodded, still not convinced about anything beyond the fact she couldn't remain locked away in her realm of false happiness, despite how much she wished she could.

Celeste gave her shoulders a squeeze and looked toward the door she entered through. "Now go. Don't keep him waiting. Mates are a wonderful thing, but patience is not a virtue they possess."

Chapter Forty Five

AUGUSTINE

August scoffed at the sun.

It had no business filling the room with its light. With its warmth. Not when his heart couldn't feel it. Not when his light hung in the balance.

A storm he could handle. A downpour from the heavens that would not only wash away the blood of his people, but where the blood of his mate seeped into the earth. The thunder would match the rumbling of his soul. The lightning would mimic the rage he wished to unleash.

But no. The stars had graced him with a bloody beautiful day.

It had been two days since the Mistress decimated his kingdom. Forty-eight hours since he'd taken his father's life. But it felt like a lifetime since he'd seen the glowing warmth in the eyes of his mate.

Octavian swore the transfer of his soul had been a success, but Emery still lay unmoving where he placed her in his bed.

August could feel her on the fringes of his consciousness, as if she was just on the other side of a door. Their bond had been restored, but reaching down it was like traveling an endless hallway where he never reached his destination. He was a part of her, his essence coursing through her, but still, Emery hadn't returned to him.

A heavy sigh fell from his lips.

He needed her to come back. A king needed his queen.

King.

They'd tried to force him into moving into his father's suite, but there was no way that was happening. The fact that his kingdom had accepted him as king at all was a miracle. He'd usurped his father, and though he was well within his rights, he expected more of a backlash from the kingdom.

The few royals who survived the attack and were loyal to his father disappeared quietly into the night, and while he was sure they would be back wielding their opinions on his plans for the future, at the moment they were a silent thorn he could easily ignore.

Those who witnessed the exchange with the Mistress fully supported him, and their stories of that night had already made their way across the kingdom. He suspected Braxton's ties to like-minded vampire cells had something to do with it.

He opened his senses, listening for the rapid heartbeat of his daughter in Emery's womb. It was a miracle she had survived, but then again he shouldn't have been surprised. She was a fighter like her mother, and stubborn like her father. It was a deadly combination, but it would serve her well. He was already wrapped around her little fingers, singing to her and telling her stories until the wee hours of the morning while she rewarded him with kicks and jabs.

Their daughter was the single thing he had to hold on to. The only piece of his world that made sense.

A gentle pounding on the door sounded, and August reluctantly turned toward it.

Dorian stepped through, his hair ruffled and his eyes hollow. "You wanted to speak with me, Your Majesty?"

August studied the sentinel, his eyes narrowed. "You look like shit."

Dorian shrugged. "I feel like shit. Also," he pointed at August, "pot calling the kettle black."

August snorted. He wasn't wrong—it had been some time since August had changed his clothes or showered.

Dorian's state of mind shouldn't matter. The only thing August should care about at that moment was if he could trust the sentinel he'd come to care for. There was something Dorian was hiding; something he hadn't shared. Vampires didn't just disappear out of thin air.

But Dorian's health and happiness did matter, because August did care for Dorian and so did Emery.

Still he couldn't risk Dorian being the spy in his ranks. August stepped forward and straightened to his full height. "It isn't me you claim fealty to, is it?"

Dorian inhaled a shaky breath and released it slowly, shaking his head. "You are not my only king, but you are the one I have chosen to serve."

"Who are you, Dorian? Is that even your real name?"

Dorian held August's stare for a moment, and then dropped his eyes to the floor. With his gaze also fell his glamour, revealing the being Augustine had seen flicker into existence the night before. He was impossibly beautiful, with chiseled cheekbones and pointed ears.

Looking at the ground as if it were the most interesting thing in the room, Dorian spoke so low August almost couldn't hear it. "No. Its Dorianthian, unseelie fae of the dark court."

August's eyes widened, and he choked on his disbelief. "Fae? As in Fairy?"

Dorian nodded and lifted his head. "I am so sorry, Your Majesty."

"Holy hell." August ran his fingers through his hair, his emotions ranging somewhere between rage and awe. "What the hell are you doing posing as one of my sentinels? Are you the Mistress' spy?"

"No! I would never do anything to betray you or your queen. My prince—well he was my prince once—he asked me to help him as a favor. He wanted to know if the vampires were trustworthy. He knew your father was a piece of shit, but he needed to know who you were."

"And what will you report back?"

Dorian exercised his hands, opening and shutting them rapidly. "I've never had a home, much less one filled with love and acceptance. What I've found here with you and Emery and everyone in Scotland was more than I ever could have expected. As I said before, you are the king I have chosen to serve. I reported nothing."

Bloody hell. August's heart swelled against the rage in his chest. Dorian was a part of their family, and despite his lies of omission, he wanted to believe him. Their family had lost enough. If Dorian left them, it might break the fragile bubble they'd encased themselves in since the attack.

August locked eyes with Dorian, and listened to the steady beat of his heart. "What about your prince?"

Dorian shrugged, but his demeanor didn't change. "I suspect he'll be in contact soon, but he won't hear of anything from me. I do not wish to return to the faewilde except to replenish my magic, and even then, there are pockets I can access in the mortal realm."

Dorian's heart didn't race and there was no taste of a lie in the words he spoke. That didn't mean that Dorian's words didn't give August pause. He was going to war with the Mistress, and now he might have the fae sniffing around his door. The fae, who he hadn't been sure existed beyond myth and legend.

"Wait." A realization struck him like lightning and a growl tore through August, "You've been fae all along and you didn't help find the flower sooner for Thea?"

August took two steps forward, his hands ready to unleash hell on Dorian.

Dorian threw up his hands in surrender. "No, Your Majesty. That flower is rare even by our standards. I haven't seen it growing in the Faewilde in nearly a millennium. It's a miracle Octavian had it to begin with."

"Fucking Octavian," August growled.

"Fucking Octavian is right." Dorian scrubbed his face with his hand, trailing it over days old stubble. "He's something more, Your Majesty. I haven't figured it out, but he could see through my glamour. Only another fae should be able to do that."

Was nothing meant to be easy?

August didn't let his interest or his anger on the matters show, both of which were warring for the forefront. It was a sentiment that felt familiar, but left a sadness in his chest. He didn't want to admit there was a part of him that missed the split. It was amazing to be whole, but he'd grown used to having someone disagreeing with him at every turn. Now it was only himself.

Then again he supposed it had always been only himself.

August didn't dwell on that thought, but simply nodded to Dorian. "I'll keep that in mind when I question him."

An awkward silence washed over the room, and August was about to mention he just wanted to go back to being alone with his mate when Dorian broke the silence.

"May I speak freely, Your Majesty?"

"Do I have a choice?"

"Everyone is worried about you. Callum is holding the kingdom together, while Malcolm is doing his best with the family. Your mother is recovering, Thea's presence is helping. Lily and the witches are healing the wounded, and she is reluctantly embracing her role as the interim leader of the witches who wish to defect from the Mistress' cause. And Draven and Flora are keeping the wolves from rioting over losing…"

Ansel.

Dorian swallowed hard but didn't say his name. They were all feeling his loss. That fucking guard dog was family just as much as Dorian was. Sloane had taken him and a shit ton of Emery's blood as part of her plan. A plan he was still trying to figure out, but nothing added up.

August softened his gaze and pressed his sentinel. "You love him, don't you?"

"It doesn't matter, Your Majesty." Dorian lowered his head and August could have sworn he saw a single glittered tear fall. "What matters is he doesn't deserve to be at the hands of that vile woman."

It did matter. August may not know Dorian's story, but he knew Ansel's. And despite being the furry prankster who infuriated him to no end most days, that man deserved happiness after all he'd been through. He deserved to find love again—and that's what he and Dorian had, even if neither of them would admit it. Hell, Ansel probably didn't even know what Dorian was. But it wouldn't matter. Not with the way those two looked at each other.

"We'll get him back," August vowed. A vow he fully intended to keep.

"We need you back first," Dorian whispered, his words hitting August straight in the gut. "History is being made, and you are at the center of it."

He reached for the bond, needing its comfort, but the vacant tether in his chest taunted him. "I need her at my side," he choked out, uncaring how vulnerable it made him sound.

Dorian reached out and placed his hand on August's shoulder and gave it a tight squeeze. "She will be. You are the ones the stars have chosen to lead us into the new era of the supernatural world."

August looked up, the hope in Dorian's eyes giving him a boost of his own. "Do the fae believe in the stars?"

"Our world ends and begins with the stars. Where do you think the witches learned it from?" Dorian gave him a sly smirk and turned for the door.

August followed him and softly shut it behind him, pressing his forehead into the cold wood, left with infinitely more questions than answers.

I wonder if he knows how good his ass looks in those jeans.

The faint whisper met his ears, and August growled through the door. "Really Dorian? I can fucking hear you. Just because I allowed you to speak your mind doesn't mean you can just say shit like that."

"Dorian?" The soft voice tumbled through the room like a breeze, knocking him off balance.

August whipped around and sucked in a breath when the most beautiful amber eyes met his. He raced to the bed and pulled Emery to his chest. "You're awake." He tangled his hands in her hair and pressed a kiss to her forehead.

I won't be if you suffocate me, asshole.

He chuckled and pulled her away. "Asshole? Really? That's how you're going to greet your mate?"

Emery stilled, "I didn't say tha—" Her brow furrowing as she looked up at him with confusion. "Holy shit your eyes. What happened to them?"

Of all the ways he expected her to react to the only

outward sign that he'd fused his soul at last, that wasn't it. He'd known it would be a shock. Hell, he was still getting used to seeing the dark midnight ring that radiated along the outer edge of his ice blue irises.

A genuine smile pulled at his lips, and he beamed. "Dark and light. August and Augustine. I'm whole again...well mostly. By the look of your eyes, you house a bit of my darkness too."

Emery scrambled out of the bed and to the bathroom, and he shamelessly admired the way her perfect ass peeked out of the bottom of his shirt.

When he entered, he found her leaning over the counter as much as her belly would allow and examining the obsidian rings that now permanently lined her eyes.

"What happened to me? I died, at least I think I died." Her hand clasped her throat where the faint scar from his father's blade still healed. "My sister… and your father… and then I was in a room where nothing mattered. My soul. I was happy. Weightless. It feels like it was a dream now, but Celeste was there and she told me I had to leave, to come back to you. To our daughter. Oh my gods, our daughter, is she okay?"

August's eyes met hers in the mirror. "Yes, she's perfect. I can feel her more now that you house a part of me."

"You can?" Tears rimmed her eyes and the first bit of emotion danced along their reforged bond.

Happiness.

Pure. Fucking. Happiness.

August almost fell to his knees, both because of the bond reigniting in his chest and because his own side mirrored Emery's emotions. This was all he wanted. All he needed.

He nodded and gently turned her so he could cup her face in his hands. He just needed to touch her. He would never get enough of her touch and after almost losing her, he was pressed to find a reason why she couldn't be against him every moment of every day.

His body reacted instantly to her demanding he claim her in every way. He shifted his hips so she was nestled between them, and his cock twitched against her.

Emery reached up and placed her hands over his and slid them down his forearms. Her lips tipped up into a smile. "I'm okay."

"But you weren't. I almost lost you." He swallowed hard as the last few days played through his head. He'd tried not to think about it, but with Emery standing in front of him, every pained moment came rushing back. "She tried to take your soul from me. I....I can't survive without you."

Tears fell freely down Emery's face, and she let out a half-hearted chuckle. "You'd make it. And you would have led our people in my memory. Saved and raised our children."

"Well it's a good thing I'll never have to figure out what that's like." Not only because he'd never let her out of his gods damned sight again, but also because he physically couldn't exist without her. Not really.

Emery's eyes narrowed. "Why do I get the feeling that's a weighted statement?"

Damn his little witch, ever the observant one.

August bit the inside of his cheek and tried to figure out the best way to break the news to her. In the end, he decided to just blurt it out. "Because our lives are literally bound together now."

"What did you do?" she ground out, the dark rings surrounding her irises thickening.

"Your soul was leaving your body. My only options were to bow to Sloane and her plans or give Octavian's hair-brained idea a try. I'm beginning to think Octavian knows a hell of a lot more than he lets on."

"What did you do?" Emery asked again, this time with a significantly more menacing tone.

August reached up and tucked a piece of pink hair behind her ear where it had fallen free of the bun he'd tried to master while she'd been asleep. He placed a kiss to her forehead that he knew she'd find patronizing, but he did it anyway. It didn't matter what she thought of his decision. He'd do it again and again if it meant having her in his arms like this.

"I gave you a piece of my soul to tether yours to. Our souls will forever be intertwined, and if you die, I'll slowly go crazy like Octavian."

Emery gasped, and her eyes widened as she slowly pieced together what he'd done. "Celeste?"

August nodded. "He saved her after the first time her people tried to assassinate her."

She blinked and leaned forward, pressing her lips to his chest to kiss him before resting her head there. "Can't I just give you your soul back?"

"It doesn't work that way, Princess." He ran a hand up and down her spine to comfort and soothe her. "Your soul was fractured because of your sister's spell. It's lost, mine replaced it."

Emery pulled back and tears rimmed her eyes, which had returned to a less angry version with only thin black rings. "You did that for me?"

"I'd do anything for you, little witch."

"You shouldn't have had to, though." She bit back, her eyes narrowing and the dark circles that lined her eyes thickened again and swirled inward, creating a whirlpool that matched the desperate anger spiraling through their bond.

They were really going to have to work on harnessing the darkness within her. After the merge it had become second nature for August because Augustine had always been a part of him. When they'd become one, he'd inherently known how to do so.

"Emery," the use of her name and not one of his nicknames for her caused her to still in his arms. "You are my everything. I'd sacrifice a piece of my soul every day of the week if it meant you'd survive."

She shook against him, balling her fists at her sides. Tendrils of amber and coal snaked down her arms.

August cupped her face and pressed a kiss to her lips. "Don't let the bitch win, Emery."

Emery didn't respond right away, but after a moment, she softened against him. She broke their kiss, and when she peered up at him, her eyes still swirled. "Sloane is a monster. She killed your people. She tried to kill me. She wants to take our child and to rule the supernatural world like a dictator. I will not sit by and allow our people to fall prey to her again. For fucksake she makes your father look appealing. And that's saying something, considering he slit my throat to save his own skin."

"Just wait till you hear what Jessi did."

A downright sexy growl slipped between Emery's lips and it took everything for August to contain his need to lift her onto the bathroom counter and meet her sweet darkness with his own.

"What. Did. She. Do." Emery ground out through clenched teeth.

"She joined your sister after admitting she'd been cozying up with my father to ensure her own status."

"That fucking bitch." Emery swore, her eyes glowing as she struggled against her magic once more. "I swear if I ever see her again I'm going to—"

"I know, little witch. I know." August interrupted. He threaded his fingers in her hair and tightened his grip, tilting her head up, he locked his gaze on hers. "We are going to defeat her. We're going to rip apart every single one of those vile women. We are the intended heirs. Draven too. And we are going to bring peace to our people. Our child deserves to live in a world where she can be both witch and vampire, and love whoever she damn well pleases."

I love you.

"I love you too, little witch."

Her eyes widened and dilated, the darkness seeping back to their edges. "I—"

Can you hear me?

August's jaw dropped and his eyes widened. Emery's lips hadn't moved, but he'd heard her loud and clear in the depths of his mind. He nodded. *That was you commenting about how great my ass looks in these jeans wasn't it?*

Shit. Fuck me.

A wicked smile tipped his lips. "Oh I plan to, mate."

But first he had an important question to ask her.

August stepped away from her and pulled out the ring he'd carried in his pocket from the moment he'd lay her in his bed. It was a family heirloom, one that had been passed down through generations of Nicholson vampires. It suited Emery perfectly. A hexagonal salt and pepper diamond, surrounded by clusters of smaller diamonds, set in a rose gold band. It reflected light and dark through its beauty, just as his mate did.

He'd had hours—days—to think about what he would say, how he would convince her to be his forever. But looking in her eyes, he realized this was only a formality. She already belonged to him.

He took his hand in hers and got down on one knee.

"Emery Noelle Montgomery, you are my mate, my love, the mother of my children. I know I am a hard man to love."

Emery snorted and rolled her eyes. *That's an understatement.*

He narrowed his eyes and a growl rumbled through him, loving every ounce of her defiance. "I'll take you over my knee, little witch."

"And ruin a perfectly beautiful proposal?" she taunted. "You wouldn't."

She tried to side step him, but he caught her wrist and spun her against him, pulling her down so she lay face up across his knee.

He leaned in, nestling his nose in her hair above her ear. "Marry me. Be my queen, little witch, so I can take you over my knee and punish you for every eye roll. So I may run my hands over your perfect body and take my sweet time making you come on my tongue. Marry me, so that everyone knows you are mine."

"I'm pretty sure everyone already knows that." She ran her hand over her belly.

August growled and nipped the lobe of her ear.

A moan fell from her lips, and it was nearly his undoing. It's not like she was going to say no. He wouldn't let her say no.

But then she said the words he wanted to hear most. "Yes, August. Of course, I will marry you."

He slipped the ring on her finger and swept her up to his arms, swiftly walking back into the room.

"Hey." She protested. "Where are we going? I am sure I need a shower before we do any celebrating."

"Oh I plan to ensure you are positively filthy before I wash every inch of your body myself."

Chapter Forty Six

EMERY

The smell of death clung to the wind coming off the lake. Each of the seventy-two pyres were wrapped and prepared for a proper funeral. White cloth hugged each of the bodies, a clean slate as they journeyed to the realm of the stars. Emery's gaze fell to each one, her heart growing heavier as she moved down the line until they landed on the tiniest pyre, and she choked back tears.

She didn't know if she could go through with what she'd suggested. It was supposed to bring them closure. That was the whole idea behind putting together a day of mourning and sending off those who'd lost their lives in the attack. It was supposed to be a way to unify them. And for the most part, it had.

Looking out over the pyres, it struck her as downright poetic that in death, not a single body could be identified as vampire, wolf or witch; they were just the dead. Lost in a war started by ancestors who didn't give a shit about a single one of them.

August stepped forward to stand next to her on the platform in which the sentinels and witches would shoot their flames. She'd never thought she'd see the day they stood side by side, but it felt right. It felt like the first step in the right direction.

Four days had passed since she had woken. She and August had taken two days to become reacquainted with each other and celebrate their engagement, multiple times, on every surface of their shared suite. It was everything she needed at that moment. A celebration of life when death had come so close to taking her along. It was what they should have had all those months ago, but the stars had other plans. And even though so much of their journey was a mess, and she felt like the stars could go fuck themselves nintey percent of the time, the pride she felt standing next to her mate and the bond that tethered them was worth it.

The only time they'd pressed pause was to eat and nap to stave off pure exhaustion.

She craned her neck to look up at her mate as he stood stoically at her side, a crown glittering against his dirty blond hair. His jaw set tight. August had stepped into his role as king with all the diplomacy and dominance a ruler should have. He'd spent the past week endlessly laying out the groundwork for peace between the witches, wolves, and vampires. It wasn't perfect, and war was still on the horizon, but it was progress.

Her gaze fell to August's left where Lily stood with Malcolm by her side. She'd reluctantly taken over the role of leader to all the witches who'd forsaken Sloane and her dark magic. She refused to be called a priestess or wear the crystal crown, but despite all her bitching, Lily was made for the role. She wasn't the heir the stars prophesied to change the supernatural world, but she was the heir the witches needed.

Flora slipped her hand into Emery's and gave it a squeeze. Draven stood on the other side of her, his lips set in a firm line. Emery couldn't help the small smile that spread on her face.

The wolves had rallied behind Draven and Flora, despite both of them being hybrids. The Alpha had named them his heirs, and before the end of the year, he'd step down and allow them to rule. They were the image of hope in her heart and she couldn't be more happy for them.

Callum stood on one end of the heir and Dorian on the other—Callum a prince in his own right, and Dorian a fae warrior.

Callum had been suspiciously absent for the battle, and wouldn't give Emery a straight answer as to where he was beyond 'It would make sense in time'. Fucking cryptic asshole. His saving grace was that he'd stepped up and carried more than his fair share of the weight in rebuilding the kingdom of North American vampires.

Emery still struggled to wrap her head around the fact Dorian had been fae all along and reporting to a fae prince. Ultimately, she was glad he was on their side and pledged his allegiance to August and their child. He was family as much as anyone else.

Emery scanned her eyes over their makeshift family, and her heart ached at the wolf-size hole that should have been at Dorian's side. She'd destroyed the crystal parlor when August and Dorian told her that Sloane had taken Ansel. As it was, just thinking about it caused the darkness within her to swirl and fuel her need for revenge.

August's hand tightened around hers.

How did you know? Emery tilted her head and frowned. She'd been working on creating a mental block between her and August just as they'd each done at times with their bond. While it had come in handy to be able to communicate in their minds, neither of them wanted the constant blast of their mate's monologue in their head.

You're still shit at keeping your emotions from your face. And even if your eyes weren't swirling coal depths, I saw you staring at Dorian.

They deserve their happily ever after.

August squeezed her hand and nodded. *We'll find him.*

Emery nodded and focused on the members of each kingdom, pack and coven, as they lined the lakeshore. While there was some hesitancy, most stood shoulder to shoulder with the sole purpose of honoring their dead.

August gave her hand another squeeze and together they stepped forward.

Each of the seventy-two pyres was pushed from the shore into the dark waters of the lake.

Except one.

"Today we send our brothers and sisters to rest among the stars. May the gods welcome them and the stars sing their names with love and fury, so that we may hear it fall from the heavens and know they've arrived in peace."

Lily raised her hand, and cast a shower of shooting stars over the lake. "May their souls be at rest and their bodies embraced by the earth to give life to those yet to come."

Draven turned his eyes to the moon and let out a long low howl. When he was finished, each of the pack members in attendance also let out the same mournful howl to honor their dead.

When the last of the howls ceased, August gave the signal, and each of the sentinels notched a flaming arrow to their bows. Lily nodded and the elemental witches that lined the shore—along with Emery—called forth their magic.

"Until we meet again," Emery whispered, a single tear falling as balls of fire and flaming arrows rained down onto the pyres, sending each of their dead on to the next life.

For a few stolen moments, the only sound on the lakeshore was the soft sobs from those mourning their dead, until deep within the crowd of witches, vampires, and wolves a solemn hymn could be heard.

There was no telling who started the ancient song, but it was one even Emery knew. Not because Ada taught it to her, but because she'd heard Agatha sing it time and time again in the cafe while she worked.

August replaced his hand in hers and tugged her forward.

It's time, little witch.

She nodded and allowed him to lead her down to the lake's edge where the last remaining pyre floated.

It was a tiny, infant-sized pyre. The kind no parent should ever have to face.

Tears welled in her eyes, and her heart constricted, unsure if she could do what needed to be done. It was supposed to bring closure, but how was she ever supposed to be okay with losing her son? Burning a pyre wasn't going to fill the ache in her chest or bring back her beautiful smiling boy.

I'm with you, Em.

She looked up to see her mate. The king of her world.

His eyes matched her own, rimmed with unshed tears that may never cease.

Emery sighed, they might as well get it over with.

Together?

Always, princess.

They turned forward, and just as they were about to lean down and push the pyre that represented the end of the earthly life of their son, the telltale signs of a vision tugged at Emery's mind.

She tried to pull her hand from August's, not wanting to risk losing him in her vision, but his grip tightened.

Emery's awareness clouded, and she and August were pulled into a vision that was exactly the same as reality. The chanting of their family and friends surrounded them, but sitting on the pyre was no longer a box draped in a sheet. Instead their beautiful baby boy with the truest blue eyes sat smiling at them.

Emery choked on a sob and turned to see August swallow hard beside her. She reached down and picked up the baby, pulling him against her chest.

August's arms tightened around them, and the three of them stayed there for a long moment.

When they finally pulled apart, tears fell freely from August and Emery's eyes and their baby smiled up at them. He was perfect in every way.

Emery looked up at August and smiled through the tears. "Shall we name him?

August nodded. "Miles Augustine Nicholson."

A gasp fell from Emery's lip. "It's perfect." Honoring not only her uncle who had brought so many bright days to her childhood, but also the darkest parts of his father that found the light when his children needed him.

Miles giggled in her arms, and Emery pulled him tighter against her. She knew this moment couldn't last forever, but she would savor it always.

Tiny fingers reached up and caressed her cheek, and she saw that Miles had also done the same to August.

Both of their mouths fell open as their baby spoke in their minds, much as his sister had when they'd been merged.

I love you. I am still with you. Always. The stars have a plan.

"I love you too, baby boy."

The cloudiness returned to the edges of her vision, and Emery knew they would be sucked back to reality any moment.

They leaned down, placed one final kiss on their son's forehead, and allowed the vision to take them.

When they returned, their family had surrounded them by

the lake, and their people continued to sing, lending their support through their voices.

Emery looked up at August and nodded.

It was time. The stars had granted them the chance to say goodbye and reminded them they had a plan. Even if it seemed fucked up at times, Emery had to believe there was a happily ever after for them out there.

They leaned over together and pushed the pyre into the lake. Emery raised her hand and with August's intertwined and pressed to the back of her palm, she released a lone flame onto the pyre.

Her eyes followed it to the horizon, and she traced it up to the stars.

A weighted calm overcame her and deep within her womb she felt the flutter of her daughter. The promise that her son was with them always.

For Miles, Augustine whispered through their bond.

"For Miles."

Emery and August stepped back, and their family embraced them. As one, they lifted their voices in the final verse of the song that rang out like a battle cry. United as one, the supernatural community mourned their dead, but it felt more like a promise to honor them. To not allow their deaths to be in vain.

In the face of despair, hope flared within Emery.

War was coming, but they were a force united.

THANK YOU FOR READING

Thank you for Reading The Intended!!
I really hope you have enjoyed August and Emery's journey so far. I have so much more in store for these characters and this world. In so many ways, this is just the beginning and I am so excited for more!
If you enjoyed The Intended, or even if you hated it, I would so appreciate you hopping over to leave a review on Amazon and/or Goodreads. Reviews help tiny self published authors like me to gain new readers and get my books on fancy lists some day.
Thank you to everyone who reviews, recommends and posts about this series. I couldn't do this without you!

WHAT'S NEXT - THE UNITED

The United, the epic conclusion of Emery and August's story, is set to come out November 2022.

Pre-order Today!

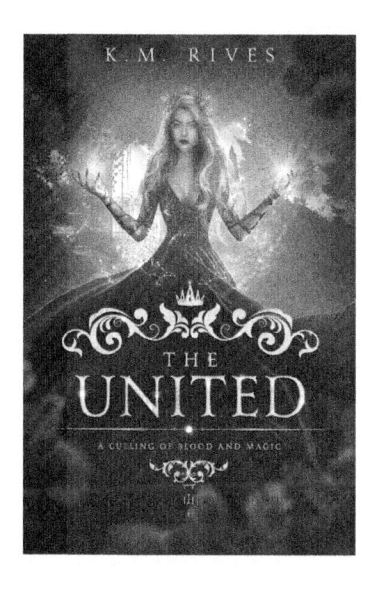

I am going to try to move up this release if possible. Keep an eye out in my Newsletter and Instagram for teasers and more information.

ALSO IN THE CULLING SERIES

The next release in the Culling series is Hybrid Moon Rising. Find out how Flora met Draven and how she became his mate.

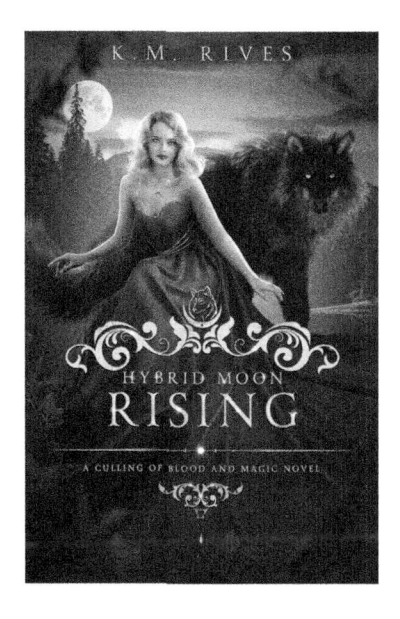

Hybrid Moon Rising

THE CULLING OF BLOOD AND MAGIC SERIES

The Replacement

The Intended

The United

Hybrid Moon Rising - Companion Novel

ACKNOWLEDGMENTS

Wow. What to say.

I'm going to just jump right in and say this book sent me through a whirlwind. At times it was extremely difficult to write and I struggled so many times wondering if I was getting the words right, portraying my characters honestly and if I was doing my readers justice. The stars did not make my job easy and more often than not these characters tended to go off script with their complex emotions and sideways decision making. If it weren't for the people in my life cheering me on and demanding I look deeper into the minds of my characters to find their story, I'm not sure this book would be what it is today.

To my husband, my rock, my home: Thank you from the bottom of my heart. You handled everything in the real world so I could escape into this fictional one and bang out one amazing story. I love you forever and always, and not only because you bring me charcuterie boards and beer when you know I need a pick me up.

To my daughters who remind me everyone needs a play break and cuddles. You guys are my world.

To my family: I love the way you believe in me. Thank you for always pushing me to follow my dreams and consistently supporting me in everything I do. I am so lucky to have you.

To the book community:

Holy hell, I must say I am blown away by the kindness and support of authors, bookstagrammers and readers who have promoted my books. Every single time I get tagged in a gorgeous photo or video I get a giddy smile on my face and it restores a bit of my faith in humanity. You seriously make my day and inspire me to keep writing worlds you love.

To my Smut Sisters: Our chats give me life. Thank you for being my tribe and making Finding Malcolm a thing.

To Brittany: I'm not even sure you understand how grateful I am that you've come into my life let alone become my PA. Seriously this release would have been dead on arrival if it weren't for you and your meticulous organizing. Not to mention you are the best cheerleader ever. Thank you for your friendship and everything you do.

To Melissa Ivers and Sienna Varrone: How the hell did I get so lucky to find you ladies? Writing a book can be a lonely journey, but with you guys it's been a wild ride of spicy conversations and drooling over covers. I couldn't ask for more loyal, funny, kind and just all-around awesome people to have at my back. Thank you for always beta reading, keeping me on task and cheering me on even though you have a million other things on your plate. I can't imagine doing this without you.

To Nana Logan: The one who started this crazy journey with

me. I couldn't ask for a better mentor and friend. This year has been one of the most trying in our lives and I can't imagine having battled it with anyone else but you. You have helped me craft a solid foundation in not only my writing but my life. Thank you for standing by me and encouraging me every step of the way. For teaching me endless photoshop tricks when I stubbornly wanted to make all my own graphics. For reminding me the pool is fun, but the ocean is deep. Love you to the fucking stars and back woman.

To Amy: You are an editing queen. I am so glad to have found you. You accept me even though I am shit at commas and I couldn't ask for a better person to work with and bounce ideas off of. Thank you for everything you do and for believing in me and my story.

And finally, thank you to my readers.
Every. Single. One of you.
I can't believe how much love this series has gotten or the overall support I've received as an author. I am so grateful I get to do this job. Thank you for every sentence you read, every review you leave, every post you make. I see you. Thank you for taking a chance on me and my stories. You guys are magic.

— K.M.

ABOUT THE AUTHOR

Krista is a California girl living in a North Carolina world… for now. After all, home is where the Army tells her husband they're moving next. She's a lover of dungeons and dragons, singing at the top of her lungs, ice cold beer and all things dessert. Most days you can find her wrangling her two young daughters and finding any moment she can to sneak away into the worlds she writes.

For more information check out kmrives.com

Printed in Great Britain
by Amazon